The Urbana Free Library

D1372423

THE LONG BLUE MOAN

By L.M. Ross

alyson books
los angeles | new york

9/02   13.95   Pub

ALL CHARACTERS IN THIS BOOK ARE FICTITIOUS. ANY RESEMBLANCE TO REAL
INDIVIDUALS—EITHER LIVING OR DEAD—IS STRICTLY COINCIDENTAL.

THIS TRADE PAPERBACK ORIGINAL IS PUBLISHED BY ALYSON PUBLICATIONS,
P.O. BOX 4371, LOS ANGELES, CALIFORNIA 90078-4371.
DISTRIBUTION IN THE UNITED KINGDOM BY
TURNAROUND PUBLISHER SERVICES LTD.,
UNIT 3, OLYMPIA TRADING ESTATE, COBURG ROAD, WOOD GREEN,
LONDON N22 6TZ ENGLAND.

FIRST EDITION: AUGUST 2002

02 03 04 05 06 **a** 10 9 8 7 6 5 4 3 2 1

ISBN 1-55583-621-6

CREDITS
COVER DESIGN BY MATT SAMS.
COVER PHOTOGRAPHY BY TONY STONE IMAGES.

In Memory of All the Mighty Souls of New York,
Past, Present, and Future.
L.M.R.

Prologue

The boy's brain screamed, *Fuck you, fuck him, fuck them, fuck all you motherfuckers!* as he bolted down the city block. Every part of him was hurting, and as hard and fast as he ran, he couldn't seem to stop. Fresh blood soaked through his pants, yet still he ran. He ran and ran until he saw a decrepit old Lincoln parked at a corner. He broke inside, hot-wired it, and sped away into the cold and crucified night. He drove with madness, weaving in and out of traffic, on a mission, ending up in a forgotten part of the South Bronx.

He left the car, stared at the carcass of the tenement that once housed his hopeless childhood. An icy wind blew, wrapping its frigid fingers around him, and he knew he had to do something to keep the cold away.

Matches! He didn't have much, but he had those. Someone once told him that the blue of the flame was the hottest part. Maybe that blue could warm him. He reached into his pocket and found a matchbook. Cupping his hand, he struck a stick. Suddenly, a blaze of red, yellow-gold, and transparent *blue* loomed from a flickering spike. Hypnotic. Deadly. The menacing heat crept close to his hand,

1

and if he didn't toss it soon it would burn him. By then, though, he'd been burned so many times his skin was raw.

No more, damn it! Fuck you!

Then he saw it, that can of paint thinner catching a wicked light. He picked it up, emptied its stringent elixir along the wooden steps, lit another match and, oh, what a beautiful sound. *Who-o-osh!*

He watched the crimson rise and run, blaze and lick the stairs and beyond. The sensation of peering back at something his anger had built transformed him. To watch it smoke and glow, burn and take new flame made him shudder all over. He watched for a moment the scattered choreography of rats fleeing in all their sleazy beauty.

Jumping inside that stolen Lincoln, he sped away, driving harder and faster than ever. He looked back, just once, at the fantastic monstrosity anger and a single match had made, and he smiled.

One

Small and Bitter

The rhythm, the rhythm of the city's soundtrack swooshed and crackled a little less loudly now. Strutting the atmospheric strut and fret of a man on a mission, Browny glided his bones through another electronic night of muscling crowds, siren sounds, and glimmering parallels of light. The Manhattan air was thick with the musk of hot pretzels and jasmine incense sold by Muslims and cats in silken robes. The traffic Roller Derbied down Broadway as mad people in mad machines streaked across the Times Square frenzy. It was almost picture postcard pretty. But *this* was *not* his beautiful city anymore.

Little by little, Midtown was winning its war with sleaze, and shiny new erections molested the sky. Browny's mind flickered like a cheap neon sign asking *Where can I get a quick hummer on a late-summer night, yo? Can't a Brother cop a bag, a vial, a hit of herbal elation anymore? Why did these bastards have to vacuum the streets and clean the dealers out of Bryant Park?* All of his beloved haunts, dens, and porn shops had been overrun by the Giuliani decency cops. "Man! Look at this shit. Yo! They done blew up my spot!"

3

It was true. The generals of Disney staged a coup on 40-deuce—a strategic maneuver the working girls, boys, pimps, tricks, pervs, dealers, and junkies never survived.

Browny figured he'd kill some free time before his meeting downtown, bounce into Show World and rent a cheap view of stripper tits and coochie. But the glare from that most excellent hootchie plaza had disappeared. It was like that Joni Mitchell line: "You don't know what you've got till it's gone."

Well, someone had paved over *his* paradise and put up a whole other neon world. He couldn't get over it. Wasn't it just a year or three ago that this Great Gleaming City was flashing and spreading its legs wide open in fidgeting, glittering, clitoring eminence? He missed the throbbing red crotch of Times Square, when whatever he wanted he could easily cop there, and then be on his way. Now that hot sleazy glamour had vanished, and Faison Brown was pissed. So he went ahead and took the train Downtown.

Of course it was a different place now. There was a gaping hole in the skyline. The absence of two shimmering signifiers of reach and enterprise was palpable.

Tiny taverns in the East Village glowed in soothing pink lights against skinny lines of varicose streets. The one he'd chosen for his meeting was as dark as a Poe short story. Behind the bar, brown and green bottles lined up like soldiers on the frontline of a tidy little war. The place reeked of old dreams and nicotine, cheap booze, mean spirits. And loneliness.

Stew, the bartender, a compressed wall of a man with dead-end eyes and a wry grin, was part philosopher, part pugilist, and part poet. Often he'd show his benevolence for stumbling bums—as he did this night, with Browny as witness—by hailing a cab and paying the man's tab from his own pocket. When asked why, Stew said, "You never know the things that'll break a man."

A clouded barroom voice replied, "That damn bottle broke *him*."

To which Stew answered, "His life was gentle, and the elements so mixed within him, that nature would stand up and say to all the world, 'This was a man!'"

"Yo! I like that shit right there. That's Shakespeare, right?" Browny asked.

"Yeah. From *Hamlet*," Stew replied, washing his shot glasses.

Then *she* stepped inside the bar. Clad in black, her once-famous eyes obscured by wide Jackie O. shades, hair wrapped in one of those *gelees* Tyrone had sent her from Africa.

No one recognized her.

She sat three seats from Browny, who was one vodka shot away from drunk. He remembered her from back in the day. He remembered *who* she was and who she *used* to be. He turned in her direction, and waited for her to notice him. She didn't, so finally he said, "Yo, Bliss! It's me."

"Excuse me? Do we *know* each other?"

"Well, I sure as hell know you, Bliss Santana."

Oh. It's that annoying little hemorrhoid. What's his name?

"It's me, *Browny*. Faison Brown. You know, from the loft downtown? Yo, am I really *all that* forgettable? I never forgot you. I always thought you was the real cream in Depina's instant coffee. How you doin', Bliss? You doin' all right for yourself?"

"Was that *your* message on my machine? How'd you get my number? You've been rummaging through his things?"

"Mami, please. Yo! I had *that* all along. I was in the inner circle. Yeah, Pass-cow and me go *way back*. In fact, I'm thinkin' 'bout doin' a book on the famous Mr. Pass-cow. Yo, once upon a time the two of us was *down*, like, like *Apartheid*, so ya better recognize."

"Pascal and *you* were down?" Bliss asked incredulously, lowering her glasses. "I seriously doubt that." She paused. "All right. I'm here. And I'm not rich, so blackmail would be fruitless."

"Fruitless? Yo! Kinda like how you musta felt when he left ya, huh?"

Bliss said nothing. She only rolled her ice-green eyes to the heavens, sighed, and let Browny continue.

"We started out as *boys*. Nah. That's a lie. But we went to Performing Arts High together. Ya *know* I can sing, right? Oh, yeah. That shit's all legend. Like to hear me? Here I go. *On-hell-lee-toes.*

Angelitos / Negro-o-oes, Lala la, skipwahdeedah / Skipwahdah-dee-dada-dee-o…" he scatted to make sure there could be no doubt of his skills on vocals. "So, after hearin' me blow, yo! They *all* wanted me. Hell. To tell the truth, they was all a li'l shady. You know what they say about show folk. But I blew with them for a minute, and the blend was tight. That's when we started our singin' group. Called ourselves 'Da Elixir,' right? But then, all hell broke loose and—"

Bliss caught one hard glimpse at the rumpled, broken Browny and choked on her gin and tonic. Though Pascal had always downplayed his past, she knew about the group. But she'd forgotten about Browny's involvement. Now, suddenly, it amused her.

"Elixir?" Thoughts of *him* being anyone's elixir tickled her into a fresh gush of laughter. She couldn't help it.

"Yo! It was *Ty's* wiseass idea. The rest of us hated it. But then *Ty* broke it down: The Elixir was a magic potion, like the Fountain of Youth, a feel-good balm, a healing tonic."

She'd forgotten how some drunks were artists at emotional manipulation. *Ty*. She'd always maintained a soft chamber in her heart for Tyrone.

"Go on," she said.

"Well. Ty talked us into the name. So me, Pass-cow, Ty, and David became Da Elixir. Then Ty messed around and wrote us a fuckin' hit, and the rest is music history."

"Really?"

"And the more I think about it, maybe Ty had that *forward sight*. You know, he was, what's that word…?"

"Prophetic?" Bliss contributed. *And this drunken little idiot wants to write a damn book!*

"Yo! If that shit means he could see the future, then yeah, prophetic! See, I think we spent most our lives lookin' for that *elixir*. Maybe everybody does. I mean, we both sittin' here sippin' on one right now. Whatever's gonna make us feel mo better, yo—maybe *that's* the elixir. And we both know Pascal the Rascal had plenty elixirs. So, I figga ya might wanna throw in with me. What ya think?"

The notion of anyone exploiting Pascal enraged her. She wanted to hit Browny, just whale all over him. "Fuck you, you desperate lit-tle cold-blooded bastard! I loved him. And if you even *think* about slandering *my* name, I'll see your little bone-picking ass in court!"

"Yo! So ya name-callin' now? Is that your new elixir? Know what my boy Ty said about name-callin'? Just a desperate act of the guilty, baby."

"So now I suppose you were Tyrone's friend too?"

"Oh, hail yeah! Yo, check it." He leaned in close. "Figga I'll start chapter one a little sump'n like this: 'Yo! In high school some kids fit in, some stand out, and some just don't give a fuck.' What you think, Bliss? Is that the shit, or what?" He grinned, nodding his head, proud of himself.

Leaning back, Bliss said, "I think it's adolescent, and that you need a breath mint."

"Oh, so you Rosie Perez, now? You got jokes? Well I ain't laughin'. One more crack, and I'll smack that pretty ass harder then Pass-cow ever did! So, yo! You wanna throw down with me on this, or what?"

"You could never write a book, Browny." Bliss Santana announced. "The pages would all just flame from that hell you're living in."

She stood to leave, dropping some green on the bar. "Excuse me, bartender…His next one's on me. And make it something stiff and bitter, and serve it in a little glass." Then, she clicked her hot tongue in Browny's direction, and exited the bar.

"Dumb witch!" he grumbled after her. "I guess you don't care if he used yo ass too. Guess ya liked being a beard, till he shaved you off with his disposable razor and threw ya both away. Hey! That ain't half-bad! Who needs her? I can do this shit by my lonesome." As he turned away from the door, he saw his reflection in the mirror. He noticed that annoying infestation of gray in his goatee.

Stew placed another glass before him.

Browny drank it quickly.

Despite his bluster, Faison "Browny" Brown had neither the knowledge, the skills, nor the self-discipline needed to write a *true* tell-all. Yet, even if he did, he was at best a slighted character in a 20-year saga. But he was right about one thing: They all *had* met in a special place, a place that nourished the sons and daughters of applause.

New York City, High School of Performing Arts, 1977-1978

The auditorium smelled of turpentine, greasepaint, the tart funk of dancer's feet, and the sweat of youthful ambition. After third-period chorus, Tyrone Hunter remained behind to plink plink on the piano while he waited for Mr. Raines. A tall, lanky kid with warm toffee skin, Ty's brow furrowed into a studious brood as his long tapered fingers stroked the keys. There was something playing in Tyrone's mind—a tune that wasn't quite yet a tune.

Out in the hallway, a squat sparkplug of a deep-chocolate bully who went by the name of "Browny" stalked ominously. It was open season for Browny, who took antagonistic delight in chasing down "special punks." He'd just cornered another unsuspecting victim. Without provocation, he punched him in the chest as hard as he possibly could, then ran away, laughing.

As David Richmond glided by, he saw Faison Brown's assault. It pissed him off. His amber eyes blazed, and he thought, *Enough with this! I got something for your ass!* Browny hadn't hit David—yet—but that didn't matter. David switched his gait. He phased into his slow jock's swagger and approached the bully. Smiling impishly, he hauled off and punched him even harder than Browny had punched his latest victim. David did it for every "special punk" in that school who was too afraid to hit Browny back. A quick left to the center of his chest, and Faison Brown fell to floor, winded.

Meanwhile, Pascal "Face" Depina was in the mirror of the boy's room. People had been telling him he looked like a young, bronzed, green-eyed Paul Newman, and he was starting to believe the hype. He'd even taken to styling his fawn hair to look like Newman's 'do in the *The Hustler*. Sufficiently coiffed, he winked a green eye and exited the bathroom just in time to witness the punch that landed

Browny on his bullish ass. Depina laughed his secretive cackle.

"You all right?" David asked, leaning over the stunned bully. "Nah? You ain't? Damn, boy, you just got dropped by a *special* punk."

Soon as he could, a dazed Faison rose with revenge raging in his eyes, "Oh, it's like that, yo? I'm a kick yo punk ass!"

With that, David ran, only, it wasn't out of fear. He ran to show he could not only outpunch but out*run* a meaningless thug. He ran, leaving Faison Brown to eat his fairy dust. At the tail end of this run, David burst through the auditorium door, breathless, every young muscle heaving.

Tyrone looked up, recognized him as that crazy-weird talented dancer cat with a knack for inventive fashion, and kept playing with the keys.

David stood in back, listening for a moment. Liking what he heard, he yelled, "Hey! That sounds pretty damn good, man. You're the dude with that stiff bowlegged Blacula walk, from the ensemble chorus, right?"

Ty didn't answer.

Mr. Thomas Raines entered from stage right, a round jovial nut-brown man in his 40s. "Tyrone?" he asked. "What's that you're playing?"

"Nothing. Not yet anyway. I keep hearing this tune in my head. I do that sometimes—hear stuff no one else hears. Is there a name for that?"

"Yeah. It's called creativity. You should work on that tune, maybe give it a name, and the lyrics will come." He noticed David. "Oh, there you are."

David sauntered slowly down the aisle, his maize-yellow sweatpants tied high about his narrow waist. He had a strong and very noticeable V-shape. Though only five foot six, 130 pounds, he was extraordinarily muscular, and a skinny kid like Ty coveted his well-formed biceps. Suddenly, his long purple tank came off, revealing a tighter electric-blue one. He hastily fashioned the bright purple top into a babushka around his head. On anyone else it would've looked completely *ridic*, yet on David, somehow it worked. By the time he made it to the stage, he was his own kind of performance art piece. At least, Tyrone thought so.

Just then, through the door, bopped a suave, well-dressed Pascal "Face" Depina, followed by a winded Faison Brown. Browny was punching his palm and deviously eyeballing David. But David ignored him. His heart was too busy racing at the sight of Face Depina.

Face and Browny seemed an odd combo to Tyrone. He wondered, *Why are they here?* But apparently they too had been summoned by Mr. Raines.

"OK, you're all present. Listen, fellas," Raines began. "Each of you is dangerously close to flunking my class. Yes, Tyrone, David, and Pascal, I realize none of you is a music major, but you *don't* get to skate through my classes. Faison Brown, you *are* a music major, so you have no excuse."

"But Mr. Raines, I—"

"Save it," Raines admonished. "Pascal, you being a senior, I'm quite sure you'd *love* to see yourself swaggering down the aisle in a cap and gown. You're on the acting track, right?"

Pascal grinned and nodded.

"Then try *acting* like an interested student."

Pascal's grin quickly left him.

"The semester ends soon, and if any of you want to pass, extra credit is due. You can come up with something individually, or work as a team. Either way, I want to see a superior effort. There are plenty of kids who would give their eyeteeth to be where you are. No one gets a free lunch here. Am I understood? Well? Am I?"

"Yes, Mr. Raines," they all said in a bored singsong unity.

Tyrone thought, *Well, it'll definitely be something individual. I'm not sure I like these cats.*

Just then, David, seeing the horny benefit of working alongside Face Depina, weighed in. "Hey, we could knock this out the box in a hurry. All of us can sing, right? We could form a singin' group, and do somethin' fly. Flyer than The Temptations even. Seriously, this guy right here, he could even write us a song," he said, gesturing at Ty.

Are ya crazy? Ty wondered. *Please, don't do this shit to me!*

"Great. Then it's set," said Mr. Raines.

"But…" Ty began.

"Any kid here can sing something from *America's Top 40*," said Mr. Raines. "Where's the challenge in that? Challenge yourselves, and get used to it, before the world outside these doors does the challenging. We're done here, gentlemen. Have a good day."

Once dismissed, Tyrone thought, *This is* not *the beginning of a beautiful friendship.*

Three Weeks Later…

"Yo, Hunter!" Browny kicked at the auditorium bleachers. "Why every time I see you, you and Raines got y'alls heads together? Ya need to stop kissin' up. People might start thinkin' y'all *funny* for each other. Whisperin' together like a coupla of bitches!"

Tyrone glared at him.

"Yeah, I said it. Whatchu gon' do?" Browny challenged, fists clenched, upper body jerking forth in a pseudo-threatening move.

Tyrone had flinched the first few times he'd done that, but he didn't anymore. "Keep talkin' junk, man. Better yet, let *him* hear you. Then maybe he *won't* get his nephew, who just happens to be a producer at Sigma Sound studios, to drop by the concert and take a look at us."

"What?" Browny asked, eyes bugging twice their normal size. "Say what, yo?" Tempestuous tenor rising to new soprano heights.

"What's wrong? Depina singing too loud in your ear again? Ya heard me," Ty said.

"Fo real, yo?"

"Fo *real*."

"I don't believe it. Yo, do Pass-cow and David know?"

"Nope. I just now found out myself."

"You know this could be big, right? I mean, Sigma Sound ain't no joke! Didn't Black Ivory record up in there?"

"Yep. And they were just about the same age as us."

"Yo! This could be crazy! Fo real. I'm gettin' psyched and shit!"

"Don't get too psyched, just get it right, brother. Nothin's promised, and we still got a lotta work to do."

"Hell, the song's *tight*, the harmony's workin' out. Yo! It's smellin' like, like *gold* up in here, man! Here, smell my finger…"

Ty smacked his hand away.

Five seconds later, Browny was zooming down the auditorium's center aisle. The boy had vanished, gone to that Happy Place squat, talented, braided-head Black boys go when they dream of being stars! He dashed into Room 308 and yelled it to David, who was in the middle of ballet class. He hollered it in an echo to Pascal Depina who was in the third-floor bathroom mirror: "A cat from Sigma Sound is comin' to the Winter Extravaganza and we go'n be *stars!*"

THE BAND

Da Elixir was the sum of four parts:

Ty, Age 16
Brilliant, Involved, Hopeful, Lucky?

Long before he'd ever heard of the playwright Bertolt Brecht, he'd written his own play that echoed that author's *Three Penny Opera*. It was Ty's entree into the hallowed halls of P.A. He didn't want to be a cog in a machine of an entertainment factory whose prime produce was cranking out performers. But there he was, knee-deep in the hurried hubbub of wandering weirdos, eccentric adolescents, stage, screen, and television vets. Those halls buzzed with the combustible excitement of the young, talented, and destined.

Strange, the things the universe hands us.

Though he stood six-two and weighed a gangly 150, Tyrone had an almost coltish charm. His face was a thin presentation of toffee skin and curious features all trying at once to be handsome. To some it was a *cool face*, long, bony, hungry. His crowning glory was a bank of pomade-assisted curls—a look some Latin chicos affected, and Ty had adapted from old Sal Mineo movies. His almond-shaped eyes were a deep, dramatic shade of sable and others were haunted by their directness. His most bewitching feature, though, was his lips— soft, puffy, heart-shaped lips. At times, they seemed almost begging to be kissed.

A lexical cat at 16, Ty spoke with a crazy verbiage, as if his words were grits served with a dash of hipster syntax, mixed, peppered, *Tyronized*, and sitting on a china plate.

During his entrance audition for school Ty riffed:

"Back in the day the Moms had all these fantasies of being a Blues Chanteuse. But Moms was far more Piaf than Bessie, so the suits at *Verve* never called her back. By the time I shot out Momma had a brand new bag: the camera. Man, she musta taken a million snaps of me, her hope, her half-cute papoose. She'd show 'em to everyone. Musta been her trip, puttin' her womb art on display. So, one sunny afternoon, she's outside the Kodak soul-freezing shop, perusing the latest batch of mugs, when some strolling woman asks for a peek. Lady turned out to be a casting agent. The Moms jets home, high on visions of better living room furniture, her eyes clouded by those spacey cataracts old dreams make, and she asked me, 'Ty? Do momma's baby wanna be on TV? Momma's baby boy wanna be a star, huh?'

"I'm like, all of 18 months old, but I must've goo-gooed something that sounded vaguely like, 'Sure, Ma. Why the hell not?'

"Cut to page 133 in a Sears catalogue, that grinning brown tot is me. That deep tan toddler in a wet diaper, making a mad telegenic sprint for a dry Pamper—me. Hey, I didn't mind being exploited 'cause it helped with the ends. But the expiration date on cute brown mutes ran out. And I was pretty much a has been, rejected at age seven."

Ty had things to say. He was, by nature, creative. But he wore a mood the color of lonely.

David, Age 15
Brilliant, Silly, Cute, Dancer

David knew from the time he could walk that one Metro-golden day he would *be* a professional dancer. He'd spent his youth mesmerized by the flickering blue glow of early MGM musicals. Soon, he became addicted to all things light, spirited, and gay. He floated with an understated snare drum in his gait. Chest out, spine and shoulders straight, the aesthetic was never a problem for David. He was very cool with his *faggotry*, unless he wanted to *play* the queen.

With the softest light-hazel overcast, David's eyes looked as if he'd just awakened from a pleasant dream. Often there appeared to be a private little comedy act going on behind his gaze.

Dance was his life, and he did it with élan. The kid was a "firebird." Everyone said so. At his audition, David was asked to "tell us a little about yourself."

"I tell people about myself through the dance," he said. "I believe dance is freedom, plain and simple. Only there's nothin' simple about freedom." And then he danced.

Tyrone just happened to see him, and as the writer would someday write:

"It was his life story that he was portraying—his whole damn life. In dance. Every muscle of David's body became an instrument of poetic expression, moving from a gleeful tap-dancing kid to a ridiculed student to an abused and battered teen. You could almost *see* the boxing ring and smell the sweat as he stomped and lumbered, floated, sashayed, and spun across the stage to the theme from *Rocky*.

"I guess it was part modern, part ballet, and part something no one in the room could put a name to, but it made me *believe him*. It made me wanna laugh with him, cry for him, and pray for him. I asked myself, *Who the hell is this strange, scary-talented cat? And what is* my *limited ass even doing here?* How do you compare a pinlight to a star? You don't."

From that day on Tyrone became a sponge to David's light.

David knew what he could do and how well he could do it, and took pride in being a "wicked body-worker." That mad dancer's heart was full of hot rhythms as it sped, slowed, and sped again—when he opened the auditorium door and there stood...

Pascal, Age 18
Beautiful, Not Brilliant, Magnetic, Troubled

One fact was never disputed: Physically, this boy was sumptuous. No matter your taste or preference or your sensibility, when you stared at him all you saw was *pretty*. There was a deep mystery, a racial ambiguity in that face. You couldn't tell his background. You knew Black was involved. *But Black and, what?* It confounded many. Was it Black and Italian, Spanish, Irish, or something more exotic, like maybe Tasmanian? Full of sharp angles and green-eyed mischief, he stood 6 foot 5 and weighed 180 pounds. Most entrancing was that chameleon-like skin in the sun, how the tones of tan turned to taupe and bronze. And everything just seemed to come alive when he smiled.

Folks said he looked like a junior Paul Newman. A strange Egyptian version, with eyes as green as Newman's were blue. Green jewels and cool lime specks of light. When people noted his celebrity likeness, he'd smile and say, "Well, it's like this. I'm Mr. Newman's love child, 'kay? But we don't talk about it. It's too painful." Some people actually believed the lie, despite the fact that he was a full head and a cluster of curls *taller* than Newman.

Lie or no lie, in a place where talented kids would give their tender young tits to be famous, Pascal's line bought him instant popularity. They noticed that face. That face launched a thousand crushes. That *face* got him props. That face became his name. He claimed he wanted to be an actor, but he already looked like a star.

His pulsar was evident.

Rumor had it someone called in a favor to get him accepted. There may have been some truth to that.

His audition: deemed passable at best, a diligent application of a finite talent.

But Pascal was a culturally mixed phallic symbol: tall, erect, recalling the athletic grace of a ballplayer mixed with the insouciance of a minor prince. Ah! He of the beautifully cool, confident exterior.

Faison, Age 17
Gifted, Unlucky, Obstinate, Unlucky

Faison Brown acted like a thug—a straight-up bully. Albeit a short, squat, obnoxious, "damn he can sing his ass off" bully.

Upon hearing him, David relented:

"Shit! That boy *can sing!* Hell, *I almost wanna do him* when he sings. Whatever's good inside Faison, it all comes out when he sings.

As Tyrone would later coin it:

"Faison "Browny" Brown had the makings of a true *artiste*: immense talent dwelling inside a miserable human being. I always thought he was full of shit, but then he opened his mouth and *sang*."

Things rarely come easy for short, dark, attitudinal boys who dream of being stars. Yet Faison had *his* hot, happy happening future all tripped out. He was Faison Marcellus Brown, the Best Damn Singer in school, and after one of those showcases some top talent agent was going to hear him, *feel* him, and sign him to a multi-LP deal. In Faison's World, *cute* was wasted on the cute-seekers; *talent* got paid.

Browny, at his own audition:

"When I was four, I started singin' in church 'cause I seen other big-headed kids doin' it. I heard all that screechin' yah-yah-yaah, and *knew* they couldn't blow. But *I* could. By the time I was six, I was a soloist in all kinds of talent shows, sang at people's parties, weddings, funerals. Show business is my goal. See, I come from Harlem. We go to the The Apollo once a month. Now *that's* show business! Everybody's played there. My Pops used to date the Sandman's cousin's daughter, and once he took me backstage to meet Smokey freakin' Robinson! There he was, all suave, beige, and *smoky*-eyed. My Pops told him I could sing. 'Go'n sing for the man, Faison,' he said. But I was way too busy messin' my pants. Smokey understood. He told me, 'You keep at it, kid. I grew up in the projects too.' That's what Smokey said. Hard to believe with all that class and style Smokey got, he came from poor Black folks like me.

"But I ain't no sweet-soundin' falsetto. Nah. I'm a mad natural tenor with a three-octave range. I don't just blow—I *ascend*. R&B ain't ready for me. You know what inspires me? Opera. Black folks ain't too used to hearin' opera. But that's cool. I'ma change 'em. This is gonna surprise y'all, but I digs me some Luciano Pavarotti. Luciano is *the man*! That's how I see myself: Faison Marcellus Brown, first tenor at the Met, performin' *Rigaletto, Porgy and Bess*— all the greats! You just watch me, yo."

And then he opened his mouth to sing, and this extraordinary sound floated out across the room and into a place where excellence is nourished.

MANY FIGHTS, REHEARSALS, AND MORE FIGHTS LATER...

Ty, David, Face, and Browny had become "Da Elixir." Conflict was a constant. Moments before they went onstage at the Winter Extravaganza, Browny was yelling, "Yo, Ty, you foul! Tryna ice us, huh? I just heard you. You and Raines was talkin' about *you own-ing* the song and stuff. Like the rest of us ain't worked hard on this bullshit!"

Just as fists were about to fly, it was *showtime!*

As Raines had promised, his nephew, genius producer "Tabby" Freeman, was present. Freeman sat attentively, digging the song, the moves, the staging—digging the whole act. After the finale, Freeman approached Tyrone about making a demo of his song. A hyped Ty quickly agreed, but only if he secured the rights to his own publishing. Reluctantly, Freeman acquiesced. Ty had one more con-dition: "It's gotta be a package deal. The other cats get to sing on wax," he said.

* * *

Together, Da Elixir made a very sweet noise. Their song was a rhythmic tale of teenage love lost, sung with David's crying falsetto, leading into Browny's soaring tenor, backed by Ty's solid baritone. And Depina...well, he gave good face. When the song hit the air-waves, everyone was *hyped!* Suddenly, Da Elixir was Number 51 With a Bullet. Premier East Coast DJ Eddie O'Jay caught the bug, then Paco, followed by Frankie Crocker. Then Vy Higgenson bit, and soon everybody was diggin' them, digging it. Suddenly Da Elixir was like, The Shit!

By early April they were the opening act at the Apollo. Local disco shows were biting for their delight, and even *Soul Train* was beckoning. But by June Da Elixir fizzled. Face Depina had just graduated, and aware of his matinee idol looks, decided he was just too damn pretty for that group bullshit. *Besides,* he thought, *I never liked any of them small-time motherfuckers anyway.*

After Depina's departure, David soon followed.

Ty thought it best to break the news to Browny in public, on a crowded subway.

"Aw, na-a-ah! No! No! Not like this! Nah! I *ain't* goin' out like that! Yo! Whose ass I gotta kick to stop this shit? David's?"

Ty wanted say, *Didn't David already flatten yo ass once?* But he chilled. Browny was past livid, and you *don't* wanna fuck with a livid, ambitious bully.

"We worked too hard, man. We on top, now! We about to do *Soul Train*, man! Make it stop, yo! Make these crazy mothafuckers come to they senses!" Browny was holding his head in both hands. He thought it might explode if he didn't. "Ty, you could do it. Fuck Pass-cow! Never liked him anyway. You and David done got tight, yo. Make *him* stay. We got plenty singers around us, we could get another one. We could still *do* this!"

"Like I told ya, Browny, it's a done deal. Now that he's graduated, Face wants to act. And David, he doesn't even wanna go on without Face. Remember what happened the night of the Extravaganza? Now David's all strung-out over that cat. Besides, this summer he's got some auditions on Broadway."

"Well fuck 'em both. Yo, you and me, we'll find us somebody else. Don't you wanna be a star, yo?"

"Me? Nah. Da Elixir was just a freak thing. I'm a writer, man."

"Well, what about *me?*" Browny asked.

"You're the real singer, man. You've got the chops. If you go to Juilliard and study hard, I *know* you could make it happen."

"Juilliard?" he threw up his disgusted hands. "Shit, man! People go there to try to be somebody. We already *are* somebody, damn it! Da Elixir is 'bout to be *big*, yo!"

"Look. I'm sorry if this messes with your plans, but nobody else is really into it anymore."

Ty placed a comforting hand on Browny's shoulder. Browny quickly knocked it away. He wanted to hit Tyrone. Just kick his ass all over the IRT.

Two

Fire in the Pews

In *The Latin Quarter* the coolest club kids danced *The Rock*, *The Patty Duke*, and *The Wop* as hip-hop came fully out the box. Spray paint cans in artistic hands tagged the South Bronx livelier than it had ever been. Urban kids spun on their heads as homelessness spun out of control. The bass and freebase was all over the place.

The Roxy, November 1982

David was dancing on Broadway. Thanksgiving eve, though, he wanted to go roller-skating. So he called Tyrone, who, being in his sophomore year at Columbia, was full of new collegiate insights and metaphors.

"There was this *family* in the neighborhood," Tyrone told David. "A whole mess of them, called the Johnsons. A gang of boys, all beautiful, all talented, all dynamic. They sang, danced, did impressions, mastered crazy instruments. They made a pretty black noise in a small segment of the world. Hell, they were like ghetto Jacksons. It was only later people discovered most of those Johnsons were never *really* family. They were adopted, trained, punished, rewarded, and conditioned to perform. Like lab rats. Then, little by little, those Johnson boys began to disappear, vanish, ple forgot all about 'em. But for a time, the Johnsons ruled the earth," Tyrone proclaimed, skating away from David.

"Tyrone?" David asked, catching up to him. "I know you're heavy into symbolism this week, but the point of that story would be…?"

"*We* were the Johnsons, Davy. We *are* the fucking Johnsons!"

* * *

Two nights later, Davy devised an Elixir reunion. Davy, Ty, Face, and Browny met for a movie. The animosity was palpable, though initially misguided.

Browny yelled at a man sprawled on the pavement, "Yo! Negro! Leave that pipe alone!"

"Easy, Browny! That's prob'ly somebody's old man," Face said.

"So what? Don't nobody give a shit about his drunk ass, or he wouldn't be lyin' out there like that!"

"There but for the grace of God, my brother," Ty reminded him. Just then, Tyrone stopped his stride. He bent down and asked the man earnestly, "You all right, sir? You need a cup of coffee, a good meal, or something?"

The man stared vaguely out of his chaos, and spat, "Fuck you, punk!"

And the others broke out in laughter—loud, crazy, uproarious laughter.

"You wild, Tyrone! Yo! What was you gonna do, ask him to step to the movies with us?" Browny joked, laughing harder than the rest, holding his stomach and chortling into the night.

"Nice try, though, Ty. So what movie we gonna see?" David asked as the gang of four strutted along Broadway.

"Yo! I hear that new Chuck Norris flick's dope. It's 'posed to be def!" Browny suggested.

"No karate flicks! Blah!" David protested.

"Karate flicks are cool," Ty said. "But dang! When was the last time any of you cats saw a good *Black* movie? Bet ya can't remember, can you?"

"I can't," David said. "Sometimes I just wanna holla: Yo Hollywood, ple-e-ease give us Negroes a chance!"

"It's 1982, Davy. Come correct: Please give us *African-Americans* a chance!"

"No, Ty. I said it right the first time. Hey, I know," David suggested. "Let's see that new movie, *Making Love*. I hear the two men actually *kiss*," he whispered gleefully.

"Yo! Sports fans! Anybody see the Knicks game last night?" Browny asked, guiding the gab away from Davy and Ty's eternally queer talk.

Tyrone and David answered in a resounding, simultaneous, "Nah!"

Browny tried again, "Yo! Facey, you used to run track. What you think of this new cat, Carl Lewis? That boy's bound to cop some crazy Olympic gold, huh?"

But Face was silent. Track? That shit was a lie he'd told back in high school. Depina never ran track. But he'd also never copped to his athletic deception, and at that point, he couldn't see a reason why he should.

David proclaimed, "Carl Lewis. There's something about that fast-ass Black boy I really *like*."

"I hear Diana's playing the Garden. Anybody wanna go? I'll buy the tickets," Tyrone said.

"Bet!" Browny quickly accepted.

"I can't, damn it! *Cats*, remember? I swear, all this steady work's puttin' a serious hurt on my social life," David complained. "Mondays are dark, though. I heard Luther's playin' the Beacon next month. And you *know* I loves me some Loofuh!"

"Who the fuck *don't* you love, ya little queer?" Coming from Face Depina, those words brought a particular sting. David tried not to show it.

"Yo! Check it. This movie, the eats, the get high, hell, this whole night's on you, right, Tyrone?" Browny made it sound like a given.

"Browny? Do I *look* like your Daddy?" Ty inquired, only half-jokingly.

"Yo! Come on, Tyrone! You's the one with all this new money, homey. You's the *only one* gettin' paid!"

"Browny, give it a rest," said David. "It ain't his fault he's brilliant."

"Fuck that shit! Tyrone? Yo, you payin' or what?" Browny hounded.

"I'll pay your way, Browny. All right? You *happy* yet?" Ty said. "But don't let this become a habit."

"Too late," said Face. "Already has."

"Yo! You mighta *wrote* the damn song, but ya didn't sing it all by ya damn self, did ya? We *all* shoulda been paid! Right, Pass-cow? Why ain't you sayin' shit? I *know* you feel the same way."

"And what *way* is that, Browny?" Ty's irritation growing.

"Shit! Ya wrote the motherfuck, but the rest of us shouldn't be paid?"

"You know what, Browny? You're absolutely correct. I *wrote* the motherfuck. I *own* the publishing rights. Get over it. Or try to stop bitchin' long enough to sit down and *write yourself* a number 1 hit. Then *you* can spend the ducats anyway you want, ya hateful bastard!"

"Yo! I oughta bust you in your punk ass! Keep runnin' yo fuckin' mouth, Tyrone!"

Tyrone stopped in his tracks. "So, you wanna *fight* me now, Browny?" he asked. "After *all* we've been through? Yo! *Yo!*" he mocked. "I'm talkin' to you, Faison! You wanna kick my ass? Huh? Then c'mon, let's do this, 'cause I'm sick with you and your petty shit!"

"Calm down, Ty. He's being Browny, like always," David said. "You know he's just jealous. Let's try havin' a good time, for once."

But Browny refused to let it go.

"Depina! Yo, Face! Don't you want some of this?" Browny said. "Ain't you got somethin' to say?"

"Oh? So now you *both* wanna kick my ass all up and down Broadway? Why you trippin' like this?" Tyrone asked, his face grimacing, then hardening in disgust.

"Well," Face said. "I ain't got no beef with you, Tyrone. It's *your* song, *your* money, man. But you know that shit was wrong."

Suddenly Tyrone was way north of pissed. "See, David. Pay attention. What did I tell you about the Johnsons? Ain't no love, no brotherhood, no *nothin'* stronger than ignorant greed! The Ojay's had that shit correct. A small piece of paper carries a lotta dead weight. I said I'd take care of you all, and I *meant* it. Don't I break you off every chance I get? But it's never enough, is it? You'll always find something new to bitch about. You know what? Fuck a movie!" Ty said, then turned and walked in the opposite direction.

"Aw, Ty! C'mon! Don't be like that!" David called out.

"Yo! Fuck him!" Browny bellowed. "Don't nobody care about his bourgie ass! Walk, bitch! Yo! David, you his favorite, why don't you wag yo little ass behind him?"

"You know what, Browny?" David said. "That shit was small and fucked up, just like you! The record label screwed us, not Ty. When he breaks you off a grip, it's out of *his* pocket. Tyrone is a fuckin' *prince*, but you can't see that!"

"Fuckin' *princess* is more like it!" said Face, nudging Browny into laughter.

"*Et tu*, Pascal?" Davy challenged.

"Fuck off, cocksucka," Face snapped. "Yeah, I said it. Now go home and cry about it like the little bitch you are!"

Turning their backs on David, Face and Browny headed for the nearest theater.

Why you suddenly hate me so much, Facey? David thought. *God help me! Why am I so attracted to them pretty, damaged boys?*

Drawn to the dual plastic idols of Good-looks and Cool-swagger, David had a history of genuflecting before false gods.

* * *

There was a kind of magic about David Richmond, and it both attracted and repelled, sometimes both at once. David was an *original*.

It mattered not if the boarding room in his head housed 127 personalities, each of whom "dressed for every occasion." All of those people under his skin were a lithe copper dancer dancing, tumbling toward grace.

Fey, silly, sexy, wise, whatever and whoever he was, he was always uniquely David. He'd breezed through tap and made a quick slide into jazz, then found an affinity for the rigors of ballet. When he was 10, he'd proudly been accepted into the prestigious Dance Theater of Harlem's Children's Summer Program. He'd worked hard, followed instruction, and by summer's end he was perfection in a Danskin. Back then, David believed that once he returned home he'd be a *firebird*, burning, flying, ready to soar.

Instead his preacher father decided he was a tad too merry for comfort. So it became the Right Reverend Daddy Richmond's mission to make a "man" of his son. And he handed down an edict: "Boy, if you gonna float around here like some fancy sissy, then you gonna have to learn to fight!" The Right Reverend Daddy took David to a gym and demanded that he learn to box.

Daddy Richmond was determined to whip that little fairy clean out of Davy.

Boxing gave David a place to vent his anger over his father's implication that what he was wasn't good enough. Under those circumstances, the kid kicked much ass. He affected the swagger of a jock, picked up the *shit talk*. It was a whole new role for David, an improvisation called survival.

The dancer-cum-athlete used his body as a brilliant artist would. With a cock of the head, a tilt of the neck, he *became* other people. He'd move from Pacino in *Scarface* to Vivian Leigh in *Ship of Fools*. People were there to be *fooled*, and fuck 'em if they can't take a joke.

But not everything was a joke. David took love, or the idea of it, very seriously. David truly, madly, deeply loved the idea of *falling in love*. Always had. Unfortunately, he had a knack for meeting the most unlovable people on the planet.

Rico Rivera, for example.

A new and noticeably robust member of Daddy Richmond's congregation, Rico was a darkly handsome Black Puerto Rican with a history of amateur boxing. 15-year-old David couldn't seem to keep his eyes or his mind off him.

* * *

Even eight years later, David couldn't stop thinking of him.

APRIL 1985

David was a queer character in many ways. Among his curiosities, he actually *liked* attending funerals. For him, they were social events. And didn't David always look fly in black? He'd slip on his one modest suit, step into a parlor, sign the register, and should he be asked, he'd say, "I used to stop by after work, and we'd talk." Which was more socially acceptable than the truth. But this day was different. More than anything, he longed to say, "When I was 15, I used to collect his sweaty jockstraps from the locker room floor. I sniffed them and masturbated myself to sleep. And *you* would be…?"

For this funeral, David meant serious grieving business. But like those times when he was 15, other thoughts intruded. As David listened to the mourners' solemn sentiments, he remembered Rico in his prime—a 5-foot-10, russet-skinned, thick-printed *wonderman*…

David had already learned to box some, but that wasn't enough. The Reverend had a notion that Rico just might be the right influence to *set David straight*. "Take my boy to the gym," he told Rico. "Turn the little sissy into a fighter!"

Rico, a middleweight with quick hands and a hot glare, once had a shot at the pros. Thus, in Reverend Richmond's eyes Rico was a worthy role model. It mattered not that Rico had recently been paroled from prison, where he'd been sent for breaking and entering. He'd paid his debt to society, and "let those without sin," and so on…The Reverend trusted Rico to get the job done.

David's interest in boxing suddenly grew.

After a rigorous workout, Rico would head for the showers,

leaving a trail of ripe clothing in his wake. Behind him, David would gather those damp articles, adoring them, sniffing their musk. There, David would watch Rico stand under a jetting nozzle: those exquisitely rounded globes, the hot carved legs splayed apart, the water running wet down his body in jeweled rivulets.

Once, Rico turned, and David stared at beauty. Sierra-skinned jackfruit in all its oblong soft-pulped beauty beckoned to him from beneath tufts of black grass. Perfect, peculiar, full. David noticed how it seemed to be stretching; yes, that bronze bar was elongating in its skin, growing hard as wrought iron. Was it begging, hissing, saying, *"Suck me"!?*

Against the pounding sound of his chest, David asked, "You OK? You need anything, Rico?"

Rico didn't answer right away. Seduction was a quiet dance around the ring of David's libido. Finally he said, "No. Get outta here, kid!"

And the world ended.

Until the day Rico said, after a workout, "C'mon, Davy. Let's me and you take a ride."

Rico drove fast that dark night, and his silence and speed scared David.

Once safe at Rico's, the boxer said, "I think we done enough foreplay, don't you?" Then he led David into a small gym-like room complete with a punching bag, mats, and the stink of old sweat. He tossed a pair of gloves at David, and demanded, "Put 'em on!"

At that point, the *last* thing David wanted to do was box. But he did as instructed. Immediately, Rico slugged him on the chin—hard enough to make him cry. He then began tagging him with body blows. As David tried to shake them off, Rico cold-cocked him in the nose. David fell hard to the mats.

"We sparred long enough. Now drop those fuckin' sweats!" Rico commanded.

"Fuck you!" David spat, lying on the mats, his feelings, his body, everything in him hurting. Except for his jackfruit, and Rico could *see* that.

Crouching low, Rico ripped Davy's sweats in two, leaving him exposed and bulging in his jock. Rico tongued along the warming cloth, and then all at once he yanked down the combustible panel and gobbled up its hot, salty contents.

Suddenly David's trembling member swam in the impulsive current of a man's mouth. A thousand sensations melded into one sighing moan. All he could do was moan. To be steeped in that crush of tongue and saliva was the most *authentic* thing he'd ever known.

It was realer than religion, realer than sin!

David very quickly—too quickly—shivered, shuddered, and spurted all over.

Afterward, ever the sweet talker, Rico warned, "I'll kick yo fuckin' ass if you ever tell, or if you do this shit with somebody else! Hear me? I swear, I'll fuck you up!" And those hot words were music to David's burning ears.

One week later, Rico redefined the meaning of "Breaking and Entering." But David would be the first to admit his little sugar plum was ripe to be plucked. What David remembered were plaid Bermuda shorts and Rico's stems: Strong and dark, they shone with mad-sexy muscle.

And those deep sable eyes that were all over him.

They parked in the woods on the edge of a lake. Rico's large warm hand crept up David's trim thigh and burned there like a brand. "You hot, ain't you, Davy? I can tell," Rico said, as his hand delved inside David's Fruit of the Looms.

They headed into the woods, stopping in the densest part. There, they rubbed their inflamed sticks together, hard, harder, until they seared, made fire.

Next, there was kissing. Long, liquid kissing. And Rico gave David a new appreciation of hands. Hands were as paramount to lovemaking as they were to the art of dance or boxing. Each finger became an individual lover, probing so slowly and deeply that David soon begged for the genuine article.

"It'll sting a little at first," Rico warned. "It's supposed to. But don't worry, you'll get used to it."

Rico mounted him with quick and eager purpose. Suddenly, a large brown blade of lightning sliced David's core. "A-a-aw!" Pain inclined the dancer's spine into leaning. Pain came hard, pointed. Pain burned and stung until it became every kind of pain at once. David tightened, contesting every thick and brutalizing inch. His legs spread and stretched like those branches hovering above him. The rough husk and scratch of grass pricked and pounded, piercing, crushing him. Bark and limb and cherry were broken in that grass, and a burning boy yielded into moaning.

"That's it. Now you got it. Mmm. Just stay still, Davy, and let me make love to it."

David heard Rico clearly. He'd said *make love!* Make love, as opposed to fuck—which was what he was actually doing. Somehow, David's agony was lessened by the fact that he was pleasing Rico.

From the moment of that erect and zealous shudder deep within him, Rico Rivera became a minor god, the beau ideal, and the shining bronze prototype for David's future choices. Perhaps we all want some form of the thing which first wanted us. Or maybe we just long for the one thing we never truly possessed.

That summer, David learned the rhythm of bliss, and the elation in what his father called "sin." He'd learned to please, and to find a painful contentment in that pleasing.

And then Rico upped and married the church's second organist. David's Father, the Right Reverend Richmond, presided over the ceremony as David watched, quietly shattered, from the pews.

And now, a man with Rico's older, sadder face lay soundly, most profoundly dead. David Richmond wanted to scream: "*Liars!* Rico didn't die of any damn cancer!" But David had been taught good Christian etiquette, so he chilled. And then he rose, excused himself, and quickly exited that stained glass grievatorium. After all, it was Wednesday, Wet Jock Night at Limelight.

Three

The Condition of One's Loafers

As they often did, the New York contingent of the Hunter clan gathered at Tyrone's Aunt Viv's place for Sunday dinner. That particular day, all things seemed familiarly tribal as they commenced digging into the mutilated bird. But then, another kind of foul entered the festivities: Uncle Jerome. A small, rain-thin, pop-eyed man with an omnipresent porkpie hat, he stumbled in to perform his long-running one-man show entitled "Let's Piss on the Family Dinner."

"Aw-w-w! Y'all done started without me again," he said scratching his backside while Aunt Hattie clicked her tongue in disgust.

"Don't worry, I ain't got no fleas, Hattie," he countered. "I's scratchin' my ass 'cause it itch, damn it. Don't you fat Black church people's asses ever itch? Or do prayer cure that shit?"

No one said a word. Tyrone could feel his cheeks puffing like blowfishes. He wanted to laugh, but he knew enough to chill.

"Well, where my chair at, huh? Ain't I 'posed to have a chair in this here courtroom?"

The eating continued.

Jerome ambled, arms stretched out as if he were walking a tightrope to the china cabinet, and fetched himself a plate. He chose one of Viv's finest dishes. Then, staring at them all, Jerome purposely let it fall to the floor. Every person present jumped.

"Yeah, I drinks!" he proclaimed. "Damn it, I'm a drunk!" He gazed around the table at the faces of his family, faces that refused to acknowledge him. "Guess I be the only sinner in this room, huh? Well, ya ain't gotta feed me and ya ain't gotta love me if ya don't want. Guess what? I don't need ya. I'ma find me somebody. That's right. Me and my po drunk ass g'on find us somebody and we g'on live our *own* long blue moan."

Ty wondered what a "blue moan" was, and what the inebriated hell Jerome was talking about.

"Ain't nobody said you ain't got feelin's, Jerome. Now let me fix you a plate," Viv said.

No one else spoke. To Ty, it seemed to be a contest: Which Hunter family member could best ignore Jerome's drunken ass? Aunt Viv fixed him a plate. And after cussin' them out for "turnin' they backs on they own," Jerome left, and everything resumed as if his anger weren't still lurking in every corner of the room.

Once the sweet potato pie was finished and the young'ns, including Ty, were dismissed, the women started in on the Jerome conversation.

Ty followed his cousins sluggishly and heard his Aunt Hattie say, "Shit! You need to put his puny ass out!"

"What am I g'on do? Better he stay here than in the gutter!" Aunt Viv responded. "Girl, where else he gonna go? Don't nobody want him 'cause he fucks with men."

The phrase was blunt, concise, and shocking as "The Truth, Black-Folks Style" often is. No pussy-footing, no vague allusions to Jerome liking show tunes, or to the condition of his loafers. No creative euphemisms to pretty-up his vulgar reality. And Ty knew by the sound, the *inflection* in Viv's voice, that it *was* vulgar. Suddenly he understood why his Uncle Jerome was the eternal family outcast. Why Jerome drank the way he did. Why Jerome was barely tolerated. Yes, now he knew. And he wanted to weep for his uncle, and for himself. The lesson lay in four short words: He fucks with men.

Go ahead! Be a faggot, and alienate everyone you love!

Later that evening, Jerome cornered Ty, having recognized traces of himself in his teenage nephew. Tyrone expected the usual mindless drunken gibberish. Instead, Jerome grabbed him by the collar and said, "Can't nobody live yo life, but you, boi. So don't you let nobody steal yo motherfuckin' joy! Ya hear me?" He took a long, anguished swig from the brown paper bag he carried through life. "See, they don't like me," he declared, his eyes more sad than red. "They don't like me. Never did. My own brother and sisters, Ty. You think I did somethin' to 'em? I ain't did shit but tried to live my life. That's all."

Tyrone wanted to say something comical or comforting to blow it off. But he knew it was true.

They walked outside, and Jerome gazed at the setting sun, toasting it and his plastic freedom with his brown paper bag.

"Boi, look at me. You think I'm dumb, but I ain't. I see *you* clear. Let me tell you this," he said in a whisper. "Don't let no man take your manhood."

Ty wondered if Jerome was drunk. He didn't sound so drunk. But like those times when he *was* truly stupid-drunk, Ty didn't quite understand what he meant.

"You go'n live your life. You go'n meet men who feel like you feel. Some men will *like* you, for a minute. And that minute is tricky. Don't you go believin' in no minutes! Even when dem minute men make you feel like you ain't alone. Respect yourself! Don't you go takin' all kind of minute men inside you, boi. Find you somebody dat understands you, if you g'on go through dis pain out here. Find you somebody and hold on to dat. Don't make you no mo or less a man or a punk if you pitch or catch. You understand what I'm sayin'? Just don't you never let no bum inside you who ain't worth it. And make sure nobody go inside you without no rubber. Ya understand me, boi?"

Ty nodded, embarrassed as all hell. But now he understood. He understood that his crazy, drunk, *bent* Uncle loved him. Whatever the condition of *his* loafers.

Jerome wandered off down the block, nodding as he passed Omar Peterson.

Ty, his cousins, and Omar—19, well-built, and deeply hip—often sat on the same stoop watching life, kids, men, women, and fools go by. Beyond noticing him, Ty was *feeling* Omar. He dug his tough boy Brooklynese swagger, and how his deep-mahogany skin caught a shimmering light. Omar had a moist little habit of grabbing himself through his Levi's when he thought Ty was looking. Yeah. Omar was kind of hot in that "I don't have to try to be, I just got it like that" way. At least Ty thought so. Sometimes, he'd shoot Ty The Ray, and it made Tyrone wonder just *how hip* Omar was.

After Jerome passed, Omar strolled over toward Ty, handed him a note on the sly, then walked away.

That night, as Ty lay in bed, he opened Omar's surreptitious note.

Do you want to be a faget? I could show you. Nothing wrong with being a faget long as you keep it secret. I can show you the 69 Saturday. Come to the Brooklyn Library, and we could hook up. Just don't tell. If you don't want to it's OK. But just DON'T TELL anybody. Peace. 'O'. P.S. Throw away this note. I'm serious! Saturday morning after 10 o'clock, call me. Let my phone ring once then hang-up if you coming. Tyrone throw away this note. I'm serious!

For one belly-aching moment, he imagined it was a cruel hoax. Or worse, a setup. Maybe Omar and his big bad Brooklyn boys would show up and whale on his "faget" ass, punch him in the throat and kick him in the dick.

Then his mind took a *negativity pause*. Maybe Omar *was* gay. Ty considered the secrecy, the constant grabbing of the dick, and how, when Omar said something funny, he'd look at Ty as if measuring Ty's glee factor, Ty's *delight*.

Everything made a vague kind of sense. *Yeah! Omar could be that way!* The prospect excited Ty because from the first day Ty saw him, he dug him some Omar with his hard-boy, dark-chocolate, crotch-grabbing, cool-ass self.

Tyrone read and reread that note, pushing, pulling, rubbing his stiffness into those words, pulling and tugging until the ink began to smudge, blur, and flood the page.

* * *

Saturday came. Ty dialed the digits, let it ring once, and abruptly hung up. Butterflies aside, he told the appropriate lies and hopped a subway to the Brooklyn Library. But if Omar fucked around and wore the wrong outfit, didn't comb his hair, brush his teeth, or any other equally unappealing shit...

Hello. Omar appeared, and he did not disappoint. In his black Levi's and white tee—one sleeve rolled up, two Kools in the crease—Omar was Brooklyn heat personified.

"Hey," he said. "So you wanna do this?" His voice was full of confidence.

"Bet. Let's go." A warm thrill rose in Ty's belly, a slightly high, slightly ill feeling of nerves, anticipation, and curiosity. They walked side by side, but not too close, and neither had much to say.

No one was home at Omar's crib. But he didn't know exactly when one of his brothers, his sister, or heaven forbid *his moms* might return.

"Wanna beer?" he asked, playing the host.

"No, thanks," Ty replied. He never much liked beer, and besides, he already felt on the verge of retching. So he sat on the couch, pretending to be enthralled by the longhaired Asian chick shaking her tail down the *Soul Train* line. Omar stood near the telly, slowly, blatantly rubbing that notorious thing he rubbed.

Ty looked, saw that growing soul train line in Omar's Levi's, and said, "So, whachu wanna do, man?"

Omar glared at him as if to say, *Damn boy! I know you a virgin, and this shit is new for you. But are ya stupid, too? We ain't about to do the nasty in the middle of my mama's livin' room, fool!* But what he said was, "Follow me."

So Ty followed him down that long thin hallway indigenous to Brooklyn apartments. Omar stopped where the deed would be done, at the end of the corridor, in an empty space near the closet by the room Omar shared with his brother. A slant of July sunlight streamed inside and hovered in that space, giving them just enough light to see, admire, trace the contours of each other.

Omar removed his shirt. The Brother's chest was a terrific traffic jam of dark, hard, muscular lines swerving one into the hard dark next. Already there were black ringlets splayed across it, and rich chocolate nipples sat erect and stony as two hardened Brooklyn projects. Suddenly there were crazy beats in Ty's chest. Omar's skin in that limited light was close to indigo, and like smoke, it swirled in Tyrone's eyes. Omar held him inside a stare. Did he know what a prize he was? Did he know his full lips were like soft, puffy rafts Ty wanted to board and, if he could, sail away on from every secret he ever kept.

More than anything, Ty wanted to kiss those lips. But he didn't know the rules yet. Still, it seemed Omar was willing him to kiss his neck, to lick his pulsing jugular. Looking at him, Ty recalled those summers of pickup B-ball games, funky Converse All-Stars, and the shooting gush of hydrant waters washing him clean, washing *them* clean. But they were boys then. And as far as he could see, Omar was now *a man*.

And the man unfastened his pants. And the man wore blazing red nylon briefs. And those briefs were swollen and stretching and taut. And red nylon never hugged a man's dick tighter. And that dick was large. Unexpectedly, breathlessly large!

Omar pulled at Ty's tee, grinding his largeness into Ty's thigh. Backing away, Ty removed his shirt. Omar placed Ty's hand on his growing bulge. A rush of adrenaline zoomed up Ty's spine. Ty rubbed and Omar's cock grew and spiked through the skinny shroud of nylon.

"Stand back," Omar warned, as if his giant dick needed room to make its big debut. Ty stepped back. And Omar rolled those red nylon briefs slowly down his hips, thighs, calves…

And there he stood. Beyond Large. Beyond Hard. Beyond words. The deepest, darkest mahogany rod bobbed long and exquisitely flawed. The dim light illuminated its head just so. Omar was *much* more man than Ty had bargained for.

"Now let's see you," Omar said.

Ty was, by then, hard as hard could possibly be. Seven and a half inches of taut, teenage buoyancy. He unzipped, reached in, and produced his erect and leaking fruit.

Omar slapped his custard apple against Tyrone's, flushing him with heat. They stood foreheads touching, breathing hard and stroking. Breathing hard and grinding, their swollen lips, wanting kisses, wanting everything. But afraid, withholding.

They stood closeasthis, breathing, sweating, breathing, waiting, anticipating.

Omar moved first. A dip, a bend. A pinch. A raw and hungry gnaw of nipple. A slow descent down chest and belly and bush. One breath through the kiss of Omar's lips, and Ty disappeared inside a hot shock of moisture. Slippery. Hot. Gliding. Hot. Heading for the throat hot! Ah-h-h! First time blow job. Everything inside Ty quickened, suddenly alive, dynamic, active, and supreme. Brand-new bliss slid, surfed, and slushed along him. His amorous hand slid across the spiraling waves of Omar's spinning skull. Thoughts of something like *Love* began whirling in his belly.

Then, looking up, his eyes fixed inside that *need*, Omar smiled and said, "Now you try me."

He pulled Ty down, and they lay on the cool wooden floor, contorting like dark and salty pretzel boys. The taste of Omar's sweat kissed Ty's lips, and with one deep, memorable breath he made that glide down pounding chest, heaving belly, and scratching path of pubic naps to that tremulous tip.

Oh! So *this* was "69"! Breaths quickened into labored panting, into strident bucks, into pitching hips and lips sighing, "Ah! Shit!" Omar's strong hand shoved Ty's head further down his long slippery wedge—so warm, so wet, so strange and heavy to his tongue. The act became a test to see if he could possibly possess its wholeness. He could not. Yet, through a river of sweat and knots and wild pulses, he tried.

Omar's sucking grip grew stronger, tighter, as he commenced sucking like street-tough roughnecks never dared to suck. Soon, he was fighting the pitch of Ty's dick-happy thrusts, and he was winning.

Tyrone devoured what he could, his lips and tongue running, his head and neck pumping against the heat of skin and drum of veins. "Ah-h-h!" he shuddered, closing his eyes, stretching his lips wider. Omar became a long blue moan caught in Tyrone's throat, and Ty didn't want that sweet choking to end. Omar plunged deeper, and together they caught the same fever, same rhythm, same fire. Moving together, tough and tender, angry and sweet, hurting and cured.

Omar pulled away, and Ty followed. Their excited hands commenced to beating proud wet stalks. The verge of eruption seemed a breath away. Ty volcanoed first, bursting, filling his fist in hot spiking rivers of white. Omar followed, shaking, shooting, spraying the floor like a black Uzi.

Ty lay there with a man, a full, bucking, squirting man. He fell into Omar's face and found himself, landing on the softest reaches of its tough owner's soul. The *thud* was so precise, it was unmistakable: Ty was falling in love with Omar, and a minute before he hadn't even known that feeling could ever exist. But his mind sighed, *Oh, Ty. You love him. Uh-oh! You love him, and he's a roughneck.*

Roughneck not withstanding, Tyrone had become Officially Queer. A new and radiant "faget." A happy, albeit closeted, citizen of the other side.

"What time is it? Quick, man. You gotta get dressed! My sister'll be back from doin' laundry any minute," Omar said, killing the mood, but never the memory. They both quickly dressed, and it didn't matter to Ty if the Brother had no postfellatio etiquette; Ty felt sure they were destined.

Three weeks later, with much coaxing and slow neck kissing, Ty *gave it up*. He experienced the agony of the anus with a man inside it, because, for Omar, it was mandatory. He remembered his Uncle Jerome's warning. It didn't stop him. But he insisted rubbers be involved.

Giving it up to Omar was the biggest, most painful, most necessary lesson of Ty's sexual schooling: Men are dicks, and dicks are cool, but let one inside you and it hurts.

After its agonizing culmination, for Omar the challenge was gone. Thus, their queer relationship ended. Omar had fucked himself another virgin. Mission complete. Omar checked Ty off the list, like dry cleaning.

It pissed-off, sickened, crushed, and toughened Tyrone.

"Omar might've been a roughneck, but he was a *bigger punk* than me," Ty would later say. "He turned out to be a cowardly clown. I could've shown him how to step inside the center ring. But he fucked around, got scared, and missed the whole damn carnal carnival."

Four

"Face" the Facts

As it turns out, Mr. Paul Newman didn't go slumming through the South Bronx and leave his seed to nest inside some sweet café au lait creature resulting in pretty-ass Face Depina. However, Face still had a color-rich pedigree. His mother, Matilda "Mattie" Dupree, was part Creole, part Caribbean. She bore a striking resemblance to Lena Horne. His father, Alphonze "Fonzy" Depina, was Portuguese and a quarter German. A real good-looking cat. Fonzy played a mean jazz sax and was a preeminent studio musician back in the day. A chronic drugger, boozer, and womanizer supreme, he put aside his pills, potions, and pandemic penis as soon as he first laid eyes on Matilda. At least, for a time.

"Dupree, huh?" he'd asked. "So, just exactly how French are you?"

Ah! Mattie of the flowing black hair and flashing hazel eyes. Their love was real, dizzying, lyrical, and so very jazzy. But their concerto caused much disharmony, as neither family condoned their coupling. Mattie, though fair, was deemed too dark for the boldly beige Portuguese Depina clan. And Alphonze was so high-yella, he was damn near white. Besides, the man was a musician—

by definition *a fancy-ass vagabond*. Yet nothing could stop two crazy kids in love.

And, ah! The things that bloom from the flowers we love.

* * *

Face: "Family? What the fuck is that? Movin' from one broke-down project to the next? One more set of people that didn't know who I was, or *what* I was. Just 'cause what I was didn't *look* like them, it was all right to call me 'half-and-half,' 'octoroon maricoon,' 'mixed spick,' 'butter pecan nigga.' I heard all that shit and worse. And *this* was *family*. Every last one of 'em was stone broke and hopeless as they fuckin' jokes! Treated me like shit. I used to run away just so I could get lost somewhere, anywhere. Never got all the way lost, though, 'cause don't people try to find you when you lost? I don't remember nobody ever tryin' to find my poor yellow ass."

Pascal Depina was punted back and forth between relatives like a worn-out soccer ball. He heard it all, from "You take him. I got six kids, and I never did like his daddy anyway" to "Foster parent? Well, how much do it pay?"

Finally, he landed in the streets of East Harlem, keeping company with stripper chicks, dealers, pickpockets, and cons. He lived by his wits, stole what he could, panhandled when he had no choice. More than once, he slept in a dumpster. Other times, he relied on the kindness of carnal-minded strangers.

Then, one day *she* saw him.

February 1974

"Boy? Whatchu doin' out here on these streets? Ain't you got someplace to be? Somebody home waitin' for you, son? You hungry? You ain't on nothin', is you? Fess up! Don't even try to run no game on me!"

Lavinia "Precious" Stone was a streetwalker who saw a lost, green-eyed boy trying his best to be brave. And that green-eyed boy awakened a memory in her. She imagined Pascal as the *What if?* on the other side of her first abortion. She offered him room, board, and a taste of her terminal freedom. Because he was looking to love someone, Pascal loved her. She had the softest hazelnut skin, too soft and pretty for the dirty work she did.

"They rent my body," she told him. "That's it. Not one of these played-out three-minute sons of bitches evuh gets *my* heart!"

Then she smiled a smile reserved only for him, and he snuggled in her bed to sleep with her. He was 14; she was 33. She was everything: mother, father, protector, provider, and finally his lover. Some nights she'd let him suckle her, and she'd pacify him to sleep. But that kind of intimacy began to feel wrong to Pascal.

"People *always* put they damn hands on me," he told her. "Women was playin' with my peter when I didn't want nobody playin' with it."

The men were no better. Nor were the crazy aunts and cousins, and uncles, and the kids down the street.

He was a pretty, yellow, green-eyed novelty, and *that* was all anybody ever wanted to know about him.

"I remember my only birthday party. I was 6. Aunt Claire made a chocolate cream cake. Don't remember how it tasted. All I remember is crazy Aunt Vera yellin' 'Happy Birthday, Pascal' and jammin' her fuckin' tongue down my throat. They made me run around naked, and they pointed and laughed at me. 'Let's see if little Pascalito's pee-pee grown!' That shit was wrong! They was supposed to look out for me."

Lavinia listened, the shielded pieces of her heart unraveling to him. "I'm sorry, honey. I thought you *wanted* to be close to me. I…I didn't know," she said, lightly kissing his shoulder. "I swear on everything left to believe in, Pascal, I won't never touch you wrong again."

She kept her word. And she died of cervical cancer the following spring.

So Pascal Depina was 15 and back on the streets when he wandered into a midtown parish. It was said to be a *safe house* under the care of good Christian men, with caregiving eyes and arms spread wide open to welcome children of the skid-marked night. But despite their robes and talk of God, they were no different than the rest who saw beauty and abused its golden boyish body.

Pascal met Angel at that safe house. Angel, a vet at 10, had the safe house thing tricked out by 13. He was a street-scarred 16 when he got into a fistfight with Pascal. They battled to a draw, and Angel's iciness thawed a bit.

It was the winter of a growth spurt. Pascal went from 5 foot 10 to 6 foot 3, and Angel dug how the new height, voice, and premature beauty got them inside liquor stores, movie doors, and cool restricted clubs. Yet, it didn't take long before Angel grew to resent that shit, too.

When you're walking down 42nd Street and the whores tease *your boy*, oohing and ahing at his prettiness and offering to fuck *him* for free, it can piss you off. Everything seemed to come effortlessly for Pascal. Angel would gawk at that dreamy puss, looking so damn smug and so fucking pretty, and he'd almost want to fuck him himself. He wanted to kick his ass, then fuck him. But Angel couldn't, because Angel was straight. So Angel kicked his ass and left him in the gutter.

MAY 1975

Erik Von Ness was Viking blond, ice-blue-eyed, and brick-headed. He was New York's *other* extreme, Fifth Avenue–bred, a former pilot, mountain climber, full of daring-do. Von Ness was born with a fortune, and added to it by investing well. He met Pascal outside of Port Authority, where Pascal was running his latest hustle: picking pockets under the guise of helping travelers with their bags. The tip was usually 50 cents, a dollar, a five-spot tops. But Von Ness *looked like money*. Pascal swooped up Erik's Ralph Lauren bags and placed them into a waiting cab, deciding to leave his wallet alone. Von Ness, liking the cut of Depina's jib and that mad young cobra lounging in shrink-to-fit, purposefully tight 501's, handed him a 50-spot.

"Keep it. It's yours."

"For real? Thanks! Thanks a lot, man."

Then Von Ness wagged the dick of his finger and asked, "Would you like to take a ride?"

Opportunity smelled of expensive cologne.

Pascal told Von Ness his story, emphasizing the parts rich white liberal horny people would want to rectify.

"So...what about school?" Erik was fascinated by the kid's tale of urban survival.

"School? When I went, they called me 'ghetto trash' 'cause I didn't look like them or wear the right clothes. Hell, I don't *got no* clothes."

"I don't *have any* clothes," Von Ness corrected.

Pascal told him he was going to be somebody "Large." Maybe even an actor. "In junior high, they put on that play *Guys and Dolls*. I was Nathan Detroit. Folks say I was good. Man! I sure *felt* good on that stage, with that applause, and all that good shit! I wasn't ghetto trash no more. They got schools for kids with talent. I know this kid who goes to one. So maybe if I save enough cash, I'll find a place, cop some fly rags, and look into something like that."

"Well, you certainly have *presence*," Erik said. He stared at Pascal and saw a grit that wasn't yet grimy. Inside that contemplative eye-fuck, Von Ness was trying to decide if he could trust Pascal. But who didn't want to trust a face so damn pretty? "Listen. I travel quite a bit, and my houseboy recently went back to Singapore. Would you like to housesit for me? Just for the summer. I'd pay you, and you'd have full use of the pool, the tennis court, the entire house. What do you think?"

"What? No shit? You serious?"

"Yes, I'm serious."

"That's fuckin' fantastic! What do I think? I think, yes, man! Hell, yes!"

Erik laughed, and Pascal laughed. They sealed the deal with a handshake and a rigorous ass-fuck. The whole time, Pascal closed his eyes and imagined himself lord of that magnificent manor. Soon,

Erik was grunting, groaning, and gushing on his belly, and Pascal detonated over the whole vision-of-richness trip. They lay heaving, staring at the high marble ceiling, as Erik issued one warning: "By the way, kid. It's crucial: My business must always remain *my* business. So, no company. No sleepovers or hanging with your homeboys. No one-night stands here, ever. Should I find you've deceived me in any way…well, for your sake, I hope you never do. Understand?" Von Ness gazed at the set of ancient machetes on his wall.

Pascal did understand. So he never talked about the orgies with Fortune 500 guys, or the day a man he watched raise a family on TV showed up at the door, ready to get his not-for-prime-time freak on.

And so began his summer of living less dangerously. A summer of cleaning pools, dusting masterpieces, waxing fine wood floors. He answered the door, took Erik's calls, and a poor boy got to live a part-time life of Riley. He was a *good* lad *most* of that summer. It paid to be. Erik, bless his horny, liberal soul, managed to get him into that school of performing arts, and purchased him a fly new Italian designed wardrobe to boot.

Five

The Book of Ty

Teddy "Trick" Brown was Faison "Browny" Brown's older, hipper, more *down* brother. Street-smart, industrious, seemingly more sophisticated, Trick was the one Brown Tyrone actually *liked*. Trick had that mean independent gene, and was way too enterprisingly cool for anybody's "lame-ass school," so he quit in the 10th grade and hit the road.

Trick was 5 foot 10, two hundred pounds of mocha imperfection glazed in cinnamon, and Ty dug his flavor from the start. Maybe it was those sleep-sexy eyes, or those big ol' puffy lips, or maybe it was that wide, well-muscled body full of mojo. He looked like a fullback, all arms, chest, thighs, and butt. Homey had bluster for days, and one glance at him rolling down the sidewalk sporting his Trick-grimace and cool-ass simian bop was enough to fluster most into crossing the street. Maybe it was that mean, I might just beat yo ass and take your shit toughness. Maybe it was that the Brother was straight rebellious. But there was more to Trick Brown than met the naked eye.

Trick had a habit of calling Ty "Junior." Ty had been called worse, but he hated that shit coming from Trick. "Junior" inferred he hadn't attained enough hip points to hang with a Brother.

But suddenly Ty was 17, with a pencil-thin mustache, a fluent vocab, a miniscule celebrity, and a head full of pomade. Tyrone magically achieved his cool-enough credentials from Trick. They became not only boys, but *boys* who slap-boxed down Lennox Avenue, who flowed with an easy homeboy cadence, and who liked to dance.

Trick couldn't read so well. He was, in fact, illiterate. And once Tyrone discovered this secret shame, it became his mission to teach a Brother. In that teaching, Tyrone managed to *reach* a Brother, and a Brother reached back. They'd meet twice a week in secret, at the Schomberg Center in Harlem. Their lessons began slowly, as Trick's pride and frustration were obstacles. But Tyrone never judged him, and once Trick could trust him, baby-steps became larger steps, and larger steps became bounding leaps. Pretty soon, Trick was reading *Native Son*. He was asking questions, venturing opinions. And Ty found himself having a secret romance with Trick's impassioned mind.

"Trick, you never were stupid, man. Truth is, you're one of the smartest cats I know."

"Yeah, right. Don't bullshit me. I'm just gettin' by. But you get props on that," Trick acknowledged. It was his way of saying *Thanks, Ty. You made a diff in my fuckin' illiterate life*.

"Somebody just failed to teach your ass basic phonics. Once, you got that shit down, you were off and jettin' like Bob Beamon, man!"

Often, Trick would look at Ty, when Ty was unaware of being watched, and he'd think, *What's up with him? All this good shit is because of him, and the cat's humble. He's gotta be that way. Gotta be, or I wouldn't be diggin' his vibe. Look at him. Man! I can feel all the good shit this cat brings.*

Away from reading, they would get wasted on talk and *chiba*, and it seemed talk, weed, and each other were all two homeys needed to be content. Soon they became *true* aces, smiling covert smiles, keeping what the rest would never understand close to the vest. Besides, it was nobody's business if they were secretly queer for each other. Whenever they found time or some place to *be together*, it became their oasis, even if that oasis was the back seat of Trick's metallic green Deuce and a Quarter.

Each *sneak-end* they would live out their hippest dreams on the dance floors of the city. The two of them became larger when they danced. They transformed, shifting into something bold, bronze, and handsome. With a fly glide to their stride they would slide inside the dive, and you knew them by their walk, that sheen in their game. They meant serious disco business. Other guys stood around envious, because few could move the way they did. Ty and Trick, Trick and Ty were hot shit in rayon and gabardine, cutting masculine figures when they danced on the city's dream floors, where their swollen secrets and the poverty tucked inside their pockets didn't show.

* * *

It was an unusually chilly October afternoon. A breeze was kicking in from the north and Tyrone acknowledged that shiver on his skin as he left Empire Barber Shop, having had his fade tightened. Fine vines and sharp hair were all that really mattered in 1979. Ty was taking notes from that notorious spiral bound *slang book* being passed around school. When he finally got a glance, it read like a rumor of who was cool and who was *phine* and who could vine and who wasn't phine and who couldn't vine and what they thought and what music they listened to and who threw the best gigs and who knew how to dance and shit like that. And the coolest kid, the hippest dude in the whole damn school, already at the height of his legendary drool factor, wrote: "Appearance ain't everything. It's The Only Thing." That attitude fit Tyrone for a cool autumnal season.

That particular night he dressed to finesse—his skinny pimp frame in a suit of shiny blue rayon. Even Niagara Slim, the Elegant Neighborhood Bum, tipped his bag in Ty's natty, ghetto-dapper direction, saying, "Boy, ya lookin' like a hundred dolla bill!" and Ty beamed all the way to West 117th Street.

With a quick lively bop into Trick's building, Ty rang the buzzer to the sound of: "Whoisit?"

"It's me, Trick-diesel. Let me up!" The buzzer buzzed, Ty entered, and climbed the tedious project steps leading to the third floor. Tapping on 3-H, he hollered, "Hope you're ready. I ain't payin' no full admission tonight. Let's roll!"

Trick Brown opened the door, looking like a squat, powerfully built white tornado—totally out of season.

Though the impression put a rise in his rayons, Ty lectured, "Trick. You're the Black Travolta, all right? But it's fuckin' October, man! And it's *hawkin'* out there tonight!"

"But don't a Brother look fly in this?" Trick asked, fishing for props.

"You look like a fuckin' star," Ty said, and he meant it. But those gushy words sounded *too* sweet.

Trick didn't like it when he sounded too sweet.

"A fuckin' star?" he asked dubiously.

"Yeah. A thick-ass costar on the top of a thick-ass ghetto wedding cake. Where's the wedding, huh?" Ty turned his sweetness around.

"But, yo, Poetry Man, check the twill of this polyester. Damn. I look good in this here motherfucka! Good enough to be buried in this here bad boy!" He grinned his gap-toothed Trick grin, checking his cool quotient in the mirror.

Ty stood beside him, gazing at their dual cool images as he said, "Whatever, man. I'm tellin' ya, it's after Labor Day, it's cold out there, and you'll look played-out. But don't let that stop you."

"All right. I'll sport the money-green jammy. Still say I should be buried in this here white one." Dropping his pants, he gave Ty the *so you want some of this before we go* gander. Ty declined with his eyes. The night was so young it was infantile. There was juice in the Deuce and plenty of time to rub dicks in the crazy dark.

"Let's do that club in the east 80s. Remember? That joint, Pegasus?" Trick suggested.

Fifteen minutes later they were on the block, floating by cool jerk juveniles juiced on Tanqueray and bravado. People dug their style, decked out like ghetto kings, Kangols tipped acey-deucey, with Trick in his lime-green marshmallow shoes.

It was a typical Friday night's hang in a straight disco, where enthusiastic white girls became urbanized sirens, and the men resembled blasé gigolos. It wasn't *supposed* to be *their scene*, yet the two hot-danced themselves electric on an evening full of speed and the promise of ecstasy. Trick stood, full of elements, taking a rest before grabbing the tallest chick he could find and dancing his thick ass off. On the night's hungry dance floor, he and Ty reigned like kings, players, Somebodies. The floor was full of sex and its strobe-lit possibilities, party freaks, and cliques of hedonistic hands reaching out to touch them. So Trick and Ty, they'd look at each other, chip in a few Latin hustle steps, and no one dared try and best them. Along the mirrored walls, under red specks and flashing blue balls of light, they caught glimpses and dug themselves in all their profitless beauty. When you're 17 and 19, with moves like fuel-injected pop lockers, you tend to believe in your own providence.

Girls, chicks, the few sisters present awaited their turns to burn inside Trick and Tyrone's radioactivity. Trick and Ty would grab two at a time, spin them wild and fast like 78s until they'd be all dizzy, man. Dizzier than Gillespies. And for a while, those chicks would be crazy dizzy in love with Trick and Ty. Ty and Trick. They owned the joints they inhabited. These boys were bad, and fast becoming Legends.

If "appearance was the only thing," Trick Brown didn't *appear* freaked or stressed that Friday night, though he'd vaguely mentioned "a debt." "Man, I hope big-headed Razor Morrisey don't bring his crazy ass 'round here, riffin' 'bout that damn debt. Spotted me a little loan. Nothin' heavy. But sheeit. He can't get what I ain't got, right?" he yelled, between beats.

He said it with that quick nervous energy he had, like that of a speed addict having just popped a fistful. Trick laughed it off, so Ty laughed with him. Laughing was the second best thing they did. They laughed hard in the bricked-up face of their circumstances. Mostly they laughed at themselves, because they were young, strong, horny, and testing the limits. High, stupid, and completely ridiculous, they laughed and danced as the music played its loud and thumping bass for the swaying, rhythmic pop-ulace. Ty was in that wild place he'd go when he was dancing and feeling alive!

Ty was still in that wild place, dancing, spinning, and drawing a charismatic sweat when Razor Morrisey bopped in with his big head lidded under the cruel shade of a beaver-fur fedora. Razor's rep, like the rats in the city, infected the community at large. Razor was a local hot-boy with *juice*. He had his hot hands in a little of everything: drugs, extortion, numbers, prostitution, chop shops, loan sharking—anything as long as there was profit.

Ty never saw Trick and Razor's animated conversation, or how Trick's graceful hands began to fly like frightened birds, trying to explain themselves. That absurd night's fractured pantomime went unnoticed. And Ty was too busy dancing to see that long slow drag out past the doors of Pegasus. He never witnessed that quick flicker of panic darkening Trick's gap-toothed smile. Never saw Razor break mean with a switchblade.

Ty was knee-deep inside the screams and whistles of a frantic dancing room where he and Trick reigned. He didn't *feel* Trick's absence, *sense* his terror, or *know* something was horribly wrong. Until someone tapped his dancing shoulder and said, "Trick's hurt, man. Razor and his boys, they stuck him. Real bad."

Ty ran like a brand new madman. He ran with a wild heart beating in his ears. Outside, there was a fresh smear of blood on the pavement. It must've been six feet long. Strange. Ty felt a twinge of *relief*, thinking: *That can't be Trick's blood. Nah. Trick ain't that tall!*

But further down the street, he saw something. A small ball, bloodied and still. They'd beaten him badly. They'd slashed his throat. Blood was all over his face. If it wasn't for the blood-stained money-green suit, Ty would've never recognized him as the same Trick he'd laughed with, danced with only minutes before.

"Trick? Trick. Get up, Trick! Trick? No-o-o!"

The human voice was never meant for that kind of frenzy.

Ty held his hand, and there was nothing but cold. He held it until he couldn't hold it anymore.

A large thing was welling up in him, a tightness in his chest. Tyrone couldn't breathe for the rage in his broken heart. He thought he was going crazy. Maybe he was. He wanted to hit and spit and whale on everyone, everything and every person on that street. He walked around, pacing in his raging skin. There was no sane place left in him.

* * *

Ty: "I still have dreams of the blood. A million times in my dreams, he's stabbed in the slowest motion. His arms, they flail in a kind of flourish, a sad and fractured ballet. And everyone just dances around him, or stands there, watching his life drain away. They just *stood* there, letting the blood run. Did any one of those motherfuckers out there *know* who he was, or what he was going to be? He was somebody's son, brother, somebody's friend, and I could trust him, and we could dance. Didn't they care that he'd never fuckin' dance again?"

* * *

Theodore "Trick" Brown was buried in that fly white suit he'd so admired himself in. Tyrone and Faison served as pallbearers. Ty elegized: "He was a smooth chocolate heartthrob with crazy legs. He was tough and tender too. But when he put on a suit, there was a new glide in his walk. He never stuttered when he talked, and the poverty in his pockets didn't show...much."

SUMMER 1985

Many times, Tyrone tried to write it all down. He'd tried, but the words stared back from his word processor until even *he* didn't recognize them. That's when he'd *sense* Trick. His presence, or pieces of him, began to hover inside that writing room, seeping into Tyrone's consciousness. Trick Brown was haunting him, slowly.

"Why don't you just write the fuckin' truth, man? You taught me how to read. But I could always read you, Ty. What were we? Best friends? Just two cool dancin' fools? I don't think so. I did you, you did me, and didn't we both like it? Damn it, Poetry Man. Start again: 'Once upon a time, there was this dark-skinned, Harlem-bred, thick-muscled, big-dicked Brother named Trick, who rocked my fuckin' world.'"

Omar was *the first*, but Trick was *The Memorable One*, the long blue moan that caught in Tyrone's throat.

September 1979

Trick's ride was parked on 169th Street.

"You afraid of it?" Trick asked, with a touch of the braggart-with-a-big-ol'-massive-bozack in his voice.

"Afraid? Nah," Ty said. "I've done this before." But his mind was howling: *Don't you know the truth, man? It's got nothing to do with the size of your joint. Which is huge by the way. The truth is, I'm in love with you, fool. And I gotta tell you, lovin', really lovin' another man scares the absolute shit out of me. Where will all this secret love and lust take us? It feels super-scary stupid-dangerous to me. But there you sit, bruh. There you sit.*

Yes. And there sat Trick's pickax, protruding high from his lap in the backseat of that dubiously owned Deuce and a Quarter. Eyes met, then lips and tongue were drawn to its crest. He tasted like stewed plums, like sex and honey and chili, like secrets and sweat, and a little like the pulse of love. Ty never took sex or sexing lightly. Emotions, senses were all involved in the mix. He wanted to remember every fold, curve, and twisting vein of Trick. And of it.

That always lush romantic ditty "Get Down Tonight" played loudly from Trick's cassette: K.C. and his Sunshine Band urging Ty to *get down, get down, get down* on Trick's freaky fat freakishness.

But, oh! The hot things two horny Brothers can do in the back of a '76 deuce. That deuce with its lime-green metallic sheen rocked, sighed, and drove Tyrone full-speed into a whole other kind of liberation.

CENTRAL PARK, AUGUST 1984

Ty said to David, "Even though it was only my second voyage onto those warm, slippery shores of The River Fellatio, I was convinced in my bones it would be OK, because he *liked* me. I had a bad case of love's wicked itch, and no one could scratch that shit like Trick. He showed me I could dig a man deeply as a friend and still want to be kissed, touched, sucked, and fucked. I could talk and laugh, be silly or intense, and *just be*. And given time, I *know* he would've realized and admitted he loved me, too."

"Baby, that's so queer I could gag on the beauty of it," David joked. "You were such a mental boy, even back then. I remember you tellin' me once that you could never love a vacant pretty boy. And I thought, *How tragic*. Sex and beauty are *the* key components of our culture, baby boy! And here's my little rebel, breakin' the laws of our God-given superficial nature. Why? Because he wants someone to talk to who can talk back. Dionne Warwick and me is *both* gonna say a little prayer for your sad-ass."

Tyrone laughed. "I'm not blind, baby. I recognize *fine* when I see it, ya beauty-whore! I just choose not to chase after it with my mouth wide open, 'cause it's only fast food. It can't sustain us. Beauty's just a cock or a pussy staring back at us from the crotch of time. It's gonna rot and shrivel and dry up sooner or later. And when beauty hits the wall, Duchess, it can be plug ugly. Substance lasts. Believe me, the quick, meaningless fuck is highly overrated. 'Kay? Self-identity is sexy to me. I knew *more* than the biggest part of him. I knew the *best* part of him. Sometimes he'd look at me, and this pure and brilliant love poured from his eyes. It was spiritual. Besides, the pretty ones are never very interesting or dynamic."

"Or dangerous," David added. He knew Ty's choices even better than Ty himself. "Trick wasn't everybody's pretty boy, but he *was* pretty dangerous. Hell, he personified that shit. He was Black, hard, and tough, and yes, that can be beautiful. But he didn't look or sound or act in any way gay, baby. You liked that, too. Ya still do!"

"Nah. Trick looked, sounded, and acted like *himself*. And I dug that. Dealing with my first Real Man was some serious shit. I wasn't just looking for a quick hummer in the backseat of a deuce. What we had went *beyond* knocking gongs in the dark. For me, the Brother had to be down—"

"On the *down-low*, you mean. I *know men* just like Trick. Even if he'd lived to be 100, he would've never stepped out of his cool cock-clutchin' closet. Don't kid yourself, baby boy. Cool-pose was his god. And if you think you could've changed that, you's a fool. Please don't take this wrong. But the day I met you, I *knew* you were that stiff, "God please don't let me mince" type. Sometimes I think you're just another uptight straight boy trapped in a queer man's body. It's OK. That ain't a judgment. This is your best friend talking. I see all, feel all. You never wanted to be gay. That was one of those hilarious jokes The Creator played on yo ass. If you had your way, you'd be straighter than John fuckin' Wayne. But you can't be, so you settle for quietly queer. You got a bit of that *Rock Hudson* complex in you, boy."

"That's bullshit! For you, anyone who doesn't come into a room leaping and screaming like a freaking siren is a closet case."

"No. But the siren of my buck-wild blatancy must scare you. Why do you think we never bumped nasties? I *know* you love me. Hell, who wouldn't? And without gettin' all Hallmark about it, I loves you too, Porgy. But I'm so far from being your type, I might as well be from Uranus!"

"That's the first thing you've gotten right all afternoon," Ty fumed.

"Problem was, and still is, ya want too damn much. Ya want dick. Oops, excuse me. Penis. But not just any penis will do. Will all the big Black intellects in the house please whip out your long, thick, 10-inch IQ's? If you're queer, but not *too* queer, Ty would like you cleaned, stripped, and sent to his tent!"

"So I'm asking for the impossible?"

"No. Not if you happen to have Barbara Eden's bottle on hand. Listen, you want love. Believe me, I do understand. But trust me, not prayers, not a genie, not even the best, most upstanding queer cat on the planet can deliver all the stuff *you* want."

"I'm about 10 seconds from kickin' your soft ass all up and down this fuckin' park! What the hell does that shit mean?"

"Simple. Do ya want a roughneck, or a rough wit? Trick was a budding roughneck. But in *your mind* you've painted him with all kinds of intelligence, sensitivity, romance, and Technicolor movie shit. Because *that's* what you want. But you ain't bein' real, baby. Hello! Trick was a hustler, a get-in-where-you-fit-in type of Brother. He'd do what he had to do to survive, look good, drive a fly ride, and stay high. Obviously *that* was the real bait, the boyfriend juice back then. But you can't accept that, can you? You're afraid that truth would cheapen what you felt for him. You're afraid if you write that shit, he would only come off as a colored cliché."

"I hate this conversation. I hate you. You know me too fuckin' well, ya li'l spooky bastard!"

"Hey. We're all products of pain. But the question is, what you g'on do with yours? Damn it! Tell the truth, and shame the devil!"

Six

Suddenly, That Duplicitous Summer

JULY 1985

Inside the walls of Don't Tell Mama's, under dim lights and hipster chatter, this one cat spoke the staccato of the fatally cool. Sitting at Ty and Browny's table, he kept running his fool mouth, riffin' and vampin' 'bout *his* music. His voice itself was a kind of scat as he prattled on about Diz and Prez, Bird and Billie, the whole ethnomusicology of jazz.

Although Ty didn't know him from a can of paint, he seemed a little too everything: too pretentious, too slick, too fake, too much like a player. In dark shades and a carefully cocked beret, he was way too precious for the room. But Ty's Uncle Jerome had taught him to live by the c'mon get happy phrase, "No fools, no fun," so he left himself the freedom to be amused. But the dude began stroking Ty's thigh under the table; and though he was smoothly shady with it, he sent Ty a vibe that said: "Yeah. I see ya diggin' me. Bet you wonderin' how you can be down with all this!"

Ty pushed his hand away, gave him the *Mixed-Negro-Please!* look.

The stranger rasped, "Yo! What's your prob, boss? What up with the stank attitude?"

"Don't ask questions if you'd rather not know the answer," Ty cracked.

"Well, fuck it, I'm askin'," Mr. Too-Suave-For-The-Cafe insisted.

" 'Kay. The low-budget Miles Davis lounge lizard trip. It ain't real, ain't authentic. No disrespect. I think ya fakin' the funk, bruh."

"You don't know *jack!* Authentic? Miles is my daddy!" he said in a hurt voice, getting up, walking away in a slow bop.

Ty turned to Browny, who'd brought him along to sample a new play.

"You know that cat, right? So what up, Browny? Was he legit or what?"

"Hell, no! Sucka! He clowned you! You don't know who that is? That's Pass-cow! He's in the play. See? Fuckin' mouth got ya spittin' out Tang before you know the flavor!"

"Pass-cow? Pascal? That asshole was Face?"

"Yeah. *Some* people called him that." Faison still held a secret grudge. After all, his name was *Faison*. Why didn't people call *him* Face? So what if he wasn't gorgeous? He had *talent*. Why were people too damn lazy to shorten his fucking name? "Call me Face," he'd tell them. But it never stuck.

But that hidden resentment went unnoticed by Ty, because for him the night had just become electric. All at once, his head flooded with memories of that fine-ass Depina boy. When he first met Face, Ty was leery of him. He'd thought Face was all mutton and no chops or potatoes, and not nearly as talented as he pretended to be. And those tales of his background were shaky to Ty's discerning ear. Face had the best haircuts, the most expensive clothes, but why did he always have to turn his well-formed nose in the air? Still, he made a beautiful entrance, and he had that uncanny gift of being whatever you projected him to be. Blink your eyes, and he became a duke, a thug, a crush, a get-high partner, a homeboy, a potential lover, a friend, maybe even a savior. When he tilted his fine head and smiled, no one—except Browny—was immune to his charm. He was the bomb-diggity.

Most handsome.

Best-dressed.

Mr. Popularity.

Ty felt that odd excitement reminiscent of an earlier time, a time of promise. In that romantic state, he almost forgot the ugliness of Da Elixir's demise. Then he realized, *Oh, damn! I just embarrassed myself, right here in Don't Tell Mama's! Face Depina, of all people, just* clowned *me!* Suddenly, he'd lapsed into that hopelessly uncool high school chump. But now, as a highly evolved, socially adroit college grad, Ty *had* to do something. Improvise. Say something quick. Recover from the stigma of being punked. "Face, huh?" he acknowledged, in a decidedly beige tone. "That low-budget Mario Van Peebles wanna be! Homey needs to go back to Acting 101. I didn't buy his rap, his spiel, his thing."

Browny shot Ty the quick *gas face*.

Then Depina took to that small, blackened stage, and something unexpected happened. He was absolutely riveting. He'd dug deep, applied himself, studied, hung out with musicians and junkies, and junkie musicians, and, as a result, all you could see was a sad brilliance. He was strong, *authentic*, and so radiantly real that Tyrone believed every word he rasped in his portrayal of a doomed jazz musician. Ty was tripping on that experimental theater stuff, but no one told him there'd be *a nude scene!* Hello! Pascal "Face" Depina stood naked, as if it was the most natural thing in the world to be naked, and blowing his sad horn as the other clothed players ignored him.

But Tyrone did *not* ignore his ass. He couldn't.

Naked as new birth, Depina gave new meaning to the phrase *Les Jazz Hot*, and *long* too! His sleek body had a Palomino-like quality, all shiny, defined, and gleaming. Ty's eyes clung to the skin of his dangle, lingered on the tense light-skinned mold of an ass strong enough to crack walnuts. Tyrone thought, *Ah! To be, or not to be, a fucking walnut!*

When Depina's character died from an overdose, nude, alone, even his gonads became collapsing actors. Oh, yes, Face did his thing. He'd worked his performance into Tyrone Hunter's most sensitive of review areas. When the show was over, Ty was the very first to stand up and cheer, "Bravo! Bravo, my Brother! Encore! Encore!"

"Tyrone! Calm yo monkey ass down! Shit! He won't all that good!" said Browny.

But Tyrone felt he'd just watched the dawning of a star, because whatever *Star Quality* was, Face Depina was lousy with that shit. Against the roar of usually jaded New Yorkers, Ty wanted to bolt upright, charge like a mad new fan to that stage, and just take him. But he chilled.

"He's good, huh?" a stranger sitting at the next table asked.

"Good? He's fantastic!" Ty yelled back.

Shortly thereafter, at Ty's insistence, he and Browny tipped backstage to sing Depina's praises. As they approached the door, Ty wondered, *What will Face say? How will he act?*

Face opened the door, saw them, and immediately flashed his newly improved, well-capped actor's grin. "Tyrone Hunter." His arms flung open and the two embraced, hard and full, like old friends, or lovers even. The warm reception seemed odd to Ty. The last time they'd seen each other they'd argued over money. It was always about the money. And like Browny, Depina had wanted his cut. But apparently Face had let go of his grudge. (Browny was another story.) Face appeared to be genuinely happy to see Tyrone's ass.

"Tyrone Fucking Hunter." Face was still holding him.

Fuckin' homos, the hater in Browny hissed.

But then, in a shock of all shocks, Face pulled back, leaned forward and *kissed* Tyrone full on the lips.

So he one of them bold fuckin' homos, now? thought Browny.

Ty was stunned.

Browny couldn't believe it: Face and those fuckin' kisses. Browny remembered when they were Da Elixir, singing, dancing, spraying their postadolescent sexitude for the terminally teenage masses.

But even then, it was all about "Pass-cow."

At some point, David had decided it was time to test the power of his *boyfriend juice*. He told Ty and Browny on the subway, "I think I'll have me a piece of Depina." David assessed his own appeal: "I can bag him. I'm cute, verging on adorable. Plus I'm a dancer. Check the gams. And my ass? Please. Rico told me I could open a jar of caviar with this thing."

Dancing *had* given David a superior ass. But would all that ass be enough to bag the coveted Face Depina? David thought so. Ty and Browny didn't.

Then, the night of the big show, for some queer reason, Face decided, in the middle of the applause, to do the unthinkable, something most popular-cool teenage boys would never dare to do. He turned to the only openly gay member of the group, the little dancer who'd patiently taught him the moves, and, to everyone's amazement, picked him up and kissed him hard on the lips.

The crowd went wild. And David went on a jag of love from which he never fully recovered.

Tyrone was *most* amazed by that spectacle. It didn't mean Face was *gay*, necessarily, only that he wasn't afraid to be *gay-friendly*. On that count alone, Depina scored 50 extra Cool Points, and Ty lost a bet. He had wagered 50 bucks against David's ever getting *close* to a dude like Face.

Ty listened to the crowd chant, "Face! Face! Face!" and thought, *Bow down to the queen. Look at that. Little Duchess and big fine Face. Damn!* Browny stared as Depina brought David back down to earth. Then he thought, *If I hit one good long note, these motherfuckers will know who the real star is!*

But he didn't, and so they didn't know.

Now, watching Face plant one on Tyrone, he wanted to say, *Don't kiss him back! You don't know where the fuck them lips been, fool!* But like that time on stage, he chilled. Besides, now it was too late. Ty had already been *indoctrinated* into the cult.

"You was the Black *Oliver* up in this muthafuck tonight," was Browny's forced critique. Browny was keen enough to know the difference between Sir Larry and the fictional street urchin; he *meant* the latter. "Didn't know you had it in you. So, you got a agent now, or what?" *And how long did you have to blow the motherfucka to get this fuckin' role?* is what he *really* wanted to ask.

Depina ignored his question. He was too busy staring at that skinny kid from school, the one with more luck than talent. He was falling into the new idea of Tyrone Hunter. *Damn. He grew up good, didn't he?*

Recovering from that Vampire's Kiss, Ty offered his breathless assessment. "Man! I got no adjectives for you tonight. You did the old school proud, bruh. Sure had me fooled. Sorry for being such an asshole earlier, but—"

"Don't stress it, man. Fuckin' with people's heads, seeing how they react gives me new material." He looked different than that piece of *jazzed-out strange* from earlier in the evening. He had a mad mane of curly springs all over his head, as if his hair couldn't decide whether to be an Afro or dreads that week. And his arrangement of riches looked damn good in those tight black jeans. As he began stuffing belongings into his bag, he grabbed his script and a copy of a popular stroke magazine fell to the floor.

"Uh-huh! I knew it. Fuckin' closet case!" Browny hissed, just loud enough for Ty to hear.

But the sight of the magazine was a happy vision to Ty.

"Uh, that's not mine," Face lied. "I know somebody in there, though."

"Small world, ain't it, Sister? Ty the Tyke is still writin'. Ain't you, Ty? Only now it ain't about music. It's about the smut thing. You spit a little sump'n in them queer magazines, right?" Browny teased.

Both Ty and Browny witnessed a small sensation as they watched Depina's face brighten into an intriguing Cheshire cat smile. He was beautiful—very, very beautiful—when he smiled.

"Damn! Uptight, Ty? First you write a hit song and now *jerk juice words?* Damn, boy. You must got a wild imagination!"

"Don't be fooled by that boy, Pass-cow! Under that game face, he's a true freak, just like you." The bitch in Faison was trying to annoy them both.

"It's *Face*, man. Nobody's called me 'Pascal' in years," Depina said, a slight irritability in his tone. "So, you're a freak now, Tyrone?

I mean, you seemed pretty lame back in the day. You were always runnin' around with that li'l effeminate thing…what's-her-face?"

"David," Browny said. "Come on, Pass-cow, you remember that shit!"

Face thought, *If I have to tell this half-drunk Negro bitch my fuckin' name one more time, it's on!*

"Yeah. Ain't seen him in so long, I forgot. David. The Dancer. Wild little pussycat. Whatever happened to him, anyway?"

"He's tapped in, man," Ty bragged. "He's always working or touring in a revival, or doing something showy. Right now he's in L.A. shooting a video."

The three shared a cab uptown. Ty wisely sat in the middle. The ride was quiet, considering all the things and places and people they had in common. Browny whipped out his flask of vodka, which he finished by himself, never offering the others a swig.

Ever since the break-up, Browny had a new act: eternal victim, drinker, attitudinal Brother with a perennial bruised look. He'd been trying to break into the music business, without success. He was still dreaming, still trying, and still getting his drunken heart smashed to smithereens. Everything *bad* that ever happened to him was someone else's fault: crooked agent; lazy, crooked manager; lousy crooked songwriters; the advent of crooked video; fear of the Straight Black Dick. Everyone conspired against him. Plus, he was dark and small: For *that* he blamed God.

"Where the hell a Brother gonna sing opera? How'm I gonna flex my chops in the fuckin' chorus of the New York Philharmonic?"

Tyrone suddenly remembered, and missed, the singer with the crystal tear in his voice, the three-octave tenor who reached operatic heights. He missed that other side of Browny, the one that soared over the *hater* he'd become.

Browny got out first, on 28th Street, stinking of liquor and a foul attitude.

"Yo Pass-cow! I *would* give you my number, but you'd just lose it again. Tyrone, I'll holla at you later, bro. Peace out, *Pass-cow,*" he taunted, and with that he slammed the door.

"Diz-zamn! What vile bug crawled up his ass tonight?" Ty asked.

"Hell if I know," Face said. "We cribbed together for a minute. You know, two strugglin' artists tryna make it. Then he fucked around, got in some deep shit with Razor Morrisey, and I had to bail his little drunk ass out. Motherfucka never even thanked me."

"Razor Morrisey?" That name still sent a little tremor through Ty. "He's the one who stuck, who killed—"

"Yeah, Trick. I know. Well, I guess Browny's love of dope musta been stronger than his love for his brother. So, *I* got Razor off Browny's ass. Took a whole month's rent and *then some*, but I did it. After that, Browny's ass *had* to go. Too much heat around him. You know yourself how it is when you do a solid for somebody and they end up resentin' you. That's why I'm cool now with you and the song-money thing. So, enough about him! What's goin' on with you? Did you *really* like my performance?"

A lot was coming at Ty, and none of it sounded *legit. Browny dealing with Razor on any level other than mortal combat? Face helping Browny's ass out of a jam?* These events could only occur in an alternate universe.

"Well?" said Face. "What did you think? Do I got the stuff, or what?"

Ty remembered now. It was all about Face. He had almost forgotten that it always was. In that space between answers, he thought of David, his "li'l effeminate friend." *Why did Face have to say it that way? David wasn't so effeminate. Didn't Face get it? That was just David being playful, and in love.*

David, at the age of 15, had lived, breathed, and dreamed of only Face Depina: "I mean, day-yum! Why does Face have to be *so* damn fine? Face is, like, superfine! Did you ever jerk the gherkin thinkin' of Facey? I do. Regularly. You think Facey likes boys, 'cause he makes me feel all wet and giggly inside. Who is Facey fuckin', anyway? You think Facey fucks as good as he looks?"

"Probably fucks as good as he dances," Ty had replied. "Which ain't bad for a White girl from Long Island, but…"

In the taxi, Face's question still hovered like a gadfly. He sat closer, one strong knee pressed achingly against Tyrone's.

"Your skills? Your skills are tight, man. You were really on point," Ty said, and he meant it. What he didn't say was: *Yeah. You're tight, all right. Tight and toasty. Ever have any man-honey on that toast?*

"You think I got what it takes?"

"Sure. Why not? It's all a crap shoot. When I wrote that song, I never expected it to be a hit. Besides, I—"

"I mean, because I go the whole nine, you know? That play is real *hoard* on me, so many lines, emotions and shit." *Hoard* was Faceyspeak meaning *extra hard*. "Now, I just need to kick it," he sighed. "So, you got any ideas…?" Face's voice trailed off strangely. He was *trying* to be sexy, Ty could tell.

In that silence, something was crackling between them. Then, without warning, Face's hand crawled up Ty's inner thigh in a smooth and confident glide. He must've known in his balls he could have Ty, or most any man or woman he desired. His shiny green eyes stabbed through the dark, focusing on the intended target.

Damn, Face. That's your hand on my thigh, dude. Whatchu tryna do? Next, that slow meandering hand settled on Ty's lap, rubbing, caressing the strap of his thang.

Face smiled. Tyrone glanced forward to find the taxi driver ignoring them.

The exhibitionist in Face made him bold enough to unzip Ty right there in the backseat.

The first touch vacuumed Ty away from the reality of a New York cab ride. His head spun. *Face Depina is touching my dong!* There was always a certain strain of wildness, a fearlessness in Face, and maybe Ty had forgotten that too. *Yo! Mr. Taxi-driver! Do you see this? He's stroking me off, man!* Heat was baking every atom in Ty's body. *Oh, my damn!* It was a mighty bumpy, bouncy ride through the streets of Gotham. Tyrone wanted to grab a shock of Depina's hair and drive his beautiful lips there, to that percolating place. *Does he give head, too?* He could only imagine the wet warmth of Face's mouth and lips going down on him. But *this*, this was cool too because Depina's manipulations were making him drool. Ooh! He had skills in those hands! Ty was moaning low, and he hoped the cabby couldn't hear him.

When that monumental moment came, Ty pushed Face away swiftly, and he sprayed in a thrust to the floor and the seats and his jeans. He was breathing harder than a long distance runner. *Look at me! I'm a fuckin' mess, but I don't care!*

"That's act 1, baby. Tonight's your lucky night. Let's swing by Mirage," Face whispered.

Tyrone and his shocked penis consented.

A few minutes later, they'd checked their clothes down to their jocks and hiking boots. Ty was in deep lust with Face's physique. His eyes perused the lean, almond-hued sweep of him. Face's outstretched supporter loomed abundant with unseen buttered-pecan treat. The club songs began to pump, and they hit the crowded floor. Seemed like every hot, horny cat in Manhattan was out cattin' that night.

Ty and Face moved in a screw of hips, writhing in their jocks, on fire with rhythm. *Damn!* thought Ty. *Even his dancing has improved!*

It was too loud to talk, to think of anything other than sex, so they let their grinding bodies speak for them. In mid nasty groove, Depina grabbed Tyrone's neck, pulling his face into his. They stared and breathed, and then they kissed, long and hot, daring and wet. Ty's fast heartbeat was a bass line. In a heated tremor, Face clutched Ty's ass, pushing his writhing body forth. All Tyrone could feel was that long bank of meat mounting under a damp jock.

Ty planted sucking kisses all across the taut savory scape of Face. He lacquered Depina's neck and sweat-glazed shoulders, licked the dense wires of Face's pits, and nibbled those delectable tits.

"Wanna fuck around some?" Depina howled, so boldly, so straight out with his shit. Tyrone and his dick answered, "Hell, yeah!"

Depina looked around, then slowly peeled down the front of his jock, and motherfuck! A very long and still elongating tan joint took Ty's breath.

"Diz-zamn!" was all he could say. From his view in the audience, Tyrone knew Face was blessed. He'd expected a big, firm, Urban-Legend-type Boner, but *this!* Diz-zamn! Close to 10 inches of lean, uncut, tapered, pecan-colored tube reached out for Tyrone, willing him to do something hot with it.

But then, Depina tucked his prize away.

Sufficiently excited, they left the dance floor in a quest for privacy. Their pricks stabbed a path through the dancing, romancing mayhem, en route to the back room. Which was jammed. The high reek of sex was everywhere. Moaning, groaning men coupled in every freaking corner. No way two tall, erect ethnics would fit comfortably in that serpentine mix. Strangers would be all over them like bacon on greens, hot on salsa.

"I used to DJ here," Face said. "There's this old booth upstairs, real private." Depina gestured in that direction. Ty nodded, and Face led the way. In the darkened glass booth, he switched on a red lamp. Face looked even hotter bathed in red light. There was an old turntable, a leather chair, and a gang of vintage disco albums. A small army of spent condoms littered the floor like defeated latex soldiers. Face dropped his jock. His meat torqued upward—tall, tan, and lovely as its owner. He sat in the chair, and led Ty's head down, down… "Suck me off, if you can," challenged Face Fine-ass Depina.

Ty was hypnotized. Yes, *naked* was Depina's color. Still, there was that *shadiness* about him. Ty didn't know where the hell he and his elegant pecan prick had been. So he reached for his wallet, pulled out a Trojan.

"What the hell is *that* for?"

"Safety. I'm not down with the DNA slurpee. All kinds of diseases out there. Gotta suit up if you wanna play with *me*. Besides, you don't know where I been either."

"No glove, no love, huh?" Face smirked. *Fuckin' punk! What's wrong with him? I'm clean, and he's lucky I'm payin' attention to his fortunate ass!* But Depina didn't say anything as Tyrone rolled the rubber down his lengthy span. Then, in a New York minute Depina grabbed Ty's chin and fed him warm raging knob and lengthy shaft, then more shaft. Damn, how much shaft did he have! And with more shaft came more vibration. Rising from the chair, Depina and his *pinga* bucked and struck the back of Ty's throat. Ty choked it back, then lapped to the sound and beat of the bass at his feet. As the flaunt and strut of sexy, sweaty men freaked below, Ty ingested the tip and shaft of a dream. Was it *real?* Was he *really* gagging on a spit and red-lit *dream?*

"I *knew* you dug me back in school. I could tell," Face said with hubris, as he stood, pushing Ty against the desk. Then, all at once, his moist lips locked on Ty's naked schlong.

Wait! Wait! Don't you want me to put a rubber on?

But Depina didn't care. Like some reckless predator, he was all over Ty, smacking his ass, twisting his tits, throttling that mounting piece with lips, mouth, tongue, and throat. Ty never imagined one man could be so sexual. Face was a rattler, licking, hissing through Ty's prickly bush. He was rough, full of slobber and rushing breaths, but a suck-sore Ty was surprised at just how much he *liked* it.

Then, he switched turntables, mixed it up, scratched it, and surprised Ty with a brand new beat. "You know," he began, "I done a coupla men before. They just love to sit on this long hot motherfucka and ride!" His voice wore a tough guy catch when he said that. He smacked his lovely to Tyrone's thigh. "And I just love to hear 'em squealin' like first time faggots!"

Is this your seduction rap, Face? Because as good as you look, that shit could use some work.

"I got that fuckin' part down cold," Face said. "Now I need to know the rest."

"The rest?" Ty asked, not quite feeling his flow.

"Yeah. The rest." His hands sailed down Tyrone's belly. He grabbed Ty's limb and jerked it into a long, strong, wicked hardness. "Get up. I think I want you to hit it."

It had been a night thick with surprises. But Tyrone couldn't quite *believe* this one.

Face, with his long straight bone beautifully erect, lay face-up, his back on the table.

But looking at Face Depina head-on would've made Ty come too quickly—so he ordered, "Turn around."

Face did, and Ty slowly massaged the red-lighted slopes of a perfectly glazed rump. He could smell the excitement in the air. Tyrone, who never left home without his rubbers, slid one on. Depina tensed, teasing the hell out of Ty, who was now one hard and juicin' Brotha.

It was showtime for Tyrone and the Face. And Ty was primed and ready for his close-up.

Crouching, he divided Depina's cheeks. Then he slowly let his crest, his shaft submerge inside that leather-knotted Cheerio. The clasp, oh, the clasp was so maddening.

"Aw! Oh. Shit!" Depina groaned that groan of anguished pleasure.

Ty eased in and out, giving Face more and more of his measure.

"Aw! Shit!"

Ty pierced him in one impatient thrust. Face grunted hard against the slice and slide. A warm tightness enclosed Tyrone. Like a deep and magnetic furnace, it seemed to will him, pull him deeper into its heat. Being inside Depina was like plunging one's dick into the eye of a crushing, twisting cyclone.

Flipping himself over, Depina glared defiantly at Ty. "Come on! Hit it! Damn it! More! Harder! Harder, damn it!" he demanded.

So Tyrone hit him rougher. Applying more muscle, his hips drove harder, his body plunged deeper.

"Come on! That all you got? Fuck!"

Ty set a meaner rhythm, squeezing Depina's cheeks, sending his cock forcefully through him.

Depina rose up, devilishly winked, and gnashed his teeth against Ty's nipple.

"Aw! Face, man! That shit hurts!" he complained as Depina rolled the other nip between his strong, menacing fingers. This, coupled with his long history of curiosity about Face and the intensity of actually being inside him, sent Tyrone to that spacey edge. He could feel his whole body flooding, pulsating against the rub, the groove, the smoothest friction. He had maybe three strokes left, and that was it. He lunged and instantly felt his shudder. Slipping into that strange *shiver-place*, he grabbed Depina's long rigid dick and pistoned it quicker. A vibrant charge rumbled through Depina's bone, and its quivering set Ty *off!*

Depina heaved as wild skeets ripped forth, blasting, one after the next. Fisting him wet, Ty pulled back, slammed, shook, and fired great glistening gobs of electric fire. *I can't believe it. I can't believe I just did Face fucking Depina!*

"Man!" Face sighed. "That was wild, baby. Real *wile*. But don't go fallin' in love or anything 'cause I ain't like you. I ain't gay. So keep this shit between us. All right?" he said, his green eyes weighted in seriousness. "This was just one of them experiments. You know, like a actin' exercise."

Tyrone heard him. He watched those lying eyes. But it was all sort of dreamlike, or more like *waking up* from a dream, where everything sits in its own quiet haze and nothing is quite yet real.

"I mean, it felt all right. Can't say I was *really* into it. But—"

"What? Come on, Face! Don't bullshit me with this whole elusive, veiled, *misterioso* trip. You give head, and you take it up the ass. Last time I checked, that's gay!" Tyrone fumed.

"See, the old Face would be kickin' yo ass right about now. But I'll just call that shit a compliment. You're all hung-up on labels. Ain't you heard Tina Turner's new cut: "What's Love Got to Do With It?" Well, what's *gay* gotta do with it, huh? I ain't like you, Ty. Hey, you ain't gotta believe me. You can ask any one of my *many* chicks. See, I'm up for this role as a gay athlete, and I'm supposed to know what the hell I'm doin', right? Besides, shit, man, I went to P.A.—I was *surrounded* by you guys. And down here, dealin' with the artsy farts, I'm *always* bein' hit on. I've been around, man. Not much turns me off anymore. See, this part, it ain't no buck-wild dick-swingin' porn. But I'm supposed to be a young queer cat. I have to *get* being queer. I mean, what's it like to kiss? Did that. You close your eyes, and it's like kissin' your damn arm. But I had to go deeper than that. I needed to know what it feels like to *be* with another man. Now I know. See, I'm in this for real. I'm tryna be a artist, not some fly-by-night. I'm dead serious about my craft."

Tyrone stared back at this *actor*, this supposed thespian, and for the first time, Face didn't seem so damn pretty. Who was he, really? Maybe Ty should've felt clowned again. But the laugh, this time, was on Depina. Tyrone wanted Face to know he *knew* for sure now that Pascal Ornette "Face" Depina was *not* legit.

"Acting?" Ty said. "Nah. Trust me, you were *never* that good. Sucking dick once might be an experiment. Sucking it twice then taking it to the rim and demanding *more* just makes you another deluded faggot! You think you played me? No, bruh. Ya played yourself!"

Ty began his shrivel process. That eight-inch thing which let him know how it felt to be Black, gay, and *alive* was descending into a little brown sliver of pissed-off twine.

"Come on, Ty! I picked you outta all the guys I coulda picked, 'cause I knew you'd keep it quiet. So don't feel used. You *enjoyed* it. I *know* you did!" Face blustered, as Ty walked away. "Yo! Just keep it between us, and don't be all mad at a Brotha! Hey! Ain't you ever heard of The Method?"

"Whatever's clever, sista! You played yourself, but whatever's clever," he said, heading back to the room filled with men who knew, acknowledged, and embraced what they were.

Seven

Claims and Proclamations

Tyrone was studying journalism at Columbia, which was cool and all, but journalism, at best, was literature in a hurry, and Ty was in a hurry to make literature. In his 19 years, he had been through so much he *knew* there had to be a novel (or two) in him. He had just spent a long, hot, industrious summer *feeling* and writing. So now he stood, in the offices of a publishing house, holding his own little piece of earth, believing it to be the whole fucking world.

For his date with destiny, Ty had worn his hunter-green corduroy jacket and carried his serious-business briefcase.

He hadn't expected the editor to be so young, so darkly handsome. But Constantine Feld was.

As Feld leafed through Tyrone Hunter's Great American Novel, all 93 pages of it, Ty began to *feel* the buzz. He imagined it was greatness swooping down from the air to kiss his angst-ridden ass, embrace his teenage tragedies. He could smell the fresh ink on the pages of his contract, hear the champagne uncork. Constantine Feld was going to rise from his desk, call in the big boys of literati, alert the media, and, damn it, phone Liz Smith! Yes, Ty could feel

70

it. All that good shit and glory was just a page-turn away.

But then Feld, his eyes never leaving the page, delivered not glory but a hard smack of condescension: "You want to write, kid? Learn *how* to write. Finish school. Get a life. Pay attention to things around you. Question everything. Lose your hang-ups. You're young, be promiscuous! Then try celibacy. Don't speak for a year, maybe two years, and then *shout* everything. Write. Rewrite. That's the best advice I can give you, kid. Now, good luck, and good evening."

Ty could not believe it. He'd put blood, sweat, and a summer of hot tears into that manuscript, and here was this man disrespecting him and it. *Typical. Fuckin' fat-cat elitist! And that page of advice from the Bohemian's Handbook? This is the '80s, in New York City, and he wants me to go out and be* promiscuous?

Every man has his own petri dish. And while Ty was born to experiment, none of his experiments were of the *très* kinky variety. Instead, he took turns embracing the various "isms." He had this mad itch to learn more shit than anyone needed to know about mysticism, vegetarianism, Buddhism, Jungianism, plus a whole lot of other "isms" most people couldn't even pretend to understand. That past summer, after reading *Das Kapital*, Ty had been down with the proletariat. David was in East Oshkosh at the time, dancing for the money as hard as he could. When they touched base long-distance, all Ty talked about was embracing socialism while all Davey talked about was embracing the long, brown, thick dicks of chorus boys.

Some ideologies, like some cocks, fit for a season.

Inside that fancy 42nd Street office, Ty imploded. And for one, self-doubting, introspective moment, he thought, *Maybe I don't have what it takes.* But his Uncle Jerome's voice piped into his consciousness: "Boi! Don't you let them motherfuckas steal your joy!"

So Ty, who'd thought he was a genius since he wrote that freak hit song, said to this high-and-mighty editor hunk: "Excuse me, sir. I've worked very hard on this. You read one page of one chapter, and you say I can't write? Maybe I can't. Or maybe you don't read so well, which is pretty sad, for an editor." And with that, he snatched back his prized if unappreciated manuscript in an indignant blur.

Ty returned to school, taking a deeper, more soul-investigating interest in people, everyday people as well as the city's *perceived* freaks of all types, classes, genres. He sat in parks and observed the way people behaved when unaware of being watched, listened to. He spent time on the streets and slept in a shelter. He volunteered in a soup kitchen, hung out with skid poets, underground artists. He submitted his short stories to major magazines, and was never more alive than when sitting on fire, exchanging ideas with writers in workshops. Ty was determined to sharpen his literary chops. Whenever he could, he spent time around young kids, desperate to never lose touch with the rejected 7-year-old child within. He was accepted at four writer's colonies, and he never stopped working. Homeboy wrote and scribed his aspiring ass off.

Tyrone became a kind of urban chameleon. Every day brought a different suit. He'd try it on to see if it fit, sometimes reaching beyond the drag and assuming the identity.

Along the way, he met Jamaal. No last name. Just *Jamaal*—a struggling poet–radical visionary artist–thinker–primal screamer who spouted Allah and Nationalism to the casually beige cliques downtown.

Jamaal said it *loud*, shrouded his body in kente cloth, wore his political hair in knotty, unkempt-and-I-don't-care locks. He was a dark, towering performance art piece with a voice deeper than God's or James Earl Jones's. His trip was to anoint avenue blocks with his Big Black Sound. Black people were being gunned down, chased into traffic, beaten to death. Cops were shooting Black grandmothers, like Eleanor Bumpers. Blacks, like graffiti artist Michael Stewart, were beaten into comas from which they would never awaken. And they took out 16-year-old Yusuf Hawkins, who made the fatal mistake of looking for a used car in the wrong neighborhood.

Jamaal spoke out against that shit. He was a freedom seeker, seeking like-minded thinkers and new Afros in a terminally Jheri curl city. He'd talk *Revolution!* to most anyone who'd listen, and Ty was down with the sound. Theirs was an educational hang. Ty was a Knowledge Groupie and Jamaal was big on dropping the science.

Being five years older, he took a liking to Ty's anxious mind. Jamaal was a known criticizer of most everything and anyone that did not play a part in Uplifting the Race, yet he was torn between the *Koran* and the *Kama Sutra,* between hostility and lust.

The first time they *did it* was on the train, between cars on the number 6. Though his talk was bigger than his penis, Jamaal's warrior tool was heroic enough as he unleashed it to the cool rapid night air. Holding on for dear life, Ty crammed his mouth full of Jamaal's throbbing black anger, but he didn't swallow. His tongue sprinted and rattled along the jolt of it as the train screeched and scraped along the tracks. The dark underground with its rapid shafts of light and wind sped against them as Ty's lips, tongue, and anxious breaths engaged in their own electric transport. It was all so quick. It felt dangerous, and hot. Afterward, there were stains on Jamaal's dashiki.

But Ty was *not* seeking the position as Royal Cocksucker to the new African King of Radicals. In an East Village bar, he struck up a conversation with a longhair who'd once run with the Beats. Ty had always been intrigued by the Beats. But something the man told him sounded a warning. The history he recited was about love. It seemed that Allen Ginsberg's love and admiration for Jack Kerouac was so deep, Allen would often fellate Jack under the Brooklyn Bridge. Did brilliance shoot out? Could Ginsberg swallow it and from the bitterness be somehow better? According to longhair legend, whenever those acts were performed, it was Allen going down on brilliance. Jack never gave brilliance back.

"Oh, hell, no! I'm not gonna fall for Jamaal or any other on-the-fence angry straight man, no matter how brilliant his ass might be. Nah! See, I do not crave cock in that blind, love-me-short-time way. Hell, I've got one too. No reciprocation is the first sign of lack of sexual respect. What's the fuckin' profit in that shit?"

The subject was moot, as far as Jamaal was concerned. For him, there was nothing vaguely funny, cute, or advantageous in being openly gay. And besides, "Ain't no evolutions nor revolutions to be gained by taking it up the ass."

"But revolution is change," Ty countered. "Change redefines things by the nature of the word. Your version, that's the old version, and it's gonna have to change. Love is so much wider than your narrow definition my soldja! I'm sick of people tryin' to tear love apart, like so much meat. It is what it is. Love is love, brother. Man lovin' woman, woman lovin' woman, and no matter what face you put on it, men lovin' men is *love*. You try to maintain any kind of lasting revolution without love, my homophobic mutha-brotha, and you're gonna fail."

Ty boarded his next train *alone*.

Eight

The Season of Bliss

Once upon a time there was a sweet-faced *chica*-sista who went by the name of Bliss Santana. Bliss was a very sassy, sexy girl. As Face indelicately put it: "All I know is she's hot. When my Akita, Sasha, saw her, he popped a boner! Before that, I thought Sasha was a fuckin' queer hound!"

Maybe it was all that long cascading gypsy hair, blacker than a raven's wings, or maybe those liquid eyes, as stunning and hypnotically green as Face Depina's. Whatever it was, the moment Face laid his mean greens on hers, he heard the noise of a galloping heart. In Bliss, he saw his feminine equal. Naturally, he was attracted. She was tall, surfacely refined, and her breasts were real strident girls. She had a scratch of a voice that made him think of a *dame* belting back bourbons with the boys in a smoky pool hall, a cue in one hand, a Camel in the other. And when she laughed, it caused little earthquakes under his skin.

He liked her from the beginning when she turned, did a double-take, and asked, "So, what's your bag?"

Acting was hers. She excelled at that gig, but portrayed *real* much better. Bliss Santana was a fighter, cusser, shit-talker, and a take-no-prisoners brawler if you pissed her off. That wild streak gave her a hipper edge than the rest. On the exterior, she was another pretty actress with chops. But when the lights went down, she turned the player off. Then she became that Jersey girl, burning with spirit, who'd worked on herself, cleaned up her act, and went from tough chick with pool stick to daytime TV's leading Blacktress. She began that trek at Arthur Murray's, teaching samba and other Latin dances, but decided after one more misplaced brogan landed *hard* on her baby toe, *Fuck this scene! Hell! If I can fake-teach these rhythmically retarded bastards to dance, and smile like Rita Chita Rivera Moreno, then maybe I* can *be a freaking actress!* So she paid her dues as a waitress, barmaid, and hat model while she studied the craft and read *Backstage* religiously. She found parts in plays, showcases, and prayed for her big break.

She never fucked her way to the middle.

Face had never met a more confident woman. He called her a "complex carbohydrate." Later, he'd compare her—as he did all women, screwed and unscrewed—to a car. Bliss was a Jaguar: expensive, fast, lovely to look at, and yes, *trouble*.

They met when he auditioned for the boyfriend role on her soap. Face was nervous, and it showed in his aspect. He had that frightened glaze of a half-assed player who'd forgotten what the hell he was doing onstage. *He's damn cute, though*, Bliss thought. *Maybe a little too cute for comfort.*

"So what's your bag?" she'd said, followed by, "Calm down, honey boy. It's just a read-through. Tell you what: Imagine everyone here except *you* is buck naked. They look pretty ridiculous, don't they? Now breathe. Breathe… There. That's better."

That was how it went down. But Face would change the story in later years to protect his facade.

Face didn't get the part.

"He's a bronzed Ken doll, only stiffer and less talented," said the casting director.

Maybe Face didn't snatch the role, but he did get the *snatch*.

"Know why you didn't get cast? I saw the test. You were prettier than the rest. Hell, you were prettier than me," Bliss teased.

"Bullshit. No one's prettier than you. I sucked!"

"Well…yeah. You *did* suck. But you're just starting out. I'm telling you, you're just too damn pretty! People will think you're gay. Are you?"

"Hell no! Want me to prove it?"

"Puh-lease! All actors can *act* fuckin' interested. It's OK, hon. I have lots of gay friends. Well, a couple style-conscious bastards, whom I love dearly. Come on. You can buy me a drink and tell me your story," she said, swinging a big bag over her shoulder.

She pulled Face's arm and he followed her down the hall, into the elevator, and out the door. It was autumn, and darkness had fallen on the West Side like a cool translucent shade. Despite her low-key beret and dark shades, Bliss was recognized. Her fans waiting by the studio doors, called out: "Zina! Zina! Don't let that new bitch get the best of you!" "Zina, when are you gonna find out you were switched at birth?" "Zina, can I have your autograph?"

Face watched this scene with an envious fascination.

"How that shit feel, Bliss? They *love* you! Damn. Must be a fly life, so many people lovin' your ass…"

"It's all very sweet and gratifying. But *love* me? Please! They love Zina, the eternal doormat with a good heart. They got no idea what makes me tick."

"Well, I'd like to," a suave Face countered. He took his finger and dabbed it lightly to her soft cheek, smoothing away a fallen lash.

There's something about him, she thought. *Something distinct and disturbing. Something as bright and harsh as sunlight.* She said, "Careful what you wish for, pretty one. So, what's your fuckin' tag again?"

"Face. Face Depina."

Upon hearing *that*, Bliss began a long and wicked journey into laughter. She couldn't help it. A loud burst of it just rolled up out of her, and she guffawed all down West 57th Street. Face watched her lovely green eyes tearing, the tightened cords in her long, delicate neck, and felt cheapened by that sound. He was used to laughing at other people. It had been a long while since anyone had laughed at *him*. He'd forgotten what it felt like: that creepy sensation of Mr. Stupidity, standing still. *Is she high or what? Fuckin' actress! She better stop that shit! What's so fuckin' funny, anyway?*

And still she laughed, stopping only to take a breath and then resume. The subway rumbled under their feet, and he could feel that fucking train, speeding like a dangerous thought. For one equally dangerous moment, he wanted to haul her cackling ass into the nearest storefront and rip that noise from her laughing throat.

Finally, she saw the wounded look that had claimed his handsomely confused mug, and thought it best to cease. "I'm…I'm sorry, baby. But that name, it's…it's too fuckin' precious! Face Depina? That can't be your real name. No one could do that shit to their kid. Sounds like you want to be fuckin' porn star."

"Well, my real name is Pascal," he said. "But everybody calls me—"

"Pascal. Pascal?" she asked, repeating it in her mind, like a schoolgirl nursing a mad little crush. *Pascal and Bliss…* "I like that. I'll call you Pascal."

Face had always hated that name. But hearing it purr from Bliss's lush lips, he didn't mind it so much.

As they walked, a fashionably dressed male couple glanced at them. Bliss thought she'd been recognized yet again. *Oh, well, get out the pen.* But their eyes settled on the studly Face in a slow, deliberate glide. Feeling strangely protective, Bliss immediately grabbed his arm.

What is it about your sway? I see Adonis. But who do they see, Pascal?

"So, you never told me. What's your bag? What do you do when you're not busy being so damn cute?"

Face couldn't tell her he installed carpets, DJ'd, and "modeled" some. His sexuality was already in question, and modeling would give fire to the kindling of her suspicions. And so he lied. In that huge inky universe of Big Black Lies, it was a small high-yellow one.

He said, "I'm in advertising."

All at once, it no longer mattered what he did. She shuffled him into Bloomingdales and headed straight for the lingerie department. "What's your favorite color?" she asked.

"Green. Mint green."

He studied her innately exotic skin, her tight-boned erotic beauty as she meticulously browsed the racks for just the right article: a mint-green teddy. She held one up. Face nodded in approval. But instead of whipping out her slew of credit cards, she turned to him and said, "Come here and kiss me." Face eagerly obliged, and as their tongues searched the newness of each other's mouths, she stuffed the teddy inside her big leather bag.

Oh, shit! She's wile. This chick is wi-i-ile! Maybe even craze-e-e! I dig her. I can see myself bangin' this. So you think I'm queer, huh? Well, you won't when this night's over.

Hmm, he's a pretty good kisser. Nice slow tongue. Not too wet. I wonder what else he's good at.

The couple retired to her lair on the West Side, a trendy little symphony in avocado green. She was still in her 20s, yet she had acquired *things*. There were citations honoring her work, photos with New York swells and power brokers. And, most notably, a life-sized nude portrait of Bliss that seemed to ask, *Are you man enough for this?* Observing the quietly elegant way she lived, Depina was made all the more envious and hungry for something *better*.

Bliss fixed them a pitcher of stiff martinis. She sipped hers slowly and purposefully.

They kissed some more, for accuracy, for Bliss to see if she really liked him. It wasn't long before she decided she did. However, she saw no physical signs of his arousal, so she boldly said, "OK, you. If you like me, then show me how much. Get naked for me. Let's see if you're *pretty* where it counts."

Face stared, licking his curling lip, lowering his eyelids, doing all the shit he thought made him sexy. He ran his hand through his newly shorn hair, which was now shorter and curlier and framed his chiseled countenance most tastefully. It all might've worked if he hadn't tried so hard.

What the hell is he doing? Oh, no! He's posing for me! Oh! Definitely gay, or bisexual at least. But damn if he isn't cute. What the hell. I'll do him, long as he's wearing a condom.

Then Face very slowly removed his shirt.

Oh! This is interesting. I like. Pascal works out. Hell, he could be a model.

Face intentionally saved the best for last. Even if he wasn't *hoard* as a steel girder just yet, he knew he had the inches. He rubbed his swelling crotch, watching her, anticipating that stunned look on her face when he finally whipped it out and she could see what he'd brought to the party. He unzipped, reached deep, and thrust forth the Depina Jewel.

"Oh, my, Pascal! Look at you. You certainly are a big boy, aren't you?"

"That's what they say," he grinned.

I don't doubt it. But who says it?

Ambition, adrenaline, and martinis mixed in a heady cocktail. Face sipped it all, looking at Bliss as the Depina Jewel slowly rose to the occasion.

They kissed with their eyes, and their lips, and their hands until they kissed their clothes away. Face performed the deed and she moved in an easy intimacy around him. But Depina had yet to discover the map of a woman, or how to be freaky-free. That was OK. He was young, hung, and willing to please. Bliss Santana knew, with his clay in her hands, that she could mold this hunk into shape.

When she disappeared into another room, Face mused on the events. It had been a while since he'd laid a chick. And *so what* if she didn't blow him as good and juicy-slick as the men he'd known. She was soft, fluid, giving, and the sly filly in her seemed satisfied by his stallion acrobatics. *Yeah. Guess I proved myself tonight.* Depina wanted to jump up, click his heels, open the 17th floor window of that luxury building and shout to all the city: "*I'M FACE MUHFUCKIN' DEPINA, DAMN IT! AND I JUST FUCKED BLISS SANTANA!*"

But that would be *très* unsuave, uncool, uncivilized. So, he chilled.

When Bliss returned, wearing her pilfered teddy, he noticed how the Black and Latin cultures fought for possession of her nose and lips and the tones of her skin. She looked, in her stilettos, like a fine and sultry gazelle. And she had a little something extra to enhance the spell.

Bliss wasn't the first to introduce Face to the joys of cocaine, but this time he indulged in ways he never had before. Bliss's stash was choice, Colombian, and copious. They sniffed, snorted, sniffed, and giggled and sniffed and cooed. When he again made love to Bliss, the effect was like losing time. He sat on her couch, and Bliss mounted his impressively long thighs. She liked being on top, her back and shoulders arched across her expensive coffee table. She stared boldly into the green of Depina's eyes, and the jolt of him made something ecstatic come into in her face, her belly, as a jiggle claimed those strident breasts. Face sank slowly inside her, tunneling through her tight wet gripping woman's clutch. Staring into her eyes, he wanted to laugh, as a good feeling began rising in his head. It was safe, and wet, like crawling around in warm womb water. And for as long the fine white powder lasted, the thrust, the pitch, the sex improved. His groove was found, and like a boomerang she threw it back. The *cock of his walking manhood* was regained between wet skins as her thighs wrapped his back like coffee-colored boa constrictors. "Ah! Yes! Oh! Pascal!"

But Bliss wanted shooting stars, comets, solar showers, and shit. And penetration alone would not take her to the silky Milky Way. Face had to go that extra distance, *downtown*, and *not* to the Lower East nor West Side.

Into a tree-lined village he stared, without a map, knowing his performance would be *the telling act*. The telling act that separated the men from the boys—especially the boys who liked men's dicks. But a dash of coke on the tip of his tongue numbed him enough to ignore his basic distaste for what he was about to do. Besides, this shit *pleased* Bliss, and she and her body, her guile, her mind, and her treasure trove of stimulants had done her part in pleasing him. So he did it. He went to that downtown place. With her steady hand guiding him, he went flicking, fluttering, and *freaking* all the way.

Face wasn't seen again for nearly three weeks. When he resurfaced, he was well on his way to full-fledged coke addict status, with a classy new wardrobe and fresh traces of expensive pussy on his breath.

* * *

Bliss, being a successful working actress, provided an entrée into the Higher Life. A life filled with New York intellectuals, budding directors, fashion fixtures, about-to-happen playwrights, and a whole crew of chilly friends willing to pull a few strings, do most anything for a friend of Bliss.

One such individual was Claudio Conte, a long-maned, red-hot model-of-the-moment. Claudio was from southern Italy by way of the Bronx. He was cool, hip, and just Italian enough to talk the talk. Face did not like him at first. He stepped hard on the long frail toes of Depina's insecurity.

Once introduced, both stepped back, as two good-looking alley cats might, eyeing, sniffing each other out, trying to decide whether to fight or form a fraternity of two. Face and Claudio were too damn fly to share the same side of a room. It would only invite confusion. At whom would people gaze first? Whom would they want to befriend, mother, play with, think sexy things about? Which one would they want to fuck?

But on the sly, Face was checking Conte, because for a stuck-up supposedly European cat, he had a lot going on. With a Michelangelo-carved jawline and a freaking granite chin that seemed to stretch into the next room, he looked like a man capable with his fists. Shoulder-length hair was Conte's trademark, and that night it was meticulously slicked back, making that hook of a Roman nose somewhat more prominent. Face thought Claudio resembled a big arrogant hawk about to strike. He was almost as tall and taut as Face—another reason to hate him. But Face didn't hate him. He was suspicious of his studly ass, though, especially when Bliss grabbed Claudio's hand and the two retired to another room.

His first instinct: Follow them. He needed to know if Claudio was fucking Bliss. It was possible. After all, he and Bliss weren't exactly exclusive. He also wondered if Claudio was all-the-way straight. But some playwright was babbling about his new play, and Face needed to at least *appear* interested. The man's conversation lasted 3 minutes and 31 seconds. Face was checking the clock on the wall, computing how long it would take that tall hot Italian male model to fuck Bliss. When the door opened, he reasoned there hadn't been enough time for anything, except…maybe a little head. *Is that it? Was she in there givin' that slick motherfucka head? Is she stank like that?*

Strange, it didn't make him mad or angry or insecure, the thought of Bliss giving Claudio Conte head. Maybe when he kissed her, he'd know for sure.

What he needed was a tried-and-true gay detector, like li'l David. David could always spot a fag, no matter his drag, his bag, or the hag with him. David would simply *know*. He could walk into a room blindfolded and scope out all the queers just by sniffing the air. But David wasn't there. As Face watched Bliss and smooth cat Claudio approach, he begged the gods of gaydar to grant him a little momentary Davy power. But the gods didn't come. So he tried the gentle insult. Staring at the dense, bone-straight line of Claudio Conte's brow, he asked, "So, it's Fabio, right?"

"No, it's Claudio. But I get-a that all the time."

"Well, Claudio. You pluck those eyebrows yourself, or does somebody do that for you?"

In a heartbeat, Conte chimed, "I have-a them waxed-a, twice a month-a. I'll give-a you her name-a. She can-a take-a care of that pesky unibrow thing for you, no?"

Bliss laughed a short polite laugh, and as it ceased, she sipped her third martini. Stepping to Face, she kissed his offending caterpillar brow.

"That's all right. I like my baby's growth. So, what do you think, Claude? I mean, really! Is he not The New Gorgeous? Don't you think Eileen's people should take a look?"

"He might-a get-a some work," Claudio shrugged, his lips curling as if he too was sniffing out Depina, his cool quotient, his temperament, his eyes, his lips, his sexual preference. "But he might do-a better with a more *ethnic* agency."

The way he said it, made Face want to hit him, *hoard*.

"Please!" said Bliss. "Eileen could use some coffee with all that buttermilk she's serving up. Pascal would be perfect."

"What you two talkin' 'bout? Who's Eileen?"

"Eileen Ford. You know, Ford Models. It's Claudio's agency, and personally, I think you're Ford material."

Face still hadn't revealed that he had, in fact, *sort of* modeled, though not very successfully. But Ford was the apex of the industry's prettiest posers. You were *somebody* if Ford represented you. Maybe that acting thing could wait. There were far greater talents out there screaming to be noticed. Modeling was feasible. But, as thoughts of cover boy glory popped like flashbulbs in his skull, something darkened the Depina facade.

Back when he was 17, still a student, going into Manhattan on casting calls, interviews and such, he had nerve. Young Depina was incandescing with the hot flames of an "I'm gonna be somebody" fire. He thought little of lying about his age, his past, his sexuality, and his credits. But his *inexperience* showed. And he remembered his last modeling gig. The photographer was dark, gay, and notorious for depicting naked men of color in twisted pornographic shapes. The money was decent, but Face didn't much like the result: his young, cool queer ambiguity, spread naked, as another man was about to mount him. A big chocolate Brother, with a large, camera-friendly penis.

"What's wrong, Pascal? Aren't you interested in modeling, baby?" Bliss asked through coke-clouded eyes.

"Well, damn," he said. "Who wouldn't be?"

The rest is pretty boy history.

* * *

As it turned out, Ford didn't want him. But Boss Models did. The agency marketed him as a young, ethnic Paul Newman. His curly hair was dyed a light chestnut but the crazy sexy cool seething eyes remained a rich green, and those moist lips like soft light-cocoa pillows a man or woman might lay his or her trembling lust upon.

It didn't take long. By June, Depina's likeness was everywhere. It was suddenly *The Face*. You couldn't escape it. Not those smoldering eyes, perpetually wet lips, sumptuous pecs, stony belly, and large come-hither crotch appeal. His fineness was all over TV and bill-boards across Harlem, Times Square, Chelsea, the East and West Village, and every-freaking-where. The face. The Face! Whetting the appetites of all who gazed at his fine 50-foot facade and who let their curious eyes slide down to his designer codpiece.

It was an achievement for pretty, not-quite-Black-or-Latin men everywhere. He'd ascended ("quested," he called it) into a whole other stratosphere of existence. No doubt about it, Face was all of a sudden, like, The Shit.

He'd walk into a place, carrying his new arrogance like a long bronze dick, whipping it out, waving it around the joint. The best champagne, the best blow, the best chicks, the biggest dicks. Semi-fame was a cute new trip, but Face never owned his grace. The industry queens could haul him in, dress him, primp him, powder him, light him, adjust him, and suddenly he was a million bucks worth of sex or class or trash. His personal style became one of full-length minks over top-of-the-line Nikes, or Armani trenches topped by Kangols. One would've thought he had stock in Kangol. He owned every style of hat, skimmer, cap, and tam Kangol ever made. Ironically, beavers were his favorite. He took to wearing showy trinkets, wrist-glistening bracelets, and wouldn't be caught dead without his five-carat diamond and platinum crucifix. He was bold enough to wear big hoop earrings, diamond-studded jammies in each ear. No one dressed like that. He predicted those with money soon would. He was often photographed with his double-gauge nipple rings showing.

From week to week you never knew what flava he liked, what color his hair would be, whether he'd be clean-shaven or goateed. Every day brought yet another mood, another friend, biker, banker,

Asian babe, B-boy, B-girl, or brown boy who *no habla'd ingles*. When he'd run into someone he'd fucked, fucked over, left emotionally stymied, he'd hit 'em with, "Yeah, I remember. We had a good time, didn't we? I liked to fun, you liked to fun, and we funned togetha. I'm tryna do fun right now. So call me. I mean it. We'll fun again. Peace. By the way, you been hittin' the gym?" Or with women, he'd end the identical rap with, "You look fuckin' great in that color."

* * *

Once Face and Claudio Conte got to *know* each other, Conte dropped the faux foreign pose. Game recognized game, and Face found his first *adult hang*. Claudio was five years older and an already jaded member of the nouveaux riche. Modeling was just a hip, trippy day job where he got to cheese and pose, party and pose, hobnob and pose, and sniff expensive *sniff*.

Snow distribution was far more lucrative for Claudio than modeling.

Hanging with Claudio, Face never had to purchase coke. It was here, there, everywhere he looked—in the car on the way to a shoot, in the dressing room before and after shoots, in the back room of most every bar, dive, and hot spot, not to mention spread out on the coffee tables and end tables of Conte's apartment.

To the ghetto-born Face, Claudio was the coolest white dude in the whole damned city, with his affected continental air, fake European flair, and that stony model-man face. No matter his mood or emotion, Conte's expression never deviated from self-satisfied. Face wanted to *be* Claudio Conte. And Claudio was the ideal counterpoint to have along when dressed to the nines, stepping inside The China Club. Claudio was the one to call when the night needed a good talking to, a rush or a toot to make things just a little bit better, stronger, realer.

Face had never been a people person, a natural friend-maker, or keeper, so he mostly let his fame and hunkdom handle the intros. He'd pay attention to the way others handled themselves, what talents they exhibited, and he'd find a way to exploit them as a part of his growing entourage. He tried enlisting Tyrone into his menagerie of men, because Ty was a writer and who better to handle his press?

Ty, however, declined. He'd lost all taste for Face. Only now, it wasn't about their clandestine coitus in a DJ's booth. Ty's disdain grew from a tale Browny, who couldn't seem to get anything but high or arrested, told him during a jail visit. When Da Elixir was *it*, Tyrone had invited the guys to his parents' apartment to get wasted on the dizziness of youth and dreams of fame. But the aftermath of that evening... Tyrone had never quite put it together. Until Browny spilled it. Browny claimed that Face bragged later of "stealing some bourgie jewelry" that night. And Ty remembered that soon afterward, a gold antique brooch, a pre Civil War heirloom and his mother's most prized possession, had been discovered missing. Ty's gambling father was presumed the thief, and with that presumed theft Ty's mother ran all out of forgiveness. There were arguments, church, arguments, accusations, church, denials, and more church. And finally Ty's mother put his father out on the street.

When Ty heard this, his first instinct was to kill Face for destroying his family, to strangle him slowly with his bare fucking hands.

David, however, had no such misgivings to Face, so he jumped the bandwagon in a heartbeat. And why not? His show had closed, unemployment reigned, and money was too tight to mention.

Ever the innovator, David had formed a troupe of avant-garde dancers and artists. They performed for free, passing a hat in Washington Square, on 34th Street, Columbus Circle, wherever, until the cops came. But it didn't amount to much, and living hand-to-mouth was a particular brand of New York bitch. He went to audition after audition but when he'd finally land a job, he'd find out the gig didn't pay. Finally, there came that moment of a talented queen's greatest indignity: begging for a waiter's gig in a midtown dive.

For that reason and others, David could not have been happier than the day he glided into Face outside The Tunnel. In David's eyes, it was kismet.

"Facey? Facey Depina? Damn, baby, is that you, lookin' good enough to eat?"

"Hey, David. How the hell are you? What you doin' these days?"

Waiting tables, and waiting for your tall, fine-as-wine ass to jump off that sexual fence you've been sittin' on, baby. When you gonna give up them snow queens and find the balls to confess your fierce undying love for me? Ya pretty bastard! "Well, I finished my run in Europa, but I'm still out there, auditioning. You *know* how grueling *that* is. Been doing some extra stuff, too. I'm working with the dance troupe, PBS. Performing Black Sissies, and—"

"Yeah, yeah, great. Listen, it must be fate, runnin' into you—"

"You know, I was just thinkin' the same damn thing."

"You still do makeup, don't you? Because, cousin, I could use you. Every artist needs an artist around 'em, and hell, they don't get more *artistic* than you! Here's my card. Get at me. Seriously, Davy, this could be very…" His mind, stranded by its limitations, searched for the right word. "Very…beneficial. Yeah."

Then he disappeared inside the crowd, and David just stood there with a stunned smile, being jostled in a mini New York club riot. Who knew David's winding journey would include riding shotgun inside Face Depina's Cool Carnal Corvette? David did! Now, he had *Face's digits*, and a job offer too. All he'd had to do was stand there, looking *fabu*.

So David was officially indoctrinated into Face Depina's Cult Menagerie. His roles: makeup man, personal stylist, and undying loyalist. This was a gig he would've done for free.

Nine

Love and Fists

In the summer of '87, amidst a city's outrage over police shootings and racial violence, some people managed to fall violently in love. But Ty's inner soundtrack blared, "I Still Haven't Found What I'm Looking For."

By the fall people were hurting out loud and right in front of him. They were hurting in shrouds and Salvation Army overcoats, hurting under newspapers, on the concrete, and before ghostly trash fires. Tyrone would open the door and find people were hurting all over the place. But the few souls huddled that cold night outside the Blue Note were probably hurting *most*.

But inside that renowned jazz emporium the music was *live!* Some bluesy cat on a slide trombone played a snazzy riff. Heads bopped, fingers snapped, people was diggin' it, man.

Then, the mood changed as a thick cinnamon-skinned man stood center stage with a sax. He took a breath and blew his horny horn in a long and *hurting* note so clear, melodious, pristine, and perfect that it reminded Tyrone of a trembling tear. Maybe this sustained resonance was that fabled "long blue moan" his Uncle Jerome had spoken of: the penetrating sound of sex and sadness, sin and surrender. Ty listened, and it seemed that angry, lonely people cried out of that horn.

After his solitary date with a mood at the Blue Note, Ty headed home. On his way to the train, a great hulking giant of a man bumped into him so hard it nearly knocked him to the ground. But the Giant kept just stepping.

Damn, dude! The phrase is, excuse me! Ty thought. But he didn't dare say it. So he chilled. That offender of his space seemed too big, too mean, and too dangerous. Dangerous as the street itself.

Tyrone didn't know it then, but the Giant had a name, and it was Chaz. Chaz Williams.

Upon returning home, Tyrone remembered why he'd left. The place was a mess. His desk was a wasteland of stillborn chapters to a wasted book about a wasted generation that Tyrone was far too emotionally wasted to complete. But the act of *writing* had become the only confirmation that he was still alive, and so that act consumed the crippled hours of his wasted days.

He checked his messages. David deeply wanted to trip the erotic light nostalgic. Ty listened repeatedly to David's voice. How hopeful, animated, and *silly* too it sounded, as if nothing in the world mattered but dancing to his own promiscuous groove. "Ty, you there? Pick up, ya cave-dwellin' bastard! Listen, this hot, hot, *hot* new club just opened on West 12th. So take your hand off your penis, 'cause it's time for some hot new dick. What are you savin' it for, baby boy?"

Ty detected a sadness in David's voice, as if he pitied his friend's isolation.

"Ty, if you're *still my boy*, when you get this, you better holler back. I repeat, hot new dick, West 12th. Be there, or be queer, and alone. Again!"

Hot new dick? Doesn't he even give a fuck that we're in the middle of goddamn crisis?

Tyrone commiserated inside his room with the ghost of Trick Brown. "I just don't know about him, Trick. There's nothing out there but crowds and cliques of loneliness. I see it on every corner, on every street, in every section of every borough, and it sits on every fuckin' fire escape. Sometimes I leave home, and it tricks me, man. I almost begin to feel cocky that it's gone. But it plops right beside my ass on the subway, and rents space inside every spectacular square and rectangle in this diseased city. Hell, Trick, I've got 50 different versions of lonely scrawled in 50 different matchbooks—and those are just the ones I've kept. But you wanna know something? If I wasn't so afraid for David, I'd almost envy his little wild ass. But my friends are dead or dying. And I'm celibate, and alone, and I guess that's a kind of death too."

* * *

Meanwhile in the meatpacking district, Chaz, the Giant who'd nearly flattened Tyrone, walked his formidable gait beyond the doors of another blackened building where the players played in leather. He walked, and the place rumbled. For years, he'd known the smell of pitch-black rooms where lust bent his limbs into falling before some long, hard, thick anonymity. Shiny metal studs oiled with sweat, chained and nipple-ringed men flexed for him. But he was skulking, stalking the night for the right size, the right skin, the right illusion. What he needed was a precise partner endowed with a hard, heavy hand, with just the right strike and burn to it.

Williams had had to *take a man down* that day. It was rough work breaking a man's spirit, his legs, his will to flee. The blood was never pretty. But hell was never *supposed* to be pretty. Now it was time for body and soul to even the score.

Inside that darkened labyrinth of sinuous contortions, men noticed the fierce six-foot-nine, 325-pound mesomorph crowded by hard slabs of muddy muscle.

Yet, inside a darker room, where candles flamed like fiery cocks burning down the wick of night, he yielded his might to a world of submission. His penance could be found strapped to a steel cross, his chest, arms, legs, feet roped. Redemption came warm, hard, and thick across his lips, its weight, girth, taste taunting him.

Amidst the erratic spasms of driven limbs, masks, and howls, wild tongues suckled on the succulence of anonymity. And the seam of Chaz's leathered crotch began to swell. And two men were driving him now, driving him with digits and plugs and latex phalluses. A sudden burst of amphetamine crackled within him, and against that sweet pain of yearning, he wanted, needed to know: Who were they? One man wore a hood, the other cop gear. They were taunting, teasing, tormenting his flesh with hot hands, hot tongues, hot candle wax. And that large knot was building under the leather, mounting, coursing with blood as it clotted with cream and urgency.

The Cop's bronzed hose was solid, thick, bloated. A Prince Albert glistened at its crest as it wagged in Chaz's direction. The other, the Executioner, eyed the inky enormity of Williams's spike: long, strong, ultrathick. The sight of it made the executioner's dick rise, quicken, emerge from its hood. Soon all three stood erect as sightless cobras, rearing in the air.

The Cop demanded of Chaz, "Suck him off! Suck it good, boy!"

Chaz spat, "Don't call me boy!"

Still, Chaz suckled that stretching projection with all the vigor, spittle, and might within him.

But the sling still awaited. Blindfolded, hands and feet fastened by ropes to the chains of the sling, he heard the charged crack of the Cop's whip, and waited for the burn. He needed to burn. To burn would be...*paradise*.

Paradise arrived, crisp and sharp. The bullwhip blazed across his buttocks. "Aw-w-w!" It sliced again. He arched, and it sizzled, and his mind howled, *Yes! Yes!* And the whip rose and crackled again, burning him, cutting him—each slice harder, more abrasive than the next.

"Aw! *Aw-w-w!* More. Yes. More! Harder! Shit! Make it burn!"

Every whip and snap made him hump and snarl, tremble and cry out, "More! More!"

Lashing ceased. That whip skimmed teasingly along the places burned. Two fat fingers launched and plowed him deep. Williams unleashed a groan. Sweat boiled on his skin. The hooded one stood by wielding a long schlong like a javelin thrust through Chaz's begging lips.

A warm coating touched down slowly, sliming, warming, filling. Chaz was lubed, probed, pried opened by fingers, by thumbs, and then, by fire. A rotund bolt of heat came sharp and singeing, a lightning strike surpassing Chaz's limits—surging beyond that threshold of foot-long latex, clashing through sweat-soaked sinews, and he twitched, trembled, *begged* for more.

"Yeah. Take it. Take it!" grunted the Cop. "Surrender to it, bitch," the other said, as waves of naked flames delivered a lovesick, insane strain of pain, baking his center, slamming his being. The gloved intruder shoved deeper then, bringing shocked pleasure and full-bodied frenzy.

Excruciatingly keen, a twisting pain pushed through curves, through grooves, through gullets, rudely reconfiguring this giant of a man.

In a state of climactic trance, everything in him lurched. A sound beyond a scream echoed in his brain, and without knowing he would, he erupted. Quick and hard, the clotted cream careened out of him in a burst of frothy slush.

Chaz was then untied, his blindfold removed.

The lean and flaming Executioner promptly took aim, lust burning too strong for precautions or warnings or rubbers.

Long steel prong pierced bluntly.

Long steel prong thrust severely. That thrust, each thrust came barbaric and swift, sent the sling shaking, chains rattling, and Chaz bellowing, "More!" In savage discord, slave voices howled, and Chaz threw his orgasmic wail inside that howling cacophony. His eyes locked into the Cop's mask of bones, chiseled, lined, firecracker-hot. That cop shoved his thick serpentine dick in Chaz's face, his mean eyes blazing, "S-s-suck it!"

Obedient, Chaz's lips became wrestlers, grappling flesh, salt, and veins, and every pulse-point tasted of redemption.

He grunted, he groaned, he yielded to the synergy of these men, piling him, driving him, ramming him, slamming him, so exquisite in their abuse.

Driven by a mutual madness, Chaz slipped into his own Paradise

Dark, and yes, nirvana seemed just a rough thrust away. The executioner drumming him suddenly grabbed Chaz's ear and everything stilled. The hooded man jammed his willful tongue through the slash in that mask. Then he gnashed his teeth to Chaz's tongue. The shock was palpable, Sucking bleeding tongue, the hooded one pummeled and slammed, pummeled and slammed. A bleeding Chaz wanted them to bleed and come *together*. He said it with his eyes wide open. The man inside him glared back, understanding, and then that foot-long slab Chaz slung shot wild, and the man shot wild inside him. That raw hot wound in Williams was balmed as he convulsed. The man collapsed on top of him, jism connecting them inside the throbbing candlelit gossamer.

And then, the man who'd shot inside him removed his mask.

Face Depina. And his cop partner was Claudio Conte.

"Yeah. It's me. Face Motherfuckin' Depina. And I just made you my bitch!" he sneered, wagging his sperm-polished knob at Chaz. Then, bunching up phlegm, he hauled off and spat on Chaz's belly.

It was the most romantic fit of poetry Face could have ever recited to Chaz's masochistic ear. Chaz Williams wanted to burn his life away; Face Depina carried a blowtorch.

From that night on, Chaz was yin to Face's complicated yang.

Ten

Fire in Young Men's Eyes

That magnificent kid between the sheets *said* his name was Ishmael. Maybe it was. Maybe it wasn't. In dawn's first trick of peculiar firelight, he looked 20 or 21. Was he? Face wanted him to be. This "Ishmael" had been good at granting wishes. Hot brown mesomorphs were becoming proficient at fulfilling Face's sadomasochistic stateside wishes.

Chaz was away at another funeral. But Depina didn't like funerals in his head, or his bed. Facey was bored. He needed to play with *life*. That morning after the groggy night, Face wanted something else. If men were going to be with men, then they should *fuck* like men fuck, hurt like men hurt. Save that soft shit for chicks. The bigger the danger, the bigger the thrill. Whenever Face found a partner willing to *thrill*, willing to take that dive into dark, he was a very, very hyped boy.

"I want you to tie me up and give me a good, hard fuck," Face said, his voice never losing its forcefulness. "Can you handle that?"

Ishmael stated that he could.

Depina was shackled by handcuffs and ankle restraints. He

motioned for the red ball, all the better to gag him with, and Ishmael applied it.

Face received him like a hot, stinging dagger. Inch after long, hard, angry inch made Face want to cry out loud, "Harder, deeper, damn it!" But the gag prevented it, and so he demanded it with his eyes. But something inside those seething eyes turned inward on Ishmael. Depina was just one more john, exacting something from him, *telling me what the fuck to do!*

Ishmael was *not* going to take it anymore. All too quickly, his attitude hardened, and the thunder of his thrusts increased. In Depina's eyes, Ishmael was suddenly that enigma in hot leather. Strange how he reminded Face of his long ago homey, Angel. That glazed look in the hustler's eyes began to frighten and excite Depina as anger claimed Ishmael's limbs, hips, and dick. In the middle of a thrust, his anger became an implement of war. Everything transformed. He was fucking something else in that moment: prejudice, ignorance, disrespect. That hot piece of tan ass writhing below him was real, raw, and tangible. He could hit it, and it wouldn't hit back. There could not have been a tighter or more *right there* place to use as an anger receptacle. Depina's anus represented the world, and Ishmael commenced fucking it hard and rapidly with body, cock, belly, gut, knees. He banged his fists into Depina's chest. He picked a cockfight with his own conflicted emotions, calling Face "punk" and "faggot."

"You like it, faggot? Huh? You feelin' me yet, faggot? Huh?"

Depina wanted to hit him; hit him *hoard!* Draw back and knock the shit out of this crazy motherfucker. But his hands were locked. Yet, somewhere between the force, pain, and degradation, everything changed. He realized nothing was ever perfect. Except anger. The anger boys like Ishmael know, live with, live through, and somehow survive. Now, Ishmael was Anger incarnate: 10 inches of rage engaged in perfect fury.

Face had raged himself, many times before. And so, in some deep and visceral place—just beyond his near-ruptured sphincter—Face Depina understood.

The hustler exploded in a flurry of white-hot sparks. He shot and shot as if his cock itself were spitting! The pellets riddled Face's body like collateral damage after a hellish war.

As Face lay bound, gagged, unable to please himself, Ishmael grabbed his long, hard, tempestuous member. Gripping it tight, he silently, violently jacked it. Face spewed wild white chunks. Then cruelty slowly left the hustler's face, and he realized what had transpired.

Ishmael quickly removed the gag.

"Shit man! I'm...I'm sorry, man...I...I just needed to throw myself into something." His apology tumbled from his mouth like blood.

"Don't sweat it, kid. And don't *ever* apologize! Understand me? Don't say nothin'," Face huffed, his body wrecked by the urban hurricane, his skin a 6-foot-5 skid mark, his cock leaking pain.

He found himself staring at the floor, which he did sometimes, when the gods of language kidnapped his voice. He stared as if whatever he was supposed to say was written there like cue cards for a brain-damaged actor. He gazed at the leather jacket on that floor, its scarred, distressed leather like the kind Fighter Pilots wear. For a moment, he saw his equal.

Before Depina was ready to let him go, Ishmael left, taking the 300 bones he'd earned with him. Sadly, Face watched him exit, knowing both had new poses to affect, new tricks to leave sore and wanting more. Were they separated at birth—two lost twins, no longer looking for love? *Love?* Whatever that shit meant. Ishmael was a hustler, and thus not interested. Face understood that.

Being with Ishmael conjured up memories of an earlier life when Face was Pascal, and worked his own hustle, swinging on a few unfortunate white boys, snatching purses, committing little acts of miscellaneous mayhem. It wasn't about copping new Jordans then—just a way to make ends.

SOUTH BRONX, OCTOBER 27, 1976

Even then a boy could see that Jimmy Carter and those other politicians were lying. Revitalizing the South Bronx was *not* a top priority. The place was still an urbanized Hiroshima. Sirens raked the streets sending wild cries through an indifferent borough. Yet even fear and dread have a rhythm. And danger has an excitement all its own. The Son of Sam was wreaking havoc. The fire escapes had eyes. Good people walked beside corrupt, drums pounding in their chests. It was not a pretty place, but Pascal called it home.

Sometimes, the sounds of Tito Puente timbaled Pascal coolly down East 183rd Street, and he felt high. That night, in fact, he *was* high, spinning off cheap wine, reefer, and sounds. He was feeling no pain and breathing the syntax of singing. That was when it all became sort of beautiful, and poverty put on a better suit of clothes. Tito's energy could do that for him. Then there were those times he passed by a "Black people's church," a storefront where the music, the shouting, and the hope never stopped. It, too, in its own goose-bumping way was beautiful.

Pascal had smoked most of his dime bag, but planned to save a joint to blow with Angel. When he was high, his mind became this free-form musical revue. But suddenly the music stopped, as he approached a shadow, too obvious in its femininity. It was Rosalita. All summer she'd been shooting offers to take the kid home and "make a man" of him. To her eyes, he *looked* fucky enough. But, as always, he smiled and said, "No thanks, Rosie."

Homeboys huddled on the next corner—vigilant, attentive as coyotes, ready to jump at anything that moved.

Pascal stepped into the nearest bodega to cop more rolling papers. He wanted the man behind the counter to remember him, but it appeared he didn't. *Hey. I'm 16 today. Remember that snotty nose, dirt-poor kid you used to throw a pack of Lifesavers for free? Well, he's 16 now, so how about a free beer, for old times' sake?* Not that he really expect-ed that. Still, it was *his* day, and someone should give a shit. But it was just another day in the slaughterhood. The tediously humming boulevard of his forgotten life throbbed on dispassionately. Except someone *had* remembered, and that was his reason for being there, to grab a piece of chocolate cake, kiss his Auntie Claire's aging cheek, and try to ignore the reek of mothballs in her apartment.

"Look at this handsome boy in my doe," said the small café-au-lait colored woman with large hazel eyes and a touch of poverty in her time-worn smile. "Well, he ain't a boy no mo. You's a handsome young *man*, that's what you is. Ain't had time to make you no cake. But there's a pack of Hostess cupcakes in the breadbox. Hid 'em in there, just for you." She winked.

How fuckin' special. A whole pack, just for my ass? Damn. Could you afford 'em?

Then, as if to smash the cupcake of his dismal day, that fuckin' father of his dropped by. A stooped ticking shadow of decayed glamour, it seemed he'd come only to renew the fuckin' hatred. Though the man was about as welcome as a cockroach crawling over the Thanksgiving turkey, Pascal had just received news of his acceptance into a special school for performers. It was dual cause for celebration, and Pascal thought, *hoped* maybe his father would lose *that look*, that cruel, accusatory grimace he always wore. Maybe just once, he might embrace the boy, tell him how *proud* he was. But the senior Depina didn't care about any birthday. He'd only just come to hit his sis up for a loan. Coke was getting to be an expensive habit.

When his father made eye contact with him, for a moment Pascal felt warm.

Shadowed by wasted years of loss and misunderstanding, a father drew closer and whispered in his son's ear, "Ya think that school's gonna make ya something *special*? You can *perform* all ya fuckin' want. It won't change change shit. You'll still be a little murderer."

In that one whisper, Pascal knew *nothing* was forgiven, or forgotten—except what day it was.

His father left, and Pascal looked in the mirror expecting to see the same wickedness his father saw in him. But he didn't see it. All he saw was his face, beginning to crack with tears. *No! Don't you fuckin' cry like some punk bitch! One day they'll be the ones cryin'.*

He lifted his chin, and in defiance of tears, something close to flames appeared in his eyes. Suddenly he was 16 and livid, hell-bent on hitting, spitting, shitting on something. Maybe tonight he'd throw himself off a rooftop and see how well he could fly. Would his body crash and burn, or glide like an angel? But teenage suicide fantasies could wait. Different day, same shit. It didn't matter, though, because Pascal's boy Angel was fresh out of juvenile hall and full of ideas on how to get the party started correctly.

* * *

"This is how it's gonna go down, *mijo*. He knows me. So you be cool, and let me do the tawkin'. Once we get him all hard and bothered, the pants is comin' off. This dude's always packin' big bills. We might fuck around and get a couple of G's off him tonight. He likes you light-skin boys, so you'll be over like Grover. All ya gotta do is act interested. Believe me, he ain't gonna run too far with no fuckin' pants on. I'm tellin' ya, this mutt-fucker is a easy mark."

But the mark was Pascal.

Someone had obviously ignored the PLEASE DON'T PEE IN OUR HALL sign. Nevertheless, Pascal followed Angel through the piss stench, up four flights to a door at the far end of the hall. Amidst the drone of '60s Motown and the smell of bourbon, a dark face appeared at the door. Strong, blue-black, hypnotic, with a menacing sheen, its lips looked permanently downturned. Its slow eyes trailed Pascal's face, then his crotch, like an overgrown boy eyeing a shiny new toy.

"Hey, dude. Wanna double your pleasure tonight?" Angel asked.

The stranger glowered at Pascal and thought, *Yes! Good work. Good fuckin' work!*

The door opened. He was in his 40s, and about the biggest brute of a man Pascal had ever seen in person. Pascal himself was tall, but this guy, *he* seemed more like a Giant. He must've been something like 6 foot 10 and 300 pounds of muscle and threat. Earlier, Angel had said he was in law enforcement. Suddenly, Pascal wondered if that was true. There wasn't much furniture in the little room, only a bed, a night table, a dresser with a TV on top. Pascal gazed at the man skeptically, and then he saw *it*. *Damn! What's goin' on in them jeans, motherfucker? You got a big black fist in there?*

Angel loomed in the background, like an extra in a technicolor porn movie starring Pascal "The Punk" Depina.

"Here, drink," the Giant offered.

Pascal sniffed the dirty glass, asking, "What's this?"

"Bourbon. A man's drink." Even his voice seemed tall.

Pascal passed it to Angel. Angel downed it quickly, not a grimace in sight. The man poured another, passed it to Pascal. Trusting Angel, he drank that one.

"Angel tell you what I like?" the Giant asked.

"Yeah, I told him," Angel said, locking the door.

"Good. 'Cause I know you fuckin' want some of *this!*" the man taunted, holding the biggest, hardest part of himself.

"Nah. No way, man. I ain't like that! I stand still, and you do me."

"Fuck that shit!" the stranger spat.

Sensing danger, Pascal shot Angel a look that said, *Come on, man! Let's do what we came to do, and book.*

But Angel just stood, idling.

All at once, the man gripped the back of Pascal's neck and applied a fierce pressure to it, forcing Pascal to his knees.

"Yeah. Give it to her, Rock!" Angel suddenly shouted, a strange, new bluster claiming his voice.

This stranger must've had over 11 fearsome inches. Pursing his lips, Pascal clinched him away.

That's when he felt that cold metal poke under his chin.

What the fuck? "Angel! Angel, get this motherfucker off me, man! He's…he's got a gun!" Pascal cried. "Angel! Angel? Let's go, man! I…I ain't down with this!"

"Shut the fuck up!" Angel shouted, folding his arms, looking on.

The man placed the cocked gun into Pascal's mouth, choking him into terrified submission.

What transpired in that room was never supposed to be about sex, but some wilder, meaner, *other act* entirely. The Giant eased the gun away as Pascal slowly rose.

"Let's go, Angel," he whimpered.

Angel grinned, then struck him so hard he hit the floor, stunned, temporarily unconscious.

In seconds, Pascal's jeans were around his ankles, and an ache like no other ache in the whole long, wide, thick fucking world was building, flaming, breaking inside him. He wanted to scream, but only a grunt of anguish came to the surface. He felt rug burns on his chest as he was lunged repeatedly into the carpet. The Giant lifted his sweater, and laid his sweating skull on Pascal's back. The moisture ran down, smelling of bourbon and sweat and victory, as the Giant pushed and slammed and thrust.

A dread, a fear for his life gripped Pascal. All he could hear was the sound of a pounding body and the eerie noise of Angel's laughter.

A piece of Pascal Depina died that night—swallowed up by the pain, the distress, by cold sweat and tears. Betrayal carved a hole in him. And he grew angry and *hard* beneath the grunting, smashing weight of a Giant fucking him. He was hard and hurting and the whole room was spinning. *The bourbon*, he wondered. *Was it laced?* Everything hurt too much to think about, and everything hurt for hours.

"All right. That's enough! Let the bitch go!" Angel ordered. Angel of all people was giving the command. Lunging at a more punishing pace, the Giant exploded, and then, unexpectedly, so did young Pascal, branded somehow by the violence of it. He rolled over, buried his confused head in his arms, and wept like a violent child.

"All right, I'm through with her. Did you like it?" the Giant asked. "Musta. You a fuckin' mess. Tonight, you got broke-in by Rock, kid. Now run and tell your daddy about that!" Then he spat on him.

"Yeah," Angel chimed. "That's right, punk-ass. Welcome to the world. And, oh, yeah, Happy Birthday, motherfucker!"

When he was let out of the room of blood and laughter, the dazed and bleeding boy ran. He ran in pain, his hurting brain screaming, *Fuck 'em all!*

But fuck Angel most.

Soon a stolen Lincoln sped away in a crucified night. He drove with madness, wondering why his boy, his partner, his *ace* had turned on him. Was it that wiseass comment he'd made earlier about homeboy getting "done" in the joint?

"Did you like it? Bet ya did," he'd cracked. It wasn't an accusation. He was only ball-busting. But hadn't he *noticed* how something shifted and darkened in homeboy's mug when he'd said it?

"Fuck you, man!" his boy had snapped. That was all he'd said, but his head had been full of its own private madness.

Still Pascal drove, and before he knew it an old tenement stuck up like an unmarked, unremarkable gravestone above the corpse of his earlier life. As he stood before that vacant building, glaring *fuck you* at it, memories of a hopeless childhood burned within him. That night, just once, he thought he could make that flaming incandescence *stop!*

Maybe the only real *angels* were the careless workmen, the alley people, or the bums who'd left behind that *can of paint thinner*. An icy wind wrapped his skin and every cold event of that night embraced him. *Fire* was needed.

Fuck Angel! Fuck 'em all! he thought.

With one strike of a match, *Who-o-osh!* became such a beautiful sound, a beautiful vision of crimson rising, running, licking those stairs and beyond. He saw it smoke and glow, burn, take on new flame, and it made him shudder all over. He watched for a moment the scattered choreography of rats fleeing in all their sleazy beauty.

And then he drove away in that stolen Lincoln, driving harder and faster than ever. In the rearview mirror he could see the blinding red monstrosity he and *a stick of anger* had made. And Pascal Depina smiled a little.

CASA DE LA DEPINA, WEST VILLAGE, LATE NIGHT, DECEMBER 6, 1987

"The College Girl" had been a new breed for Face. He remembered her as cute, if a little quiet. He couldn't remember her name, but he liked the way she giggled when she said, "You look a little like Paul Newman."

"She had a very pretty *boceta*."

"Bo-what?" asked Claudio.

"*Boceta*. It's Portuguese for pussy. There *are* some pretty ones, ya know."

"Hell. I appreciate a good twat, but *pretty*? Most of 'em look like Audrey, that man-eating plant in *Little Shop of Horrors*."

"Well, *hers* was pretty. Fine hairs, all fresh and dewy. Dewy enough to know she *wanted* it. But somewhere in the middle of wantin' it, she changed her damn mind. You don't do that shit! You don't stop my passion, my thrust, my best shit with some scared bullshit! Little tease! She was only a fuckin' freshman, though. Maybe I was her first real man. At least I didn't go at it full force. Gentle was all right for a minute. I think she wanted a *boyfriend*, but I knew I was never gonna see her again. Shit! It's the '80s. Nobody's supposed to give a fuck."

"Right. Right. So why are you still thinking about it?" Claudio asked in that chronically bored voice of his.

"Because she seemed so...so *pure*."

"Don't kid yourself, man. It's an impure world."

"But there was somethin' *brand new* about her. I was high and doin' my thing. But she was cryin' near the end, and it made me feel weird."

"And...so what! You gave it to her good. That's all."

"Nah. This felt like something else. Almost like I was forcin' her."

"Bullshit! Look at us, man. Do you need a mirror? There's not a chick out there either one of us ever needs to force himself on. And all this talk is bringin' me down, man. When did you get a fuckin' conscience?"

"I don't know. I think about stuff sometimes. Like when you're sittin' around, or you're in the shower, washin' your dick, and rememberin' all the places it's been..."

"Oh, yeah. Sure. I've done that."

"Well, it got me thinkin', that's all. I get into some kinky shit sometimes. You *know* that. But no matter how hard and fast I *do wild*, it's always been…what? Help me, buddy. What's that word?"

"Consensual?"

"Yeah. Consensual. I never wanna think I forced somethin' foul on somebody. Maybe I'm just depressed or somethin'. Give me a 'lude."

Claudio complied.

"Thanks. You know, the world can be one big bowel movement. Sometimes life is one smooth shit and everything's goin' good, ker-plop. Me? I can't be happy with kerplop. I'm always lookin' for the bellyachin' diarrhea."

"You know what, man? You're nasty!" Claudio dipped his silver straw into a long white line and sniffed.

Eleven

How Do You Say "Faith" in Your Language?

Café Wha, Greenwich Village, January 1988

Adapting to the skin of the melancholy soul he'd become, or perhaps always was, Tyrone made a lousy first date. You couldn't shut him up to save his miserable life.

"I've been called a romantic. But that's not entirely true. Like everyone, there are times when all I really *want* or *need* is some head. You know? You meet someone. You dig each other. It's purely animal. You're not even checking each other's credentials. Somehow you click, and before you know it, you're rubbing genitals in the risky hole of night. The sex, it's so hot it almost has *meaning*. You shiver. It's over. He looks at you. You look at him. And all you've shared is sweat and come and this pregnant pause that never gives birth to anything real.

"Just once, I'd like to shudder in the cool blue hue of the moment and not stress my impending mortality.

"See, I do not *identify* with 'The Life' out there. Would you mind getting to *know me* before you suck my dick? I wanna talk to people, know who they are, who they wanna be. I wanna be kissed by somebody who knows how, and who *means* it. But nothing is that deep or spiritual anymore. Maybe it never was.

"You front and pose and maybe get blown, or you fuck and pray the condom don't break somewhere in the middle of all that meaninglessness.

"In 1980, I was still shell-shocked. My best friend had just been stolen from me. Before I knew it, it was time for college. But I wasn't ready for the fuckin' world. I was 18. Wasn't I supposed to be full of dreams, semen, and good cock-strong intentions?

"In '81, every now and then, I'd hear whispers of a 'gay cancer.' Queer little oxymoron, don't you think?

"In '82, at school, I had everyone using that motto: 'No fools, no fun.' I was young, fairly cool, somewhat hung. But I didn't suffer fools, and never gave myself permission to have big fun.

"1983 was the first season of young white men in the village wearing purple sores. They were sweating, losing weight, and falling by the wayside of this fuckin' wasteland. Remember? And they'd given the cancer a proper name.

"By 1984, I was walking petrified. People I was really intimate with had died from an intimacy disease. First you grieve, then you never stop grieving. And that voice in your brain, the one you can't seem to turn off, tells you, *Get your ass to a clinic!* So I tested. For two weeks, I sweated. I prayed, made promises to God, on my knees pleading, crying—for myself, for all the rest.

"I tested negative.

"By 1987, my new friends were in heaven.

"It's 1988 now, and I'm celibate.

"There's no shame in surviving, is there? My friends are missing my life. Hell! *I'm missing my life.* I *need* to know why I'm still here and they're not. I have to believe they were just unlucky. I do know this: They never got the chance to feel *realized*. Now, they're gone. But some things you hold on to, like *him*. I wear his tattoo where no one can see it. And the one you *can* see, I reserve for an intimate few. See? This blue stain inside my bottom lip? It's really a tattoo of a name. The asshole artist fucked up and etched the word 'Tick.' It's *supposed* to read 'Trick.' But sometimes I wonder if it was *really* a mistake, because maybe it signifies *tick, tock, tick, tock.*

"Am I crying? Do you have a fear of gay African-American men with eyes full of tears? Better tell me now, if you do. You. You sit there in your cool strong face, like no one and nothing can break you. Just wait. It *will* happen. If it doesn't, or worse, if you don't let it, then wherever you are, I'll feel sorry for you. The last thing you want to be is one of those solitary old queens on the playground, in the park, or alone in the streets, overcoat hanging 'round you like a shroud.

"Two people together, maybe that's a miracle. Maybe I've already had my share of miracles. But you have to go on, right? So now I'm a designated war correspondent. This is a war, you know? I guess it took death to get me off my pacifistic ass. But I'm finally fighting because I have to, even with a pen full of bullets."

And Ty's first date of the new year asked, "Yo, man. It's gettin' late. So, you still wanna fuck, or what?"

* * *

"The Duchess says all the time, 'Ty, just try puttin' your dreams and desires out there. Tell the universe.' Shit. When was the last time the fuckin' universe listened? Trick? Are you listening? I don't need the eyes of a saint with a godlike body, or a wet dream with a Watusi's cock. All I need is someone who calls me by my naked name and makes me feel like I'm laid out on the hottest, most exotic, most quixotic get-away inside my skin. See, I had that once. I'd like that again. Where can I find someone who can catch a knife in his throat without *spitting up blood?*"

TY'S KITCHEN

The following morning, David regurgitated the tale of his latest conquest. "'I hate to be indelicate,' I said, 'but how much dick you slingin'?' And he just chuckled at my ass. *Love it* when they laugh right off like that, cuz I know they like me a little already. Then, it's, 'Hey, check me out, baby. I bring *all this* to the table, *and* I can dance.'"

"Oh, yeah, Duchess. You can dance. I've seen you shakin' that ass. Ever think maybe you shakin' it a little too fast?"

"No. I shake-dance fine. You just can't get with my rhythm. People are tryna find something certain out there, something to celebrate, baby bubba. Laughin' releases endorphins and shit. I swear, *you* really need to try it—along with *several* tequilas."

"Nah. We're diff, bruh. I can't be you. I'd never jet-propel myself toward anyone who showed signs of being uninterested in my thrust."

"True. We are diff. *I get laid* on the regular. Wanna know why *you* don't? Sure, I bet you thought it was that long-ass, sad looking horse-face of yours. But, nah. It ain't that. You're one of those particular, uptight queers that other less uptight queers don't particularly like."

"Oh? Guess I can live with that reality. But being discreet and being *easy* are two completely different species of whore. Never took you for an easy sissy."

"Well. What you call easy, I call *free!*"

"Yeah, right," Ty said. "Next time I want my *free* ass kicked, I know the secret password: 'I hate to be indelicate, but how much penis you slingin'?'"

"Dick! Dick, damn it!" An infuriated David threw up his hands.

"Calm down! What are you, fresh from lockdown in some woman's prison?"

"Me? Me, Ty? I'm not the one in prison. Shit! That's why ya gets no play. First, learn to say *dick!* Learn to look at that riDICulous thing between your legs and love it, and share it, and laugh at it, and maybe someone else will do the same. Laugh, Ty. Me? I love the sound of my laughter. I plan to keep on laughin' till the day I die."

"I *have* a sense of humor. I never gave up that habit," Ty protested, then he lapsed into melancholy. "But that habit abandons a Brother a little more every day."

"Well, get out the fuckin' house! Step into the metro! Hit a bar, spot a tall dark intelligent mother's son, and make that eye-fuck count! Mosey up and say something smart-ass caz-z-zuel, like, 'Do you wear Jockeys? I love the sight of expandin' jockeys in the mornin', don't you?' You'd be surprised, he might smile, start a convo. Hell, you might even get some."

"You know, Duchess, not everyone has your sense of buffoonery. Not everyone has your need to shock, or that straight out raw fag dawg mentality."

"Well, they should!"

* * *

Everywhere Tyrone went, be it a train, a club, a jazz bar, even the street, he heard that same blue moaning note. Maybe it was only in *his* ear. If so, what was he supposed to do with that sound? Was it an emotional tear only he could detect? Should he compose a new song? Trip into lust, just go crazy and fuck a stranger? Should he manufacture new tears? Who were all those solitary men on the street, blaring their horns in sad and haunting dirges? Ty imagined those dirges were postmortems for the boys who were lost, getting lost, or would soon be lost in the fray of the times.

February 1988

Ty often took the Number 1 train. The ride was longer than the number, and it gave him time to read or think or people-watch on the sly. That's when it occurred to him: There are all kinds of Brothers out there—Brothers who aren't screaming retribution before revolution, or holding their bozacks on street corners. Brothers who aren't living lives of denial, coping with lies and failure through drink or clever chemistry. They aren't out jackin' people's shit, or suckin' the devil's dick, and they don't care or give a damn what Alexis Carrington-Colby is wearing. Ty had almost forgotten there were others left, worlds away from his orbit, with little interest in doing the *très* artistic thing. Yes. There were others, with middle-class leanings, a growing fraternity of them: elevated, educated, well-bred Brothers becoming Buppies.

He immediately caught Tyrone's eye on the subway platform, his big, thick nut-brown body swathed in gray flannel. On the train, Ty noted how comfortable he seemed in his skin. He didn't swish, lisp, or emit an ambiguous impression. Quite simply, he was the ideal specimen for a long-repressed GBM with hopes of love's second coming.

Then came a question: "You finish that yet?" It seemed to float above the static rumble of the car.

Tyrone looked up into full questioning lips and liquid eyes. It was that ol' lovely near-chocolatized Brother, and he carried sex on his face, his lips, and his legs like a stallion that never slept.

"Grisham. He's a good writer. Don't you think?"

"Uh, actually I haven't read it yet," Tyrone replied. The Brother peered about the indifferent straphangers for a seat. Then his eyes settled to a narrow space next to Tyrone.

Does he want to sit with me? Ty wondered, as the train stopped at 14th and the car emptied considerably. He could've sat *anywhere* then, but he chose to sit right next to Tyrone.

"I was in law for awhile. He writes the way a lawyer thinks," the man said.

His history was exotic: "I was raised in Germany until the age of 6, Italy through 13, then all over the USA." A chic, well-spoken cat, he bragged of sharing classes and "notes once" with John Kennedy, Jr., and he'd even been to Africa.

"Really? I'm dying to go," Ty said.

"I'd highly recommend it, as long as you're not afraid of needles. You'll be in for a battery of them."

This man never stopped talking about himself and how he figured into the world of high finance, mergers, and cutthroats. Before Tyrone knew it, the next stop was his.

"I get off here," he said, standing and beginning to rise in his jeans.

"Hey. Here's my card. If you ever think about dabbling in the market, I'm your man."

"Thanks. Maybe I will."

They shook hands, and as he left the train Ty glanced at the card. It read: ZAIRE T. MONK, ESQ.

The penis wants what it wants. But Ty was not overtly looking to bag a Buppie. Finally, he decided, *Maybe I'll just tip home, bust a nut, and be over it.*

There was an old Sam Cooke song his mother used to play when Tyrone was just a tyke: "Another Saturday night, and I ain't got nobody…" Well, it *was* another Saturday night and it seemed like *years* since he'd had anybody.

What he *had* was a hard-on. This came on uninvited sometimes, whispering lust by its hot first name, crying its impatient song, written in blood and *raging* like a fever. Often, he'd catch hold of its burning, and try to put it out, manually…play with it like it was an old friend, or a bully prone to spitting. And like a bully's, its aggression often came from a lonely place. The penis had few options but to rise up, fight for attention. Some nights he could *not* ignore it. Loneliness unaddressed manifested in a hard-on of the soul, until he slowly rubbed it away, like a tear.

* * *

In the bar's soft blue neon lighting, *his* face shone like a hot, dark carving full of ancient mystique. And Ty thought, *If I were a sculptor and molded that face, I'd call it Africanus Man.* There in a room full of eyes, attitude, and spiked crotches, Tyrone saw the closest thing to *home* as he checked their reflections in the mirror. They were different shades of the same color. He was 6 foot 2, Tyrone's height, and his naked head caught an arresting light. A white Lycra shirt clung to his body like a possessive lover. His posture was so erect, so regally dignified, so sexy that his presence evoked the image of a majestic piece of mahogany sculpture. He gazed back at Ty with unfathomable lush-shiny eyes, and Ty couldn't imagine why the others weren't all over him, fighting to embrace his magnificent succulence. It occurred to him how *still* this man stood in a night full of pretense and games and movement. Was that regal stance only a pose? If so, he seemed to be posing for Ty alone. A faint suggestion of a smile crossed the man's face, and Ty played it off by looking in another direction. When his gaze returned to the mirror, the man was gone. *Shit!* he thought. *Fuck me! I'll never get it right!*

But as he turned away in disappointment, the mahogany sculpture had come to life. It walked up right behind Ty, and with a slight accent, said in Ty's ear, "I'm Imani. Let's dance." He extended a large firmly carved hand, and Ty took it.

They danced slow and hot, skulls touching, hands stroking the unfamiliar maps of each other's bodies. Ty sighed what he hoped was an intangible moan. The man hardened, a slip of precome coating sweet warm promise on his secret skin. Then, this man called Imani stepped back, and his full-frontal *lovely* was *massive!* Pulling Ty close, he ground that excitation into him. Fires rose, set, and caught flame against their flesh. His eyes were heat-seekers darting over Tyrone. The shrouded vision coursed a seductive trail further down his thigh, asking the one essential question of the night.

Hungry as the evening was, courageous as desperation sometimes makes men, Ty wanted nothing more on this deep brown earth than to touch *it*.

Sometimes, by nature, or by a silent shout of the eyes, by God or by fluke, people *do* manage to find each other. They are not always at their best, but they are men, full of urgent limbs, flaming minds, and bone-erect complexities in their jeans. They smile, and solitude takes a sabbatical.

"I'm Tyrone."

Ty wondered: *Do you think I do this shit all the time? I don't. Do you know how long it's been since a man, any man, has entered the wet warm asylum of my mouth? Do you know that the taste of your neck is like solitude's serum? What did you say your name was? Oh, yes. Imani!*

They hadn't spoken another word. Yet Ty had a feeling that both he and Imani were well-versed in the Blues. Did Imani feel it too— that sensation of falling? Ty stood outside of himself, watching himself recede into some dark hard calamity of need. But he *needed* to fall into something or someone who could support his scared-shitless descent into carnality.

"I do not live very far away," Imani said. "Come home with me tonight. Let's be sexual men together," he offered, his long lashes sweeping over nearly Asian eyes. Ty was charmed by the way Imani said things.

* * *

A bang against the wall echoed inside an uptown apartment building, on the seventh floor, as Imani cooed, "Take it easy!"

But I am gagging on you, you beautiful African fool! Ty *was* gagging, gagging on his story, his truth, his vibe; and those sloe-brown eyes sang down on him with such lewd tunes. Strange, how they vibed with seemingly new rhythms. Were they really new? It felt as if they'd *rhythmed* before.

"Yes. Yes. No. Not so hard," Imani begged between sighs. "Please. My deek! Take it easy!"

But it had been a long time since *easy* was Tyrone's for the taking.

A plunge of his hips told Imani just how deep, sooty, and boundless *longing* could be.

Tyrone closed his eyes and let nothing exist but that *deek*, that Island of Imani on his tongue. Imani threw his hips in slow rotating dances, and oh! Ty danced along. He imagined tangy plantains, sassafras root, savory mangos swaying in a swift breeze. He imagined Imani's sweat trickling, then running like the Nile down the brawny continent of his flesh.

You're close. You're so close... I can feel you!

Imani pulled away, and his bounty vaulted high, filling the room with the voice and vision of his coming. He managed to still the air pumping in and out of his lungs just long enough to say, "Oh! You don't know how much I needed that!"

"I think I know," Ty said. "I think I know."

Ty's hungry eyes glimpsed his naked body, taking in all that dead-gorgeous African manhood standing before him. His nipples hard as rock candies, his panting chest washed in luminous sweat, his sweeping shoulders pitching with the very caps of them jumping from that explosion. Imani's face was a thunderclap of dark, haunting masculinity. His was a terrible beauty, so sharp it hurt the untrained, unappreciative eye. Ty was suddenly his art groupie.

"In my country, we've no places such as the place we met this evening. I like this country for its freedoms and its opportunities, but I miss my home," Imani said sadly.

He'd come to America from Liberia to study medicine. He had one semester left, and then it was on to his internship.

"I want to go back. I must go back to treat the villagers. Though some parts of Liberia are quite rich, my village is small and very poor. I am needed there, and so I must go." Imani peered back at Ty, his gaze a silent howl.

And then, both of them stared at the cock Tyrone's emotional fist had pumped into iron. In one rash move, Imani gobbled Ty down as if he were the raw esoteric food of a god.

"Ah-h-h! Mmm, yes!" That coiled tongue seemed to have been created for pulling deep pleasure from another man. Ty could feel his *life* inside Imani's mouth. The room spun and took on color and light, then heat. *Yes! Keep spinning! Keep swirling! Keep sucking me outta this world!* Ty's skin sizzled. Whirling his hips, gradually, sensuously, he felt Imani humming a most hot and savage hum.

"Oh! I…easy. E-e-easy, baby! I'm…I'm gonna come—I don't want to come yet!" Ty said.

"Then I must stop. Together we are far too good to end so quickly," Imani said, looking at Ty and smiling.

I love your accent, your smile. Imani, you are a Long Blue Moan maker, that's for sure: shy, intelligent, cool, hot, happy, and sad at the same damn time.

Imani's vine rose mightily once again, and Ty decided it was best to say what had to be said before the two of them went any further: "I don't get fucked," he said plainly and just a little too forced.

Imani looked a little stricken by such dick-deflating candor.

"Understand, it's not a faggot issue. Really, it's not."

"Are you afraid of catching something from me? You need not worry. I am nearly a medical professional, and I am, how do they say it here? I am clean."

"No. It's not that, really. It's just never been my...erotic orientation," Ty managed.

"Are you afraid? That the plague is never far away?" Imani's eyes searched for an answer.

"No. But I think a man should know what he likes, and, well, I don't like ass-sex very much. For me, it's a gift a man gives to a man he loves. Even then, it's a gift that hurts. And looking at you, Imani, I figure I'd hurt for a decade or two." Ty laughed nervously, trying to take the shade off the mood.

"Sometimes a man needs to hurt," Imani stated.

Oh, damn... Is he gonna try and rationalize or finesse me into this shit? Nice try. Won't work, though, my erect African King!

Imani didn't know Ty's history. He'd no clue of Tyrone's trust issues. Of Omar.

Omar had hurt *a lot*. And did Omar *dig* him? Not.

Now Ty stood before this man called Imani, and it seemed Imani was waiting for him to say something. But Ty couldn't tell if his no-fucking-in-the-ass policy had pissed Imani off, or if Imani was the type who was *going to* that night, with or without permission or policies or prophylactics. Was the man merely being philosophical when he said, "Sometimes a man needs to hurt"?

"Well, have you...been tested?" Imani asked, slowly, as if wanting to know yet dreading the answer.

"Yes. Many times. I'm negative," Tyrone said. "And you?"

"I am negative also. So you see, things aren't so bad. Do you have any condoms?"

* * *

In the dreamy afterglow, where cream pooled on bellies and ran down mocha thighs, they kissed, hot tongues igniting like venerable flames.

They became fast, furious friends. Imani seemed to be the answer for Ty, the elixir for what lay dark and alone inside. Strange how a good, cleansing, bone-shuddering climax can sometimes kill the scream of lonely chaos.

Many times Ty collapsed contentedly into Imani's firm stretch of sun-roasted skin, thinking, *Damn! He's so fuckin' strong! Where does all that strength come from? Is it something they teach young boys in Liberia? Maybe I can learn something* better *from his naked example.*

"Imani. That's a beautiful name, man. It's Arabic, right? What does it mean?"

"Faith," he'd said. "Faith."

June 1988

The doctor did indeed go back to his country to tend the villagers. He and Ty wrote long, sad, beautiful letters, swearing they'd be together again—one day.

But "one day" was thousands of miles away, and sometimes Ty found himself daydreaming about that cat on the train. Zaire Monk. And the fated thing about the city is that sometimes people you haven't seen in ages suddenly show up shortly after the thought of them, or *him* in this case, has stroked your mind.

Months had passed, yet the recognition factor was instant. Ty nodded and Monk included a smile in his nod.

"Yo, Bruh. How you doing? Listen, I've got a great inside tip for you."

Ty was so happy to see him that Monk's words didn't quite register...at first.

Monk was beyond warm for his form, and sometimes a lonely, needy, carnally interested Brother has to stand with his horny dick in hand and just say *fuck it!* Besides, Monk's "great inside tip" was steadily rising inside those Brooks Brothers.

"Why don't we shoot by my place, and I'll tell you all about it?"

Inside Monk's apartment, the hard glide-'n'-slide of Monk's thickness sputtered against Ty's thigh. He grabbed Monk's bountiful ass and slammed into him with a desperate violence. He just about *lost it* to that sweet slide of heat and need and want. The freaky sensation of Monk's wide tip swerved against the fine hairs of Ty's breach. *Is he makin' that move? Of course, he is! But do I want him to?* Monk's ripe mouth gently brushed the swell of Ty's upper lip. Monk's skin was smooth, his bozack so hard and so damned tempting…

"We don't have to fuck, Ty. We can do whatever you want, man. We could just jerk-off together, and that could be hot too." Monk said as he pumped his rotating rump, skimming his moist lips along the slender nape of Ty's long-unkissed neck.

Together they were a sexy composition: rhythmic, funky, hot, sweaty. They moved like two experimental jazzmen, their improvisational hands stroking the other's pulsing keys. The attraction between them was so strong they could've stood grooving, moving, lunging, lusting, and come like that.

But Monk's slow hand descended Ty's belly, clutching what stood waiting hard and hovering. Monk's fingers played down Ty's spine, and the music rose. With a quickness, he dipped and blew Tyrone's lonely horn, hard and loud, pausing only to lick the engorged reed with a slick uncorporate-like madness.

"Oh, yes. Suck me!" Already, Ty was edging—a deep crescendo rattled his balls. Running his hands along infinitely dark shoulders, he eased Monk away.

Theirs was no staid meeting of the Mutual Penile Admiration Society. Ty knew it was time to get wild—wilder than the tangible urge to scream, "*No!*"

They took it to a primal place, the floor. There, face to face, legs akimbo as they straddled each other, Ty entered him. "Aw! Ark, Ah!" Monk's mighty arms lowered and rose as he undulated downward, controlling Ty's impact. And soon their hips worked in pumping, slapping, thumping unison. Ty thrust, Monk humped, Ty hammered, Monk surged and his eyes never left his partner's. Soon their music reached its thrashing crescendo. Monk rocked and rolled, smiling as Ty plunged and pummeled.

"Aw! Ah! *Aw-w-w!*" Tyrone groaned. Monk brought his feet to

Ty's chest, grimacing as Tyrone lit into him. "Aw-w-w! Come on, baby. Work it! Throw it on me!"

Their legs entwined, breaths echoed breaths, heartbeats collided, and tongues drummed the skin of lips, prying, dashing toward warm rattling wetness.

And after climaxing, Zaire Monk, Esq. said, "You just don't know, man. I've been celibate for almost two years, and that, that right there was ah-h-h, my Brother!"

Ty couldn't help but smile.

Yes. They were a rhythmic *song* for a while. Zaire and Tyrone. Ty and Zy. But not everyone was diggin' it or trying to hear their music. Monk's parents, for instance, just straight-up didn't *like* Tyrone. Oh. They knew *who* he was and *what* he was, and what he and Monk were *doing together*. That was never the issue.

No, Ty was simply deemed not quite up to snuff. He didn't play the right sports, or belong to a fraternity, let alone the *right* fraternity. He did not vacation in the right spots, or own the right suits. Hell, Ty half-expected the old brown paper bag test to see if his skin was light enough.

The Monks decided, after one chilly dinner of Cornish game hens, that Ty's golden-brown luster lacked sufficient polish. And after three months, apparently Zaire—a grown-ass man with a grown-ass career (and a grown-ass penis)—agreed.

Twelve

The Discontented Season

Blood never looked more murderous than on that snowy concrete in back of the Windsor projects. But to hear Faison Brown tell it, the stunned and bleeding motherfucker had it coming.

"You know that cat, Ty? Huh? Well, that motherfucka is boys with the cutthroat motherfucka that done ripped holes in my brother."

Suddenly a part of Ty, a part Browny couldn't see, was stunned and bleeding.

"And he's gonna *step to me*, smilin' and cheesin', talking 'bout, 'Your brother shouldnuh went ta Dairy Queen if his po ass was lactose-intolerant!' Like it's all some fuckin' joke. Let him press charges, I don't give a shit! Ain't no fuckin' punk gonna throw shade on *my* brother's memory and grin in *my* motherfuckin' face!"

Ty understood. But, damn it, here it was Browny's first day back in the world, and already he was throwin' up his fists. He'd called Ty and asked him to pick him up, and, of course, Ty had agreed.

Despite their miniscule bout with high school recording fame, and Ty's *getting paid*, and Browny resenting that shit, he'd decided in his hour of need to *forgive*.

The only *real* connective thread between Tyrone and Faison was Trick. But now Trick had little to add to the relationship, except his absence—which was *a felt thing* whenever Ty spent time around Faison. Yes. Trick and Faison looked alike. That same angry dark child grimace claimed their foreheads whenever something upset them. And they had a similar hyperkinetic energy. But the similarities ended there.

I knew Trick. You'll never be him. He never went looking for a fight. Hell, Trick was the coolest nig I knew.

But times were rapidly changing.

Earlier, the sky was a vast and limitless blue page. All at once the intrusion of slate colored the day as the sun grew red and low in the horizon. And there Faison Brown was in a T-shirt on a cold winter's night. Tyrone saw a sad kind of irony in the nickname "Browny." *A Brother out of season.* He dropped him off on 110th Street in Harlem. As Browny was about to leave, Ty shook his hand, slipping a new $100 bill in Faison's palm. "Merry Christmas, Browny."

"Thanks, man. You too, yo…"

For Faison, everything seemed just a little sweeter, if more barren, than when he'd left. It was Christmas time, yet the city stood uneasily still, like a shark at leisure wearing a garland. Where was everyone? While he was still in prison, his mother had died, and on that day, he'd promised himself to live a more righteous life. But it was going to be a tough promise to maintain. The only people hiring were Mickey Dee's and Burger King. Less talented Brothers were bringing in five tax-free G's a week, slinging vials and baggies on the street. His people were genuflecting to a different king now. *The Pipe* was lord and master. No one was paying much attention to the signs, nor the Keith Haring billboard over 125th Street advertising: CRACK IS WHACK. Sheeit! Half of *Bush's America* was strapped, high, dying, or dying to get high.

During his incarceration, Browny had grown addicted to smuggled porn, and was thus a ruthless masturbator. Titties, titties, titties! He was obsessed by thoughts of sucking on somebody's titties. He remembered one chick with big ol' chocolate beginning-to-sagsome titties. She didn't have too many flies on her yet. And she wasn't too particular.

* * *

Juanita Lewis *owned* her sexuality, and she wasn't adverse to taking in the occasional brawler, baller, less-than-gentlemanly caller. Though some mistakenly considered her loose, she was never a member of anyone's cliché Ho Club. She'd long ago transcended the stigma that her four kids were by four different men.

"What I got to be ashamed of? Shit! All I'm guilty of is four bad choices. I love my kids to death!"

She was an urban Assagai woman, a makeshift warrior fashioning spears against corruption, and making an example of herself. No one, much less a man, ever raised a hand to her, and she never rode the welfare merry-go-round. She organized rent strikes, spearheaded a neighborhood watch, and once clocked a man who'd spat on her freshly swept sidewalk. She was a mother *and* a father. Most of all, she was a woman who held on to the same elusive dream; even overweight Sisters with four screaming kids and big-beginning-to-sagsome titties dream. Nights alone in her bed, she'd sometimes sing those "I Just Can't Find Me No Good Man" blues.

"Hey, Faison," she said almost inadvertently. "Heard you was back."

"Feels good to *be* back, yo," he said, thinking it a positive sign that her apartment door was done-up in green aluminum wrapping paper and a big red velvet bow. When he entered, it *felt* like Christmas. "Nice tree," he said.

She could smell jail all over him. It was unmistakable: a musk of desperation, coupled with a dash of bravado to disguise the stink of fear. But Juanita wasn't scared. She liked it. Brothers fresh from lockdown usually gave a good fuck—for as long as the fuck lasted. Unfortunately, most blasted quick loads and pimp-walked out her door, not calling again until a hungry night begged for more. But Juanita had grown used to it. "Ya hungry?" she asked.

He nodded.

She wore her hair in a short natural. Her eyes were large black saucers. But they weren't cold, arbitrary eyes. She cooked too; cooked like nobody's mama's business, and knew about 19 positions to a one-night stand. All but six she might perform if she *liked* you. She had a warm smile, too. She brought Faison a li'l something to nosh on in the form of a heaping helping of smothered pork chops, collard greens with ham hocks, potato salad, macaroni and cheese, hot cornbread, red beans and rice, a slab of peach cobbler, *and* a Diet Coke. Yes, the food was smokin'. But Browny had been so long tucked away on an extended Hell's Holiday, and there sat those breasts. Strange how they kept staring back at him, like two bombs in a pink sparkled spandex turtleneck.

Look at dem shits. I need dem shits.

Her kids were at her sister's, and she was thinking she *might* just give him a piece.

Faison looked different to her. She liked his newly hard prison bod, and that he had *enough class* to bring her a six-pack (and not a one was opened). She didn't even mind that little nervous Browny habit of tapping things, the table, his thighs. She liked how he wasn't so concerned with time, or checking his watch like other fast cocks before him.

She turned on the radio. DJ Frankie Crocker, the Chief Rocker, was smoothing it out on the R&B tip, and radio station WBLS was settling into "The Quiet Storm." Faison blessed Juanita with a song, and magic happened. His vocals were his aphrodisiac, and so *it was on*. The song of seduction was "Never Too Much," and he was never too shy to sing it.

Da-a-amn, bruh! Make a sister feel all gushy and wet and serenaded and shit. She felt special, felt like… *Negro! Why don't you just…just go on and take me?*

Soon, he fell into all of her, every crease, pleat, and comforting ripple. But all of a sudden, his dream of a pussy paradise stalled. When he pushed inside her, he went limp. Memories of prison. *Oh, Nah! Oh, damn!* Browny rolled over, devastated, pressing his frustrations into a pillow.

Juanita slowly fingered his back, trying to stroke his phantoms away.

"You ain't got to prove nothin' to me," she said tenderly.

He wanted to scream, *It ain't you, stupid bitch! I need to prove this shit to me!*

A soft sweep of her gargantuan breasts swayed across his restless shoulders. How huge, damp, and comforting they seemed. With a swiftness, he rolled over and kissed her hard. His tongue sailed down each earth-brown mountainous tit, probing, lingering on that luscious chocolate areola. Yes, he needed *dem shits*, and everything was coming back to life, *rising, jerking around*.

He mounted her then, much like a rusted bike in the rain, remembering the wetness of the ride. Inside her sopping-wet spicy folds he lost those prison visions and every brutal memory. Hard time slid like random precome from the dick of his mind, and he almost wanted to cry against the awe-inspiring float of those breasts. As she juggled and jiggled about him, he pushed and grunted his way back into the world.

She was *A Find* when the rest of his clique was doing time inside a prolonged nightmare of living crack whores. *Show her some attention, some simple, genuine respect, and Juanita and her cooking, and her kids, and her pride—and her titties—could be yours.*

All women were strange fish to Browny. This one drove him delirious, turned him into an elastic, spastic, sputtering madman between those grateful sheets.

Only afterward, he wondered, *Is she for real? Do she got the gift to see my gift?* Could she look beyond the rust and swagger, see into the faint signs of his luster and recognize he had a shinier future in mind? Or did she possess the power to turn on him? Would she try to stick a Brotha for his papers? *Papers?* All he had was enough for cab fare and admission to a titty bar and maybe a lap dance. His only prospect was a homemade demo tape of his unhappy ass singing. *Papers?* Soon, he imagined he'd be making crazy-mad papers singing his bruised heart out. Where would those chicks be then? Biting for his *rich* dark delight? Women. He didn't trust them very much. Yet, now and then, one would fuck around and genuinely surprise him.

"You can stay here, if you want. Sleep right here on my couch. At least till you get back on your feet," she softly volunteered. Brown was far too needy to refuse. She let the truth be known as she prepared the sofa with blankets and a pillow. "But you got to get a *job*, Faison. I ain't yo mama. And I don't plan on takin' care of you."

"You all right, Juanita," he said, looking at her, and for the first time seeing *more* than just titties, titties, titties.

"I *ain't* your ho, and I ain't no Saint Juanita either." She turned off the light, leaving him warm, satisfied, and thinking—thinking about a future.

What he did not know, and what Juanita in her generosity was afraid to tell him, was of her connection to a man who once broke mean with a switchblade.

JANUARY 1989

Browny had to humble himself. He took a janitor's job at his old high school. But he made his own glamour, singing arias from Puccini while buffing floors. Meanwhile, bigger doors closed with loud-ass *slams* in his hopeful Black face. Rejection could depress even the best of Brothers, let alone The Maestro of Low Self-esteem.

As hard luck would have it, he ran into a man, recently in the green, with a familiar face and an even larger arrogance than he remembered.

"Pass-cow Depina! Yo! Is that *you*? Ah, shit! Look at you," he appraised, his envy evident. "Hey! Digs the ride, man. Hot to death! This is slick!"

"Hey, Browny. Steal any Jettas lately, or you an entertainer now?" Face asked, laughing to himself.

"Yeah. Well, all that's about to go down real soon, man. You know me, I'm still doin' my thing. Got prospects out the ying-yang. So, uh, what you doin' 'round here? Somebody told me you's the next big thing! About to be large!"

"I *am* large. It's the petty li'l motherfuckers I used to run with that got smaller," Face jabbed. But suddenly his David-styled hair stood on end.

Browny noticed Face looking around nervously, those green eyes shifting, darting up and down the street.

"Yo, man. Now's not a good time," Face warned.

"But yo. This must be fate 'cause I got this tape and you sho gonna wanna hear it."

Face panicked. "Yo! Shit! Get in. Just get in, now!"

Seconds later, they were hauled back out of the car and Browny's hands were forced behind his back. He hated being touched, especially by cops, and what the fuck were they trying to shackle him for? He was nobody's choirboy, but for once he was living clean. Yet there he was, fighting off a cop, being "one of those aggressive Negroes." Cops hated that shit. So they yoked him, then pushed him face-first to the pavement. He was Mirandized and shoved right next to the man who'd never *really* been his *boy*.

A terror spooked those green eyes, as all Face saw were vile visions of a life behind bars. That vision was not, repeat *not* in the Grand Depina Plan. "Psst. You owe me. Tell 'em the duffel is yours. Cop to this and I swear, you'll never want for nothin' again. I can hook you up," Face whispered to a stunned, confused Browny.

"What? Whatchu talkin' bout?"

"Razor Morrisey. Had ya cryin' like a drunk bitch, beggin' for your life. Broke as I was, I bailed you out. Remember?"

* * *

Face and Browny were living together, right after P.A., trying to be artists. But Browny had fucked up, got hooked on coke, and his foolish ass ended up owing *Razor Morrisey's* boys. Razor, of all fucking people! Now there was no rent money, no cash for food, no nothing. Face was in survival mode, looking to pay rent. Browny was too, but more literally. He *needed* that money.

Where can that little fool get that kinda money? Pascal wondered.

And what the fuck I'm gonna do 'bout the rent, my acting lessons, and food, and some fuckin' get-high?

Of course, there *was* someone who could help. Someone with money who probably wouldn't even sweat him about paying it back. Someone who'd liked him back when he was still "Pascal." But what would he want in return? Maybe just a little suck-'n'-fuck for old times sake? Hell, Face could do that shit with a quickness and be on his way…

Long Island, Two Days Later…

Erik Von Ness lay in a chaise lounge on his deck, his jeans undone, his Hamptons-tanned feet propped up. Once more, Face Depina had provided a decent suck-'n'-fuck. But after the gush, Von Ness just wasn't gushing anymore. "The Kid" had provided a service, and that was all Von Ness wanted from him now.

"Erik, listen…I hate to ask, but I really need to borrow some cash. See, I'm tryna be a actor, and it's *hoard* out there. Rent's due, and there's food, and…"

"Save it kid. I'm not your Daddy. I'm not even your *friend*. Was once, a few summers back, until you got what you wanted from me. Maybe you don't *do* friends very well, kid. Hell, I almost *admire* you for having the nerve to come and ask me for another favor. And for that, I will give you something. What's the going rate these days on common boy-whores with uncommonly pretty green eyes?" He reached in his pocket and threw a 50 at Face. "Goodbye Pascal," he said, and walked into his house.

Face stood there feeling cheap, insulted, reduced, fucked, and fucked-over. *Oh, yeah? Ya stuck-up fancy faggot son-of-a-rich-bitch! Nobody disses me like that no more!*

Besides, Browny *needed* that money. Browny was sure-as-dead without it! And Face needed some cheddar too. So he was *going* to make that visit pay, if even in a fancy piece of crystal; that Lalique vase, or maybe some artsy-fartsy knickknack. Face was gonna *get* paid—and a helluva lot more than a 50.

So Face followed Von Ness inside.

Why did Von Ness have to get physical? Face wasn't trying to fight him, just *use* him. Why did he pull that machete on Face? Why did he have to cut his arm? Blood pooled through the sleeve of Face's shirt. Face *had* to hit him then. Hit him so *hoard* it knocked him down. Struck him in the belly and he flew across the living room. His head hit very hard on that hardwood floor, which knocked him unconscious. Face took a Cartier watch, some diamond cufflinks, a gold slave bracelet, and some other shit he knew Von Ness had insured.

Von Ness was still out when Face left, never looking back.

In his fall, however, Von Ness had knocked a burning candle to the floor. The burning candle, flames, curtains, flames, hardwood floor, flames.

Face saw it all on TV that night. *I didn't do that. That wasn't me...was it? I know I didn't do that.*

"Oh, Erik. Oh, fuck!"

But Browny got bailed out from Razor. And Face's rent got paid for another month.

* * *

"I paid him off, and I never called you on it, did I? Well, I'm puttin' in my marker now, Brother."

Browny thought, *I didn't think you had heart till you took it out yo crusty pocket*. And in one mad greedy ambitious desperate moment, Browny shook his head. Before he knew what shackled him, he was back behind bars. But this time, he had a promise, a guarantee from Pass-cow Depina.

Thirteen

Heard It Through the Grapevine

Back in 1980, when Tyrone had arrived at Columbia, he'd been pretty much clinically depressed. It wasn't easy living the special loneliness of being an 18-year-old secret widower, grieving in a place most people couldn't see.

By Ty's junior year, his new roomie was a constant source of comic relief. Jasper "Jazz" Thomas swept in like a fresh breath of real illy Philly air. A sanity saver, Jazz was a buff, handsome ebony Brother, with a smooth rap, a mischievous grin, and a fast-ass zipper. Yeah, Jazz.

Now for old times' sake, Ty placed a call to touch base with Jazz. He just had to send a shout-out to his boogie boy from the wilds of Philly. "Hello… Ms. Thomas? Ms. Nina Thomas? I hope you remember me. This is Tyrone… Yes, that's right. Ty Hunter. Jazz and I were roommates. How are you? Well, I haven't spoke to him in almost two years, and I just wanted to find out how my big head-boy's doing…"

* * *

"Ty, did you hear? Did you hear about Marvin?" Jazz asked, the afternoon of April 3, 1984.

"Yeah. But it's just a rumor, right? It can't be true. I was in the student lounge, and some girl came in crying, saying she heard it on the news…"

"It's true, man. They say *his father* shot him. What could make a man do that shit to his son? I've been sittin' here, rememberin' all the good times I had with Marvin in the background. I…I can't believe he's gone, man."

Jazz had just taken a shower and was draped in a short white terry cloth towel. He stood, staring at Tyrone in silence. A spot of clear elixir slid down his naked thigh like a transient tear. Perhaps what he did was necessary for both his and Ty's lucidity. He hugged Ty tightly, and somehow his large dark hands drifted. And then Jazz just *went there*, boldly unzipping Ty's jeans.

Jazz ran his cheek along his friend's warm crying flesh. Ty trembled. Jazz blew him like a saxophone, sadly. And every place inside Ty moaned as lips slid across him in an act of confusion and need and music remembered.

Marvin's voice singing "Sexual Healing" was all either of them could hear as Jazz let his towel fall. He was vertical, his flesh tall, warm, stiff as a girder. Ty gently reached out and traced his boy's broad, indulgent thigh, and soon Jazz was drowning in the wave of a tongue that couldn't save him or anyone.

* * *

Hanging up the phone, Tyrone reflected on the irony of how *sex* was *not healing* a damn thing. It was killing people. Sex or drugs or both had killed Jazz a year and a half earlier. Ty hadn't even *known*.

And just 10 days after hearing of Jazz, there came a glib call from Ty's long-estranged and gambling father. The message was simple: Ty's Uncle Jerome was dead.

Oh, no! Not Jerome.

Tyrone had been feeling optimistic about *him*. After Omar, Ty's visits to Brooklyn had become less frequent over time. But the last time he'd pushed through, he'd noticed that something was beginning to melt the frozen claw that had a hold on Jerome's life. A casual observer wouldn't have perceived the change, but Tyrone did. It gave him a strange sense of hope for his Unc, because inside those ancient gin and juice ruins, Jerome had found *love*. Or love had found him. Suddenly his uncle's heart was full of vaguely remembered palpitations.

Love was decked out in long and happy bones, taped glasses, and brand new teeth. A tall skinny dude named Clifford. He was a friendlier drunk than Jerome. But he was crazy, too. Crazy with spring. A live cock squawking, chasing after a new feathered friend.

Seeing them, Ty was struck by how oddly precious they were together, whether arguing over what to have for dinner, or debating over jazz and blues greats. Jerome's posture had improved too. And he had a brand new porkpie to match the new stride to his step. With Clifford, Jerome didn't seem so hell-bent on killing himself with booze and self-pity. It was really something to see. It confirmed a hope in Tyrone, a slender thread-thin belief that strange and wonderful shit could actually happen; furthermore, it could actually happen to anyone, even gay Black drunken men.

Two Men Together *could* work, beyond fucking or sucking or games. So many people were marching through quick, ineffectual lives, snug in their collective blindness, racing with a chaos that passed for heartbeats, but Jerome had found *love*.

Ty imagined they would bond and form a life, Jerome and Clifford, two Black men together. Yes. It was crazy and sweet, calamitous and deep. And he had never believed in it, until they gave him that possibility.

Now the possibilities were falling all around him, like mortal dominoes with well-loved faces.

After the news of Jazz and Jerome, Ty retreated into himself. He got himself tested and retested, and he continued to read negative. It didn't matter. Fear was the mother of all paranoia. Maybe those tests were *false-negatives*, because something *felt wrong* inside him. Did he have *it*? Did the cute boy with the trusting brown eyes, who slyly bit his nipples a little too hard have *it*? That uncertainty lived in his every pore. Because, real or imagined, every siren represented another death. Every siren became another broken heart, another kind of pain, another unfinished work of art, another unfinished dream, another unfinished life. Every siren. Every fucking siren. And New York City was full of sirens. Tyrone lived every day in *terror* that maybe this day whatever lay sleeping in him would awaken.

David said to Ty in his kitchen one evening, "Know what your problem is? You spend way too much time thinking about death, wondering who's next, pondering and worrying about dying and loss, and you're starting to *become* something lost and dying. Ty, this shit is *becoming* you! This, right here, it's what *death* is. It's the absence of life!"

Ty argued, "If a *bullet* killed them, would you still play with guns? Well, *sex* killed them! It's as true as the tag on their toes. Sex killed them, and I'm no longer a fan of the weapon that took all my friends!"

"Whoa! Get a grip. You startin' to sound hysterical! Listen, let's get the hell out of here. Open some damn windows. Let's go out, baby boy."

"What for, Duch? There's just death out there. Death in Levi's with a hard-on and a cock ring, stalkin' our asses."

"No, *life* is out there! When hell freezes over, buy a fuckin' Dorothy Hamill wig and slip into some ice skates! Come on, Ty, let's go dancin'! Don't you wanna dance anymore? Shit! I do. This whole thing is a conspiracy anyway! A conspiracy against us dancin' people. Look at who's getting it! Just us. But if I'm going down, shit! I'm going down dancin'. Just watch me, shakin' my faggot black ass. 'Cause that's how I fight! Ain't you the one who told me, 'Never let the motherfuckers steal your joy'? Well, where that joy boy at? I liked him. Is he even in the house? Ty, I know you got dreams. You lettin' *it* steal all your fuckin' dreams, baby boy! Don't you want to be happy?"

Ty stared out his window at the twilit activity of the metro, and he didn't speak. He couldn't seem to find the words or the strength it took to say them. He did that thing he often did with his dreads, running his hand through them until they stood on end. Finally, through slow and crazy tears, he turned to his best friend in the whole world, and he said, "I wanna be something radical. I wanna be a happy Black and gay senior citizen."

Meanwhile, life was a sunny beach for Face Depina: sipping coladas in Jamaica, shooting jism on the island of Java, snorting fine snow in Lhasa. In his popularity, Depina did not simply puff up or even blow up; he just expanded inside his own filtered reality.

And David…
Sometimes words come back to bite you on the ass.
"If I'm going down, shit, I'm going down dancin', 'cause that's how I fight."

The dance is a fragile art. You leap and bound, spin and soar like a firebird, full of flames and light and music. But at any moment, you can descend from flight and find yourself touching down *all kinds of wrong*. And all you know for sure is that the flame is still there, but the music in the limbs is gone.

July 4, 1989

While happily humping in Hempstead, little lithe dancing Davy was finessing a new move, a fierce, frenetic fandango with Hector, his spicy *nuevo boricua*. Always sexually inventive, Davy thought nothing of scoring a few extra coital style points on a spiral staircase. And so the adventurous dancer and the heroically hung Hector busted a move with David's left leg propped, quite literally, in a daring-ass split atop the banister. It was all so hot, rigorous, and athletic, until David lost his balance.

Hector slipped out, David tipped over.

It would've been *très* hilarious if David had not broken his leg in three places. Gone would be the days and nights of dancing on stages and of doing that daring terpsichorean shit he did.

Davy wanted to scream for Ty: "My fuckin' leg! They're telling me I'll never dance again! They say it's over! I *need you!* Come quick!" But then David realized: He couldn't tell *Ty* the truth. *Tyrone would only look at me, shake his head, and see me as some frivo- lously foolish fag foiled and fucked-up by his own fucking faggotry! Maybe he would never say it, but he'd think it the rest of his life. How do I work this? How, in this crazy mad stupid fuckin' unfair world, do I tell him my career is dead? Shit! As much as I hurt, and I hurt to my core, this would only hurt Ty even more.*

So David wove a tale of a particularly treacherous step, a leap he was trying to perfect that *went all kinds of horribly wrong.* At least then he could hold his head up and earn some sympathy. *Sorry. I love you, baby boy. But this one I'll take to the grave...*

It was the only *real lie* David would ever tell Tyrone—and he felt broken by it. He thought he'd found in Ty that *one person* he could tell anything, no matter how crazy or sick or unflattering, and know it would be guarded from judgment. Maybe the line of trust had its own invisible limit—invisible, until you crossed it.

But Tyrone had his own dirt. After all those years, he'd never told David about his night with the deceptive Facey. Knowing David's adoration for his idol, Ty couldn't hurt him with the knowledge that he'd *been* where Davy longed to go.

The tally in the naked honesty count was even.

Ty had lied by omission, David by creation. But the fact remained, David's dance was done. In a low, abysmal period, Davy lost himself and became susceptible to all sorts of vile, un-Davy-like shit. Rough and nameless fucks became the norm. He'd find a *vato* who liked to box (like Rico), and he'd let that boxer *whale on him.* The emotional beat-downs of beat angels, beat devils, and beat apartments with roaches and rats rounding corners like locomotives were the dark places David roamed.

Sometimes all he could do was look in the mirror, and cry those "Why did I ever lay down with this musty moody macho mad moth- erfucker" blues.

He purposely avoided Ty.

A Pale Blue Room

"Tyrone's got all these impossibly high standards for what he *dreams* people can be. It's almost fuckin' romantic how he wants to believe in people's potential. Shame how we always disappoint him," David maintained. "Ty's got ways of saying shit without saying anything. And maybe he don't judge me with words. But I know his silences. He'll just quietly moralize everything to fuckin' death, just like my father, when his ass ain't no way perfect."

Fourteen

Facing History

Snorting, cavorting, and whoring around, painting the nightlife red and tan in every city, town, and island, Face Depina lived a fabulously sweet and spinning life. Suddenly, he was one of the *deified*. He fell in with a fast-track pack of spoiled, closeted playboys who languished in the joys and pains of the flesh, and they joined him in his hedonistic quest of snorting, consorting, trafficking, and laughing. They ate peaches on the beaches of Belize. In France, his famous mouth was known as La Bouche, and his busy penis, Le Baton Beige. While in Spain, he was El Toro Cremoso. Inside that new netherworld, Face became a divine being in a land whose beautiful denizens existed outside the lines of self-control and responsibility.

Beyond the Age of Excess trip, there were some particularly ugly incidents for which Face never fully took responsibility. But Face couldn't have any foul shit messing with all that fabulousness hurtling toward him. He knew he'd acquired a few ugly behaviors, but he had excuses: bad environment, bad breaks, bad influences.

If he fucked up badly, or hurt someone, he still never apologized unless it benefited him. Later, Claudio schooled him on the ritual practice of sending flowers, but… "Why bother apologizin' for shit that happened in a moment? A moment is only here for so long. There…feel this one? Now it's gone."

And Depina's hectic schedule didn't allow for much self-illumination. One day he was posing in his drawers in Milan and the next in a natty London Fog backdropped by Big Ben. Women and men were all over him, swarming like pigeons to a brand-new, wide-shouldered statue.

Women and men vied for his green-eyed attention as he donned matador pants and cape to challenge a charging imaginary beast in Madrid. Everyone loved him. He was showered with expensive gifts and treated to fits of ass-kissing extraordinaire, both figuratively and literally. And the sex, oh, the sexing was fierce, frivolous, free, freakish, and sometimes even felonious!

This was *The Good Life*. Away from the Nikons and Canons, the world was *his* to drink in, fuck with, or fuck. But whenever he was alone, the sharpest part of his idling mind would rub against the scabs of old wounds.

He was picking at the one he'd worn since birth, and it was beginning to bleed again. Under rainy London skies, he left his hotel room looking to escape the dead matches floating in that urinal of his hidden life. He was in a strange place and he wanted something *more* from the pace of that foreign night. He wanted to make the night freak inside its navy skin, shiver strangely from a little random excitement.

East-end reed-thin boys of cockneyed fathers stabbed holes through their hurt in the doorways of Soho. It felt like the darkest part of home. That night Depina was spinning and full of the madman. He asked the right questions, copped the right bag, and joined the scag-fest.

Snorting horse was boss for a quick minute—though he'd sometimes get that abrupt urge to vomit soon after.

But then came those insolent little tells: the vacancies of time and thought, that sudden clutch of despondency, those ill-timed nose-bleeds.

And so, after yet another fabulous party, he decided to up the ante. There he lay, naked in another bedroom, next to yet another pale boy with another set of translucent eyes who kissed slyly and was clever with his tongue. The boy rolled over, suggested in a woozy after-sex tone that they both ride a provocative little dragon called China White.

"I've been using since I'm 14, mate. I'll fix ya, if you'd like."

And the rest is addiction history.

Suddenly he'd found his new med, and it was a whole lot better than that Peruvian shit he'd *been* fucking with. It even had a *cool-jerky danger* to it.

Mainlining was the *real deal*. It was as if God Himself waltzed into his bloodstream and made everything tranquil and light, radiant and radiating. For the first time, Depina could hear the music of himself, and he felt like he'd just grown *a soul*. Pain evened out, then vanished inside a floating mind made suddenly golden and wise. A mind wherein lay the answers to all questions, even those he'd never asked.

And then there were no questions, no answers, no worries. Only the exquisitely quiet hum of peace.

It felt more than fantastic to lounge inside a crazy calm adrenaline of the new, to not stress the haze and horror of the old. Ah! Smack! He wanted to submerge his body, his mind, his reckless thrill-seeking soul in the cool crush tactility of it. It was such a radically different concept for the promiscuously nomadic, naughty by the nature of his gonads Depina to be thrilled, actually thrilled by a sense of calm.

By the time he boarded the plane in Orly, he felt all mooged and synthesized, his mood marvelously modified. Everything in the life of his mind was fly. He wasn't the same Facey anymore. Uncle Heroin was bouncing him on his thin and bony knee. Uncle? Hell! Mama and Poppa too. It was his sister and his brother, his friend and lover, his teacher, preacher, and he didn't need anyone else, any-motherfucking-thing else, except cash.

* * *

On the other side of the pond, shattered women and broken men he'd befriended, fucked, and fucked over awaited his long overdue return. Including Bliss Santana, who was by then in a bad way.

It was Tyrone who finally came to her rescue.

"Face. It's Tyrone. Bliss is in trouble. Have you seen her? Don't you care? She looks bad. Her fire's gone. She's losing weight. She showed up at my door this morning at 5:15, crying hysterically over your ass. It's got me worried."

"Well, who the hell asked you to worry? Mind your own damn business. Fuckin' drama queen! That's all you are. Better not be fillin' her head with no goddamn lies about me!"

"This conversation ain't about your fuckin' paranoia. Why don't you just once try being a fuckin' man? It don't pay top model dollars, but it's a noble gig. Tell Bliss it's over, and *why* it's over, man. Then maybe she can go on with her motherfuckin' life!"

"You sure it ain't her faggot-fuckin' life?"

Tyrone hung up. But he had become involved.

* * *

Bliss had come to Ty because she needed help. She was all hopped up on blow and delusions of grandeur, and she hooked him with her story.

She had recently tried to *work* her show's producer, schmooze and smile and do what sexy women do to make *the suits* pay attention. She'd styled a plan for a new Black-Latina story line. But he flat out rejected it. So *the coquette* left the room and Bliss "Boom-Boom" Santana, the coke-charged seductress with a smart word and a "Lick my cat, you bastard!" for everyone, took over. She demanded a mad-outrageous salary. When the producer rebuked her, she went back to her Jersey roots and cursed him out. Then home-girl punctuated her tirade by hauling off and *spitting* dead in his face. As if that wasn't enough, she reached into her big black trick bag and whipped out a pair of cuffs. "I'll show you just who you're fucking with!"

TY'S HARLEM APARTMENT BUILDING ROOF

Ty shifted in his chair. "And so, this fierce, fantastic jazz flower of a double-jointed woman *cuffed her own wrists* to a chair and had

139

to be bodily escorted from the studio, crying and screaming like a formerly well-paid banshee. In one day, her part was recast and they cancelled her contract."

"As if she didn't know how cold showbiz could be," David said.

"She said she turned to her dwindling stash to recharge her broke-down bitch battery and to widen her scope. But besides her disappearing dope, the first person she tried to seek solace in was—"

"Please. Let me guess: *Mi corazón*, Facey."

"You are correct, ma'am."

"But Facey was in Milan," David volunteered.

"Damn! You're vurry scurry. I know you've got it bad for The Man Who Would Be Fag, but hell, Duchess! You got some kind of trailing device stuffed in your Danskin, or what?"

"Don't be catty, gonad-breath! It's very unattractive on you. And, by the way, so is anything sleeveless. Pick up a barbell, damn it! Personally, I like to think of *my* Facey Face as The Once and Future Fag! All right, Pissy Poo?"

"Well, I guess a girl's gotta dream, doesn't she?"

"You know, Facey's thinking about letting me do something different with his hair!" David angled his head and shook it in haughty *sniff-sniff* arrogance.

"Stick to the subject, please. Ix-nay on Ace-fay, OK? I'm sick with it."

"You just *hate it* that Face and me are close, don't you? Because I won't let you say harsh shit about him without callin' you on it. That's how I do friendship. I'd do the same if *he* dogged you out!"

"You know what I *do* hate, David? How every conversation you have is about you and the wonderfulness of Face. And that you don't see how he plays people until they *bore* him, then moves on to the next. Because one day soon, he'll get bored and shoot some toxic shit at you, which will undoubtedly leave you quiverin' like Raid on a fuckin' roach. You'll be wondering, *What did I do? What the hell happened?* Well, what *is* gonna happen? Have ya even *thought* about that? I don't wanna see in you in one of those three-cornered paper hats making a La-Z-boy of your own excrement, mumbling, 'Facey...Facey...' Face it, he's a playa. I want better for you. Don't you think it's time *you* started wanting better?"

"See, Ty. That right there tells me you don't know jack! He might be *complex*, but they don't come any *better* than Face!"

"*That's* your comeback? You makin' a joke, right?"

"No. I'm serious. You really don't *know* him, or what he's been through, or the wonderful things he's done for me. Introduced me to a whole new world. I think that threatens you. Cool out. You're still my girl, friend. But you need to shut the fuck up on the subject of him playin' me. He only plays people he don't respect."

That cold bayonet of words stabbed Tyrone slowly, and he wondered if the stun showed. *Does David know? Did Depina get high and babble his Depina-ized version of... Nah. I could see him to doin' that shit to me. But not Davy. Unless, of course, he wanted to come between us.* "What exactly is going on in that dancing head of yours? What do you *know*?" Ty quizzed.

"I always pride myself on being a *good and graceful* queen. Not some cruel, bitchy, resentful shrew like, well, some people. I don't spread rumors. I *give* good fact. You know that about me."

He knows. Definitely. Come on, girlfriend. Hit me with it! Let's just have our Geraldo *moment, take off our earrings, get to swingin' like two bitches and be over it.*

"Tell me something, Ty. When did you get so concerned about Miss Bliss and her terminal New York times? Ya startin' ta sound like a princess all entranced by the Queen Mother! Please." He shooed away a bumblebee. "These things never work out. Let them handle their own risky business. She was just a phase, anyway." Traces of hope clung to David's every syllable.

"Well, for her sake, I hope he doesn't play her like that."

"Not thinkin' about switchin' teams, are you Queenie? I've *seen* that movie. You go through a drought, someone curvy shows you attention, and suddenly the sad young sodomite is magically cured by the Miracle of Pussy? Somebody say, Amen! Now, please repeat after me: A woman, even a good, understanding, *sexy* woman is not, repeat *not* the boot camp for homo rehab. It's ridiculous for you or Facey or anybody who's runnin' scared and desperate to think so. It only hurts people. Just 'cause you can get it to stand up and cheer for the other side, please! A bored dog might lick a *pussy* cat. It don't make him any less a dog. Just a bored dog."

"You forget that in the quest to be liked and accepted, desperate people do desperate shit. And when desperation rubs against desperation, it can make fire, or some other form of deeply sick pornography."

"That's probably true. But there's a limit to the things we can do with our dicks."

"But who sets those limits?"

"The owner. Fuck the rest."

"Yeah, David, but even *you're* insecure. We all are. And whatever the insecurity, sometimes you just want the world to see you as less of a freak. Face, he's obviously got some freak shit with him," Ty said. "And he doesn't want that fly shit to go away, so he's operating from a place of fear."

"I know about the fear. I'm tryin' to cure him and the *rest* of my friends of that."

"Please, David. Cure yourself! He ain't seekin' no cure. He's too busy publicly dating beauties and doing his dirt on the down-low. That's all he knows. Queers either amuse or terrify him. So, he and his devils make a stab at being straight. Why? Because it's just so much more convenient, man!"

"Convenient? Fuck that! Who says anybody's life is supposed to be convenient? You are who you are, and you like what you like when you like it. That's the name of Facey's sex. He just needs to own that. There's a hell of a lot more *gray* than black and white out there. You're supposed to be this insightful writer, ain't you? Haven't you noticed that yet, *mijo?*" David asked. "See, I understand Face. I've been a student of his most of my *vida loca*. So all I'll say is, Face belongs to no one. No woman, no man, no one but the Universe…"

The Long Blue Moan

After her meltdown in the producer's office, Bliss couldn't find work. She suspected she'd been blacklisted, which she later found out was the truth. She tried to take her case to the press, but no one would touch her. Except Tyrone Hunter, who'd quickly grown to like her far more than he'd ever liked Face.

One month after they met, there was a reading for Tyrone's play-in-progress, and Bliss accompanied him. He asked her to read, and she did so most eloquently. Ty fell a little in love with the fantasy of her. But that fuzzy pink reverie went black, bronze, and green when Face Depina strode into the theater. At that point, the winding road where Bliss and Face merged and intersected was filthy with skid marks.

Bliss was by now beyond furious with his chronically missing-in-action ass. Where was his support, his sympathy, his wide shoulder to cry on, his long cock to slide down and forget the darkest hour of her career catastrophe? After she'd helped launch *his* career, he *owed* her. Didn't he?

Now *he* stood in that theater door, unexpected, unannounced, smiling, and causing little earthquakes just by hanging in the back, arms folded, looking like, well, Face.

Check 'em, checkin' me. Shit. I could do anyone I wanted to up in this queer little camp. Hell. See a few I already banged. Yeah. That's right. Depina's in duh motherfuckin' howse. Look at poor Ty up there, still tryna be somebody. Look at his hair. What homey do, sit in the barber's chair and tell him, "Make me look like a goddamn fool"? Run a comb through that African mess, boy! Where's my woman? There she is. Gettin' kinda light in the ass, ain't you baby? Bliss? Hey! Over here. OK, smile. Daddy's home. Come to Daddy. I said, come to Daddy. Bliss? Daddy's waiting. Bliss, come to Daddy, you hard-headed bitch!

After the reading, Bliss grabbed Ty's hand and they retired backstage.

Hey! What up with this shit? She tryin' to change him? She givin' that little fag a little head? Motherfuck! Is she hummin' him? Is she? Is he...? Are they stank like that? Nah. What would she want with a fuckin' fag?

Depina checked his image in the darkened glass of the door.

Depina saw their heads together, going over lines, and he waited for that diabolical pussy-machine magnetism thang he slang to take effect. He'd expected kisses, maybe even an embrace from his quasi-homeboy. What he *got* was ignored. But Depina determined he'd make his presence felt, even if it stung someone.

"So. This here thing, this *play* needs a lotta work, huh, Ty?"

"Hello Pascal. Actually, I think it's just about perfect," Bliss said.

Depina didn't like that defensive stance, or the way she and Ty *looked* together. The level of comfort they shared was all too evident. "Tell me sump'n, how long you two been girlfriends? And what the hell you got to talk about, anyway?"

His question died a silent death.

"Nice seeing you too, Face." Ty kissed Bliss's cheek, and whispered, "I'll call you." Then he walked away.

Depina actually felt spurned.

But he was feeling too good to let small shit upset his axis. "So, baby, let's grab somethin' to eat and party and fuck like it's 1999. C'mon. Grab your coat!"

"Can't. I got a doctor's appointment. Besides, you look…tired. Maybe you should get some rest. Bye."

"Yo Bliss! Hold up! You hummin' Ty, now? 'Cause you know he's a fag, right?"

"What I know is, he's my friend. Unique concept, huh?"

"Friend, huh? Well, what your *girlfriend* say about me, huh? I *know* you talk about me!"

"Tyrone is too busy to spend his time *gossiping* about you. And what could he possibly tell me that I don't already know, huh? Bye-bye."

*　*　*

Face's question about whether Bliss and Ty were an item was not as far from the truth as one might have guessed.

Stimulated by Bliss's style, conversation, and mind, Ty couldn't help but imagine being with her. What would it be like? It was certainly doable, at least in his flinty imagination. Every now and again, the thought stroked the dick of his mind, like once when she leaned in close, rubbed his thigh, looked into his eyes with those pale green lights, and said, "I'm starting to believe it's just not in a man to love completely. Even you think it's impossible for another man to love you totally and faithfully, right?"

She cuddled close to him. "Maybe you're not so gay after all. Maybe you're just, terminally *tender* for men. Maybe you just romanticize the best in them. Did you ever think of *that*, my not so happy and gay friend?"

"Well, if I'm not gay, I've pulled off a damn good imitation of it. And believe me when I say there's *rarely* anything *tender* about it."

Yet, in those most vulnerable moments, in the thread-thin silence of thought, he'd revisit her words, and he'd wonder if she was right.

But he also knew it didn't matter because Face still rented space in her mind. A melancholy gaze would cloud her eyes. Then she'd breathe deep, and it would subside. But Ty knew. He'd seen that same struggling look in David's eyes. Both tried valiantly to overcome it, yet still suffered from that lingering sickness: the Acquired Depina Disease Syndrome.

David's case was just more overtly acute.

TY'S HARLEM APARTMENT BUILDING ROOF

"I know in my bones we're gonna happen. I even checked with Madam Zoreena, and ya know how accurate her stuff be. Well she lit a candle for me. Then she says she sees me 'walking hand-in-hand with a tall, impressive Latin man.' That's exactly what she said, Ty. Then, out the blue, I run into him, and he offers me a job that keeps me *very close* to his fine ass."

"Ah, Duch, no disrespect to the clairvoyant Zoreena, but what about Chaz?" Ty asked.

"Chaz? Please. I ain't mad at the Brother, big and gruff as he be. But he's just too much *manimal* with that big ol' butt, big ol' body, and big ol' voice. He's always taking big steps with them big ol' feet, and suckin' up *big* oxygen. Makes me nervous. Always brooding. Chaz ain't Facey's future. But recently…I've discovered something."

"Yes, Columbus…"

"How do I put this *discreetly?*"

"Ya can't even *spell* 'discreetly,' so just spit it."

"Let's just say that when the native is restless, homey, and trust me on this, even the *horses* flee in fear. This Brother's vine, it's…pre-historic! I almost expected to see *Tarzan* swingin' from it. Just *ah-h-he-e-e-ah-h*, glidin' from one tree trunk thigh to the other!"

"Easy, baby. You're talking to a celibate queer, here."

"Please! Are ya chargin' for it, now? *Sell-a-bit?* Baby boy, ya can't even give it away!"

"So, what *else* is going on?" Ty asked.

David, however, was too busy *talking dick* to answer. "Listen to me! I'm talkin' 'bout record book bozack here! This was some *Ripley's Believe It or Not* type cock. Ridiculous dick! I seen it up close. I've scoped it, watched it do Slinky tricks. Every part of me winced! He couldn't be *doin'* Facey with it, could he?"

LOS ANGELES

Meanwhile, Face wanted to expand his budding thespian thing. So he flew to the West Coast with Claudio to see and to be seen.

"Like it or not, Gloss Angeles is the spot pretty people pimp they potential," Face said.

The two rented a Mercedes and cruised Sunset. Conquering L.A. was always part of the Grand Depina Plan in his quest for total world domination. When flying on First Class Smack Airlines, there wasn't a part written Face didn't feel he could play. He'd accepted a couple of small roles as "male decoration" in some independent films, and it made him hunger for more. He was always chronically lousy at auditions. But one coveted role in a soon-to-be-major direc-tor's indie flick seemed picture-perfect for him. It wasn't the lead, but a potential breakout part in a drama.

He'd heard the talk about the pretty boy who hit the motherlode for being *only that*. Depina was determined. Almost as much as he wanted to fix, he wanted to show the world his chops. He read and reread with the kind of edginess needed for the part. Then, he actually did a pretty good screen test. Still, it was expected a Big Name Actor or hot newcomer would be the chosen player in the end. But the director had an aesthetic crush on him.

The rest is Lucky Pretty Boy history.

Face portrayed a conflicted young man, a hustler and a weasel who gyps a small-time hood, who in turn takes vengeance. In the end, Depina's character is responsible for his own mother's death.

It was a role he was born to play.

BROOKLYN, 1960

Two years after Mattie and Fonzy Depina jumped the broom, they discovered she had a rare blood disease—making pregnancy a dangerous affair. But Mattie loved Alphonze, and desperately wanted to bear him a child. She was willful, and this was *her* sacrifice to make.

Mattie didn't tell her husband until the sixth month. Alphonze was furious and frightened. He pushed her against a wall, and suddenly she was bleeding. She thought she'd miscarried. Alphonze rushed her to the ER. Things turned chaotic in the labor room. She was crying, breathing, crying, bleeding, crying, screaming, crying, and pushing to give the world a shiny new star.

Mattie died in childbirth. Alphonze was inconsolable. Though his son was strikingly beautiful, he wanted no part of "the little murderer."

Alphonze thought of smothering it, snuffing out its life as *it* had his beauteous Mattie's. *Flames.* Eventually he dropped *it* off at his sister's and disappeared into the sanctuary of alcohol, then, in time, hard-core smack. Alphonze never stopped loving Matilda or blaming the child he'd forever need to believe caused her death.

* * *

Flames. Bounced like an unwanted kickball from place to hard-luck place, Face never had a real foundation or any sense of permanence. *Flames*. Being exceedingly pretty drew others to him, but the child learned to never rely on anything, *anyone*, or any feeling hanging around for the long run. All friends, family, lovers—people in general—had expiration dates. *Flames*. Ironically, the intensity of his most memorable relationships lasted roughly *six months*. Such was the nature of things. *Flames*.

LOS ANGELES

Face had three scenes, one requiring emotional pyrotechnics.

Since his arrival in L.A., he'd been trying to wean himself away from heroin's seductive teat. But the pain coiled inside him, weakening his charm, making him nauseous and withdrawn. A day without smack was a day too long and distressing. What he needed was a little speed-ball, just to take off the edge… *Just one,* he thought, *and I can do this shit.*

When he strode back onto the set, his eyes were green windows, cracked by the telltale vandals of coke and smack. He stood with legs heavy as rocks, calling on strength, willing his brain into focus.

Sometimes all a man has left to *trust* are his bones. He trusts them to guide him, push him forth, and suddenly he's walking, talking, putting on a Personality Light Show until no one knows he's a crumbling fraud. Face did that shit to remarkable effect. Most *functioning* junkies do. The script required tears, so he cried. He stooped and roared in savage guttural grunts, in smears of snotty babbling chatter. He cried, screeched, lamented the most brilliant tears a half-Black bisexual closeted junkie had ever dared to cry on screen.

Was it acting or was it a public breakdown?

Those sounds he made, those rants, howls, and caws of the heart, they were *outside of human*. He was more authentic than Brando, Pacino, Dean, or Denzel. Few men ever had the balls to reveal *that kind* of intimacy.

He could only play that scene once. Luckily, once was more than enough.

"Cut! Beautiful, Facey! Just beautiful. That's a print!"

But the wild tears didn't stop for Face. Every crippled feature in his aspect darkened, reddened, and wept. Wept uncontrollably.

Face was, at his core, a user. In rare and coldly sober interludes, even *he* knew that. This time he'd used and abused his tender unformed memory of the mother he'd never cried for. But this one particular act of using burned like a branding iron. How does a boy, or a man, any *real man* recover from that?

Six months later, Pascal "Face" Depina received an Independent Spirit Award Nomination for Best Supporting Actor.

Fifteen

Bluesy Love Songs

When Browny made parole, no arms greeted him. Juanita wasn't outside waiting with a pot of greens and ham hocks, and a ride back to a warm Dream Street apartment. If Browny were to record the soundtrack of his life, the title song would have been: "Why My Arias Always Gotta Sound Like the Fuckin' Blues, Yo?"

Making matters worse, the all-too-alluring call of *that rock* beckoned.

For the longest time, Depina was away, giving pretty face in crazy fly exotic places. Browny could never find him to hit him up for cash. He saw no choice but to sing in the subways for pocket change.

"Yo! Man. You got a voice. Why you down here, actin' like some Step-'n'-Fetchit fool?" a stranger barked.

Where the fuck is Face? I need to see that motherfucka! But it behooved Browny to sing because singing brought quick dollars and quick dollars bought quick rocks. He had this hot new career with the rock. Even other crackheads were beginning to call him "Rock Star."

Faison lost himself a little more each day. Was it one month or

150

two before he was begging for loans, selling off his few belongings? Gone were his raggedy Mustang, his friends, his trustworthiness, a job, then another job, then another. None of it meant anything. Nothing mattered except that fucking *hunger*.

He often called Ty, using Trick's memory to secure cash. The cash was for the hunger, for the crack, then the cash was for the help to quit the hunger for crack.

Message From Tyrone Hunter Left on Face Depina's Answering Machine, April 1991

"Listen, Pascal. I don't know the deal with you and Browny and I don't want to. But I finally got him into a clinic, and now he's AWOL. Damn fool seems to think that only *you* can help him. Everything's falling apart for him! He seems to think *your* life is intact. If ya got any decency left, and if you owe him like he claims, please don't turn your fuckin' back on him! 'Cuz I can't help him anymore. I'm out."

* * *

Face had assumed that whatever the lingering aftereffects of prison, Browny could drink or smoke them away. But Browny was *not going away*. The phone call from Ty, and other things, too. Like Browny would suddenly *appear*—outside a corner store Face frequented, or in the middle of Central Park during a fashion shoot. Sometimes in a crowd, sometimes all alone. Sometimes Face thought he'd only imagined Browny, that somehow the past or *his high* was fucking with him. But no. Browny *was there*, staring at him, smoking a borrowed cigarette, saying nothing.

So Face decided it was time to take him upstairs to his digs and buy his pathetic ass off, fucking once and for all! He wrote a check, a *nice* check.

But for Browny cash was not sufficient. "You tryna buy me? Nah. I ain't goin' out like that. A few bills for three years in hell? And it *was* hell, Pass-cow. I ain't the same big tall strappin' buck as you. Why was *you* shittin' bricks, anyway? Huh? Was ya scared of the sound of them steel doors closin' you inside? Did ya figga you was too pretty for that shit?

"Scared ya wouldna survived, huh? Bet ya thought they'd line up, hold ya down, and take turns raping yo pretty ass… Well, guess what? It don't matter if you pretty."

"Look, it's too bad you had to go through that. I never meant for—"

"SHUT THE FUCK UP, AND PAY ATTENTION! You ever hafta put on a fuckin' halter top? You ever have one real fight in your fuckin' life, worth fightin' to the death for, huh? Well, between them poundin' fists red with your blood and them kicks to your insides something clicks, man. You realize, I'm gonna die like this. And for what? 'Cause some motherfucker wants my ass? My short, thick, black piece of ass! What's a straight man's ass, anyway? His last piece of pride? Do it make him a punk if somebody take it? Why? Wasn't like somebody was battlin' for me or my ass to survive on the outside. So what was I fightin' tooth and nail for, when it was gonna get took anyway, bloody or not?

"Men in prison, they ain't into that warm, fuzzy shit. Foreplay don't exist, except for *you* suckin' *his* dick." Browny paused long enough to wipe his mouth. "That first time hurt, man! And it never did *stop* hurtin'.

"You wanna know what kept me sane and alive? *You*, Pass-cow. You and the future beyond that big dark beast of a motherfucka drummin' down on me. I had me a future on the other side of that razor wire. That was all I needed to keep breathin'.

"I seen boys stop breathin', stop fightin' altogether. Gettin' they jugular slashed or a rusty shank stuck in they scared shitless chest. I seen a young boy, even prettier than you, hangin' from his own sheet because he just couldn't take another beatin', another pair of women's panties, another man, another dick after diseased dick rammed up his cryin', helpless ass.

"Yo! Now you wanna offer me a check, and say we even? *I don't think so, Pass-cow!* You just don't get it, do you? It ain't about the money, fuckin' asshole. I want a *life*. A *career*."

"I ain't God, Browny! I can't just snap my fuckin' fingers, and presto, you get a life!"

"I don't see why not. Yo! Ya played God before when ya guilted me into sayin' those four little please fuck *my* ass words: 'The stash is mine'!"

Depina almost wanted to laugh. Browny was the ultimate suck-er. *Stupid, stupid motherfucker! Yeah, you copped to it. You got in the damn car, and shit happened. Didn't take much beggin', did it? Yeah, I said I'd hook you up. I was desperate, you crazy Negro! All that time on the street, you still don't know when you bein played. Fuckin' hemor-rhoid, that's all you are! Startin' to make me real uncomfortable. Need to have your naggin' milk-bump ass lanced. I know people, too. You don't wanna fuck with me, Browny!*

"Know what, Pass-cow? Once, when I was tryna build myself up into a big, strong *man* like you, I ordered the Charles Atlas kit from the back of a comic book."

"Yeah-yeah. What's your point?" Face asked, his buffed arms folded, his long legs spread wide in defensive stance.

"Of course, Pass-cow. Yo! Wouldn't wanna waste yo time, you bein' one of them in-demand type motherfuckas. See, I got the kit, but it was just a lotta pictures of a half-naked Atlas workin' out, and some instructions and shit. I felt ripped the fuck off! But they kept sendin' me more shit. Same shit. So I quit. Stopped payin' through the ass for some dumb-ass photos. Yo! Now, *you* pay attention. This is the good part: Mr. Charles Atlas, or somebody in his muscle camp, wrote me a letter 'bout debts. They was tryna shame me, sayin' how a *real man* pays his debts. Then they went all Oriental on my ass.

"They got this ancient Chinese sayin' that the worse thing any real man could do was to *lose his honor*. Without that, a man ain't nothin'. They called it 'losing face'!"

"Yeah, so, and…"

"Don't you get it, fool? You don't attend yo debts, boy. Ya ain't got no honor! You ain't no man! You, Pascal Punk-ass Depina done LOST FACE, motherfucka!"

Depina eyeballed Browny, wishing he possessed the supernatural power to make him disappear. Make the world forget there ever *was* a Browny. *Little black singin' Sambo motherfucker! I could take his thick ass down, right here and now. Squash him like a fuckin' cockaroach, 'cause that's all he is. I wish his little black ass fit in my microwave!*

Still, that term *losing face* buzzed like an annoying black fly in Depina's aggravated ear. A fly he couldn't shoo away.

As Depina phoned his agent to try and make *things happen*, Browny walked around the place, looking at all the new fancy shit that could've, should've, would've probably been his: the big screen TV, the top-of-the-line stereo system, the plush Italian leather furniture, and that fly-ass view of Manhattan staring back in its steely majesty.

Depina hung up the phone, took a deep breath, wrung his long elegant hands, and hit Browny with his latest plan.

"Listen man, there's a role in this independent film I'm workin' on. It's got a nightclub scene that needs a singer. Now, hear me, Faison, *I can't say it's yours.* It's just my fourth film, and I ain't got that kind of power. But Benny, my agent, is gonna represent you this one time as a favor. He'll pull some strings, get you an audition, and the rest, pal, that's up to you."

Every feature in Browny's face lit up brighter than the Rockefeller Center Christmas tree.

"Yo! An open door. That's all I want."

* * *

As it turned out, Browny sang magnificently. But he wasn't *the right type*. The director hired him for his "incredibly melodious voice," only to use it as a dub for another, more photogenic performer, which turned out to be Face Depina.

Browny was livid. Homeboy was ready to go the cops, the authorities, the press, to whoever might hear his story of how rising model-actor Face Depina was a dope addict and a punk ass half-a-fag, minus the balls to come forth and admit it.

Depina realized his best defense was a good offense. "Look! Don't be sweatin' me. I'm tryna make things happen, but it takes time, man. You say ya don't want charity. Bet. I can respect that. But stay here. Crush place, right? Plenty of room, lots of fringes. I'll make you my assistant. You can answer the phones, check my fan mail, whatever. I'll pay four bills a week, plus free rent and food. Hey, you even can take the money, pool it together, rent some studio time... Hell, you can record a CD, market it yourself. Sound like a plan?"

What it *sounded like* was Depina running scared. But hell! Browny had seen, slept, lived in, and been kicked out of far worse places. That fancy loft had *potential*, and so did Facey's plan.

"Bet. But only for a few months, until I've got enough to do my thing. You know what, man? I might just have to change my opinion of you, Pass-cow."

"That's anotha thing...if you livin' in my crib, eatin' my eats, and receivin' a check with *my* name on top, you're gonna respect me! Try gettin' used to callin' me *Face*. Aiight?"

Browny wasn't about to let the opportunity slip, and decided he could manage that.

Actually, an entire family of misfits was harbored under Depina's roof. David, of course, spent a lot of time there. At least when Face was around.

* * *

One warm June morning, after a long night's freak, David reentered Depina's apartment to prepare for the Gay Pride Parade. In two hours, he created magic, transforming himself from a brown downtown club kid to a gold, copper, and gloriously platinum-wigged temptress.

Sometime during David's *tedious girl's work*, Depina had returned and grabbed a quick shower. When he emerged, wet and naked to the waist, the ripe pacifiers on his chest resembling cinnamon jujubes, the sight just about floored David. In all his painted-up platinum regalia, at first Face thought him some freaky female intruder. But David softly vamped, "Oh my! Mr. Depina. Can't a girl have *any* privacy?" Then he changed voices. "Not bad, huh, Facey? I know. I see you're breathless."

"David? Da-a-amn! That's *you* under all that?

"On my way to the parade. I wish you would go…"

"Can't. Glitter ain't my scene," Depina quipped. Those ripe brazen nipples entirely stole David's vision, not to mention his libido. "Besides, that damn queer-fest lasts all day and night. Ain't you got work to do?"

"Not to worry. I've picked three outfits for you," David laid out the selection of clothes he thought Face should wear that evening to a fashion awards show.

Still, Depina's nipples were whispering silent love notes.

"Know what would look really good on you, Facey?"

"What? The suede? The leather?"

"Me."

"A suede the color of your skin, I get it."

"No, I don't think you do. Remember when you hired me? You wanted a consultant, a stylist. But later, you wanted me to teach you a new word a day."

"Yeah. I remember. Yesterday's word was *insouciant*. It means cool, nonchalant, like me, right?"

"Very good. Well, today's word is *the word*. C'mon. Let's go to your bedroom and *spread it*, baby."

"David. I like havin' your little fly ass 'round here 'cause you help me look fly, and I need to look fly, so I appreciate that shit. In fact, I'm kinda surprised how much I like your fly ass. In fact, I like most every queer bone in your little body, Davy. I just don't want *my bone* in it. Aiight?"

Color David Donatello Richmond devastated.

"You wound me, Facey. You think I'm too delicate, too femme, don't you?"

Depina didn't want to say yes, so he kept quiet.

"Never don't judge *this book* by its smooth copper cover, Facey.

Hey, I'm a dancer. You give me one chance between those sheets, and I will *turn you out* with my rhythm!

Depina took one hard look at him and broke into a booming round of laughter as he walked out of the room.

Once the laughing ceased, Face peeked his head inside. "Yo! Before you go, I need a touch-up Davy, or whoever you are this week. You see these lines here under my eyes. That ain't pretty. People don't wanna see that."

"You mean *right now?* But I don't wanna be late!" Then, seeing the slightest upset claim Depina's mug, David quickly snapped, "OK, OK, I'll do it."

Touching Depina became the only fodder David needed to erect new exotic fantasies in his flaming mind: *It happens beneath a radiant sun, on a beach in Martinique, where Facey lies luxuriously along a mossy cliff. Ah! The ocean breeze rouses the peaks of his nipples. Like Facey, they burn so easily in the sun. He applies the elixir I created especially for him, soothing it into his shoulders, his chest and his belly where moisture collects like a pool of gold, and oh! I detect a stirring in his tight black Speedo. He skims his hand along his striking pecan torso, massaging the slick fluid into one tightening areola. He slowly traces his hand down inside his suit. And I watch him, shivering like a frond in a tropical storm as ever so slowly he glides his hand along his waistband. Then that suit descends down browning hips, thighs, knees, and he lets it fall to the green moss. Woo! I'm all wet by then. But suddenly his feet leave the moss, his thighs and chest become perpendicular. And Facey being so tall, so lean and so long, I think he's going to… My, damn! He's going to suck his own…yes! A slow drop of liquid falls to those bee-stung lips. Just as he's prepared to receive his tip, the sun streams down in warm honeyed light, and I, his watcher, make myself known. A sweat-bead forms at the lips of his excitement, and his sigh rises like a song on the breeze.*

And Facey Depina sees me standing there. And gravity begs those long legs to the ground. And he smiles that sultry smirk. With no words between us, I walk to where beauty lies, and I fall, toppling to its chest, belly, and hard slippery prick. I'm warm and wet as his long greasy dick coasts between my thighs. We kiss slow and electric. We slide and moan as we hump pole to hard and glistening pole. Oh! My dancing legs spread in grand jetés. I look at him, and he knows my grotto is a warm, safe and welcoming haven.

When his span journeys through me, it doesn't hurt at all. Once inside me, my hurting, his hurting, all the hurting finally stops. A turbulent tide washes through my love-hungry soul, and I finally know the feel of him. Oh! Birds sing from wavering limbs of Banyan trees. All rivers flow into the boiling sea, and the sea foams like we do into the clamoring Atlantic. "Yes! Facey, yes!" The feel of him embedded inside me is so fuckin' sweet and right and necessary that I bury my head inside his flawless pecan chest, and silently weep.

Yes, fantasy can be an elixir for the lonely, unrequited lovers of the world.

But Face Depina had his own motto about sex with men: "the bigger the dick, the bigger the pussy."

Chaz, for instance. Though he might've been blessed with a *Superpenis erectus,* he rarely used it to fuck. A contented submissive, he lived for the thrill of the whip, the agony of the victorious fist. He reserved his acres of ass and valleys of machismo for only the most robust of dominants. And Depina fit the bill.

Whenever Face breezed back into town, it became an event. That emptiness in the pit of Chaz's being would suddenly fill up. Depina's lean shiny presence was his needle, and the junkie in Chaz would swoon as soon as Face entered *The War Room*.

Leathered-down, keyed-up, and flying in his skin, the High Hard One was still in good and sturdy working order. Face's chest would become a beating drum, his body, a seismic boom of driving bronze, his dick erect, thrusting through muscle, skin, and sweat. By then, The Williams Log was hard as iron, a mast wavering high from the fuck and the fuck's crescendo.

Flying and feeling strangely tactile, Face had a habit of touching himself, flicking his own nipples, grabbing his own ass while whipping into Chaz with forceful jolting jabs. Submission was never better or mo wetter.

But whatever the force of the fuck, it barely registered with

Chaz. "Punch it. Damn it. Hit me. Hard. Shit. Where's your force, you soft mothafucka? Hurt me!" he'd call out like a wildly different kind of creature, a creature addicted to its own slaughter.

* * *

One afternoon, when neither Face nor Chaz nor any other Depina hangers-on were around, David talked Faison into having his first facial. "You *do* have a rich, dark, pretty complexion, Black man. You just need a little exfoliation, that's all."

"Exfoliation? What the hell beatin' off got to do with my skin?"

"Honey? Were you always so *this*? I mean, so hopelessly, retard-edly, grotesquely dense? Uncouth, yes. Ya never had any couth whatsoever. In school, all ya had was mouth and those damn Farina braids that looked like they hadn't seen a comb or pomade since—"

"Bitch, I'll kick your—"

"Now, now. Calm down, boyfriend! It *does* get better. I'll say this only one time, so you need to listen: Faison, you are so much more than a rock and a pipe. You bigger than that. God musta looked down and said, 'I'll kiss this one's throat so he'll sing like a angel.' Back in school, I had no doubt *you'd* be the one to shine. Well, stars shine, baby. Black holes don't. You a star, and you owe it to yourself to stop acting so defeated. If you ever leave that crack pipe alone, you'll be who you were *born* to be. You got some shine to you. Baby, your star quality just needs some work. Today, I'll start with your skin."

"You know what, David? You ain't half-bad for a little fruit. And I mean that shit."

Sixteen

A Season of Clarity and Blur

Nelson Mandela was free, after 27 years in prison. It was a time for jubilation.

On top of that, yet another singer had covered the song Ty wrote as a teen, and two other artists had recently sampled it with platinum results. *Hunter luck* had struck again. Ty couldn't believe he was able to live comfortably off some freak beginner's luck. But those frequent royalties were mighty sweet.

Harlem was in the throes of gentrification, and the money enabled Ty to buy an apartment just off Striver's Row. Ty never acted liked a Black man with money, though. No jewels, fly rides, no trophy sex, or high days and nights. He donated heavily to the GMHC, the United Negro College Fund, Meals-on-Wheels, the Red Cross, Hale House, and the Make-a-Wish Foundation. Ty was nothing if not charitable. And though neither David nor Browny was aware of it, Ty always put aside a little something for them, purchasing shares of blue-chip stocks in their names.

Was life fabu yet? From the outside, it seemed everything was mildly fabulous, but his interior felt deficient. His soul, empty. A lifelong shutterbug, he took his camera to the streets, on a mission to interview the city's downtrodden disaffected. Victims of drug addiction, homelessness, and disease became his new passion.

"What about *real* passion? You know, like a partner? Don't you want someone to share your life?" David often hounded.

Davy wasn't wrong. At 28, Tyrone was a man in sore need of getting laid.

"I seriously think you're undersexed, Ty. Lookin' like ya ain't had a decent blow job since Diana had a hit record!"

"Blow job? Not part of my new '90s vernacular. I'll settle for a mind job."

"Please. You'll nevuh meet a man with enough plumbing to reach *that* far, baby boy."

"A companion in the struggle would be hip. Well, besides you. A partner would be doable. But that's a luxury, not a necessity, Duch."

* * *

Ty took some shots of Princess Diana when she visited Harlem's Hale House. She was holding a little jittering crack baby and everyone oohed and ahed, *How brave!* A couple of Ty's shots were published, and suddenly he was a *hot shit celebrity photographer* getting assignments to go out and schmooze with 15-minute cool ones in the-hip-to-the-nanosecond downtown scene. It was either a part-time distraction or a slow death—he couldn't decide which, but thought, *If it's got to be done, shouldn't someone do this shit correctly? People have a need to know other people's business. There's a hunger for it.*

Gossips are bitches by definition, but Ty tried to up the status.

He couldn't seem to *give away* a homeless photograph, or a story of an American Dream deferred. People didn't want to buy the *real* shit. You could see too much real, sordid, distressing shit in the city for free.

He became a kind of downtown dilettante, asking nonessential questions of nonessential people: Who's zooming who at 4:32 am in the Cat Club's bathroom? Who was that blond on Grace Jones's arm, and *what duh hell* was she wearing? Who's disrespecting their 12-step program, and what were they wearing for their public vomit? Who's stepping out on their old man with another man in a sedan? And just what were they *not* wearing? Who's hot, who's not, who's come out, who's back in the closet, who's strung out, doped out, played out, ovuh, and do we really care anymore what *they're* wearing?

It was another night of that stuff Ty termed "mindless megalo-maniacal shit and tales from the metro maniacs." He slipped into his omnipresent leather coat, tossed his dreads into careless disarray, slid on the shades, and as he headed out the door the phone rang. *Fuck it*, he thought. *The machine will pick up.*

"Hello. You've reached Ty Hunter. Please leave your name and a coherent message, and I'll holla. Peace out."

He heard no words, only breathing. Ty had no time for it. He was working on his mental mendacity-at-its-best mode. It was a special brand of fakeness he had to affect because, with all the turmoil around him, *Why should I really give a shit about your fuckin' stupid wasted shallow lives?*

He was *there* mentally, and had the night all scoped out... But then, that voice on the other side of the machine said its name sadly. Mr. Death was leaving another message.

* * *

Jimmy Lee "Razor" Morrisey had made more money than ene-mies, more greens than Sylvia's famous Harlem eatery. When he walked his rooster's strut, you got the impression he'd seen one too many Eddie G. Robinson flicks. He was a broad caramel man, with a disturbingly large head. It was so large a dome, word was Razor had to get his pimp hats custom-made. He never drove his Caddie, his New Yorker, or his new Mercedes S-class. He was always chauf-feured. Only two kinds of people existed in Razor's orbit: those who admired him, and those who were deathly afraid of him. He embodied power, juice, intimidation, and yes, murderous intent. And he wore his prestige like a fierce sharkskin suit.

Trick's death never left him, nor had it settled itself into a dimmer, gentler memory in Tyrone's psyche. In the years since, it became more like a sensation of being robbed. There wasn't a day, night, or carefree moment when Trick Brown's demise did not wound him slowly. Once Ty had a dazzlingly imperfect smile, where everything dark in his face would just blaze with light. That dazzle was gone. Razor had swiped it. Just as he'd stolen the light from thousands of smiles before and since.

A large thing had been taken from him, and Tyrone never forgot or forgave its taker. Years went by, and still he paced inside a silent rage over Razor's lethal hand in Trick's death.

Yet, there was little he could do about it.

Or was there?

Ty rarely left home without his camera. It was his third eye, his best eye. He photographed New York life in all its chiaroscuros of light and dark: A homeless man sleeping in front of the Met. A debutante ball on the West Side juxtaposed with an old woman in tattered clothes eating from a garbage can. Contrasts were the true stories of the city.

Harlem was a study in contrasts as the doers and workers kept rapid time beside the casualties of crack and heroin. Bodies were stockpiling, and Morrisey's rep as a major scourge around town was peaking. Was it fate's accident that Ty saw him stepping out of a local numbers-friendly bar? Ty's loaded camera seemed to howl, *Shoot! Shoot him!* His hands literally shook as he brought him into focus. He managed to snap a half-roll. Back home, as he developed the proofs, the face of a murderer came into view, and Tyrone's hatred only intensified. How smug and sure and Teflon-coated: the garish gold rings on every finger, the fool's gold smile.

Like the image of Razor's thuggish mug, within that instant, an idea came clearly into focus. It seemed predestined. Had Tyrone gone to school, earned his degree in journalism for this very moment of clear-eyed realization? *Damn it! Do the world a favor.*

Kill him with words and pictures. Right then, Tyrone hatched a plan for an exposé on the dominant drug lords in his community. The story received buzz after he sold his words and pictures to an underground rag. Ty then met with a producer, and soon the story appeared on *A Current Affair*, where Tyrone testified on what a few foul fat cats could do to ravage a community. His face was shadowed, but people paid attention.

Trick's ghost warned him, *"Leave it alone, Ty. You messin' with the Big Boys..."*

But for once Tyrone ignored him.

Along the way, he discovered something even *he* had not bargained for.

* * *

Morrisey's family tree was more twisted and gnarled than an arthritic hand. Ty accidentally stumbled over a root of this tree, uncovering facts that could destroy Faison's chance at a happier existence.

"Hard-headed bastard! Didn't I tell you to leave it rest?"

But the righteous, crusading reporter in his bones would not let it rest. Tyrone went straight to the source: Juanita Lewis.

"It's true, isn't it? He's your first cousin...and you never..."

"Yes. Yes, damn it! It's true. But please, please don't tell Browny," she begged—and Juanita was not a beggar by nature. "You don't get to choose who your family be. I'm ashamed. Been ashamed of him even before he started killin' his own people. I'm the one who started our neighborhood watch, remember? Believe me, Jimmy Lee ain't no friend of mine. But if you told Faison, Tyrone, that would just kill him. It would kill us."

"But Razor killed Trick, Juanita! And the slimy motherfucker just walked away from it. He's killing half of Harlem right now, and people walk by seeing and *not* seeing it! I swear, I'm not tryna hurt you. I like you. You're *good* for Browny. But maybe if the truth came out..."

"Destroy Jimmy Lee! Go on! I won't give a motherfuck! But ya just gonna end up destroying *us* in the process! Is *that* what you want?" Then Juanita went in for the kill. "Don't you think *Trick* wanna see his brother settled down and happy for once?"

"OK, Juanita. It's not my secret to tell. But before he hears it in the streets somewhere, maybe he oughta hear it from you. He deserves *that* much."

* * *

Ty thought about the consequences, then forged ahead—without using real names. Still, it was evident that Razor was his main focal point.

Morrisey didn't read the news, let alone underground papers. But the word did get back to him, via one of his underlings.

"Tyrone Hunter? Who the fuck is he?"

"Ain't nobody really. Some faggot at a newspaper, that's all," a henchman offered.

"Well, he don't know me. But he 'bout to…" Morrisey huffed, lighting a Cuban.

Shortly thereafter, Ty was heading toward the subway when some thuggish cat approached him.

"Yo? You Tyrone Hunter, that writer?"

"Who wants to know?"

A black car with tinted windows quickly pulled onto the sidewalk. The back window rolled down and *that mug* he'd seen in his darkroom demanded, "Time we meet. Get in."

The thug forced Tyrone into the car and drove it away in a squeal of rubber.

"You got some beef with me, fool?" Razor's voice was as big as his head.

"Why would I?" Ty asked, shuddering in his skin.

"Now, see, *that's* what I wanna know. 'Cause word is, you's just a faggot. I got somethin' big and hard for yo ass. Ya might not like it, though," Razor joked, his deadly serious, seriously large head expanding. All the while he was stroking not his deadly cock, but the handle of a deadlier Glock. "What's yo beef? I don't know you, boy. Don't *wanna* know you if you's tryna put me out of bidniz! Is it like dat, huh?"

Ty feared his odious ass. He feared for his own life. But the quiet wrath he'd maintained for years far outweighed his fear.

"I don't know what you talkin' bout, bruh. I'm just a man, tryna do his job, that's all," he said, breathing in easy waves. Though he was beginning to sweat, he tried not to show stress.

"Well, the only *job* a faggot can do right is a *blow job!*" Morrisey rasped, as his boys laughed higher and giddier than most faggots ever laughed. "See, that's what I don't understand. Why a weak-ass bitch like *you* wanna knock heads with somebody like me? Is you workin' for *the man?*"

"Nah. I'm working for myself. It's just a little part-time job, man. That's all. It don't pay much. I'm sorry if it upset you. I…I was just tryna to get ahead."

"I'm sure you get plenty *a head*. But why one Black man tryna hold another Black man down? See, I don't play that shit. You scared of me? You *should* be! Don't worry. I ain't gonna hurt ya, yet. I'm a bidniz man. Just wanted to see who you is, and let this little ride be yo warnin'. You keep writin' shit I don't like, and yo queer bitch-ass will be dealt with. Do we understand each other, punk-bitch? Huh?"

Tyrone Hunter shook his head. All the while, he was thinking of his next attack. With Razor's threat complete, the door opened, and Tyrone was pushed from the car as it neared the pier where working boys strolled and sedans slowed to barter before letting them inside.

"I just dropped the little bitch off in Fag's Paradise," Razor laughed as the car sped away.

Tyrone, though bruised and shaken, escaped with his life intact. But instead of mortal fear, he was overwhelmed by a kind of runner's high. Big and bad as Razor was, Ty could smell the fear one *meaningless faggot* put inside the cocky air he breathed.

Nevertheless, that particular nightmarish ride had a sobering effect. In lieu of further stories, Ty wrote long words and took compelling pictures, and sent them to his congressman, both senators, and the district attorney. In his own way, Tyrone became the catalyst in Razor's decline. Within a few months, the tyrant toppled. It was classic that he went down the way Capone had fallen. The IRS snagged his delinquent ass for failure to pay over 11 years of back taxes.

Razor strutted his bad-ass act a little too boldly on Rikers Island. An argument came to a quick and deadly head when he was stuck with a shiv in his cell, and he bled out, and nobody cared.

* * *

That was the phone message from Mr. Death that stopped Ty in his doorway: Razor was dead. Maybe no one at Rikers Island cared, but Ty cared plenty. And when he finally did head out for the night, the air smelled a little fresher, the streets felt a little safer, and the ghosts in Tyrone's head haunted just a little more quietly.

December 1990

Though his columns had grown in popularity, Ty felt underused. He decided to quit. But as he walked into his editor's office to shout the news, he ran into The One.

Blur.

Smart. Ambitious. Beautiful. Deceptive.

Blur Antonelli was a new jack law student, hired to cover the legal beat. When Ty saw him, he was thunderstruck. Not since the sad day he'd first laid eyes on Face Depina had he seen a more staggering arrangement of beige architecture.

Black and Italian features made Ty's eyes cling to Blur in awe of what lush beauty two races could accomplish. His skin was not the preferred cup of rich hot chocolate, yet Tyrone was sinking inside its soft taupe shade. His hair hung in loose dreads and fell like thick chestnut cocks to his unusually wide shoulders. His deep hazel eyes pierced Tyrone's discriminating core. Suddenly, Ty's emotions were clumsy acrobats, tumbling, falling, fumbling, sliding around. He found himself wondering: *Are you here for me? Could you be the one? Shit! Baby, baby, please be the one!*

"Tyrone. I'd like to you meet Blur. Blur Antonelli," his editor said.

Well, hello! He's flawless. Not very tall, is he? Maybe Trick's height. Diz-zamn, you's a fine boy! God! Is there a mind behind all that fineness? If there is, I might just relax my rules about fallin' in dig with you pretty boys. Please don't open your mouth and squawk like a fool, 'cause I'm feelin' you.

"Tyrone is one of our contributing editors," the bossman said.

"Well, hey, Tyrone!" Blur said, shaking Ty's hand rigorously, a trace of genuine excitement in his voice. "I read four papers every morning. But honestly, man, your column makes my day. Great stuff. It's perspicacious and consistently poignant. I digs, man. I digs."

Sometimes, the color in a person's voice turns on like a beautiful green light...

"Thanks, man. Good to meet you," Ty said, still holding Blur's strong hand.

In a nanosecond's all-important *joint check*, Ty's eyes darted down: faded jeans worn at the crotch, and a big ol' lovely print. No briefs or boxers whatsoever. *You're a nasty boy, ain't you? Looking like somebody's casual sun god, and swinging all big in the pants. You managed to use 'perspicacious' and 'poignant' in the same damn sentence, and somehow the shit didn't even sound pretentious. Packin' ample penis, lugging extensive syntax, and you're a fan of my stuff? Oh, my goodness! Nuts up!*

Ty was *intrigued* as he and Blur often found themselves meeting face to face, belly-to-belly as they quickly squeezed past each other in the narrow office hallways. With each encounter came a smile and a slightly naughty physical twinge. Each had already mentally undressed the other. Hell, Ty had already rubbered and fellated Blur between those mental sheets, and they'd yet to have a *real* conversation.

Then it came, that first minor heartbreak. Tall, rugged, and *blond?* He dropped by to see Blur in the workplace. The two yapped it up, talking and laughing like intimate idiots. Ty immediately resented that handsome blond's athletic ass.

But Ty was nothing if not *cool* in his pursuits. He showed no sign of interest until he felt 99% sure the urge was mutual.

Come 6 o'clock, Ty collected his work, grabbed his coat, and headed for the elevator. Seeing Ty, Blur quickly closed shop and made it to the elevator before the doors opened. "Going my way?" he joked.

"I'm not sure yet, Blur. It *is* Blur, right?" Ty asked coolly.

"Yeah. Well, that's what everyone calls me. Actually, my name's Roger Antonelli Daniels. I'm a product of the Italian mom's Black daddy free-love hippie trip. Antonelli is my mom's maiden name." he explained. "Yeah, I know, I don't quite look either one. But I'm an Italianigga," he said as if he would never tire of defining himself.

Even though Tyrone hadn't asked his pedigree, it did save time.

"Right now, you're probably wondering about the *Daniels* part," Blur continued. "It's the name on my birth certificate, but I rarely use it."

Ding! The doors opened and the two stepped inside. Ty knew talking about one's *self* was most everyone's favorite subject, and wanting to keep their flow, he asked, "Does *Blur* have any significance?" as he pushed the lobby button.

"I ran track in high school. Don't wanna brag, but I still hold the school record for the 100-yard dash. Coach used to say, 'When you run Antonelli, you're a fuckin' blur zooming toward that finish line!'"

"So, uh, Blur... You're known for your speed, huh?" Ty asked with a touch of innuendo.

"Uh, yeah. But some things are better with modulation," he grinned, flashing the sexiest smile since, since, ever!

Good fuckin' answer, Mr. Blur Antonelli. Now, all ya gotta do is casually slide your hand along your crotch, and damn it, we can just let our soul song begin.

But Blur didn't grab the dick. Instead, he suggested they grab cappuccinos at the Black Sheep. The vibe between them was easy and comfortable. Blur was a Brother Ty could riff with. He liked the glint in Blur's eyes, the sound of Blur's voice. Everything Blur said was music, even when the music was blue.

"I've got the most dysfunctional family still raising hell on the planet, man," Blur confessed. "We started out in the 'burbs. Then the parents split. My mother's one cool chick. She was Madonna before Madonna was born. Maybe she was rebelling against Catholicism, or maybe she just had a thing for Black men. Married three of them. The last one was a one bum with a perpetual hard-on. We were enemies from the start. I kept waiting for my father to ride in on a big black horse and rescue me. But he was a weak man."

Blur called his father, "a serial impregnator of the world's exotic women," explaining to Ty that he had a half-Swedish half-brother, whom he called "the Swigga." A half-Korean sister: "the Korigga." And presently, the old man was Down Under, spawning a new tribe of "Austriggas."

"Seriously, I've got a mess of half-brothers and sisters. Two brothers I barely know are on lockdown. Another's strung out on rock. I've got the cutest sister you've ever seen. She's my heart. Sabina, my bright tangerine girl." He smiled, though his eyes held a quiet sadness. "Besides myself, she's the only one who went to college. But something horrible happened to her. During her first semester, she and some fast girl went to a club. 'Bina's not a party girl, and she didn't know what was out there. Well, she met some piece of shit, and he, he raped her."

"Oh, that is…horrible. Unfortunately, it's not so uncommon. But it's horrible," Ty said.

"You have to meet 'Bina. You can't really tell, but she's blind in one eye. It always made her sensitive and withdrawn. She's a real fragile girl. The last girl on earth who could handle something so fucking vicious! She hardly ever smiles anymore. After that, there was only one thing to do: Become a lawyer. A prosecutor. Bring some fucking justice back into this world."

Blur's story moved Tyrone.

There was something rare, shining, bordering on *heroic* about the dude. Unlike the others, so focused on the naked fact that Ty liked men they forgot to ask him about his own background, Blur wanted more.

"So what's the deal with *you*, Tyrone? Somebody told me you were a kid actor. Then I heard songwriter. Someone else said poet, photographer, playwright? What the hell are you, really?"

"The unknown Gordon Parks, I guess," Ty offered. It sounded odd, even to him. Maybe that was how he came off, as either a Renaissance man or an unfocused kid who'd yet to grow the fuck up. "I wrote songs when I was younger," he admitted. "But that's when there was something to sing about."

"Yeah. Unless ya got a hip-hop flow and you can bitch to the beat, yo."

"Hey. Don't dis hip-hop! Sampling's been beddy-beddy good to me. 'Kay, the original plan: Have my first play produced on Broadway by 20, my first novel published at 21, my first Pulitzer win by 25, and then branch into scene-writing. The short version of real is I started out as a kid who acted. But I never was an *actor*. So in a place full of actors, I rebelled by writing, reading, taking pictures. Guess I'm an art mutt. There, I said it."

Blur's thought: *You've done a lot of living between the sheets of books. But I bet you don't fuck much, do ya?*

"C'mon, bro. Let's break out!" Blur suggested. Ty wanted to stroll Tompkins Square Park, maybe sit, *roll a tree* and vibe inside a cool night's breezy dark. But it turned out Blur no longer smoked cheeb or drank, and he wasn't much of a nature boy, either. So, of all places for a first date, Blur took Tyrone to a live sex show. Ty didn't know whether to be insulted, or to take it as a form of public foreplay. He chose the latter. The two walked into the small red-lit room and took a seat. As Sade's "War of the Heart" played, a dark rippling god sauntered onto the small platform. He was brawny, caramel-glazed supremacy from the tip of his shiny dome to his huge-ass feet. A sensuous moneymaker, his G-string bulged thick with 20s. Every man sat erect, waiting to see what lurked beneath his leather jock. As he poured thick gold elixir along dark poking jujube nipples, his eyes locked with Tyrone's. But Ty was not a cat in the habit of stuffing cash into baskets that come. Cheap thrills and coppin' feels from paid sex machines didn't interest him. Yet he still wondered, *Why is this man throwing his stuff at me? What's his story?* And when finally the leather jock descended: *Oh damn! That sure is a big ol' penis...*

Suddenly, a pouty blond joined the god onstage for a little interactive—though choking all the way—fellatio. For his second act, Blondie was splayed across a wooden bench and deeply fucked to the entire Isaac Hayes *Shaft* soundtrack. Long after the blond came and the music ceased, Fuckenstein continued to *shaft* him to his own beat. Soon there was just him and the rhythm of the meat-beaters around him, pounding and staring, astonished. When at last the god shot, strange mouths gaped to catch his white-hot slosh. Even Ty wanted to whip *his* joint out before he exploded from writhing in his pants. But Blur just looked upon that fancy dancer with not a boner in sight. So Ty and his joint both chilled.

"Did you like it? The show, I mean," Blur asked in the lounge outside the showroom.

"Far as *watching* goes, yeah, I sort of enjoyed it," Tyrone hedged. "But I noticed *you* didn't get into it much."

"I'm as kinky as the next bastard. But, my half-brother never did give me a hard-on. *Incest* just ain't my trip."

With those words, a *little sick feeling* crept into Ty's stomach. *Why* had Blur taken him there? What kind of mad-ill shit was that? He was just about to ask that question when Blur explained, "His name is Ray. Looks like my stepdaddy, if you catch my drift. I've got no use for him, or his dong dancing. I'm all for an individual's right to dance the filthy-nasty if that's his trip. But truthfully I don't even think he's gay. Ray's just a cheap, cocky hustler with a big joint. See, I've been monitoring this place. Look around, check the trade. It's just a front for a thriving drug business. When I make my fury in this world, this, places like this, and the motherfuckers behind them will cease to exist." He said it coldly, with a sure and determined intonation that made Tyrone believe him.

Ty found himself admiring the things Blur had yet to become. The prospect of all that power excited him, the way the sight of a big, hard, *Latin pinga* excited the promiscuous pants off David.

Blur grinned. *So righteousness gets him hard!* He gave his joint a squeeze, and shot Tyrone a this-could-lead-to-some-serious-fuckin' look.

But it would be weeks before they'd finally *knock Tims*. After work, they'd hang out, and the conversation alone proved highly stimulating. They'd share kiwi and passion fruit, and listen like students to Billie's bluesiest blues. They attended off-Broadway plays, or they'd check the Yankees on the tube. Sometimes it *felt correct* for the two to just chill in silent meditation.

Was this Blur Antonelli The One, that exceptional being who could produce in Ty a *Long Blue Moan?*

* * *

Sometimes your lips touch someone else's, and you know by the soft brush of certainty your heart's in trouble.

That magic night at Tyrone's, a month to the day since they'd first met, Ty was ready. Nothing if not prepared. He had everything: towels, oils, lube, candles, incense, condoms, and Najee's jazz. Tyrone was feeling, for the first time in a long time, fucky, lucky, and bursting with new semen. 'Twas the season to spew.

He and Blur kissed till their tongues hurt from rattling, till their eager cocks teared and jostled painfully in an incessant grind. Blur's strange near-Egyptian beauty didn't cease at the neck. Fumbling, bumbling, Ty ripped open Blur's shirt to find his nipples hard, dark, tight as stars! His chest, a heaving breastplate of golden skin, distinctly ripped. The slightest trace of pale-brown hair trailed his taut belly. Ty licked his flesh, unzipped him, and Oh! How immaculate this new penis seemed, full of heat, veins, and skittering in his hand. Unleashed and erect, it swayed side to side. Its head wore a trace of chili-vinegar. Ty knew it could only get hotter, and it did. The minute Blur's long, naked *equus* meat touched his lips, its pulsing heat, its weight, its palpitation, the thrill of it throbbing in Tyrone's mouth instantly hardened him. He surged down. Even with a rubber, it felt hotter than cayenne pepper, sweeter than brown sugar melting down his wet trachea. Blur swerved those taut golden hips and lunged his 9-inch cure for loneliness deeper, deeper...

Blur.

He came, he saw, he conquered.

Blur and Ty fucked for 2 hours and 49 minutes, and when Ty came up for air, it felt like *love*.

From the moment Ty hit Blur's groove, it was *certain*, a done deed. A fait accompli. Ah! In a sweet grunt of unity, Blur bristled and constricted around him.

"Go on. Give it to me."

And Tyrone pounded *love* into a man that night. And love's first thrust was sublime. Full of power and drive, momentum, and slow trickling sweat. Full of shudders, grimaces, and gasps of, "Yes, Ty! Yes!" That fuck, their first fuck, was excellent and new and hot in all of its gooey resplendence.

"Is this your baby?" Blur asked, huffing, puffing repeatedly. "Is this your baby?" It was Blur-speak for *Are you close? Are you coming?*

"Yes. Yes," Ty chattered. "It's my baby!" And Love's first sublime hum came on like a quiet hysteria. And they pitched, sighing, shooting, and embracing tight for a long time after.

Afterward, cradled against Blur's racing chest, Ty's mind sighed, *Be still my beating heart and cock. I'm laid up here with a* man!

Two months later, Ty was writing love songs again:

We're buying appliances, pooling finances / Even talkin' 'bout adoptin' a little knotty-head / Sex is electric, so stimulating / Each night I debrief him, and he purrs me to sleep / Now ain't we somethin', this world's never seen? Ain't we somethin', my lover man and me?

But Blur's damn blond kept reappearing. What were they to each other? Friends? Classmates? Buddies? Old lovers? Ty's curiosity was only compounded when Blur never introduced them. Pride and the fear of appearing too possessive prevented Tyrone from asking that one nagging question, so it slowly ate at his jealous gut.

Still, Blur and Ty were volatile, passionate, sometimes even apocalyptic when they rattled between the sheets. When Blur's dwindling finances dictated, Ty suggested he move in with him. A hesitant Blur finally acquiesced. He brought with him his long cock, his tight ass, and a fat bag of manhood issues. Unlike Ty, he wasn't *out*, and he'd no intentions of coming out—that wasn't how he rolled. He cared for Ty, but caring too much might spell trouble in his future plans. Leading a secret life made the one attempting to keep it secret corruptible. Thus, living with a man and establishing *a home* frightened him.

At times, Blur would get moody, never wanting to talk about his career disappointments, family entanglements, his issues with homosexuality. And the blond kept returning. One day, fresh from a seminar, Ty came home to find them giggling like two secretive queens in his bed.

"What the fuck! Get out! Get the hell out of my bed, out of my apartment, out of my fuckin' life! And take blondie with you, you fuckin' asshole. I trusted you, you fuckin' lyin' bastard!"

"Calm down Ty. It's not like that! This is my brother. My fuckin' *blood* brother!" Blur snapped. "My brother Lars."

"Fuck you very much, Blur! I'm far from stupid!"

But then, the hulking blond pulled out his wallet, and showed Tyrone his driver's license. Beneath his blond, blue-eyed mug it read true enough: Ingmar Lars Daniels.

"I told you my dads got around."

"One was a Swede," Lars added. "My momma, Greta."

Color Tyrone dumfounded by a Swigga.

* * *

When Sabina, Blur's "sweet chestnut sister," came to call, Ty was enchanted. He related to her soft eyes, her skittish movement, and empathized with her fragility. She brought out a side of his savior complex.

"She's not disturbed in a pathological sense, just morbidly withdrawn, afraid of people," he diagnosed. "Maybe it's just social anxiety."

Ty bought a stack of self-help books, and genuinely tried to get through to her. But Blur would have none of it.

"What is this shit? She's not *yours* to fix!"

A few months later, after the dust settled, Sabina was over again waiting for Blur to take her bike riding. Blur was showering, and she sat in Ty's living room, looking around at familiar things. Then she glanced at Ty's coffee table where a glossy men's magazine lay staring at her. She stared back, and suddenly became very agitated. Sabina was slipping away, slipping into the darkest place she'd ever known. She began to moan and rock and cradle herself. All at once, she had to run, run or something horrible would happen to her again. She ran out the door, down five flights of stairs and into the street, crying and flailing uncontrollably. Blur, who'd heard the commotion, rushed in to find his sister had vanished. No one knew or could fathom why. Except Sabina, who had just looked into the eyes of her rapist.

The man on the cover of that glossy magazine was Face Depina.

Seventeen

Jacking Davina

Davy was decked out in full drag during the Halloween parade when he ran into an old friend from his days on the road. At 6 foot 2 and 300 pounds, Adeva was a fierce, flamboyantly maternal drag queen strutting *toughly*. Soon as Adeva saw him dressed as "Davina," she said, "Honey! Ya gorgeous! You simply *must* be in my show! It's an all drag revue. Maybe you've heard of it: *For Multicolored Queens With Dreams Deferred When These Freakin' Platforms No Longer Fit?* I wouldn't call it a big boffo hit, but we do pack 'em into that little theater on Sullivan."

And Davy, being such a natural ham-hock, you just *know* he said yes.

* * *

"Drag is only a costume for David," Adeva told a fellow performer. "He'll never be a fully let-out diva. He loves his manhood way too much. Quiet as it's kept, he can be very virile."

December 31, 1990

The New Year's Eve show ran late, and Davina decided to leave the theater in costume. That night he'd called Tyrone to ask if he wanted to hang out, but as usual his home-skillet refused. So there was Davina, all glammed up and no place to show. But when did that ever stop him?

As he tipped down the street, he thought to himself, *Miss Audrey Hepburn would be proud!* And it was true. Davina was rockin' this little black Givenchy knock-off *she'd designed*, and killer six-inch patent leather pumps. She went the whole nine. Had a pink chiffon scarf draped to dramatic effect along her head *and* Adeva's Holly Golightly shades. A Virginia Slim blazed from her long, lacquered ciggie holder. She was cool like that, glam like that.

Yes, girls. Miss Audrey has arrived, and she is takin' no shorts!

Timbales played mad rhythms in Davina's chest when she spotted him by the bar drinking a Corona. Didn't he know Davina was a sucker for cool-pose *boricuas* with oh-so-smoldering eyes?

He was young, just out of his teens, with big, drooping Al Pacino eyes.

"*Hola, mami.* You lookin' *muy caliente!*" he purred.

Of course she was. But that was beside the point.

He sat next to her, and began the novella of how he was drop-kicked out of *la casa* for being a *maricón*. He'd just found his own place, and was determined to make it inside that Great Harassing City.

Davina felt for him. She sat listening, watching him watching her, knowing at least one of them was in the groggy stage of falling dick-first into some dizzy crazy affinity. Did he have a sweet thing for *her?* He was certainly working that *cholo* charm, and Davina was snatching it up quicker than a two-for-one shoe sale at Screaming Mimi's.

He mentioned that he needed some "decoratin' tips for my new crib."

"Oh. So, you're inviting me home? How sweet. But I'm a lady, and I'm really not *that* easy, honey," Davina giggled, digging the kid's thick caterpillar brow, the mold of his hands and arms, and that way he had of stroking her warmly with those eyes.

"*Mira mami*, lookie here. My place is straight-up booty. Maybe you could give me ideas how to hook it. I mean, look at you. Yo! This place here is booty, but you dress it up, sittin' in here lookin' so fine and shit. Besides, baby, I never been with nobody like you. You like me too, don't you? C'mon, straight up, you know it. So, let's do this," he teased.

There ought to be a law against butta boys whose eye-fuck is strong enough to make you say *Fuckit*. Davina found herself saying just that, thinking, *If this boy plays his pimp cards right, he'll be purring like El Gato by night's end.*

Soon as they stepped outside, Davina began to hear new exciting sambas play in her lonely drag queen's heart. "So, what's your name again, sweetheart?" she asked, wobbling behind him.

"None of yo fuckin' business, faggot-ass bitch!"

The hairs under Audrey's elegant wig immediately stood at attention. Suddenly, Davina felt That Shiver Thing: a cautionary reaction centered in her viscera. Why hadn't she felt it before? Was her barometer busted? She felt it now, though, in spades.

"What did you just say to me?" she asked, staring a hole through the back of his head.

He spun around and repeated, "None of your fuckin' business, *faggot-ass bitch!*"

"Look! Don't you be tryna ruin Davina's night, now! Ya hear? And don't take my evening attire to mean I'm some punk, aiight? 'Cause these heels *can* come off with a quickness, and I *will* kick your puny ass all over this uncaring street!" she proclaimed.

"Yeah right. You know, you full-out faggots shouldn't be allowed out in public! What did you think, I'd let you suck my pipe?" The hood looked around. "I said, *you like suckin' pipe?*"

"Yes. I've been known to. But I like kickin' ign'it ass even better!" Davina snapped, kicking off her heels.

Those meticulously painted nails came off in a flash, balled into two formidable fists, and Ms. Davina, a.k.a. David Donatello Richmond, sprang into ass-kicking action. Slow black and white visions of his earlier self pummeling some street kid in the ring danced through his skull. "Knuckle up, guard yo grill, you coward-ly motherfucker!" David warned, taking a pugilist's stance.

Just then, another voice asked: "You like sucking pipe, huh, faggot?"

"Yeah. Look at this, bitch! You know it sucks pipe," still another voice chimed.

Hard boys streamed out of the alleyway across the street.

David turned. He was surrounded by six diabolical brown and black faces. A flood of panic rushed over him. But he refused to go out like a sucker. "Oh. So, you brought your boys, huh? Afraid you couldn't handle a soft, unsuspecting faggot by your lonesome? All right, Julio, Raul, whatever the fuck your name is, bring it!"

What they brought was a tire iron.

"Ya like suckin' pipe, faggot? Well, suck on this!" With a blunt ram someone yanked the scarf at the back of his neck and everything turned black. Strange how in that state of semiconsciousness David's mind and body recorded every assault: the quick *slam* of a boot on his back; the taunts of "Take pipe, motherfuckin' ass-bandit!" The stun of fist after fist after fist, kick after kick hammering his flesh. They'd no mercy for a dress-wearing, sashaying faggot on the prowl. They were crucifying him.

Dragging him into the darkness of that sociopathic alley, they continued their battery. They did it for fun, for shits and giggles. A swift and sudden kick to his mouth knocked out two teeth. But how many kicks would it take? How many times would that iron need to rise and plummet down, rise and pummel down before he could close his eyes and no longer *feel* anything? He wondered this as he lay there, semiconscious, waiting for a neon sign from God. *Is God in this alley?* his hurting skull questioned as the warm river of blood trickled down, seeping through Audrey's little black dress.

The final humiliation came as the young thug from the bar ripped into Ms. Davina's purse, found a bright pink lipstick, and scribbled on David's bleeding forehead: FAG!

Then they ran away hyena style, laughing, howling into the cruel Manhattan night.

* * *

A day later, his wired jaw prevented him from speaking. His only communication was through pen and pad and those eyes.

"Know what hurts most?" he wrote. "Deception. It hurts more than a tire iron."

St. Vincent's Hospital, January 1, 1991

"Is that all you can tell us? Average height. Brown skin. Caterpillar brow. Sad Pacino eyes. Is that your best description?" the patrolwoman asked, her Latina features contrasting against the pristine whiteness of the hospital room. She was a handsome woman, though her expression was one of vague, sympathetic boredom. "You've described half the population of Spanish Harlem."

The closest thing to a tear glistened, welling in David's left eye. But in steely queen's defiance, he refused to let it fall.

Maybe it's the price for being outrageous. Maybe it's just my lot to suffer the slings and arrows of outrageous fortune in this big bad hateful city. But like Ty says, I won't let those motherfuckers steal my Joy.

David wrote back, "No Polaroid," and thought, *Am I supposed to say, "Uh, before you proceed to beat me down to a bloody pulp and break my face and my fuckin' stilettos, would you mind terribly striking a pose?"*

For David, a bigger question than who was his attacker loomed: Where was his support system? And how the hell, with no insurance, could he afford his medical bills? He closed his eyes and flipped through the rolodex in his skull.

* * *

"If I told him once," Depina said to Ty, "I've told the little ill bitch a million times: 'It's risky enough being out there!' But he still takes that soft, saccharine-sweet faggot ass on the stroll like he's lookin' for a beat-down! Fuckin' freak! Told him, 'Don't tempt strange men into shakin' yo tree without tellin' 'em bout that extra limb!' I don't feel sorry for his loose, stupid ass. I don't feel nothing. The phone rings at 5:30 in the fuckin' mornin', and it's some drag queen callin' me: 'Face, honey. David's in trouble. He's hurt. They got him laid up here in the hospital, and…well, he sure could use a friend…' Well, I'm sick of his shit!"

"Excuse you?

"Yo, Ty! Bitches get treated like bitches."

Ty searched Face's eyes for the foggy, tripped-out signs of a soul.

"Listen, I only came here because of David. He feels connected to the *real* Pascal. Remember him? David does. He's always been your champion defender. I'm asking you to do right by the Brother."

"Yeah, that's funny. You, *Dudley Do-right* asking *me* to *do right* by a Brother! That's why we clash. You were always too righteous and bourgie for my tastes."

"Still trying to fade me, Depina? I'm not all hard and cold, but you sure as hell can't fade me."

"Everything you say *sounds white* to me. All you represent is a bourgie lie!" Face countered.

"Now look who's callin' the kettle indigo! I don't even know what you mean when you say that shit. Bourgie? Is it that I come from people who loved me, people who *tried* to keep it together? You resent that, don't you? I think maybe you hate seeing people happy. David was happy. Faison was *happier*, at least. I imagine Bliss was even happy once. Hell, I *know* my parents were before Hurricane Face blew in through our apartment window! Is that why you tried to sabotage them, is that why you stole the brooch? Yeah. I know all about it. Look me in the eye, damn it! I deserve to be looked in the fuckin' eye!"

Tyrone expected Depina to lie with a straight face. But for once, he didn't bother.

"Oh, that. Don't worry, I'll write your mama a nice big check, with interest," he said all nonchalant.

Tyrone wanted to hit him. Hit him in dead in his throat. "You can't fix it now, Face. And you can't downplay the shit you do. Not with me. It won't work."

"But I can buy and sell your ass," Face bragged, though it was a lie.

The phone rang, and Face grinned as he walked backward to answer it.

"Talk sense to me," he said into the receiver as he waved to a little Korean man, who appeared to be unsure if he should enter that particular battlefield. He was carrying a basin full of suds, and was flustered about where to place it for Face's bi-weekly pedi-cure. "Yeah, I heard. Yeah. I got one of his *girls* here now, bitchin' about it."

Tyrone heard, just as Face wanted him to hear.

"No. The other one. The one that thinks he's the shit. OK, Claude. I'll holla at you later. Cool. Sounds good. Hmm-m-m. Bet. Later Brother." Face hung up, then yelled at the little Korean man. "Damn it, put the tub down, ya little fool! Right there! Yes, in front of the sofa." He pointed. Then he turned to Ty. "Are we finished?" he asked.

"That was Claudio Conte? You call him *Brother*? Interesting. Here you are, flaunting this light-skin privileged life under the pose of *brotherhood*, and the *real* Brothers you dismiss."

"I'll never call *you* my brother. You too fuckin' saintly for that gig! If I *did* have a brother, he'd be one hard and sexy bitch. At least Claudio *represents*."

"A bitch? I don't doubt it," Ty quipped.

"I used to laugh at you, Tyrone. Sometimes I still do. Now you want *everything* I got. My fame, my money, the women I already knocked out. Go on and take her, Ty. But I better warn you: Bliss uses her teeth."

With that, rage overtook Tyrone. It boiled up in his hand, and it made a fist, and it grew with heat and purpose, and it hauled off and swung. The punch landed square on Face's chin and bottom lip. This was no bitch slap.

Placing his hand to the spot, Face brought back a trickle of blood and laughed. "Watch it, Ty! Fightin' over a woman? Ya bet not be lettin' her hum you! I'll fuck around and report your queer ass to the queer union, have 'em take away your purple carryin' card."

Ty was glad he'd hit him. He was also mad at himself for hitting him, but mostly *glad*. "You're a pitiful excuse for a man, Face. The subject is David. David, damn it! Good, bad, Black, or miserable, he's your friend. He's your fuckin' friend, and he needs you."

"You wanna talk about the little fag?" he asked, sitting on his Italian-crafted sofa, removing his socks. He placed his precious feet inside the basin and his servant went to work. "All right. Let's talk. You say he's *my* friend? I don't know about all that *friend* bullshit. David's run outta time with me, and his shit is stale."

"Fuck you!" Ty yelled. "David is our history. Now he's down, and you're gonna walk away? Write him off? It's a pattern with you: You just *junk* people!"

"Damn right. I junk people who hit me up for money. I junk people who sashay into one of my shows lookin' like a Black-ass Joan fuckin' Crawford on crack! David ain't Davy anymore. He's a fuckin' basket case, and I'm tired of him, his goofy dreams, and his stupid way of hittin' on me when he knows it ain't gonna happen. I'm sick and tired of his whole queer *shtick*."

"What? Worried about the negative publicity? Relax. You could always put a spin on it, make it seem like you're one of the beautiful, sensitive, sympathetic motherfuckers that kiss known queens on the lips at all the right functions."

"Fuck you twice, mothafucka! I could always drop-kick your ass too, ya know."

"And I'd be a mess, wouldn't I?" Ty replied. "What would I *become* without *you*? A nasty drunk on rock, like Browny? A sad, muscle-bound marionette, like Chaz?"

"You steppin' out of bounds, now! Ya hear me, you negro homo-erectus with a confused dick! Ya leave it the fuck alone!" Face warned.

"Or maybe I'd just put on a dress and paint my face and step into that lonely trip of backrooms, suck-holes, and toilet fucks, thinking of *you* with every anonymous cock I suck, like David!"

"That's it! Get the fuck out of here! Right now. I mean it. Out!" Face screamed, pointing to the door. He stepped out of his soapy basin and splashed his Korean pedicurist. His eyes were livid. Only when he was truly pissed did they have that strange green supernatural glow. *He* was now ready to hit *Tyrone*.

But Tyrone wasn't afraid of him, and no longer felt *punked* in his presence. There were things he'd wanted to say, hot words stewing and boiling. "You know, Face, I can be a friend despite the way my friends might trip, fall down, and bust up the leg of that friendship. You think you're better than the rest of us? Truth is, you're not, and you never were. Browny's more talented, always was. I'm a lot more accomplished. And Davy's got more humanity in his tight hip-swinging ass than you can pull from your deepest opiate-addled imagination. But guess what? Fate smiled on *you*, even though you've never done a damn thing worthwhile in your fuckin' life. You're famous because of an accident of genetics! And this mad cool apartment and flier-than-fly lifestyle won't change the fact that you're empty and fucked up."

"I give less than a clipped fuckin' pinkie toenail what you think of me, Tyrone. And right now I'm wonderin' if I got any *real true blues* besides Claudio. Friends who understand me. You know, the kind that don't *want* nutt'n from me."

"Yeah. Nothing but your *soul*! And how do you *understand* somebody that's not even *real*, Face? You ain't real. *David's* real. Remember him? He's real and he's hurt real bad. You can either deal with that or *not* deal and just shoot up, and nod it all away. Whatever. I'm out."

Face watched his road dawg head for the door. It felt like the end of *them*.

But in reality, there was no *them*.

"Oh. One more thing, Brother," Tyrone added, sarcastically. "We fucked once, and never again. Personally, I've never asked for a single thing from you, right? I'm not on a leash or a stipend. I don't bend to kiss your ass like your other sycophants. No, whatever I felt for you died a long time ago. Stupid-ass me. I keep forgetting to bury that stank fuckin' corpse!"

"Well, who the hell asked you to come here, faggot?" Depina's face reddened.

"You're right. I'm trespassing. This is *your* place. But I came here to remind you that somebody actually loves you. He loved you when you was nobody, when you didn't have this place, and now he's in pain. There's a lot of that out there. I figured maybe you could relate, just a little." Ty sniffed. "Pain. Hell, I smell it all up in this place. If you ever come down off that shit you're snorting, or shooting, you might smell it yourself, you stuck-up, counterfeit, mixed-up super-bitch! Your life is a joke, Pascal. And *you* are the fuckin' laugh!"

Then he slammed the door behind him.

Face snapped at his pedicurist, "Well? Whatcha waitin' for? My pinkie toe could use some buffin'!"

* * *

During the cab ride to the hospital, Ty recalled the first time he'd laid eyes on David: An openly queer teen, he wore a cape-like *shmat-te* that was black with a lavender lining. His eyes were raccooned in mascara and he virtually glided down the hall. Ty reasoned that he *had to be* a dance major.

"Honey boy, relax those stiff shoulders and bre-e-athe. Walkin' 'round like, like somebody's *Blacula!* Vampire vogue is very mid 70s. We'll work on you, though. Just relax, breathe, and be yourself!" were Davy's first words to him.

Now, in that cab, suddenly Tyrone felt haunted by the things he'd never said.

I never once told him how much I admire him or how transparently beautiful he is.

Maybe he hadn't said it, but Tyrone always felt that when David grew into a himself, he would be one of the most *lovely* and intriguing human beings anyone had ever seen.

With "the Duchess," Ty saw no need to be plastic or malleable, or to live that schizophrenic existence he inevitably lived on the street. He wasn't required to speak several languages, use different gestures, vocabularies, demeanors, senses. His armor didn't have to be intact. The Core Tyrone, *the Ty no one else knew*, he presented to David.

David understood him, and Ty *got* David.

Ty knew the whole gayer-than-thou thing was a costume David could change in and out of like a Broadway musical cast member. He knew David always feigned an absurd *machismo* around his father, and did so up until the day he'd died, because Daddy Richmond's acceptance loomed high in the sovereignty of David's heart. Though he never received it, David worked *hard* toward that goal of love and acceptance. Before he realized he could gather and create his own, the concept of family was very important to David Richmond. Thus, he would affect boxing, jock posturing, the "You should see the fox I'm datin', Pop" rap, and most any daring-do, short of marriage. Life around Poppa Richmond was a manly war on a sunny beach of lies, but David thought he was winning.

His father *had* given him a spiritual base—from which David often toppled—yet it somehow sustained him.

His father also saw to it that David learned to use his fists.

Knowing the Duchess could, if provoked, *swing* on an assailant and put a serious hurting on his ass made Ty feel easier. Only now it was one more reason to be angry, confused, and guilty. Hadn't David *asked him* to hang out that New Year's Eve? Hadn't Tyrone brushed him off with the excuse that he'd finally shaken his writer's block?

* * *

Tyrone had been forewarned: The person in that bed would *not* resemble the David he knew. Still he'd not been prepared for the shock of seeing that broken poodle of a boy, a tube extending through his nose, the heavy bandages, or the contusions littering that sweet face.

He called upon the long dead comic in him. "Da-a-amn, baby! I know this place is a dump, but it looks like someone took one on you!" was his pathetic offer.

"Facey with you?" David scribbled anxiously.

"Uh, no. Maybe he'll bop through later. The Beautiful People

keep different hours. So how you feeling, Duchess? I mean, really?"
Ty's voice was heavy with concern.

That wasn't David lying there. It was a worn theater marquee
with a broken facade.

"Like Garbo," David wrote, a limp wrist to his brow.

"Come on, Duchess. I've seen that movie. Garbo didn't really
'vant to be alone' baby boy."

David wanted to say, *Thank God for you, Tyrone. I'm so glad you're
here. It's no fun playin' Camille all by my lonesome.*

"Davy, I was gonna come in here and pretend, just fake my
scared ass off. But I can't do it, baby boy. Look at you! You look hor-
r-rible!" Ty confessed, his tone colored by a mirthless chuckle.

David's head jerked in a familiar gesture that said, *Get over here
and knock me a kiss.* Ty did. He placed the softest butterfly of kisses
to his bruised left cheek.

*Oh God! His teeth. His beautiful teeth! What kind of cretin would do
this? I could kill those heartless motherfuckas! Kill 'em with my bare
fuckin' hands!*

Ty hoped the tooth horror wouldn't register on his face. But his
voice was choppy with regret. "What can I say, man? I should've
been by your side last night. None of this shit would've happened if
I'd been there with you. I'm sorry, man. So sorry…"

David scribbled, "Stop! Can't control me. Fuckin' cock-blocker!"

"But I never thought you'd wind up like this!"

Telegraphically, David said, *Save it. It's raw, ain't it? I know. Shit
happens. Feces occur. Not your fault. Whatever bleedin'-heart shit you're
feelin', save it for that damn book you'll finish one damn day. Just don't
clown me. Please don't stare at me like some soft, pathetic, eternal victim,
'cause when I'm healed I'll have to kick your ass!*

"I'll drop by later with some fashion mags and crossword puz-
zles. I could kick by your place and grab your most fetching robe so
you won't be all assed-out in this joint, 'kay?"

Ty's words hovered on the silent antiseptic air.

"Duch? Davy? What do you think? Would that be cool?"

"Thanks. Love you. Re-e-eal tired now. Sore," David scribbled, thinking, *Please just leave me the hell alone! I've had enough of this puttin' on a good face bullshit. Just go!*

"OK. I'll leave. But I'll be back. We all right, man?"

"Always," David scratched softly, turning painfully to bury his broken face in his pillow.

As Tyrone left, David closed his eyes and wondered why Face hadn't come to visit. It was so cold. Clearly, Face didn't give a fuck about him. Why?

* * *

Neither Face nor David shared the plug ugly truth with Tyrone, or the details of that desperate phone conversation. But Depina's final *fuck you* had deeply wounded David.

With Face Depina, you never knew which *face* you'd get. Would it be the Depina Brood or the Depina Grin? Would you be staring into the green pools of The Idol, The Moment Maker, The Boyishly Cool Heartbreaker, The Junkie, or The Jester? The one Face that David loved best was the dependable Face, who remembered their history and sometimes even said, *I think I love your fly little ass,* even if only with a wink of his eye.

But his *favorite* Face suddenly *turned all kinds of ugly* on David. That Face didn't wanna speak to *another freak in a fuckin' dress.* Fuck Adeva! No. He wanted to speak to the *original freak.*

"Whoever you are, fuckin' pervert, put David on the goddamn phone!" he demanded. "David. You there? What's the fuckin' profit in helpin' you? Huh? Ya ain't worth it. You done used that pitiful faggot routine one too many times. Now, if I paid your debts, would ya wanna *work* it off? Ya know, I could turn you out, put ya on the street and have you suck dick for profit. How's that, freak? What? Why you so quiet? Go 'head, tell me that shit *don't* appeal to you! Hello? David, you still there?"

After a long and painful pause, David handed the phone to his friend in drag.

"Whatever you said, you just broke his face. Are ya happy? Why you tryna hurt him? If this is about that stupid show, he apologized for that. He's sorry. But, he's, he's in trouble here. Please. At least come see him. You could talk, like you used to… Face? You know how he *feels* about you… David *loves* you!"

"Get a fuckin' life, faggot. And step the hell out of mine."

Click.

You stabbed me, Facey. I'm crouched down, doubled over in wild pain. Don't you see me? Don't you love me, even just a little bit? I'm bleeding. Did you really mean it?

Had Depina meant to stab David with the thought-out precision of those words? If you asked Face, he'd say: "Yes. It was his moment, his time to bleed. Now get over it!"

Still, worst of all, *why*, after the last harrowing hours of disturbing clarity, had David become so stupid? Was he one of those *love me love me please love me* people? He'd always pitied those needy human beings, who, no matter what was said or what vile thing was done to them, would still die *loving* their persecutors. David used to ask, "What up wid dat?" But, was *he* one of *those* tragically stupid people now?

* * *

Tyrone returned home, emotionally ass-kicked, and there, fresh from winning an important civil case, was Blur, stretched out on Ty's leather sofa. His locks were gone, replaced by a Caesar cut. But he was still hot in his staid wing tips, black socks, cock ring, and nothing else. He emitted his blatant *let's get fuckin' wild* gaze at Tyrone. And *getting fucking wild* was exactly what they were going to do. Tyrone took one look at that nakedness and propelled himself at it. No talk. No hellos. No, *I missed your hot, yellow, ambitious ass, now knock me a kiss.* No. Ty threw himself at it with a bullet's speed. Soon, all he wore were his Nikes…and Blur's fat balls as a muzzle. Maybe the veins of that stiff shaft could stifle his tears; Ty was practically inhaling it. Blur reached down and smacked Ty's ass, his heart suddenly beating in raving rhythms that mirrored his frantic lover's. Tyrone's hands, mouth, and emotions were everywhere at once. The crush of prick, belly, and groin fur couldn't smother him. But he *wanted* to be smothered. Then Blur aimed two spit-wet fingers inside his lover's anus, jabbing them, and Ty gripped hold like an angry vise. And still he gulped and lacquered as if to drown in, be strangled or impaled by pure carnal abandon.

"Easy! Ease up, babe-e-ee! It ain't going anywhere!" Blur sighed, half-joking, yet close to erupting down that savagely sucking throat. "You're gonna make me shoot before we fuck!"

Ty pried away, stared into those cocky eyes of Blur's, and with his voice the closest it had ever come to sounding menacing, hissed, "Let's fuck."

He was stiff and dripping when Blur slid a rubber along his inflamed firearm. Tyrone was ready to launch it inside his lover with a speed and force uncommon to his sexual norm.

Pulling Blur's legs to the end of the sofa, he grunted and lunged hard and deep. Tyrone wasn't on a thrusting mission just to bust his nut. He could hear his own heart beating a thousand times a minute, and it scared him. Fucking might cure it. Fucking might just be the elixir. Fuck something! Fuck everything. Fuck hard, and come. Fuck and maybe the world would make some small kind of temporary sense again.

David was hurting and so was he, and so was Blur for being there. Ty lunged with a swift velocity of pounding flesh, making the leather sofa beneath them screech from misery. Bucking and sweating, his wounded eyes filled with a wildness Blur Antonelli had never seen.

"Fuck! Fuckin' wild, Tyrone! Easy, man! That shit hurts!"

But it didn't ease the ire or calm the ineffectual fire in Tyrone's loins, heart, head, cock, and balls. With every hard and punishing lunge, he saw David's battered face with its missing teeth, multiple bruises, and heartbroken eyes. He remembered the embarrassed way those beautiful honey eyes could barely look at him. Tyrone's vengeful dick stabbed at the image of Face Depina for the cruel way he'd dismissed David. He slammed those faceless thugs, those motherfucking gay-bashing bullies who'd taken something unspoken and precious and *felt* from little David.

Blur roared the *roar* of a near-raped lion. The noise brought Tyrone back to the time, place, and *reality* of this weapon he punched headlong through his lover's anus. A lover howling in anguish, shaking and shooting, trembling, ejaculating from the pain of a man inflamed.

Shooting sparks rained in a gush to Tyrone's pounding chest. He dismounted Blur and heaved, and the anger shot clean out of him in violent white tears. And it seemed he couldn't stop shooting, hurling his hurting seed past Blur's dizzy head. It leapt from the cliffs of his pain to the floor like wet white suicides.

Eighteen

The Past Is a Hard Song to Dance to

The Duchess was still nowhere to be found. David had vacated his West Village pad, and left no forwarding address. Ty was frantic. He placed call after desperate call to mutual friends, turning up nothing.

"Why do people leave like that? It's like he just fuckin' died on me! Where is he, Blur?" A hopeless Tyrone asked what had become a suitcase of rhetorical questions. "Is David out there? Is he somewhere walking alone in this narrow-minded place, with all its narrow-minded hates and fists? I don't know where he could be, or if he's even in the city. Do you think he's still in town?"

"I don't know, Tyrone. But I've never been his keeper."

"You know, since being on the streets, volunteering at the soup kitchen, and just paying attention, I've stopped wondering why so many of us are stone drunk, or sucking pipe, or sticking a needle in a good vein at 3 A.M. I've stopped wondering why so many people are escaping and just saying 'Fuck it all'! I understand."

"Well I don't, and never will. I don't understand why there's even such a thing as crack, or horse, or even drag queens," Blur stated bluntly.

"That's because you never once tried to understand David, or any of my friends. A thousand people in this city will say fuck it today. Someone is saying it right now. They're saying 'fuck it' to life, or they're *fucking life* and its jagged little fucking days to shit. Or they're smoking, dropping, snorting, shooting something; anything, as long as it makes the mean and vicious shit go away. I really do understand the urge to say fuck it."

"Maybe it's just a 'fuck it' generation," Blur added.

"No. You're a lawyer and you don't even see. These are lost and shaky times, Blur. It's so much easier to say fuck it when you're lost."

Was David *lost?* It's easy to get lost in New York City. Tyrone imagined ghastly scenarios: David alone, in pain, and babbling in the Bowery. David carted off to Bellevue by the men in white. David bombed out of his mind on Thorazine, moving from place to place like an aimless ghost. David addled by amnesia, sleeping a sleep swept clean of dreams.

Ty read in the *Village Voice* about the brutal murder and burning of a drag queen, and wondered if somewhere out there David hadn't suffered the same kind of appalling slaughter. *No. I would know. Trick taught me to know. David's alive.*

Carrying David's picture, Ty walked the streets, cased all the haunts Davy once frequented. Area, Danceteria, Limelight, America. Where the fuck was he?

"Have you seen this cat? He's 5 foot 6, a hundred and thirty pounds, delicately muscular. His name is David."

Think like Davy. Where *was* that Wednesday Night Hot Body Contest? More than once, Ty stood in the middle of Washington Square Park, and shouted from the top of his scared and frustrated lungs, *"David Donatello Richmond, where the fuck are you?"*

If anyone knew, they weren't telling.

Ty saw Davy's disappearance as a personal rejection, though he was stymied for a reason. He blamed everyone for the vanishing. Face, for obvious reasons. And Adeva, with that silly tribe of drag queens. He blamed David's own foolish quest for love and attention. But most of all, *he blamed himself.*

Then David was gone so long, Ty grew pissed at him. *If I do ever see him again, I will kick his little troubled ass, and then I'll kiss him.*

* * *

David couldn't explain it at the time. He didn't want to explain, because *telling it* was far too painful. But after that beating, a vital light had gone out in his head, and he realized it was up to him to fix his faulty wiring.

It was the season for self-examination.

Do you really love yourself? Are you addicted to sex? Or are you just a contact junkie? Will you ever find Face waiting for you on a Martinique beach, in a backroom's dark, handing love's cock to you like a gift? How far does love go? Where is all this lo-o-ove getting you? What is it giving you, David, but a chronically broken heart, broken ribs, broken teeth, and broken feelings?

A PALE BLUE ROOM

Dr. Ted Horowitz was a balding man in his mid 50s. He wore wire-framed John Lennon specs housing pale blue eyes that were keen observers. He had a tendency to scratch his wrist at signs and subtle gists of deception. Initially, with David, there was excessive wrist scratching, until they managed to scratch beyond the surface of the truth.

"There's a very telling saying in my profession," Dr. Horowitz told David. "'If it's hysterical, it's historical.' In other words, whatever triggers a destructive behavior usually has its roots in childhood."

"My father was all I had. Without him, I would've had nothing to rebel against. I'm the man he made me, and he never learned to love the queer in me," David confessed. "I'm here to get well. And I'm not gonna if I don't tell the truth. See, Doc, my mother raised me on MGM musicals. Sometimes, she'd wake me up at 2 A.M. so we could watch Fred and Ginger, Fred and Cyd, Fred and Rita, or Fred alone just tappin' up a storm. See, she *understood* the dancer in me. When I was accepted to the Dance Theater of Harlem's Children's Program, no one was happier than my mother. She came to see my final recital, alone. My father couldn't be bothered. But she, oh, she was very proud. On the way back home she was telling me *just how proud* I'd made her feel, and then she was…tryna…say something else…"

David began to cry. "My mother was a very *graceful* woman. But all that grace, it suddenly left her. Then…she sort of *slumped* forward. A massive stroke. She was gone. I was *hysterical*. My father, he was something else. He never forgave me. I mean never! It was *all* my fault. Me and my faggot dancing! I really do believe he *wanted* Rico to beat that little faggot dancer out of me. He never understood that if Rico coulda, I woulda let him. Now I'm a broken boxer, a broken dancer, a broken little faggot, and I still like dick—even when the world wants me to believe this ain't the Decade of the Dick. Well, screw my father and *fuck* the world! I'm not gonna stop being gay, even if I do stop having sex with men."

"David, are you OK?"

"No! Why the fuck do you think I'm here?" He laughed, as he often did to cut through the pain.

"Well, if you feel you're ready, I'd like to hear about Face Depina."

"Oh! God! You don't ask for much, do you?" David sniffled, drying his eyes.

"High school was sweatin' season for curious fags. I saw a *vision*, and I *had* to know, 'Who are you? What are you? What are you into? How big is it? How dark is it? Can you make it do tricks?'"

"Seriously, David. This man's affected you in ways only you, your heart, and your mind can reveal. I think it's crucial that we talk about it."

"Ah, Facey," he began, his eyes clouding over. "He doesn't want me. I know that now. He wants a man he can spit on and still respect, like Chaz. They spit on each other, you know? Some people say hello. Those two hock on each other's faces, and it becomes something almost *sacred*. I can't compete with that."

"David, you're talking around the subject," Horowitz reminded.

"A long time ago, I taught him how to *dance*, and we shared our own private tango. We were people of the night, ya know. I remember the stars and streetlights cutting through the darkness that sharp cold winter night, and how we laughed. We were all coming back from the recording studio, after we'd cut our first song. We were high on the idea that we were about to be somebody.

"Tyrone's folks were gone, so we partied at his place, getting drunk on Hennessy, and high on Facey's spacey weed. We laughed like we were all such good friends, like the way I wanted it to be. But we never all got along at the same time, except when we were singing. Well, Ty and Browny passed out, and Facey and I sat up talking. There was a moment when I felt so *safe* that I broke down and told him my childhood horror story. He felt sad for me. And in return, he told me *his* horror story. He'd never told another soul those things. It all came spilling from his mouth. I knew he wasn't acting. No, Facey was *being real* with me. Suddenly, I felt closer to him. He'd never let anyone get that close, and once I got there, I thought I'd never lose it. It was in his eyes. We'd shared *this thing*, this *hurting thing* that most people would never even know about either of us, let alone understand.

"We were having the quietest conversation with our eyes. Then he went into Ty's bathroom, and after a while I followed him. It seemed like he was *waiting* for me. Waiting for me to come inside and go down on his sadness. For a minute, I think I actually sucked that sadness away. When it was over, that big pretty sad boy kissed my forehead and whispered, 'Thank you, Davy.' I never heard him sound more tender or fuckin' sweeter.

"But then, he acted like he was *too drunk* to remember any of it. We were one person that night, Doc. And he pretended like it *never happened*. Why? Did reaching that honest place with me make him feel too naked? Well, my attitude's always been, 'let's just be naked with each other, baby.' Naked can be beautiful, and revolutionary, too.

"For days his scent was everywhere, everyplace he was. He can pretend until we're dust that he was stupid-drunk. We were *both* drunk, Doc, and *truth* was our elixir."

* * *

"The other day, I saw this man. And I use the term as limply as a überqueen's wrist. He was berating his lover out in the street, just talkin' all kinds of cruel shit. 'Look! I don't want yo ass! I don't like bein' 'round no *faggots!* Brothers want somebody to come strong and hard like Black men should!' he yelled. It was my father and Rico and Facey all over again. I can't tell you how that affected me, Doc. Once, you said 'the goal was self-acceptance.' Well I *do* accept me. I ain't ashamed of who or what I am. I happen to like men. I happen be a superb fellatrix. I embrace that part of myself. It's my nature. People who think I'm *vulgar* can kiss this faggot's natural black vulgar ass!" David declared.

What Dr. Horowitz realized was that what David feared more than anything was the thought that he'd someday be alone.

"The lips, the throat, and yes, the anus, they're such selfish masters. They want what they want, and they usually get it," David announced. "Today's my birthday, Doc. I didn't get what I wanted. But that's OK. I'm here, I'm queer, and damn it, by now you must be used to it!"

"What was it that you wanted, David?"

"A gold-plated Eveready battery–operated foot-long dildo, of course," he giggled. "No, seriously. I wanted me some new love. Hell, it ain't even gotta be new. Any love."

For the most part, the boxer kept his guard up around Horowitz. The doctor was fairly sure that David's lisping, mincing queerer-than-thou spiel was a ruse. It seemed to color his speech when he was being comical or defiant. But his voice turned to a smoke and gravel baritone those times he allowed his truth, his *core truth* into the room.

"I used to want so many things, simple things, really. You think I'm *fine* now? You shoulda saw me at 15. I was ma-a-ad-crazy-sexy-cute. I had wild limbs, and a desire to live, dance, *love*, and do everything twice. I had energy, and this *do it fluid juice* runnin' through my veins. I was comin' into myself, and comin' all the time *with* myself. She-e-it! I was a raw piece of hot fruit just dyin' to be plucked from the vine. Remember being 15, Doc, when everything was new and in working order? All you're lookin' for is the opportunity to *work it*.

"I used to see straight people in love, walkin' hand-in-hand, kissin'. It seemed like the whole fuckin' hetero world was kissin' to remind me just how *wrong* my nature was. But what kind of freakishness lives inside me that makes me so fuckin' unworthy of love, huh? Hell. Every song on the radio was a love song. Didn't it ever occur to those songwriters, many of them queer, I'm sure, that queer 15-year-old copper boys needed love too?

"So I learned to *front* for love, for respect. I learned to hold the dick, scratch the pubic scratch, walk the cool, hip simian bop, throw a rap. Hell, I did whatever was required of me to snatch a little piece of love from the jaws of suffering. I used my charm, my muscles, my fists, and finally, my tongue. I wrapped my lips around Rico and something in that pulse *felt* like love. Well, I know now that ain't love, and that's OK. Right now, I'll settle for the respect to walk down any street and not be called a faggot, not be reduced or dishonored, disrespected, discarded, or *dissed* in any way. Even if I'm flamed-out to my boa-flourishin' extreme, I want people to look in my eyes, and see me, Davy, because what the fuck does the rest of it really mean, anyway? See, David! He's a helluva cat, and a kitten too, sometimes.

"I'm pretty sure I've had more sex than most of your patients. Trust me on that. Yet, I still remember the few sweet times somebody made *love* to my ass. No pun intended. But what I keep missin' is that one in a million motherfuckers who loves me for me. Not because I'm a fly dancer, or because I'm available. I want a man who sees all the good shit inside me. Then we could fuck till they hear our hot howlin' asses in Hoboken."

* * *

"Taking inventory, today I glanced in the mirror, naked, and I didn't blanch once. Well, maybe Black folks don't blanche. But I thought, 'G'on girl! You ain't so vile.' Got this nice smooth copper Venus skin. My friend Ty once described my eyes as 'luminous orbs of amber fire,' and I *like* that. Still got a dancer's body, and I got it the hard way. Plus, I got an ass like a Chevy pickup. So what if I tend to laugh a little too loud, or swish just a little too much. I don't live for the comfort or approval of uptight assholes. I'm a good person. I've been around, Doc. I see how people are. I realize, I don't *have* to be a good person to achieve great sparkling things, or to have great things thrust at me. But I am. I've got a good heart, too.

"I have a life. But it's not the life I want. I have friends. Some are gone, and some don't want the same things I want. When I'm feeling alone and unappreciated, I go to the theaters. There's too much loneliness out there, Doc. Sometimes you have to swallow it, before it swallows you. But in those hot places I go, loneliness sits erect inside a stranger's fist, and it says, *'Hello. Look at me! I'm just like you!'*

"You find a strange kind of popularity in those places, Doc. And everyone's cute in the dark. So I go down slowly on loneliness. I make it sigh and melt away on my tongue. Because, believe me, this is one Sissy-of-Color who truly knows the flavor."

The Doctor looked on, surprised at last by the raw honesty of David's words.

"Now, some judgmental people might think that's pathetic or sluttish, or dangerous these days. And maybe they're right. But those nameless motherfuckers, shining and erect in that theater, they're *all* my lovers. Doesn't matter if they're black or brown, white or yellow. When loneliness comes down and it hurts too much to talk about, they need to sink inside something moist, deep, and boundless as their own longing. Maybe I *am* just a whore. A little man who dances and dresses in drag sometimes. But I'm an *artist*, damn it! I create pleasure. If you could ask any of those men spinnin' under my tongue, they'd swear I was some rejected angel come to light on them. And when they unload, I spit it out so quietly they can't even hear their loneliness hitting the come-stained floor, baby Doc!"

He wiped his willful mouth, refusing to be ashamed. The room grew quiet with the silent rhythm of things felt but left unsaid. David had taken to smoking. His hands fluttered about, tapping, reaching into his chest pocket, needing, itching to light a cigarette. But he knew it was prohibited in the doc's office.

"Well, Doc. Looks like you've got your work cut out for you."

"Next week, David, I'd like to delve more into the issues of your private life."

"Day-yum, Doc. Do it *get* any more private? I'm runnin' out of material!"

* * *

That night, David drifted into the Adonis Theater. A man bathed in flickering silver light sat next to him. His breathing, his lust came in a scent that rose slowly between them. He gazed at David. David ignored him. Then this man exposed his erect bronzed beauty. David quivered. With no words, only hot eyes and that disembodied sigh lust sometimes makes, David went down on him.

The man tasted restless as the night—long, hot, and lonely.

When the magic was over, David expected nothing. It came as a happy shock when this burly brown shadow kissed him and said, "Oh! I want some more of you. Let me take you home and fuck you all night with the lights on."

It was an invitation David seldom received, and it sounded like Latin jazz, like salsa, and the harp strings of an erotic heaven all at once.

His name was Carlos. David liked the way he rolled the r.

Together, they stood, letting their cocks lead them up the aisle and out into the warm, enigmatic night.

* * *

A different David walked into his next session proclaiming, "I'm in love, y'all! Sweet, sweet, thick and juicy, gooey-rich *love*, Baby-doc! His name is Car-r-rlos. He's a big ol' luscious russet Daddy who doesn't fuck. But, *ay caramba*, he makes slow, levitating *love!* And *love*, my sissies, is The Best Dick of All! I tell you, this is *big love! Mira! Mi hombre es gusto! Mi corazón es muy GRANDE!*"

"Random encounters ask nothing more of us than gonadal inter-est," Dr. Horowitz offered. "True love rarely happens in an instant, in the course of a night, or a few weeks. What is it that you love? Is it the physical, or is it something spiritual you feel you've found in this Carlos?"

"It's both, Doc. He calls me 'Puppito.' Just the sound of it gives me a big ol' warm-fuzzy. He looks at me with shiny eyes like I'm some-body precious. And the sex. Oh! God! Have you *evuh* had a man spend an entire hour on your nipples? Just your nipples? Pulling, licking, slowly suckin', I mean to the point of being worshipful. Tellin' you how special they are, how special *you* are. And when you come, damn it, you want to cry from the pure and joyful nut of your *soul!* That's *bliss*. And that's what Carlos gives *me* nightly."

The doctor crossed his legs to hide his erection.

* * *

"The other day, I was walking home from the clinic with Carlos. He has his good days, and his bad. This one wasn't such a bad day until some *punk* yelled as he passed us, 'Fuckin' faggots! Hope you all fuckin' die from that shit!'

"I ain't no punk. It made me so mad, I *know* I coulda kicked his ass! But there's Carlos dying a little more and my fuckin' back's against the wall and I can't kick *everybody's* ass. And the world's tellin' me to *be a man*, and all the time it keeps kickin' me in the fuckin' balls!

"Doc, if you listen very close, you can hear the sound of balls breakin' all up and through this room, and this city. Sometimes I just wanna cry for days. We've all been beaten down, broken down, black-balled, gay-bashed! We've been told we're too this and not enough of that! Can't be trusted. Despised worldwide. Diseases takin' us out like fuckin' assassins! Multi-colored motherfuckers workin' 24-7 tryna break your spirit! It's hard, damn it. It's hard!"

The room was full of emotion. David's eyes watered, his face was breaking in two.

Dr. Horowitz thought maybe, just perhaps, they'd reached a breakthrough. "Well," he said, "*you* more than most understand the crush of that kind of isolation, pain, and humiliation. So you might very well want to hit something, strike out, break or take something, because you feel some part of your being has been broken and taken from you. It seems to me that experiencing some of mankind's ugliness would give you better insight. If fighting against the Power outside you isn't working, maybe you need to fight *for* the Power within. Trust whatever you believe in—God, divine justice, karma, or whatever to take care of the confusion, the ignorance, and all the rest of those mean and hateful things out there."

David embraced "Baby-doc" for the first time before leaving.

* * *

It had begun to storm. Rain and wind whipped his skin like shards of broken glass. David headed home to Carlos. They kissed for 30 minutes, then *did it* doggie style on the kitchen table. Between thrusts, Carlos sighed, emitting the poems of Federico García Lorca to David's taut, cocoa bung hole.

When it was over, Carlos noticed tears in David's eyes.

"Puppito. What's wrong?"

"Nothing. I'm just happy to be out of the rain."

Nineteen

The Play Is the Thing

One day, out of the clear indigo, Tyrone's phone rang. Because he was on his computer and not wanting to lose his flow, he let the machine answer. Suddenly, the voice on the other end cooed: "Imagine, if you still can, you're sittin' in the dark. A large dark man stands behind you. You turn, and all you see is *crotch*. Lots and lots of crotch. I mean it's all up in your face. And unless he's packing a plantain inside a double pair of tube socks, he's *huge!* And the music and the drums, and your pulse are all thumpin': 'Gotta get you some. Go'n get you some!' Are you with me?"

Ty dashed to the phone asking, "Whoisthis?" though, through weary rainy eyes he already knew.

"It's your queerest half, baby boy. I'm ba-a-ack. Have you been a good boy? Of course you have. Wanna hear somethin' unbelievable? So have I, and we both know that's so much *harder* for me."

"Duchess! You fuckin' heartless, negligent, absentee bitch! Where the hell have you been? *How* you been? You know I've got gray hairs worrying about your callous uncaring ass! Would serve you right if I stopped caring and junked your ass altogether."

"Please. You couldn't if you tried. Listen. Tonight, we'll get very drunk, and we'll talk and laugh and cry and maybe I'll try to explain it all…"

* * *

"I've met this wonderful man. His name is Carlos. I've never been happier. You'd like him. He's a poet of the heart." Then David's face hardened. "But my poet's leavin' me, Ty, in a very unpoetic way. We're running out of reason and rhyme. And the saddest part is, I think I know now what it is to be *truly* devastated."

"Do you need anything? Does he? Tell me what I can do," Ty asked.

"Yeah. I need you to tell me something good and wonderful and true about yourself, 'cause I've missed that."

"Well, let's see… I missed you man, and missing my peeps, it's made me very introspective. I'm writing again, from the soul. Things are happening." Ty launched into a tale about irony—about how youthful disappointment can lead to adult fulfillment. "Remember me telling you about this white cat who tried to kick a young ambitious Brother's creativity to the curb?"

"Oh, yeah…"

* * *

Neither man acknowledged remembering the other. Though Feld recalled the tall brown boy in green corduroy with something to say, but who lacked the experience or mastery to say it. And Tyrone most definitely recalled a terse, slick taker of dreams.

Tyrone had to remind himself that he wasn't a glutton for punishment, since this time he'd been recommended to Feld by the editor of a lifestyle magazine.

Feld now presided over his own agency; and sitting across from him at a large oak desk, Ty noticed he'd acquired this *Omar Sharif thing*. Those clinging dark Pepsi Cola eyes. That old-world mustache, cut thin, but not so thin as to be *merry*. The thick bank of mixed gray waves that had begun to recede a bit. At 44, he was a striking man—suave, polished, urbane. A seasoned intellect emanated from his cosmopolitan demeanor, tailored Italian suit, and perfect manicure. He smelled divine—subtly French, and expensive. Ty could invent all kinds of stories about a man such as this. *But why would I bother? It's not like I'm attracted to him...*

"This has promise," Feld said, tracing the pages with a sensuously thick index finger. "There's potential, here. But this is all very..."

Uh-oh. OK, you elitist fuck, you better come correct with me or I'm out!

"Your characters talk, a lot," Feld said, followed by, "Take a deep breath. That's not necessarily a bad thing. I feel this could be reshaped somehow. Mamet's big now. Lots of realism and gritty language. What do *you* think?"

What Ty thought was *Bet! Then, let's do this!* He'd never set the world on fire with his first *enfant terrible* diatribe. But with this, a play about the cool skin of strangers, the cruel heartbreaks, fast flirts, the false starts and flutters of love, and the pain of being Black and gay in the diseased and fear-ridden '80s...

The work was rewritten, but not without creative differences—maddening battles, tantrums, and other tempestuous shit. Ty wrote and Feld critiqued. One artistic clash of wills resulted in a blowout: "Don't you dare question the legitimacy of these feelings. These are *my* feelings, damn it! Every black and blue one of them. Either you want it real, or you want it fake. If you want fake, find a beige synthetic writer. This is what it is, and if you can't relate, fuck you, this play, and the rest of this fake half-baked shit!"

Neither gave in, and Tyrone walked away from the project, unwilling to surrender completely to another man's wishes, to give up *his* good fight. He would rather have written for free and never let another soul read his words. After a week, Feld called, and the two talked and squawked like two opposing intellectual bitches. Then Ty thought of Trick, Jerome, Jazz, and all the rest. And he agreed to forge ahead.

There were more demands, changes, and disagreements. But

then a miraculous thing occurred. The play, in previews, received *extremely* favorable notices. One early review read: "Electric! Angry and hopeful. *Bestest Friends* is a play of biting characters and razor-sharp words that cut through the pathology of our times. This story attaches itself to the thinking gay brain like a tumor." By the time the show reached off Broadway, there was a buzz, and the word-of-mouth was: *Baby, pay attention!*

Tyrone was pleased that most everyone he knew came to see the opening of his long-nourished creation. David, and a nearly sober Browny, the guys from the paper, folks from the magazine, people from his writing class, student friends, his college drama professor. Even Face showed up, with Chaz—of all people—in tow. Everyone was surprised to see Face blow through. Tyrone, especially. Blur, with whom Ty was "on again," was working in D.C., so he sent flowers.

It was a fantastic opening, followed by a fabulous party, but before it was over, Tyrone left. He went back to his apartment to be alone with his thoughts, and to quietly commune with Trick's ghost: "You should be here, man. You should be here, laughing, dancing, and drinking. You should be here makin' love with me until we're both fuckin' raw! All I got is a fucking ghost whispering the way in my ear!"

"But you ain't never needed *me* to do this, Tyronni. You the Poetry Man. You make things all right. Did little white Dorothy need the Great and Powerful Oz cat? Shit, no! All you needed was a peep inside your heart. Now how about a life? Don't ya want one of them? You cheat me and everyone who ever believed in your ass if you don't live your motherfuckin' life, Poetry Man. This here is *your* time. What you *need* to do is get your ass back to that party and dance like we'd *both* be dancin'. Live a life, Ty."

"A life? A life, Trick? Haven't you been watching? That was one of those tricky Trick dances I never did get quite right."

"It's all in the steps, homey. The first one is a left, then a right, and before you know it, you out the door," Trick advised before his voice, and perpetually crooked-smiling image, disappeared.

When Ty opened the door, there stood Feld. Ty was surprised, but happily so.

Tyrone had noticed that while the play was in previews, Feld had stopped wearing a wedding ring.

Feld said, "I came by because you left the party before I could tell you I'm proud of you, Ty. I've watched you work, struggle, question, and explore. And you've developed into a very good writer. More importantly, you're an extraordinary young man. And I like you a great deal. But being around you, lately, has been fucking with my perspective. I just can't do it anymore."

"What are you saying? That…"

In one leaping action, Feld grabbed him by the collar, silencing his words with the sure and blunt punch of dick sliding against dick. Feld's flesh was hard.

"I don't know about you, Ty, but I think we're good together," he said, eyes fixed, lips dangerously close.

Tyrone experienced an uncertain flush of weirdness. What was Feld going to say? What words of wisdom, warning, or woe was this agent whom he now considered a friend going to say?

"Your play is about truth, isn't it? When you break it down, there is just the truth, right? Tell the truth! Just say it!"

But before Ty could say anything, Feld grabbed him by the swing-low. Feld's lips moved in close, then suddenly were on top of Ty's, smashing hard, strong, and savage, saying everything he'd wanted to say, everything he'd felt and tried to hide. In one burning flash, Ty's blazer was ripped away.

"I've been wanting *this* since the day I met your cocky green corduroyed ass," Feld said, his large hands tugging at Ty's sweat-soaked shirt. "We're about to do something dangerous."

"Yeah. Lets do it."

Shirts flew away. As Feld boldly locked the door, Ty found himself strangely at odds with *a whole other aesthetic*: A thick and shaggy pelt so dense the man's nipples were barely visible. Everything about Feld was shaggy and heaving, and the pipe down his leg was threatening to burst through the seams of his tuxedo pants. Feld ran his lips along Tyrone's torso, feasting on the lean brown slopes of his shoulders and chest. He gripped the firm dark nipples, suctioning each keen tit. With hands tracing, racing over each other's flesh, they fell to the sofa, gripping, groping at zippers.

Yes! What a long hot tool, you've got, Tyrone... Feld thought, staring at Ty's ringed phallus. Dipping down, he coated Tyrone in slow and sensuous sucks. Then, taking a breath, he swallowed the spike to its root. Ty studied the full pulsing cap darting between Feld's bushy legs. It was much more than an ample *shmeckel*. It was hard, sturdy, and attached to a man Ty could respect. Just as Ty was deciding whether to descend or not to descend, the buzzer buzzed—and buzzed loudly.

It was David, with a bottle of Dom and a big Hawaiian gift of a celebratory shlift.

"Sweetheart! Open up! I know you're in there! Don't start playin' the star with me, ya literary bitch! I still got a key, you know?" he said in a singsong reminder. "Don't make me use it!"

"Ignore him!" Feld insisted, sucking, gasping, running hands along humping curves of cheeks. His slurping nearly drowned out the noise of the rain, buzzers, and indecision. His tongue lashed feverishly at Tyrone's crevice, lapping, teasing its dark bud out of hiding. Ty stroked a trailing web of down to what lay plush pink and rigidly poking from Feld's fist.

Feld hissed, "Yeah, let's see if we fit."

Ty gazed at those thirsty brown eyes and that raw-red erection, which, having doubled in size, had become just about the fattest cock he'd ever seen on a man who wasn't Black or Latino or enlarged on a screen. Feld rose, all six feet, 200 pounds, and nearly nine inches of him.

"I'm growin' old and haggard in this fuckin' hallway! All right?" Davy huffed. "You bet not have nobody in there..."

"This...this can't happen," Ty said suddenly. "We can't let it. This wasn't meant to be, Conny. We both know that." Ty pushed away and tucked himself away and buzzed up David.

"It's the *race* thing, isn't it? Isn't it?" Feld said. "Admit it! You're afraid I wouldn't be the right arm piece, huh? Not the *acceptable* scenery for your pro-Black stance?"

"You know me better than that! It ain't political—just too personal. And this place we were about to go, it's not a *professional* place, Conny. I'd like to keep you, and your presence in my life, but only as a friend and a *professional* colleague!"

It seemed a most *ridic* statement, considering he was still wet with his colleague's spit, and the irony was not lost on either of them.

"Besides," he added, "in my experience, friends last longer when they're not fuckin' each other."

Feld eyed him with vague disgust as he quickly dressed. He felt *used*. Maybe it *was* political. Maybe all Ty ever wanted was to be a success, at any cost.

David entered, flying through the door, bottle in one hand, playbill in the other.

"Oh my! What have we here? Hello," he said dubiously to Feld. "Leaving so soon? Why Tyrone, you little coquette!" he teased, rolling his eyes.

"Shut up, David! It's not like that."

"No. Not when *I have a key* it isn't. Well, Mr. Feld you're welcome to share in some bubbly with us…"

"Thanks, but no thanks. Three's a mismatched crowd." He exited, leaving the door open in his wake.

"Well, I just hate to be a saboteur!" David yelled, cocking his head around the corner and watching Feld walk down the hall. Then, noting the open door, he said, "Symbolic, don't you think?" David sniffed the air. "Mmm. I just love the way that man smells. It's all Paris, and Greece, and (*sniff*) *dick*! Dick? And sweaty ass? *Ooh!* I'm a tell somebody!"

"Shut the hell up, *Swish* Cheese!"

David smiled devilishly, "Well, Tyronique, looks like timing *is* everything. Now, let's get our party started."

The champagne opened with a *pop*, and flowing white foam exploded into the air. "So," Davy asked, bringing the suds to his lips, "my youngish, but rapidly aging Black man, you sure there's nuttin' you wanna *tell* me about you and the oh-so-dashing Mr. Almost Sharif?"

There *was* something to tell him, something Ty couldn't quite believe himself. There was no denying a part of Ty might've enjoyed a little interracial bozack to *shmeckel* mambo with Feld. But that vital Africanus Ambitious Rex who dwelled within would've forever questioned what part *emotions and dick* played in his success.

In the midst of champagne and chitchat, the phone rang and a half-drunken Ty allowed his machine to take the call. Suddenly, Bliss Santana's voice filled the room:

"Hey, Honey Boy, it's me. I am so sorry I couldn't be there for your big night. If you're celebrating, good for you. But listen, we have to talk. It's about Tyra. I can't do this on the phone, OK? I'm in Atlanta, but I'll be in New York next week. We'll talk then. I love you, Honey Boy. Bye. And Ty, congratulations!"

"Who the hell is *Tyra?*" asked David.

FEBRUARY 1991

One seasonably chilly day in Chelsea, Ty and Bliss—two weeks out of rehab—were walking together when Ty happened to catch their reflections in the glass of a passing car. *Hmm*, he thought. *Interesting couple*. For a split second, he'd forgotten who they were. He thought he looked sexy with her on his arm.

"You look *new*," he said. "You really do. Daddy's proud, baby-girl."

"About time, don't you think? My fuckin' life was about big hair, big jewels, big drugs, and big men. I'm downsizing, now. Sometimes a girl needs a new face and friendlier eyes to show it to," she said. "I'm starting from scratch. No crutches, no pretty-faced assholes, and no more fucking anesthetizing," she proclaimed in that seductive scuff of a voice.

Tyrone actually believed her. "You know, sometimes the best way to *get out of yourself* is to get involved in something larger," Ty told her as he lead her *not* to a glitzy premier or a groovy downtown überclub, but to a bare-knuckles soup kitchen in the heart of Chelsea. There they helped serve and feed 150 strangers.

A frequent volunteer to that and other shelters, Ty had gotten to know many of the people there. "That's Sonny over there in the frayed hat and raincoat. He lost his whole family in a fire and gave up on life. The lady in the black scarf, she lost her job and after two months was evicted. Had to leave her kids with a sister until she could get it together. Then the sister up and moved. Took the kids, and never told her where. No job, no house, no kids, no hope."

And so the stories went.

Bliss noticed that Sonny's attire seemed vaguely familiar.

"Tyrone? *Please* tell me that man's *not* wearing the $450-dollar raincoat I bought you two Christmases ago!"

"Oops, sorry. But it never *was* my style. Besides it was a very *dry* season."

If Bliss was pissed she didn't reveal it. Instead, she shook her head, exasperated, yet exhilarated. "This is some fuckin' date, ya stupid-ass bastard! But you know what? It's just what my spoiled and pampered ass needed. You think it would be all right if I come again, and maybe bring some clothes and things I don't need anymore?"

Ty looked at her and smiled, glad that his prized instincts were on the money.

What a rare and beautiful man you are, she said in her mind. *A person like you should have a powerful force of love in his life.*

But at that moment he didn't. He and the ballistically ambitious Blur were once again on the outs.

Back at Bliss's apartment, as Ty was saying goodbye, the look in her face became strange and devious and tangibly sexy. Something had grown between them. Bliss Santana *had* play, and the play was the thing. She gently touched his hand, kissed it softly, and then placed it on her breast.

Bliss! Stop! This ain't gonna work, baby girl!

She placed his hand lower, and then lower, and lower still. He was amazed at how easily she made tears in his hand, and how she turned misunderstanding into flashes of lightning. "Come to Mami," she purred. And she fashioned a place for him to fall, a net of moist wet skin to catch his sad and endless longing.

No rubber was involved.

October 1991

"So. Guess I have to give it one mo try. Who the hell is Tyra?" David asked.

"Tyra? I...I think she might be my daughter."

A champagne-swilling David stood up quickly, very quickly, and then he promptly *fainted*.

"Well, mine or Face Depina's," Ty said.

But David was out cold and did not, *could not* hear that little addition.

Twenty

This Is Not My Beautiful Decade

THE '90s

It was the dawn of Generation X. No more slick, glossy extravagance; everything was downsized. Even the Gulf War proved a streamlined affair. It was time to *keep it real*. Real as gangsta rap, real as a Rodney King beat-down. Real as the L.A. riots. Real as the *unrest* in Crown Heights, Brooklyn. Real as a sailor slaughtered in a men's room. Race and race violence, sex and sex abuse, gays and homo-haters were screaming on talk TV. Oprah, Geraldo, Imus, Stern, Sally, Phil, Jerry, and Ricki—it seemed everyone would get their 15-minute groove on. TV screens grew bigger; phones, smaller; and cellies were glued to most every ear. Personal computers gave way to the Internet.

The City elected its first *African-American* mayor.

A sprawling disease clenched its fist and took on *new* prisoners...

In 1991, Magic Johnson got *it*. Upon this sobering news, Tyrone called his homey to ask the question most everyone was asking that November night. "David? Did you hear? Did you hear about Magic?"

"Yes, I heard. I spent some time in L.A. But I swear *we* never knocked Nikes! Or in his case, clacked Converses," he deadpanned.

"David, I'm serious. Please! I *want* you to finally get tested."

The silence on the other end was deafening.

"David, do you hear me? Hello? Hell-the-fuck-low!"

"Maybe I don't wanna know. Maybe I wanna live my life without fear. *Maybe* I'll die not knowing."

"Oh, yeah? Well, *maybe* you're just a pointless, unapologetic ass-hole on a suicide mission. Maybe you're not as decent and right-minded as I *thought* you were. Maybe you're just some fuckin' serial killer on the lam. Ever *maybe* think about that?"

David hung up. The two would not speak again for months.

The following day Tyrone left the U.S., and the Third World awaited.

November 1991

Ty grew a soul in Africa. More precisely, he *realized the existence of his soul* in Botswana amongst the Bushmen moving across the Kalahari Desert. They were a yellowish-brown people, short in stature yet tall of spirit. They worked cattle posts and farms, spoke in clicks, and each year, after the first rains of November, they moved en masse 20 to 30 miles from their villages. And Ty photographed them. Their survival depended upon killing prey with poison darts and digging up the roots of plants for food. Still, they trekked through the desert toward a new home.

It was a humbling experience, and it succeeded in teaching Tyrone just how little was needed to replenish one's life, to start anew.

Spring 1992

Ty was back in the states working as a photojournalist for *Current Magazine* when he got a call to fly out to the West Coast. His editor wanted him in L.A. to cover the Rodney King verdict.

Tyrone, like most of the country, had been watching and waiting for America to show her true colors. Tyrone would be there for the aftermath. From the back of a rented van, he managed to freeze-frame the flames of unrest. It was not glossy, but an up-close and personal view, in Black, brown, and bloody. While the electronic media videotaped the stunning results of Madness Incarnate, his stills illustrated a profane savagery waged by the Frankensteins that injustice created: men, women, kids, whole families enraged. He captured people running in tantrums, looting in droves, frantically pulling drivers from vehicles, bashing heads, beating them down and screaming: "*Fuck the police!*"

For three days a city burned. For two of them, Ty didn't sleep. There was no time to sleep.

His photographs cold-cocked the public with truth. Violence as a spectator sport, granting Ty another of his bouts with miniscule celebrity. But he did not *want* celebrity, especially at that cost.

"In this country, you kill someone and suddenly *you're the shit, mad famous*," Ty wrote in an opinion piece. He wanted better from life, but the riots put a tragically sad face on his childlike view of the future. Sometimes he thought he was born to feel things deeply, and that the pain in him might be generic—not wrapped up in God, or lost lovers, or ego, or mother, or father, or race, or sexuality, or even disease.

JANUARY 1991

Chaz walked in on Face in The War Room performing a crude fist act on a young blond prince. Howling mad, Chaz tore up the place. The nude offender ran screaming from the loft. The incident was squashed…and that night the sex between Chaz and Face was hotter than ever. Things were back to kinky-as-usual until about two weeks later when the lusty blond in question approached Face at a film opening, and boldly kissed him hard on the mouth.

"Motherfucker! Who *are* you? Don't you ever put yo fuckin' mouth on him! Mangy ass son of a skinny bitch! " Chaz blared. Then Chaz hit him hard, just once. Blond boy landed soundly on the red carpet, completely unconscious.

"My bodyguard. Just got a little carried away, that's all. It's cool, it's cool," a quick on his feet Face told the curious paparazzi behind flashing cameras. It sounded reasonable.

"Fuck you! Bodyguard my ass! You think anybody believes that shit?" Chaz bellowed.

"Shut up, Chaz. Shut the fuck up, man!" Face warned through clenched teeth, visibly nervous and angry.

A local gossip rag picked up the story and decided to run it as a blind item: "Which once red-hot male model got caught in a melee with his famously always-there bodyguard and a society prince with a penchant for S/M? Looks like sooner or later these princes of denial will have to come clean…"

January 1991

Bliss Santana waited in a rented Jaguar in the The West Village. It was that misty hour custom-tucked for sleepwalkers, tardy vampires, slut renters, and men who believed tricks were for kids. The Jaguar was parked outside Face Depina's loft. When he finally bopped home fresh from a long day's journey through another abusive night, she shouted, "Pascal? Pascal! It's me. Get in. We need to talk."

Oh, no, not this clingy bitch! Not today! Not now! "Hey, Bliss. What's goin' on?" he said in the chronically bored voice he reserved for people with vaginas.

"Get in and I'll tell you," she said, opening her leather trench to reveal the soft, light-caramel planes of her nakedness.

Aw shit! This crazy, desperate freak! I can't do any more sick chicks! "Look, Bliss, it's either too late or too early for this shit. Go home! We'll talk or fuck or talk while we fuck later."

"As charming and tempting as that shit sounds, Pascal, we really need to talk now. So please…get in now, or be madly, deeply, truly sorry tomorrow."

"What? You gonna kill yourself again? How the hell you s'posed to kill yourself jumpin' out a basement window? This shit's getting old, and so are you around the eyes."

"I never did like you like this! When Pascal switches into Face, and Face is all high and spacey, saying things he doesn't mean. But you're high and spacey a lot lately, aren't you?"

"Fine," he agreed. "I'll get in, but just a minute 'cause I'm feelin' sick and I'm real tired."

The two took off onto the Westside Highway. Bliss didn't say anything, but her eyes blurred with tears.

"So what the fuck's goin' on, huh? You got me. What the *fuck* do you want, Blister?"

She mustered her strength, took a deep breath and she said it. "I'm pregnant. It's yours. Do we abort or what?"

"Aw-w-w. You pregnant, for real?"

"For real," she said, taking his shaky hand and placing it on her belly. "Wanna feel?"

But all he could feel was ill.

"Seriously? You pregnant, and it's mine? Not Claudio's or Julio's or maybe *Tyrone's?*"

"Sorry. I'm not half the whore you take me for."

He held his head in his hands, rubbing his eyes, trying to make it all go away.

"Bliss, you *know* how I feel about kids. I don't want none. Never did, and you knew that. Nothin' worse in this fuckin' world than some unwanted kid! Are you stupid? Did ya think you'd keep me this way? No. No babies. Not now, not ever! Damn you! You shoulda been more careful."

He looked wired and nervous. He was starting to tic inside his skin. By then, that creepingly familiar gnaw settled in his belly. He knew what it was.

"Pull over. I'm sick. Pull the fuck over!" His voice was shrill as a siren.

It wasn't an easy trick pulling over on the Westside Highway, but Bliss found the skinniest of shoulders. Face got out and vomited all that was left inside him. *She's pregnant? A baby? And it's mine? Fuck, fuck, fuck, FUCK!* He opened the door, got back inside. Then, with green eyes weighed down by a sickly seriousness he said, simply, "Get rid of it!"

"So, we abort," she said coldly, staring at the white lines of the highway exploding beneath the wheels of the now speeding Jag. She applied more pressure to the gas pedal.

"And you need to slow the fuck down! You too emotional."

"The sky," she said. "Look at all those colors. You know, the sky hasn't cried in such a long time. But I think the clouds have been meaning to," she said.

"What the hell you talkin' 'bout? Just take me home!" Face clutched his belly and leaned against the passenger window.

"I'm talking about crying. Don't you want to cry with me, Pascal?"

"Fuck no, I don't wanna cry!"

"Then would you like to *die* with me?"

"Don't fuck with my head. I'm sick, damn it!"

"Yes. I know you're sick. And except for that one time three and a half months ago, I've long stopped fucking with you!" She looked at him and wondered in that moment if his beautiful pitifulness had succeeded in driving her crazy, and if she *was* crazy, would she *know*? And could she stop being crazy if she just said "no"?

"Pascal. You said to get rid of it. So I'm about to, right here and now."

It was that first yellow shout of dawn. The highway hadn't yet been overtaken by rush-hour traffic. The road was dotted by delivery trucks and 18-wheelers, lots of them, zooming, zooming, z-z-z z-z-z-z z-z-zooming by. The speedometer glided from 70 to 75 and pushed up on 80.

"See, now I know you're crazy. You better stop fuckin' around, Bliss! Slow down!"

Eighty became 85, then 90.

"Slow down, Bliss! Baby, slow the hell down! See that, you missed that last exit. What you doin'? Take your foot off the gas, you fuckin' crazy pregnant stupid bitch!"

Nothing he said registered. Even if it had, *she* was feeling sick now. Sick of his voice. Sick of his promiscuity, his moods, his friends, his jiggling Lolitas, his excuses…the whores, the boys in leather, the groupies. She was sick of how he and the rest of it made her feel. Most of all, she was sick of loving him.

But she couldn't stop even though she wanted to.

She wished there wasn't a baby in her womb. And she wished it wasn't his. She wished it was Tyrone's. Maybe then it would be kinder, gentler, loving, and *healthy*.

"Oh God, I'm so sorry, baby." Face said out of fear. "I'm sorry. Sorry for everything. *Everything*, you hear me?"

He said *everything* as if he knew he had *it* and had *given it* to her and their baby.

"I never meant to hurt you Bliss. I don't know why I do shit sometimes. I'm sorry. I mean it. Now, please slow the fuck down!"

"People used to say we looked good together, Pascal, and you ate it up. We were elegance, walking hand-in-hand with a lie. They even wrote about us in *Vogue*, remember? I doubt they'll recognize that same beautiful brown green-eyed couple after our violent abortion. Do you think? No, of course you don't. You never do."

"Slow. The fuckin'. Car down, Bliss. Please! Slow down, before you kill innocent people!"

"Nobody's innocent anymore," she said.

For some reason Face rubbed his one physical flaw, that nasty scar on his left arm, and a question posed long ago by Claudio flooded his mind: "So whatever happened to old Erik? You know, that Viking dude with the machetes and the mean streak. The one who hooked you up?"

"He died in a fire at the beach house," Face had admitted, his voice tinged with a strange octave of memory.

"Yo! Bliss! Look out for that truck! Get away from the fuckin' truck, Bliss! Please, slow down!"

"You afraid of trucks, Pascal? There's still so much I don't know about you. But I know you used me! I was a perfect beard for you, wasn't I?"

This mad-crazy bitch is doin' 100 MPH on the fuckin' Westside Highway!

"That's why I'm naked under this coat. Your public will think we were two insatiable lovers who couldn't keep our hot hands off each other, and that we were fuckin' our brains out when we reached our wailing, bloody-red climax. See, even after everything, I'm still trying to protect *my man!* Now ain't that *love?*" She swerved around one 18-wheeler into the lane of another. Horns blew.

God, not like this! Not with this crazy bitch! Do something to stop this shit right now. Say something!

"Bliss, this is stupid! Look. Let's don't be stupid, let's be crazy. Let's do completely nuts. Let's get married. I'll…I'll marry your ass if you want! You hear? We can do this. Bliss, we could raise the kid, together. Bliss, slow down! Bliss, baby, you hear? You my boo. Bliss, there's a kid in this shit. Slow the fuck down, baby. Slow the fuck down, baby…" He finished in a whisper. And the *baby* in that whisper reached her.

She eased off the gas, and she did slow the fuck down. A baby was worth more than this. A baby, even sick, was worth more than him or her or them together.

A baby. My baby! This is my baby!

Early November 1991, a Week Before the Phone Rift Between Ty and David

Ty was talking out loud to a ghost again: "I'm perplexed. I mean, I like Bliss. I find her fascinating and sexy, but that shit scares me. She reminds me of myself, always wanting what she can't seem to have, and it never stops her from wanting. Face, the Face she wants or imagines she wants, he's as dead as you are. And she can't *see* that."

"Ty? Who you talkin' to? Please tell me you were on the phone, and not buggin' the fuck out." David, key in hand, had stopped by to drop off a shirt he had designed.

"No, David. I was just talkin' to Trick."

"Trick? You mean…"

Ty immediately regretted his confession.

"You been smokin' trees? They got some ganja out there that will totally fuck with your senses. Tell me you smoked an ounce of that shit! Tell me you're all blitz-blasted, blunted on reality."

"I haven't been smoking anything. Trick is real, and I'm regular." Ty said it calmly.

"Hold on. I'm gonna have to sit down for this one."

"I never told you how tight we were."

"So, tell it."

And so Ty told the story of his relationship with Trick and Trick's ghost. Through it all, he kept looking around as if waiting for some word from Trick, or for permission from the cosmos to speak.

"We shared an energy. We still do. A spiritual connection that makes me think we probably walked this earth together before. I *knew* him before I knew him, and when I met him it was *home*. I know it *sounds* crazy, and if it is, I've been crazy for years. But Trick is here. See, we were on this road together, a short-lived but very cool Electric Avenue, OK? I *know* he's left the physical plane. But a part of him remains. I can feel it."

"Trick's here. Oh, yeah," David mocked. "There he is with a diamond on his tooth, in a snow-white suit, diggin' the scene with a dead gangsta's lean, mmm-hmm-m-m."

"Fuck you! He's *here*. If you don't see him or *feel* him, then you're not supposed to." It all sounded perfectly sound to Ty.

"Ty, I love you. Even if you crazy as a shithouse rat, I'll still love yo crazy rabid ass. But this is scarier than Madam Zoreena's parlor that Halloween night she made fire in her hand. Is he here right now?" David asked incredulously.

"I feel him over there by the chair. I feel the vibrato of him laughin'. He *knows* you don't believe me."

"That chair right there, by the window? What he look like? Is he still black as tar? No disrespect. Or is he white, and all see-through?"

"He's not Casper, ya wiseass. He's not some murky ectoplasm movie ghost. He's like a shadow or a flicker of light. His voice is in my head, like I'm imagining it, but it's his voice. Sometimes, not so much anymore, his face will flicker inside a shadow. He's different from how he is in my dreams. In my dreams he's whole and fully Tricked out. Here, he's just pieces of light, wisdom, comfort, counsel, and sometimes just company. And stop looking at me like I'm illin'! I'm not crazy."

"Hey, as long as he ain't some vengeful *haint* wreckin' up shit, we cool. My southern grandma used to talk about these haints comin' back all mad that they've been done wrong and their earthly shit ain't finished. They come back raging, makin' life hell. But let's don't dwell. In fact, let's not talk about this shit anymore, 'kay?"

And so they didn't.

LATE SUMMER 1992

While getting his blackjack fix in Atlantic City, Ty's father collapsed and suffered a fatal heart attack.

Ty and Blur were on the outs again, and Tyrone didn't try to find him. He'd no lover to stroke his dreads or spoon him to sleep, and he thought maybe he didn't *deserve* one. Most of all he missed David. He placed call after desperate call to David's crib. But David never returned them. Tyrone had killed their friendship.

* * *

"Duch. Please answer. How many times can I say I'm sorry? I opened my mouth and hurt you. David? I'm just back from another service. Got another funeral on Wednesday. Seems I've painted myself into this role where everyone blows their noses on my sleeve. I met a man whose job was collecting nipple rings, cock rings, wedding rings from the bodies of elegantly dead boys. He said the worst place he ever found someone dead was just outside a tearoom— corpse's pants around his ankles, a night's worth of stranger's DNA all over him. I don't ever wanna see you elegantly dead on the other side of a glory hole, David. I'm selfish like that. When I love someone, I'm way too crude. So, shoot me. There's a Timex in my head, and it's ticking off time. Where are you? I always thought we'd endure this shit together. David, how's it gonna turn out for us, bruh? Straight up. What's gonna become of us?

"Sorry for this message. I guess I've outgrown or outraged the friends I ain't outlived. But you're still my friend, aren't ya, Duch?

So how many apologies do I have to leave before you step out of your chilly dance of intolerance? Look, I opened my mouth and I hurt you out of love. I'm sorry for lovin' you that much. Goodbye."

* * *

Ty could've simple said, *David, my father died today. I need you, man.* And David would've surely come running. But Tyrone didn't say it. He didn't want sympathy, he wanted the *love* back.

Intervention was needed.

Say what you will of Faison Brown (and people said all kinds of shit), he understood the *importance of support*. Browny managed to contact David.

"Yo, David. You got yourself a friend in Tyrone. Ya ain't go'n find no better. Shit! Let's face it, ya don't deserve none. Ain't sayin' he perfect, yo. But he good people. You know his father died, right? Well, he did, and the funeral's Wednesday. So, is you go'n be a bitch, or is you go'n be his *boy*? Huh?"

TY'S ELEGY FOR HIS FATHER

"Funny thing about secrets: Sometimes they can sit still and untouched, like so many figurines gathering dust. Secrets, they were our family possessions. They did not leave the house, and we did not share them—not even with ourselves. There wasn't anything sinister going on inside our tiny box in the sky. We simply went about *robbing ourselves* of feeling and living our quietly tragic lives. Because of this, for as long as I can remember, I've walked around with something *gigantic* and unshared.

"I've no skin memory of the texture of my father's arms wrapped around me. This isn't a Daddy Dearest elegy. You see, there were two kinds of men in my family: the *bums* and the workers. My father was a *worker*. He'd come home each day in that bent, broken-down waltz of overworked bones and I'd think, *Oh, it's just Pops after another day of slavin' for The Man*. He'd pitch some tired utterances at me and he'd be gone again.

"But there were decent clothes on my back, food on the table, and my mother was no ghetto widow crying herself to sleep. Though I've no doubt *anger* was a very real part of my father's composition, we were never victims of its flying blind rages, never bombarded by its words or fists. In his way of thinking, he was a "man" because he *provided*. If we didn't ever toss a ball, or have a conversation more than three minutes, it's because he was always too busy, or tired, or afraid. The little monster he spawned now stands before you with a sharper brain, newer clothes, a better education—and I flaunted those things in his face. Shame on me! Shame on us.

"I'm older now. I understand the complexity of men who spend so much time locked inside their skulls that they never *live* what's in their hearts. For my father, respect was never a given. It didn't come on the job, on a corner, or on the shelves of any liquor store. And respect didn't come calling with a malnourished wallet. For my father, respect showed its best face during a night of Poker or a game of 21 in Atlantic City, and later Vegas.

"'You never did understand the things I do for *me*,' he once told my mother as he headed through the door into the superstitious darkness. Well, maybe we never did. He leaves behind a shamed and broken son, a new blond companion, and a host of muttered voices that now sound a little like love."

* * *

When Ty's elegy was done, he looked up and standing in the door in his one sedate suit was David. They embraced very tightly. In that moment all was forgiven.

"I can't remember. Am I the good twin or the evil one? And which one is supposed to say 'I'm sorry' first?" David asked. "Ty, come out tonight. Screw the always absentee Blur! Ya know he the *Anti-Nelly*. We'll get ya some new bone. Bet we could rustle up a big black bone, a big brown bone—hell, maybe even a big ol' *imported* bone. Believe me, bonage is *needed!*

"Imported? What? You mean, like *beluga bone*? Is there some of that in town this week? No, thanks, Davy. I've got a bone of my own, thank you."

"Yes, but you ain't that young or that hung, and you *never* were *that flexible*. Listen, Tyrone, I know it's a sad day. But come out with us and just be young and gay again. There's a high that comes from shovin' your hand down a new pair of pants, man—and you missin' way too much of that good shit!"

"David. You're *such a 'mo*. Love you, man." Ty smiled sadly. "Thanks for coming. Goodbye."

APRIL 1993

In the age of "Don't Ask, Don't Tell," David was asking, "Hey Ty, how much you *weigh* these days?"

But Ty wasn't telling. Always the queer iconoclast, Ty didn't seem to mind aging. He'd fallen out of his gym routine after snagging the coveted Blur Antonelli. Then Blur never bothered to clarify their blurry relationship. Then Blur had his own place, his own haunts, and his own agendas. Then Blur for the most part was gone and there weren't any new prospects.

Tyrone was in his early 30s and beginning to look *every single day* of it. He'd gained 25 pounds sitting on his ass trying to be brilliant. Then David began calling him "Richard Poundtree" and "Salami Davis Jr." and that shit hit the fan of Ty's ego.

So Ty joined another gym, and he witnessed a strange phenomenon: beefy Brothers, V-shaped bodies, men with tans and terrific teeth. Not just hunks, but *hulks* with shaved scrotums and waxed asses.

These beings swarmed throughout the city. Queer young men were no longer walking around looking sick. Suddenly the bars, the streets of Chelsea, the boys on Riverside, the bangee boys of Harlem and Brooklyn, the beach boys in the Pines and the Hamptons were transformed into a buffed, waxed, and clipped parade of strutting, stripped-down stallions. One warm day while he and David were sunning in Washington Square Park, watching one fantastic ballooning creature after the next file by, Ty complained, "Look at this shit. I don't get it!"

"Of course you don't. Celibates rarely do. I think that's the whole concept, Blackie Gleason."

"One mo fat joke, and I'm all over yo fag azz! Aiight? And I'm tellin' you, this Invasion of the Titty Men looks like a Wonderbra ad. It's *not* hot!"

"Yes it *is* hot! Give me mo naked bodacious beef. Beats flannel shirts, faded Levi's, and that oh-so-tired mandatory lip hair. Face it, baby. The Clone is dead. Long live the New Clone!" David trumpeted. "If a *aging* brother wants to be *bar bait*, he needs *body*—cut, ripped, shredded *body*, I tell you! But you wouldn't know jack about that, would you, Thick Wilson?"

Tyrone punched him *hard* in the arm.

MAY 1993

As with the majority of David's stories, *it all started out innocently*. Enrolled in his final year at FIT, the Fashion Institute of Technology, he'd become the popular old sage. In one class there was a kid, a cute copper boy of 18 who'd been kicked out of his house. David would encourage him. One day the boy showed up to class battered and badly bruised.

"I've been through it all, baby. Violence is an American rite. This suffering you're going through, I feel it too. It hurts like hell. But it's necessary, 'cause it's gonna make you stronger. That's what the universe is telling you right now: 'Be strong, Gabrielle, be brave, be the best damn gay human being your spirit will allow.' Here we sit, suffering, and we're here creatin' these little masterpieces every day. Don't you see the connection? You nevuh create better than when you genuinely know the taste of suffering. Now, enough with the queen mother hen act. Have you reported this ghastly shit? No? Well, I happen to *know* people. Let's take your picture. That's our evidence."

David and his new friend hit the precinct to report the latest in a disturbing series of attacks. It nearly amused David that the decade had spawned a name for this special indignity. They filed a "hate crime" complaint, determined to see justice. Instead they were promptly disrespected, mistreated, patronized, and dismissed—in that order. An embarrassed Gabrielle, seeing the uselessness of it, let it go. But not David. He felt that if he were famous, the incident would've received hype and headlines. And suddenly it occurred to him that he wasn't and never would be that world-famous dancer of destiny. He'd never get his chance to win a Tony, jet propel to the Winter Garden's stage, kiss some grande dame on both cheeks, and profusely thank his lover by his masculine and most probably Latin name. Now it seemed he and Gabrielle were companions in suffering.

"Let's get you home and cleaned up," David suggested.

David called Tyrone, hoping to get some press in his downtown rag. But Ty wasn't home. He and Blur had reunited a week before and Blur "the Bore" was staying with Ty yet again. Hearing Blur's voice, David politely asked for a legal referral, but Blur—who was never a fan of David's—hung up on his ass.

So much for knowing people.

As he applied iodine to Gabrielle's battered face, David saw *himself* in that tender skin, the not-quite-brown eyes, and the firmness of those 18-year-old limbs. Gabrielle was a slight kid, which made his beating all the more senseless. For a moment, David wondered if his friend could see their physical similarities. Did he notice their mutual interests, their circumstances, and if he did, was *that* why his jeans quaked?

"See, it's real hard becoming somebody large. I know people who've tried all their lives to be larger than they really are, or were even meant to be, you know. But the hardest part of being large is keeping the your soul intact through the metamorphosis. Because that's true shit. That's the gold *and* the goal. You wanna be able to look in the mirror and know you and your God are cool with the human staring back. That person in the mirror is the only role you're responsible for in this B movie we call life, baby boy."

David's new friend smiled sadly and slowly kissed his lips.

* * *

"I slipped. Damn it. I slip sometimes. Not often, now that there's Carlos. That's why I feel like so much wrong, rank, rancid, stank shit right now. No! Don't look at me! I'm positively vile—a vile, stupid, selfish child. I slipped, damn it! I should be allowed one or four fuck-ups in the duration of this relationship, shouldn't I? Men. We're such bullshit beings. Myself duly included. I like to pop the yang and shake my thang and see if it still works. I think that makes me human and gay, with an anxious dick. I love you, Carlos. I do! But I'm scared. Because, for once in my life, I didn't want to slip and fall into some scandalous shit. Not now… And don't talk to me about no rubbers or coughs, sores or tests… I slipped. Let's get over *that shit* first," David said to himself inside that morning's mournful mirror.

* * *

Carlos lay dying in a hospital, and David was already cheating on his corpse. He felt awful. Carlos died soon after, as if he knew.

Five Months Later...

David wished he had a ghost, like Ty had Trick. But all David had was the universe and Carlos's last request: *Live your days and nights with fire.*

So the firebird made a list: "Dear Universe. This is what I'm asking to come inside my life. Please *don't* send in the clowns. No heads either. No knuckle, crack, or chicken heads need apply, 'kay? He's got to have some looks, style, personality, ambition. Some spirituality wouldn't hurt either. Let him be real. And please let him *know* how to dance—at least hustle—and I'll take care of the rest. This is your boy, David, signing off."

November 1993

"Well, Ty, my dear, the universe listens. Things are pickin' up in the booty department. I done found me a new man! You know me. I always do. Distinguished. Latino. A real gentleman, and he's older, by about 15 years. Been married, divorced, got the T-shirts and two teenage sons as consolation prizes. And now he's got me. Face it, didn't we *all know* I was just a lost boy searchin' for his daddy? Well, Victor's a *papi*. And he only spanks me when I want him to. He wants a partner, not a wife. But what he really wants is to open a club, a downtown lounge. Says that's the next wave. I can relate to an ambitious *hombre* who ain't desperately seeking the longtime wedlock headlock, cock-lock jammy. He just wants a commitment."

"If you're happy, I'm ecstatic," Ty said. "So you committed to being Victor's *partner*? Commitment is like a seesaw with two sturdy asses on board. You *do know* what happens when someone gets off, right?"

Not long after, *the men* in David's mercurial life were finally introduced.

"Ty, meet my architect, my *papi*, and the builder of that erection in my heart. *Mi hombre de la corazón.*"

"*Hola.* Glad to meet you, Victor. Now run! Run as hard and fast as you possibly can!" Ty warned.

"But why?" Victor asked, confused by Ty's knowledge of David's history and Tyrone's warped sense of humor.

"Finally, David's found a good man, a decent man," Ty said. "Know how I can tell? I don't have that overwhelming urge to dash home to take three showers after shaking your hand."

Twenty-One
We Should Get Together More Often

There is more life in the city on Saturday nights. More death, too. More beer sold to more agitated drunks, more bridge and tunnel traffic, more friction, more threats, more punks, more tits and cocks to be idolized. Whatever the choice of merchandise, Saturday nights presented more.

Some restless Brothers were far too erect to sit home in front of their VCRs slapping their lovelies in violent masturbation techniques. And one such Brother, troubled by the trials of being Browny, wanted to escape the madness and just get his Saturday night's freak on. He decided to ring Tyrone. The crazy thought was: Maybe they should take their diversely diff dicks out on the town and try getting them wet together.

Tyrone felt the invitation had sleazy fingerprints all over it.

"Yo, Ty. Check it: Meet me outside the Zebra so we can *both* get our jungle illness on. Don't give me no shit either. Step outta that cave, ya fuckin' hermit! Just be there at 11 o'clock, and cleaner than the fuckin' Board of Health!"

"No can do. Got a deadline and I'm runnin'—"

Click. "Bastard with a record!"

Ty looked outside at the speeding neon-lit activity. The night was so young it was almost illicit. He decided to acquiesce. Blur was always busy, or out of town, and lately Ty wasn't feeling very bound to that tediously tenuous relationship. He showered quickly, dressed, and stepped into the metro.

When he hopped off the subway onto 14th Street, a thin rain misted the cool city air. The energy of people moving, going, and doing played against sounds of salsa and the slow swis-s-sh of traffic. *Yes, it's good to be out among the living*, he thought as a large throng muscled toward the club on E. 11th Street.

"Yo, baby, yo!" he heard as he approached the Zebra Den. And there stood an animated Browny, talking loud, drawing a crowd, hands flying the way his well-loved brother's once did. He was rocking a vintage George Raft gangsta style, navy pinstriped zoot suit complete with matching spats. He looked like a cross between a ridiculously cool jester and Cab Callo*wayward*. He was arguing with the doorman, trying to cop a freebie, a slide by, a get-in-where-he'd-fit-in.

As dark, moody, and difficult as Browny could be, he was still *Mr. Five Boroughs*. Wherever he went in the city, people *knew* him.

"Browny! You lookin' stoopid, man!"

"Yo! Browny! You got that five you owe me?"

"Hey, Browny. Still listenin' out for you on the radio, dawg. Where you at?"

"Yo! Check Browny out! Rockin' that dope suit! G'on Browny!" They'd laugh or pat his back. It was as if he was running for mayor, except most of the folks who knew him, well, they didn't vote.

Now he was pissed at the overly stressed doorman. "Yo, man! You *no habla* English? *Mira! Moola! Dinero!* Faison's got plenty bank!"

If he *had* any Presidents in his dubiously baggy pockets, they rarely saw the light of Harlem.

"Yo!" he yelled. "Yo, Ty! Over here!"

Years out of school, and still most every sentence out of Browny's mouth began with a big loud, "Yo!"

"Yo! Ty. 'Zup. They actin' like they don't know me up this hovel! But it's cool, I ain't stressin' it."

Ty simply addressed the doorman. "He's with me. If that's a problem please tell Coco his friend Ty is outside waiting. And he's gettin' pissed."

Any friend of Coco's was, well… The two were granted entry. "Love the suit," Ty said wryly.

"Fuck all that! Look at you, lookin' like you look. You dressed *like that* in high school. When you go'n get you some glamour, boy?"

"I'll get the glamour when you get the class. I think both of our orders are on layaway. By the way, why am I here?"

Browny's reddened eyes answered for him. Three months out of his latest rehab and apparently he still wasn't clean. "The theme tonight is 'for old times sake,'" he said cryptically. It sounded like the shit liquor made men say.

Ty wondered: *How many times have I wished you clean, sober, and singing your foolish ass off?*

Inside, the first floor was a darkened cavern alive with a driving mix of muscle boys, gogo girls, bangee boys, and party girls in varying degrees of undress. Andy Warhol was dead, and as David had recently proclaimed, "So ends the wild downtown party as we real fly boys knew it." Now it was sprinklings of club kids hyped on crystal meth, second-tier fashion models, perennial poseurs, local celebs, waiting-to-happen R&B artists, groupies, and gangs of weaved-out chicks. It wasn't a specifically gay or babe-licious crowd, and those present were either twinkies or homo thugz or didn't come to stay.

Needless to say, Tyrone *hated* it!

Browny ordered his vodka straight, and perused the hard-core party freaks. But something in his temperament signaled there wasn't much freak left in his party game.

Truth was, Faison didn't want to get drunk that night. He wanted to achieve a blessed state of wonderful numbness, an everything-go'n-be-all-rightness. Ty stood next to him, expecting him to say something, let him know what was up. But Faison only bobbed his baby dreadlocked head and modeled his zoot like a lyrical gangsta. "C'mon. Let's walk," he said.

On the second floor, a more tranquilized crowd settled down to watch the live show.

"Mad lovelies up in here tonight."

"Where? Where they at?" Ty deadpanned.

A balding tuxedoed bloke tinkled the ivories and crooned almost woozily.

The inherent sadness of the song affected Ty's mood. He thought of the few lovers he'd known, the ones who got away, those taken by the times, and melancholy overtook him. But when he looked at Browny, he thought it strange to see *him* on the verge of crying.

"Yo. Step into the john with me," Browny ordered.

"What for? Ya *know* you ain't nuttin' off me."

Browny grabbed Ty's arm and forged a way to the men's room. Glancing at that strangely *Trick-like* expression, Tyrone suddenly knew something was desperately wrong.

"It's Jonathan. Jonathan's sick. Very very sick, man…"

"Jonathan?" Ty asked. "Jonathan," he repeated to himself. "You mean…" Suddenly the name, the face, the association all melded into one realization. *Oh! That Jonathan?*

"Yeah. Final stages. And it's just a fuckin' waste, man. Such a fuckin' shame."

A shame? It was more than that. In a town of tackheads and raggedy mustangs, Jonathan was a true Cadillac of men. He had a big, pure, altruistic heart and had taken in many strays over the years. Browny was one of them, but Browny was not gay by nature. Gay for pay? Queer for a beer? "Faggot for a habit," he once called it. Perhaps. Gay out of gratitude? Probably not. But Browny's disdain for "sissies" had lessened over the years; and if he had to count his true blues, at least two gay men would complete that puny total. Jonathan was his best friend, and gay, and he'd probably saved Browny's ass from spiraling into the deepest depths of alcohol, crack, and emotional hustling.

But then, Jonathan was everyone's friend, protector, coach, father figure, confessor, and all around decent cat. Ty had once written a feature on him, but he didn't know the full extent of Jon and Browny's complex trip. He figured that Jon, who was nobody's fool, saw Browny's potential to be something better, to exist beyond the broken toilets of life.

Jonathan Rogers had saved Browny, gotten him clean and bailed him out of scrapes countless times. And now, in return, Browny couldn't save him.

"I tried to kill myself. Just once," Browny confessed. "But, yo, I was young and little and Black as tar. I was tryin' real hard to be somebody and nobody gave me a fuckin' chance. Man. It's a rough motherfucka to be young, Black, and hurtin'. I mean hurtin' bad. But, yo! Big Jon, with his big Buddha wisdom, made me see only one of them conditions was permanent." He chuckled. "So you know what he did? He threw away my fuckin' pipe and flushed my best shit. Then the big bloated bastard locked the fuckin' door so I couldn't get out. What that motherfucka do that for? All I wanted was to get the hell outta there and finish myself off. Man, I cried, screamed, begged, bitched, and tore his fuckin' livin' room apart. I woulda beaten him to death too, if I coulda. Yo, I had to fuckin' hurt him somehow, so I hauled up and threw his Mr. Leather Cleveland trophy out his 10th floor window and watched that fucker smash into a thousand gold pieces, But instead of kickin' my crazy vandalizin' ass all over the South Bronx, he held me. That's all. Held me so fuckin' tight, he put new bruises all over me. And through all that hurt and pain, for the first time in my fuckin' life, I felt loved. That man showed me much love." Browny examined his stricken reflection in the mirror. "Yo, you know Jon was a real big motherfuckin' bear of a man. Well, you wouldn't wanna see him now. Breaks my balls, man. Just breaks my fuckin' heart. He got on his motorcycle and rode into the crazy night, and crashed into a pillar under the Brooklyn Bridge. He wanted to go out *his way*. He didn't get his wish, though. Now he's all busted up, and he's sick, and I..."

Tyrone watched that inarticulate language of pain race across Browny's face. He saw how his fingers were entwined as if clutched in a useless prayer. Browny's lost eyes searched the ceiling for something to cling to, and Ty embraced him. It seemed such a wasted gesture. But there they stood, two small lives, two more casualties in a world of mean and little things. Had he called just to *cry* with Tyrone? Strangely, neither of them was crying.

Then, suddenly, a shrill voice entered the cage of Tyrone's skull, asking that question he was afraid to ask, because he feared the answer. The words boiled on his lips like troublesome cold sores: *Were you and Jonathan ever...together? Have you been tested?*

Tyrone didn't want to know. It was all becoming just too sad: Alexis, Marlon, Brad, Ari, Fat Don, Kwali, Jerome, Leon, Essex, Jazz. Ty had kissed the dead lips of too many young, beautiful men—Black Brothers, white and brown Brothers, gay and straight. The phone would ring and he'd think it was Death placing a collect call. Someone was dying. Someone just discovered they had it. Someone died, their funeral was last Thursday, and *why* hadn't Ty been there?

Often he'd thank God that in his anal retentive *rubberized* journey through road posts, yield signs, and blinking yellow lights, the awareness was such that promiscuity was not an option. Still, there was always fear. Rubbers did rip. Men did lie. It only takes one. One night. One man. One lie. One fuck to become a period at the end of a sentence he hadn't yet finished writing. Now Browny? Tyrone wasn't ready to stare down at Browny's corpse and mourn his small, unfinished life.

"I just wanted to tell you to make sure you heard it from me first," he whispered.

"I know," Ty said. "I know. So, you want to book from this place and talk? What?"

"Nah. Yo! Ain't nothin' more to say. I just wanna help him, though. He ain't got no insurance, and..." Browny was about to hit Tyrone with his idea of regrouping for a benefit. But then another group, a group of rowdy club-kids entered the john, turning Browny all chickenshit.

"Let's just go inside, toast Jonathan, and party like it's all we can do to keep from cryin' like two soft bitches."

Back on the main floor, Ty ordered a club soda, and Browny another stiff vodka. Settled in a corner, nodding heads, tapping their feet like secretly shell-shocked idiots, they shared a toast to Jonathan. There was much to say, but it was not the time or place and so they let the music fill in the blanks.

Ty casually glanced at Browny. All at once, his face had changed, his eyes brightening like mood rings as he stared ahead, smiling like a brand new idiot. Ty peered in the same direction, and thought he saw what had magically brought on that big goofy-ass, gap-toothed grin. Through the thriving dance of humanity, a tall silhouette swaggered. It seemed for a minute that all attention shifted; heads turned, eyes widened to embrace this strobe-lit phantom. Shadows lifted slowly, and the realization hit: Face!

Face is here? Damn. I don't see or hear from him in months. Then I step out with Browny's ass, and... Coincidence? Or is Faison stalking him?

Face, meanwhile, was at the zenith of his Afro-Portuguese physical appeal. Café au lait sin personified. The fucky ideal. He looked *fine* that night.

Now that Face was in the Zebra Den, lookin' weirdly mahvelous, would he bother to acknowledge Ty or Browny? Would he clutch the jewels and *grace them* with a few moments of his effervescent presence?

Club voices rose in the air: "You know who *that* is?" "Damn! He fine!" "I don't do men, but he's so fuckin' pretty I'd do him!"

Face loved it. He gave them a view of that famously fine profile, to the left, to the right, as the few queens in attendance screamed: "You betta work it!"

The man was pushing up on 33, a substance abuser, and still so drop-dead stoopid *fine* it was incomprehensible—especially to Ty. *Has he had work done?* Everyone could see the Brother was still butta—the 6-foot-5, two-hundred-pound definition of the word.

"Madison Avenue created this monster. But what the hell we 'posed do with it?" asked a voice, followed by a big dark claw gripping Ty's shoulder.

Ty turned and there was Chaz. Chaz, with that tough, long-suffering mug tinged with the sadness of a restless history. Amazingly, he was still braving it with Face. Watching them over the years was like viewing a long, very tedious, very brutal S/M flick. Only no one watching it was beating off. Least of all, Ty. Still, Ty and Chaz were esoterically intimate, and often flirting in spite of themselves.

"What up, Bub?" Ty shouted, smiling as he and Chaz embraced full and hard. Holding and beholding Chaz again, Ty couldn't help thinking: *Stop, dick! Be still now!*

"Damn, Bub, when you start keepin' vampire hours?" Chaz joked in his ear.

"Bub, please! Ain't ya heard? I'm a vamp from way back!" "Bub" was short for Bubba, someone either of them could be.

As other hangers-on sifted through, Face rested his beauteous backside at a table in the shadows, his star quality darkening like a lunar eclipse. Was he live, Memorex, a flicker of virtual reality? Ty realized *it had to be* real, because Chaz was still in his arms. Chaz, the devoted and ever true, bringing up the rear, so to speak.

"Yo, Chaz Bear." Browny tapped Chaz's gruesomely wide back. "Think I can holler at Facey-Face a minute?"

Chaz shrugged. "I ain't his manager, man. Suit yourself. And what up with that suit? Come on, Ty… Let's dance." The club music boomed Soul II Soul's "Keep On Movin'." Chaz, looking oh so *Gigantor* in his white T-shirt, made his move, grabbed Ty's wrist, and they proceeded to the floor. It was wild, and Ty felt like a native again, dancing among the mad-sexy people. One song flowed into the next, and Ty was too busy getting his necessary groove on to notice Face had given Browny the usual brush-off. In mid active groove, he saw Browny walking away and assumed he was heading for the rest room.

"Easy, Ty, I's a old-aged vampire," Chaz shouted, sweating like a slave. "And you-know-who's staring holes through us. I shouldn't be dancin' with no mens in public. He's probably all pissed. I'm getting a soda, you want anything?"

Ty shook his head no, and thought: *Please. Grow some balls, Chaz!*

Ty and Chaz had almost *happened* once. Two years earlier at Face's loft: "He's in Milan, or Japan, or one of them "an" sounding places. Probably sucking some Italian dick, licking some Japanese clit. Do you think he gives a shit about what we do?" Chaz had asked. And warm blood began to flow and flood all through a Brother as Ty suddenly recalled David's mortal *fear* of what Chaz allegedly had. His shifting eyes fell below, and, *Oh, my goodness! David ain't lied! Bruh, look at what you've got!*

What Chaz *had* "on swole" was a mad anaconda, crawling along his thigh and over it, stretching, reaching across that desperate space between them. Hard as it was, and it was *hoard*, Ty left before he would have an even harder time saying no to Chaz's offer of a momentary man-to-behemoth mambo.

As club music rumbled, Face made a cool, ambling journey, coming to an impressive standstill beside Tyrone. He grinned as if a mere grin could erase all time, distance, and acrimony. "So, Ty, what's your bag, huh?" he asked, softly slurring his words in that refined purr from his last commercial.

"My bag? Gucci," Ty replied, and Depina's face stretched into 32 dazzling capped and captivating pearlies. They clutched hands and bumped shoulders like old partners who once *popped collars*. It felt odd for both, but lukewarm and familiar too.

"Been meaning to call ya. Just so *you* know, I called in a few favors, and those punks that jacked David, well, they won't be jackin' nobody else no time soon," he said.

"Say again. You did *what*?" Ty yelled.

But then Face thought better of playing the hero. Ever since Da Elixir's beginnings, Tyrone had unwittingly reigned as "The Patriarch." He had been the group's leader and father figure. Face had *no love* for father figures, or what Ty represented. Suddenly, telling Ty of his *good deed* reeked to him of a desperate kid seeking his Daddy's respect. *Fuck you. I don't need your damn approval,* he thought. So Face dropped the subject. "I'm pretty much livin' out of hotels in Europe and L.A. these days. It's *hoard-rough* being me," he joked. "Tell you what. Tennis, next Saturday at Crunch, bet? Look,

I gotta book. Promised Calvin I'd step into his new boutique, and you don't wanna piss off Calvin. Bitch holds a mean grudge. Must be that Bronx in him. Anyway, it's all the way on the Upper East Side. So, Boss. Tennis? Call me. I mean it."

"Yeah, whatever," Ty said to the air, knowing he'd see Face again in six months to a year—if then.

"Eh! Ty-ro-o-one! Honey, you are lookin' *too tired* tonight," a drag queen named David tittered, dressed in tight black drag. "Cucumbers are more than a cheap sexual device. Trust me, a couple over those eyes works wonders, darling." *Mwah, mwah,* he kissed both Ty's cheeks.

"Tired? Witch, please!" Ty replied.

"Tyrone, I *know* you don't think ya *cute* in that 1985 leather! Times and fashion change! When will you? Or *have* you? Please. I'll just have to stop hangin' with you if ya continue to roll so…archaic!" David teased, plucking at Ty's jacket. "Look, I keep tellin' you to stop by my salon for a complete fashion makeover. You *can* afford it, you know!"

"I will. I promise. But tell me something, is it me, or does tonight suddenly feel frighteningly like a reunion?"

"A reunion?"

"Yeah. Da Elixir. We're all here in the same place, in all our wasted, faded glory," he said, eyeing his best friend's costume up and down.

"Faded? You'll have to excuse me. I'm flyin' on *X* Airlines tonight. But yes, Facey is looking faded these days. We all knew he'd hit that wall sometime," David joked, again kissing both Ty's cheeks.

"So…I'm guessin' that tonight you're Ann-Margret in her Kitten-with-a-whip stage? " Ty speculated. "But why didn't you go with the white boots shaking a mad fringed tail feather a go-go Ann? By the way, how did your meeting with the people at Ailey go? You designing next season's costumes, or what?"

"First of all, check yourself," *she* admonished, spinning around. "I'm Emma Peel, damn it! Get yo leather bitches correct! Secondly, I did the Ailey thing. Met with the peeps. Complete yawn. A mess! Dame Judith, uh, Ms. Jamison if you're nasty, was straight trippin'!"

Ty didn't know *what* that meant. David had always *loved* Judith

Jamison. He wasn't making any sense. Maybe it was the *X*. Even though he wasn't getting any younger, he was always experimenting with that trippy-hippie shit. Ty wanted to scold him, but he let it go. Besides, hadn't David *stopped* dressing in drag?

"I'm just back from a wake, hon," David volunteered.

"Oh? So what did you wear?"

"*This,* of course. It was a formal affair."

"Anyone I know?"

"Rue DeDay. Didn't you hear?"

"God no! I didn't even know he was sick!"

"He wasn't. Good queen. Horrible *ba-a-ad* judge of traffic. Glitter all over the place!"

"Oh. Sad. But isn't it queer?" Ty mused. "I'd almost forgotten there were other ways for us to die. So where's Victor tonight?"

"Didn't wanna come. Flyin' solo," David answered in a clipped, that's-the-end-of-*that*-subject tone. "And how are you and Blur *this week*? At this point, is it strictly dickly?"

"Nah. Wholly ass-holian," Ty admitted. "I love fucking him. Sometimes I think if I hit it right, I might just fuck him out of blindness and he'll *come* into seeing."

"Well, ain't it hopeful to fuck so?" David snipped. "So, Ty, what's the dealy with Facey? You know, usually when I'm on *X*, I just wanna run up and kiss err-body, but he gets *no* kisses. Did you see the way he just dissed little Faisoni? I mean, damn. I know it's *his* world and he's the bomb and all, but Faisoni didn't deserve that shit. Sometimes I wonder about Face, staging his little star tantrums. He's so hopelessly déclassé!"

"Duch? Tell me you're *not* throwing shade on the shady low-low. Has the decades-long crush finally been stomped?"

"Well, I've just opened my eyes to a few things. Therapy can do that. I'm tryna love from a distance. It's healthier. I forgave all the ugliness. Forgivin' is what I do. But even *my* artistry can't make him crazy-pretty anymore. He dropped by the boutique as if nothing bad had ever happened between us asking me to style him for some event. He put his arm around my shoulder, and foolish me, I agreed.

But over at his place, he gets one of his notorious nose bleeds, flips out, ejects me, and *fires* Browny!"

"I didn't know that, Duch. You never told me."

"No biggie. Business thrives. I always land on my stilettos. It's Browny I'm worried about. With him and Face there's nothin' but drama. I smell it swirling around like skunkweed. I used to think Faisoni was just playa-hatin'. But no, *mon cher*. This definitely goes deeper."

"Way too much ego for that loft to handle. Face it. Depina's always had big probs with ego management. Even *you* must've noticed that little flaw in his character. And Browny never liked him, so that whole living arrangement thing was a queer piece of strange and unusual. But Browny's going through some stuff."

"Yes. We *all* are. Facey can be a fuckin' unappreciative pig to the people who love him. He's not alone. You know something? You can take some mixed-Negroes out the South Bronx, but ya can't make 'em wipe they asses!"

Ty wondered what the hell David was going on about. But then, he remembered he hadn't seen Browny in the last 15 minutes. Had he left? Was he OK?

Meanwhile, outside the Zebra Den, in the deepest blue tinge of nocturne, wandering artists, suffering faces, trendy kids, heroin boys, working girls, leather men, and subterraneous hip-hoppers merged on a night full of stars and unforeseen calamities.

The Depina entourage prepared to enter their stretch limousine, and Face turned to flash that famous Depina grin and wave the customary blasé wave one last time.

Five shots rang out.

Metal, hot with purpose, exploded through flesh.

The street hushed. Two men fell to the pavement. One of them was former model-of-the-moment Claudio Conte. The other was Face Depina.

Twenty-Two

The Death of Hip

The Next Day

Browny was running on a full tank of scared shitless. So he blustered, bitched, and rebitched to the cops who'd bogarted Juanita's place.

"Yeah. I *ain't surprised* somebody busted a cap in his ass, the conceited, lyin' son of a mixed bitch! I ain't gonna lie, I ain't never liked him. No big thing. I don't like the way people treat me at the bank. Yo, I don't like how them Korean grocers don't wanna touch my hand when they give me my change. But I ain't shot none of 'em."

Shit-talkin' aside, Browny had no alibi. He did, however, have a long history of cop-hatin'. The feeling was entirely mutual.

* * *

The pundits were calling it "The Male Model Melee."

In the crowded hospital waiting room, David was hysterical.

"First Martin Luther King, then John Lennon, now Facey? This is madness! What the hell is this beastly world comin' to? Who would do this? Why you think those bastards in white won't even let us see

243

him? You think he all right? You think he still look like himself?"

"I *think* you should *listen to yourself*. He's *alive*. All right? Celebrate *that* shit!"

"Do you think he was shot in the face? Why won't somebody tell us what's goin' on? Why ain't they tellin' us anything?" David begged for an answer.

"They probably know who did it, I guess, and an arrest is imminent. Or else they don't know jack. Now *please* try to calm down," Ty said strongly; then, looking at the sobbing wreckage of his best friend, he asked, "You need a good strong bitch-smack, Duch? 'Cause, I got a coupla those left in me."

"No. But a good strong bitch's *hug* would help."

Tyrone swooped him up in his arms.

A scared David whispered, "Who would want to *kill* him?"

Get a fuckin' grip! Who the fuck wouldn't? The list of New York names alone was staggering! And Depina's enemies were global in scope. To *know* Face was to *hate the shit* he did on the regular without apology. *But why* is *everything so hush-hush?*

It was common knowledge that Claudio Conte had received a flesh wound to the shoulder. Once released, he was busted for possession of an unlicensed weapon. Surprisingly, it was his first offense.

"Look," said Ty. "I've said more than once, 'I'll kill him!' And for as long as it took to say it, I meant it," Ty whispered inside their embrace.

"I know," David said softly. Then, after a pause, "I know everything."

"Everything what, Duchess?" Ty asked, stepping back.

"All about you and Face, and the DJ booth. And I know *why* you never told me. And I've hated you for it. But I'm tryna get over it. Best friends are *supposed to tell* each other shit. You're not a very good best friend. You're still, my friend, but…"

"David," Tyrone sighed, exhausted by the one secret he'd kept between them. "Please. Don't even finish that sentence. You *know*? You know *nothing* but *his* version. And you didn't come to me? Why? What does that say?"

"It says: It must be true. Besides, why would he lie? You and Facey, you broke my fucking heart."

"I didn't come to you because I *love you* harder than my own fuckin' kin. And I never wanted to hurt you. I knew it would *hurt you*. And it was meaningless. But I knew you wouldn't see it that way. So *why* bring meaningless shit into the picture?

"You know that picture of us," Ty continued, "where we've got our heads together with the same goofy expression? I look at that picture and I smile. Love's all inside that picture. I look at it, and I see two twins. And over the years we've argued over who's the good twin, and who's the evil twin, and it's always been a joke. Please don't see me as evil now. There was never *a lie*, any meaningful lie between us. Only an omission. There's big a difference, baby boy."

"Yeah, whatever. You and your words," David said, dismissing him. "Whatever *you* say is gold. You see a photo of friendship? If you remember, *you* set the whole damn thing up, how to pose and how to look to get the right effect. There's a *metaphor* for your ass. In the movie of your life, *you direct* your friendships. The rest of us are only actors. Well you're not fuckin' Cecil B. Demille. And you're *not* Spike Lee prettying up the ghetto scenes of *my* life!"

"What you talkin' about? I don't do that…I…"

"Some people don't *understand* this thing I call friendship, Ty. They don't know how to *live in it*, or to *stay* in it. All they know is how to stand like a little crippled god over it. And they decide, 'This is what *I'll* do, and this is how *they'll* act, and this is how *I'll* handle things.'"

"Calm down! I don't know what you're talking about…"

"All these years, I thought *you* were the good twin, and *I* was the evil one. But the truth is, you're not so righteous, my friend. In fact, you're kind of a slutty little closet whore! And you're not a very good queen, either. You could use a few lessons in Telling Sexual Secrets 101. So I thought maybe I'd just keep a few secrets of my own. Well, here's one for you: I've *hated* your self-righteous ass for three years and counting."

"Fine, hate me because I *betrayed* you. Hate me because I stole something from you. But you *never owned* him, and I never once—"

"Disrespected me?" David said.

"You don't want to listen to my side? OK. Then, we're *not* having this conversation."

"There you go, playing the fucking director! Cut! You think you got the power to say we're not having this conversation? Well, fuck you!"

"I'm not *playing* anything. I'm just being Ty, remember him? Probably not, I guess, because Face and *your wild-ass brain* have devised a whole other truth."

"Fine. Go ahead. Try explaining yourself. The *short* version, please." David sat and held his head.

"It's simple. That night was the quickest mistake I ever regretted. But I didn't do it *to* you, or *against* or *in spite* of you. In fact, *you* weren't even in the room. I thought I was doing it *for* myself. My *baser self*. My dick worked fine that night. He's Depina-ized his version, I'm quite sure. Suffice it to say, it was a long hot sweaty lie. He sucked me, I fucked him, he launched into a *performance art piece* called: 'I'm not really a homosexual. But I might get to play one on TV!'"

"What? Come on!" David scoffed.

"That's what the boy told me. I couldn't make that shit up. It's vintage Face. Think about it."

David did, and, for a second, he let himself chuckle. But just for a second. He figured he'd probably forgive Ty's *deceptive ass* one day. But not *that day*. His first concern was Face.

The cop's immediate focus remained on Browny. Ty hired him a lawyer, who got Browny out of custody. But he wasn't *cleared* of anything. Several people had witnessed his animated exchange with Face at the Zebra Den.

Browny explained it. "I asked him if he wanted to put the group back together for a benefit. And he laughed in my face. Then I asked for a loan, man. He *owed* me! And I only did it for Jonathan. I swear, it was for Jon's bills. And he dissed me in front of his fancy friends. And they was *all* laughin' at me and my suit! Yo! And I got pissed, and I booked. I've been madder than *that* at his ass and ain't tried to kill him."

Meanwhile, in the venerable chambers of a well-known judge, a promising, politically ambitious young lawyer met quietly with the esteemed and politically well-connected adjudicator. The young lawyer told the judge the story of a fragile girl and the terrible thing a certain man had done to her. But there was no evidence of the deed. At best, it was a case of "he said, she said." The young lawyer proposed that if said alleged man, who'd recently been shot by said fragile girl, would *not* press charges, the young woman would never speak publicly of her motive, and would furthermore agree to seek psychiatric care in a facility of the good judge's choosing.

It was a solution that, the judge agreed, seemed best for all parties involved.

December 1, 1993

"Tyrone, please! No painted black thumbnails tonight!"

"It's a show of mourning. You *know* that. I do it so I'll always remember…"

"Tyrone, you're *not* wearing *that* to this dinner. You *know* people will ask why."

"I have no problem telling people why," Tyrone said, adjusting his tie in the bathroom mirror.

"Well, it's queer, and it's eccentric, and I'd prefer you didn't wear it," Blur said bluntly.

Ty had already agreed to fashion his braided mane into a sedate ponytail, and now the man was bitching about his fingernails? Instead of jumping in his face, for once, Ty remained silent. He removed the polish, and quietly accompanied Blur to the firm's reception honoring a senior partner's anniversary. Ty remained in the background as he'd been instructed. Blur danced with the lovelies. Tyrone watched. Blur adjourned to smoke cigars with the big boys in the parlor. Ty sat at the bar. Blur made an obvious pass at the coat-check girl. Ty was not amused. For one rebellious moment he thought of stopping the Swing band, seizing the mike, and announcing that he and Blur would soon celebrate their own anniversary as longtime apocalyptic lovers, and were thinking about adopting a Korean kid. But he chilled.

When they returned home, it was *on*.

"You know, I've had just about enough your straight man act. It's too way too fucking fake for comfort. You stand there in your little suit spouting your little ideas on justice, crime, punishment, and manhood, and you don't have a clue. Ever think maybe you're just a little man in a little suit?"

"Good. A height joke. What was it you said about name-calling? An act of the guilty? Ever think I might want a discreet partner who acts like a *man* in public? And how many times I have I told you, *don't grab my hand in the fuckin' street!*"

"You know, I used to admire all the things you wanted to become, and now all you've become is *this thing*."

"Listen, I know how to play the game. Apparently, you don't have a *clue* about how they do things in the *straight* world. Maybe you should take some lessons."

"Who the hell am I living with these days? At the risk of sounding like a sixth grader with a crush: Do you even *like* me? Sign your *real name* in my slang book, and let me know."

"Don't be *ridiculous!*"

"No. I'm serious. Tell me how you feel. I can take it. Just say the words. If you don't wanna be who you are with me, then be someone else, someplace else. I'd rather *do alone* than do time with your insecurity."

"I'm only showing you a few things you need to correct."

"Correct them for *who*? Myself? Or for you? If you're so uncomfortable with who I am, then we have a serious problem here, bruh!"

Tyrone remembered their sex life in the last few weeks. How, when the two grew hot and sweaty as Coke bottles at a Fourth of July jamboree, he'd lie inside that confusing afterglow and think, *Damn! You never stop blowin' me or my mind. You're fuckin' heroic between these sheets. Too bad you're a fuckin' fraud in life!* Now those thoughts he had given no tongue, he could say aloud, and not give a shit about the repercussions.

"You're strictly homosexual, Blur. You like to kiss men, lick men, suck, and get fucked by men. Preferably in the dark. All that makes you is a homosexual. Take it from me, you're a fantastic homosexual. But I don't think you've ever been *gay*, and I don't think you want to be."

"That's not the case."

"No, I think it is. Every one of your friends I've ever met is homophobic. They make fag jokes around you, and you *laugh*? Do you hate yourself *that* much? What do they *really* know about you, or *me*, or *us* for that matter?"

"That's none of their business!"

"What the hell are you so *ashamed* of?"

"What the hell are you so fucking *proud* of? You and your damn parades, and your crazy faggot friends. This whole damn crusade, it makes me sick!"

"Damn it. Finally some truth breezes into the room. You don't want a relationship with me or my friends or the rest of the world. You just want to fuck and suck in the dark, and walk tall and straight in the sun." Tyrone laughed. "Fuckin' David was right. Again."

"The name alone says it all, Ty... 'Anti-Nelly.'"

"Please don't bring him or *her* or *it* into this fuckin' conversation!" Blur fumed.

"Watch it, now! You disrespected *me*, because that's just what I've *let* you do. But no more! And don't you *dare* disrespect David! Trust me. You *don't* want *that* fight."

"Why? What is he to you? Your bitch, your lover on the side? I thought you liked *men!*"

"What the hell would *you know* about manhood?"

"I know this much: I know when to say *fuck you!* And fuck queer David! And fuck whatever queer agenda you're on! Fuck moving to Westchester and setting up house with me, too. In fact, *fuck us!* Fuckin' forget about *us* altogether!"

"Are you sure?" Ty asked. "Are you really fuckin' sure? Because I can get straight-up amnesiac on your ass!"

Blur left with two suitcases, a suit bag, a shaving kit, and not another mumbling word.

The Face Case was magically hushed. The official word: "The act of a probable stalker." Browny was seared, but not badly burned.

Blur campaigned mightily for the esteemed adjudicator in the next election, and in return was appointed to a politically advantageous position in the district attorney's office.

* * *

Depina's wounds were not catastrophic: two bullets to the posterior region, a little gunpowder on his ego. In a star exit, under the sneaky shroud of night, he left the hospital. But while there, secrets were revealed and unlocked. The kind one only discovers after a *complete* examination, including blood work.

It was all in the doctor's face. He delivered the sentence plainly.

The cinema in Face Depina's mind played a reel of events, mistakes, and places he wanted to snatch back from the deepest depths of forever.

He became drawn, and withdrawn. He was decidedly low-key. He stopped seeing Chaz altogether. There would be no more carnal battles in *The War Room*. He broke it off coldly. Never gave a reason why.

There were lots of messages on his various machines. He listened to the distressed "Facey, are you OKs?" from the usual jaded set. There were hounding messages from the press, annoying ones from Browny, and some deeply unsettling ones from Chaz.

It was too much to deal with *straight*. He needed something to take the edge off. *Who* was he gonna call? For legal reasons, he had to distance himself from Claudio, at least temporarily. He thought, *Maybe Browny?* But those damn dealers Browny knew *stepped on, cut,* and manipulated the purity of the shit. Who had the good shit? And where could he fix? And how quick?

He thought of a cat who hung out in Tompkins Square Park.

When the cat saw Face's desperate condition, he decided he'd have a little strung-out junkie fun. "You want it, big man? Huh? You want the good shit? Well, suck me off!"

Sometimes, when a man knows he's drowning, he goes down peacefully, with no fight, no desire to rise again.

* * *

Chaz Williams, fresh from the gym and convinced the break-up was just a whim, another mood swing, decided to visit.

Face, in his haste to fix, had left the door unlocked. Chaz walked in on him and his dealer thug. Seeing those two together, an apoplectic Chaz abruptly stormed out.

Back at his apartment, he drank heavily. Chaz *straight* was a gentle giant, but Chaz polluted was Mr. Hyde, squared. Few knew that terrifying side of his eerie silence. Those who did shivered in its wake. Realizing he possessed an inner psychotic, Chaz rarely revived him via the bottle. But he did that evening. Things began to eat away at his gut. Then, in the middle of the night, he returned to Depina's loft, carrying something *extra* dangerous in his pants.

Face lay sleeping, naked and alone. Chaz stood over him, loving yet hating how peaceful he looked in postcoital sleep. It would've been incredibly easy to shoot him in his naked balls. Maybe Chaz would junk the place, make it look like some crazy trick had gone berserk. He thought of the public ridicule on top of the recent shooting, imagined the headlines: "Face Shot in Pinga! Details at 11." How sweet that would be.

Chaz had quit his job, forsaken friends. Even his prowling lifestyle had ended that torrid night in Spike's Den. And for what? Some vacant-eyed pretty-boy junkie? The sight of him burned hot coals in Chaz's eyes. He slowly stroked his .45, as if it was the last true lover he'd ever have.

Face slept with his mouth open. Chaz very quietly brought the barrel to Face's lips, slid it softly along the bottom one.

He wanted Face to wake up and *beg*. As he inched the barrel deeper, his lover stirred a little. Chaz pushed in deeper still. Face began to roll his tongue along it, sucking it, as his hand played between his thighs. Chaz could see him growing aroused.

After a few perverse moments, Face's eyes shot wide open, staring directly at Chaz, seemingly unafraid. His stoned fearlessness took away Chaz's base homicidal instinct, and Chaz removed the gun.

"Go ahead. Do it. Do it, man. Do it, and do us all a favor. Come on. I'm right here waitin', baby. Come on!" he yelled. "Look at you! All that dick, and no fuckin' balls! Pathetic. If you had *real* balls, you'd do it!" Face said, staring Chaz straight in the eyes.

Instead of pulling the trigger, Chaz Williams felt a tear pull down his cheek. "You *love me*, don't you?" he asked pitifully.

* * *

Back in Harlem, Browny's woman had once again drop-kicked his junkie ass. It was Juanita's last-ditch tough-love effort to get her man clean. She wanted him off crack, off booze, off self-pity, and off that perpetual merry-go-round and sometime savior, Face Depina.

Finally, Browny broke down and told Juanita his whole ugly, confused, stupid, nonsensical Face story.

She *still* put him out.

But knowing now the sleazy way Face operated and the way he'd played *her man*, well, Juanita Lewis just wasn't having it.

A wrathful Juanita was a thing no man wanted to endure, because that wrath was just too *fantastic!* She'd gained a lot of weight in the '80s. Truth be told, she was a sister with an acute ham hock dependency. But by then she'd grown in spirit, and in love too. All that ire coming from a woman of her size and threat, loud and ghet-to-proud with her shit. A woman with a fluency of the "motherfuck" language cussing and *punking* you, hand on her hip, fingers in your face: It was too much. Standing away from it, you could see in her wrath the wild freestyle Thelonious Monk art of it. But up close it was like fire, and that day Face Depina was gasoline.

"Mr. Depina, Face, whatever yo motherfuckin' name is. I *know* everything," she said, folding her arms, getting her posture in gear for that erratic figure-eight head and neck swerve thing she did.

Oh, nah. Here it come at me. This mad-ass Black Buick's about to stomp on the gas. And I'm high and sore, and I'm sick, and she don't care! I need to get high, and look at that Buick. Ain't no stoppin' it.

"You been jerkin' *my man* around all this time, ya punk bitch! Do you know the cops was all over his ass when you got shot? Do you *know* they come in *my* motherfuckin' place, breakin' up stuff in *my* house? And Faison, he ain't been nothin' but loyal to you. Oh! So now you's about to do right by him. I don't think you got enough to pay him what you *owe* him. But Mr. Face Depina, you *will* make it right!"

This shit was the *last* shit Depina needed. He needed to cop, to fix, and quick, and he told her, "Look, I'm takin' care of things with Faison. Hell, I'm always cleanin' up after his ass. But *that's* between me and him. It's none of your damn business! Now go away. *Please.*" He said this arrogantly, using his lowering eyes as brooms to brush her off entirely.

Only Juanita was *not* a piece of lint on the shoulder of his new Versace.

"Who the fuck you think you're talkin' to? You don't mean *shit* to me! You think *you* know people? Well, I *know people*, too. People who would just as soon as cut ya than look in them fake-ass white-boy eyes of yours! No. You don't wanna fuck with me, little boy! Hell, I'll kick yo ass myself, 'cause you *ain't* all that!"

"Please. Go home, woman."

"Listen up, you fuckin' junkie! Yeah, I said it! I know *all about you*. And what I don't know, I can figga. So you gonna listen to what I got to say: My baby needs help, and *you* g'on get him into Daytop Village! You got power, so there won't be no long waitin' list to get him in. Y'all *need* to go in on the buddy plan! But your habit is *your* damn business. Once *my man* is clean, and I'm sure he's clean, me and him is gettin' married. And you, *you payin'* for the wedding! Oh yes. I don't stutter. You payin' for it. You buyin' *everything* from the flowers to the motherfuckin' socks on his feet. We'll be honeymooning in Jamaica. And thank you for *that*, too. And when we get back, there *will* be a check in our mailbox with *my man's* name on it. A check for $50,000. And by the way, *orchids* is my favorite flower."

"Now I see why you and Browny hooked up. Glad ya found each other, 'cause you're two *delirious* bitches. Now book!" he sneered.

"Bitches! I'm a bitch? Really? Well, this *delirious* bitch is about get fuckin' psychotic!"

"Too late. That Buick done left the lot, baby," Depina cracked in his private desperation.

But he was *not* the Aramis Man in those old commercials. He wasn't, as the catch phrase said, "Ready For Anything." And he certainly wasn't *ready* for Juanita Lewis' trump card.

"Did I say psychotic? Maybe I meant, what's that word? Oh yeah, *pyromaniacal!*"

Face's mouth dropped open and all the air rushed out. He had to sit, and sit quickly. He sat, and he winced. His ass still hurt. Bullets tend to do that. He wondered what she knew, how she knew, and what she planned to do with what she knew.

"I know somebody who know somebody who got all kind of stories about some kid who burned a whole *lotta* property up in the South Bronx. Caused a whole lotta damage too. I figure, a whole lotta damage *must* mean a whole lotta time, ya think? You know, them cops still ain't solve that case? Homeboy, are you with me?"

* * *

It was a lovely wedding.

MARCH 1994

Floss Angeles seemed a perfect fit for a cool, hip, ambitious, smack-addicted, terminally ethnic New York Actor.

He rented a little place on Sunset. The thought was, after that one memorable role, his once critically acclaimed ass would be the new Flavor-of-the-Month, and he'd be offered all types of phat cash and challenging roles.

Unfortunately, Face's agent was unwilling to risk his reputation on an idling addict, and so he rarely submitted Face for parts.

In short, life in L.A. was *not* Facey's blue kidney-shaped pool! He wasn't "funning the sunshine, playing just to play," or becoming that crazy-paid denizen in his actory-foolish dream. He was just another hopeful in a city full of hopefuls, stranded amid the palm trees, sun-drenched plazas, highways, freeways, and lavish ways of L.A. It was a Whole New World out there, only this one didn't say, "Hello, Facey! You fine motherfuck! Welcome to L.A. Mr. Swifty Lazar's reserved a table at Chasen's. Mr. Geffen would like to see you. And please don't forget to return Steven's calls."

"Yo, Claude. It's me, man. Times here are *hoard* as a fuck. You go to Hollyrock, and the real estate's prettier, things seem friendlier, the people, the clothes, and the cars are finer. And everything's mahvelous. But this town will drain the heart and talent right out of a motherfucka! Everything ain't fake, just a helluva lotta pretend. But I'm hangin' in, baby. You know how *I* do. Hey, Claude...every now and then, check in on Chaz for me. I cut him loose but... What you mean, he don't *like* you? You got a dick and a whip, don't ya?"

In addition, modeling had turned a cold padded shoulder. Black men *who looked like Black men* ruled the catwalk now. The Era of The Light Skin Pretty Ones was ovuh. That phenomenon, coupled with Depina's chronic instability, his absences, and the jittery phantoms of his increasingly visible addiction, made him dispensable.

Junkies tend *not* to acknowledge a changing of the guard, of clothes, or of a decade. Face was primarily an '80s-thinker. And that thinker was looking craggier, less the *hunk du jour,* and more like yesterday's graying statue. He resembled a puny scarecrow, stripped of its vital stuffing. You knew him from that omnipresent Kangol, but what was he trying to hide? That perhaps Face Depina was no longer *the shit?* You could see the once-famous bones of his face, every one of them, exposed, gaping, and even the eyes were a sickly green color his skin was beginning to match.

MAY 1994

No new monies were flowing in, and Face was busy shooting up the cash he had. He'd scan the trades, go on open calls, put on a T-shirt, his leather, or his best suit to meet and greet and read for The Suits. He'd haul out the dusty charm, but something about him was just a little askew, the eyes weren't the same luminous green. The skin and smile were less vibrant. In certain slants under the cruel L.A. sun, one could see he was *balding!*

"Yo? What's supposed to happen to folks too cool for New York and too cold for L.A., anyway?" he asked of Conte, who was still busy funning in *New Joke City*.

"I know how it is, Facey. That's why I left the biz. You're hot, you're cold, you're cute, you're over. It's enough to make a nice Italian boy go crazy. Hey! San Francisco is a good place to go crazy."

"Nah. I miss my friends, man. Hell, I even miss you, and my little fag David too."

"Then come *home*, man. We can be on Fire Island by the weekend, nuts up!"

"I can't."

"Why not? Just come home!"

"I can't, Claude. I...I don't look like *me* anymore," Face confessed "And I'm broke as shit."

But not everything looked as bad as Face. "Say," Claudio said, "when was the last time you talked to *our* accountant?"

Face had totally forgotten those boring-ass money talks Conte forced on him. But those talks had been lucrative.

"You know what?" said Claude. "You can *thank* me later. Just come home, pretty boy. Come the fuck home and help me count some of this *moola!*"

JUNE 1994

Maybe it *was* better in New York. People wore more clothes, they covered up, and everything wasn't so wide-fuckin'-open. The hardest thing to do is to try to *act* normal, *look* normal, *be* normal when normal is a drive-in movie and you're watching it far away from inside a hazy window. Normal was a two-dimensional flick, and he wasn't the star. Hell, he wasn't even in the pic. All Face could do was *feel* his habit, and try to conceal his habit, and all the while he was yielding to nothing else in the fucking world *but* the fucking habit.

Back home he could always get a runner to deliver heroin to his crib. The problem was getting them to leave. His addiction thing was now an open secret. People wanted to *see him*, see his crib, hang out there, shoot up there, OD there. This was, after all, New York, and there were worse places to wake up dead. There was a growing group of mean boys who'd drop by just to watch him, fascinated by that palsy claiming his face, and the slow ballet against gravity as he'd nod his pitiful nod. And they would *goof* on him. The once famous Face Depina was losing weight, losing hair, and losing time.

"Yo! This motherfucker used to be somebody!" they'd laugh.

"Angel? Angel, is that you, laughin' at me?" Face asked, in his elongated way, through a haze of faceless Puerto Rican boys, who once, not so long ago, were *just dying to meet him*.

AUGUST 6, 1994

Even if his success *was* only a fit of serendipity, Depina thought, *Maybe I'm entitled to a little bit of* better.

But suddenly, *better* turned its sunny face. That dizzy spiral of days where everyone wanted Face. "Get me Face" had spun off the calendar. All at once, that cool leather coat of fame had played out of style. But he thought he could stitch a new one, because his needle and his fixings were in a metal box beneath his bathtub.

Sometimes *the elixir* betrays you. But even then, there can be a certain placidity. Even then, in that final jerk of quietude, perhaps for him, there was a long blue moan in the end.

The plaintive howls of his dog, Sasha, caused a disturbance in the building. Someone called the cops. There was nothing they could do. When EMS came to pick up the body, no one recognized him. So gaunt, wasted, and blue it took a mortician's artistry to make him resemble the man he used to be.

The few who saw him in those final months guessed his story would end badly. Knowing him, in that limited way some people *allow* you to know them, it would be easy to say he never wanted anyone to see him *looking like that*.

AUGUST 7, 1994

"He kept talking about being sick and tired. Life was becoming this crazy movie beauty contest, and he was chickenshit about his looks changing. He was talking about ending the flick before his audience got bored. He was shooting up all the time, behind closed doors, alone. But it wasn't about anaesthetizing the pain anymore. Facey was shooting for death's door—I know that. The biggest thrill wasn't the high. The biggest thrill was in *not knowing*, not *caring* if he nodded off and never woke up. That's what it comes down to when you're *sick* and tired all the time. So many nights I'd find him strung-out, on that edge. I had to smack him around, throw him in a cold shower, walk him around like a cripple. He'd curse me: 'Motherfuck you, Claudio! You fuckin' fake-ass *Guido* bastard! Get the fuck outta my goddamn life! You ain't no fuckin' God! This is between me and the Real Guy!'

"Guess I finally realized what he meant. Facey *wanted to wake up dead*. We had a way of sending each other messages. He was my friend. You don't want to see your friend looking so pitiful. So I said, 'Facey, you know what? I love you, man. You say the word and it'll be done. I'll do it myself...'cause I love you that much,' " Conte claimed in a late night phone conversation with Bliss.

AUGUST 10, 1994, FACE'S FUNERAL

"Pascal. What can you say about Pascal? He was Adonis and Venus too," her elegy began. "I looked at him and my molecules hummed. After you met him, they never quite stopped humming, did they? The first time I saw him, he was standing on the set, illuminated from behind by a spot. I noticed how tall he was. Men like my father, men with Latino blood, they seem to stand taller than the rest, because that's how a man stands when he's out to prove something. Pascal moved in a slow sway toward me, the light left his wide shoulder, and another settled on his face. My God! A cool savannah breeze swirled over my arms and every part of me was Goosebump City. Ice-green eyes cut over the room and landed like warm emerald and bronze butterflies all over me.

"'You're, uh, Bliss, right? Hey, Bliss. I'm Face. So, you ready to do this thing?'

"Who was he, anyway? A scared little boy or a cocky son of the streets? A sly fox or a sad shelterless puppy? Whoever he was, strange, isn't it, how the things we find ourselves attracted to... wind up making us cry?"

Bliss, at that point, was crying.

"Say what you want about him, but Pascal 'Face' Depina was notorious is his sway."

No one quite knew what the hell she meant, but it fit somehow.

* * *

Tyrone:

"I doubt if he ever read the book, but Face reminded me of a quote from *The Picture of Dorian Gray*: 'It's better to look good than to be good.' Maybe a part of him wore the skin of a secretly scarred kid. But he learned to overcome it cosmetically, at least. I remember he had this *move* in high school. He gave people the peace sign. He'd put his two fingers very close to his face, so if you didn't respond the sign became a scratch of the nose, a rub under the eye. If you didn't acknowledge him, screw you! You'd never *punk him*. It was a very cool move. Face was the Duke of Cool Moves. The freaky sexy ones usually are.

"It would be a lie to say we were friends. I tried, but he made it hard. Most times I thought of him as a pretty fool. Pretty lucky, and pretty unappreciative. I believe passion and *coldness* coexist inside us all, but Face's *stuff* stretched the limits of human contradiction. He wanted to be noticed, and once he was, he grew to hate it. He wanted to be loved, yet held disdain for those who tried to love him. He wanted to know pleasure, yet he seemed to almost *enjoy* inflicting pain.

"Was he in some kind of private pain? If so, it never really showed or photographed. His outside distracted us. Maybe beautiful things make us selfish. Even as we age we don't want to see *beauty* grow old. So maybe, just for us, he decided he wouldn't. When he did, he didn't let us see it. Guess the Duke of Cool Moves struck one last time.

"I'll miss him the way Batman might miss The Riddler if The Riddler ever took his bag of tricks and left Gotham City for good. Peace, Face."

* * *

Browny to Juanita:

"Listen to Ty talking 'bout him like he was some-damn-body. *The Riddler!* Sheeit! Yo! I'm keepin' it real. Do you think I came here 'cause he was my friend, my partner, my boy? Oh, hell no! I needed to see if the motherfucker was *really dead*. Wouldn't put it past his slick, devious ass to cook up some scheme, some bullshit. I thought the mofo was slicker this year, though. But I guess the motherfucka really is tag-on-the-big-cold-yellow-toe dead."

"Shh," Juanita said. "Not in God's house, baby."

* * *

"Once there was this gorgeous, gorgeous time when we were all living our dreams," David began. "I know y'all expect me to get up here, scale that gender fence, and act a fool, but today the fool has left the asylum. I see no need for folly anymore. Facey's gone. And I loved that boy. Some of you know that. And the cherry on the cake of my outrage is that the world gets so judgmental of behavior when it's only *human*. The way we are, and how we got there, it's called the survival of human beings, baby. I could tell you a few stories about it.

But this is for Pascal Ornette 'Face' Depina, devout hell-raiser of our emotions. How many of you *know* there was a kind of sadness to him? Not many, I bet. He kept that beautifully cool unflappable *other* Face in check, so the rest of the world would miss *that thing* in him. I saw it once or twice, and it broke my heart. He ached like the rest of us human beings squared, and he'd take that ache out on us or whoever was there. No matter what kind of love or friendship or solace we offered, he'd take it like a hungry desperate thief, and maybe he silently resented us for being chumps. Whatever we gave him, it wasn't enough. See, I know, he was stamped as *damaged goods* from the moment he first breathed air. That was his heritage, and no amount of idolatry could ever fix that. He didn't trust *love*. When a child is never given the keys to love, the possibility of being able to accept love dies a little more every day. So maybe we should take comfort in what he was able to give."

Sitting there, Ty's mind drifted back to one shining night in October 1991…

"Hey. Look at us, being civil. Having cocktails and sharing war stories. We've never been this civilized. This shit feels so… *Old Acquaintance*."

"Whatever, man," a confused Face said, never a fan of old Bette Davis movies. Face was in a strange mood, looking everywhere, everyplace but Tyrone's eyes. Then he just decided to ask him. "So, I guess you don't *hate* me any more, huh?"

"I never hated Pascal. He was i-ight. I just never *liked* 'Face' very much."

"Damn! Are ya drunk tonight? Or am I too high to hit you? You just said that shit straight out. Sometimes a man can be *too* honest."

"I'm guessing you must have heard that somewhere," Ty jabbed.

"Ow! See, that why we clash. People expect me to be a prick, a bastard. Not you. You try to go out of your way *not* to be. I know your trip better than you do, baby. You like to go around livin' your life like you never want anybody to ever say anything *bad* about you."

"Well," Ty began. But when he contemplated that statement, he thought, *Damn! Did Face Depina, of all people, just unriddle me?* "Well, I'm a gay Black man who's fairly successful—no target there, huh? But what if I didn't want foul shit said about me? What's wrong with that?"

"It's useless. If mugfuckers can't find nothing negative about your ass, they'll make shit up. You think you gonna go to heaven 'cause of that do-good shit? What if there's no heaven, Ty? What then? All you did was waste so much fuckin' time and fun tryna be *better* that the rest of us. Ya think I'm a heartless bastard? Hey, maybe I am. I admit it. But every now and then, Ty, you'll say shit, or do shit, or just *think* shit so hard you out-bastard the worst fuckin' bastard in me. I'm not blamin' ya for it. I understand. Maybe it's just the way we survive."

It was the opening night of his play and he'd never expected Face to show. But there he was, *notorious is his sway*, saying halfway nice things, semiprovocative things instead of bent and ugly things. If Ty looked beneath that *cool unflappable* display he might've realized Face was *going through something*. Face was, in his own way, assessing his plight.

"Tonight was cool. You did decent work, man. I kinda thought I might've seen *myself* up on that stage. But it's like I didn't even exist. I saw Davy all over the place, a little bit of Browny too. Still holdin' on to them damn grudges, huh? I didn't think you'd *resent me* forever, man," Depina said.

"Come on, man. Don't make me say something *nice* to your ass. Oh, what the hell. Here it is. I never hated you. I don't even *resent* you anymore. You just… *disappoint* me. But that's *my* trip, not yours."

"So you was trippin'? Is that why I'm not in your play?"

"You? Who could write *you* down on paper, man? You're a straight-up enigma, and that means…"

"I'm not stupid, Tyrone. I *know* what that means."

"For me, a character isn't real unless he unravels who he is and lets me *see* him."

"Oh. I remember once I unraveled and you *seen* plenty," Face quipped.

"I wasn't talking about your dick, man. I'm not talking about all the shit you've pulled. I'm taking about *why*. But you'd never give that up, would you? Sure, I could've put some vain-ass pretty boy on the page, but he would've come off as pretty and empty. I don't think you're that pretty or that *empty*, man. I just never knew *who* the fuck you really were or what filled you up."

"Don't get this twisted, man, but you and Davy, you share everything like chicks with your freakin' periods. I never wanted people seeing me bleed. Just ain't my trip."

That half-drunken tidbit speaks volumes for the man under Depina's skin, Tyrone thought.

"But I sat in the audience," Face continued, "and watched those people sayin' things out loud. And I gotta tell you, I was almost jealous of your flow. I even remember some of the lines and shit—like that thing about respect. What was it? 'Snatch respect'?"

"Snatch it anyway you can. With your fist, with your lips, with your example," Ty recited, slightly amazed that Face had paid attention.

"Yeah, that's it. You did all right for yourself, by yourself. This fuckin' thing looks like it's gonna be a hit. What's that they say? Boffo, baby."

He said it as if he *knew* it—and as if in some secret part of himself he might even be *proud* of Tyrone. It was a *good moment*. They never had too many of those.

"Hey, that's a thick watch you've got on," Ty commented, gazing at the chunky gold-plated Rolex gleaming on Face's arm.

"Ah! You *like that*, huh? It is pretty fly, ain't it?" Face smiled to himself. "You want it?"

"Yeah, right. Sure," Ty joked.

But Face began to remove it, because he was serious.

"Nah, Face. I've never been into flashy stuff. And I'm not ready to sell my soul to Beelzebub. But thanks anyway."

A kind of quiet distress settled on Depina's countenance, then he asked, "Ty? You ever think we're *losing* ourselves, *our spiritual selves*, and just becomin' people who have a lotta shit?" Those haunting eyes for the first time searched Ty's for confirmation.

Ty looked at him with a real sense of *awe*. And he hadn't done that in years. Well, not since he'd laid eyes on the Depina penis. *Spiritual selves?* "Losing our spiritual selves? Yeah. All the time," he slowly answered. "In fact..." Then someone, perhaps Mr. Destiny, tapped his shoulder, and Broadway's newest playwright left what had promised to be an interesting, possibly even mind-bending conversation.

* * *

Tyrone wondered now if things would've been different if he and Face could've learned how to *talk* to each other. It seemed the only good thing in being enemies was that at least they knew where they stood.

Who was Face, really? Ty had tried to solve the riddle. On occasion, he'd asked Face about his mother and Face had invented stories of loveliness, bravery, and sacrifice. But were the tabloids right? Was his father a chattering derelict? When Ty asked about his heritage, most specifically Alphonze Depina, Face shot him the look of a thousand deaths. Some things were better left unsaid.

David stood, finishing his elegy: "The saddest thing of all is *because he looked like a fantasy*, everyone expected him to be one. I wish I could've told him the secret. I know it now. The trick is, let people see the real you. Let them love, hate all the things that you are. Those who'll still love you, they're the ones who came to say."

Later stylish men in black and matching sunglasses removed the coffin, and the people who knew bits of Face and pieces of Pascal gathered outside in the street. Ty had never seen the Duch look more lost. Ty grabbed his arm and whispered, "Tonight, if you want, we can just get pissy drunk. Talk all night, or not talk at all. Whatever you feel would be the proper requiem for *your Facey*. I just don't want you going into some dark place all alone."

"I'm fine, Ty. Death, sex, and funeral dirges, you know how they affect my libido. Tonight's a night for dancin'. If I throw myself *hoard* enough into the music, I might just dance myself to death. Then I won't see my Facey in every tall fine man's physique. I'm dancin' tonight, baby. You can come with me if you want, but ya damn sure can't stop me!"

Bliss Santana joined them on the street. Throughout the years, she and David had never been in such close proximity. Now there they were.

"Well, hello, Miss Bliss. At last we meet."

"So you're David," she said, managing the slowest of smiles.

"I need to tell you something," David began.

All at once, both Ty and Bliss held their breath.

"Once I had a crush. So many of my stories start out that way. He was a Puerto Rican boy from Newark. Couldn't salsa to save his pointy-toe-shoe-wearin' life. So, cute as he was, I had to drop-dip him. But as a goof, we once tipped into a dance school. The point of this little review is, I watched you once. Remember working at Arthur Murray's, teaching those Latin steps to them old rhythm-free people?"

"Another lifetime ago."

"Well, you were something to see in that lifetime. You in that tight yellow dress with the feathers on the side. I thought, *Ay caramba, mami! Wow! Look at her!* You were way too pretty for that place. It was a waste of time. But every now and then, one of those rhythm-free men got a step right, and something in your face brightened, and you just *let loose*. Suddenly, you were Rita Moreno in *West Side Story*, hair flying, dress gliding, so free and sexy. You were a spirit. We should all be so free and sexy," he finished sadly.

"Free? Isn't it *sexy* to think so," Bliss said.

"I'm going to hug you now, Bliss," David announced. "Now don't get *skurred*. It'll be very short and sweet, but sincere. Are you ready?"

"Yes, I think I am." She planted her feet firmly.

David's hug was very much like him: short and sweet and sincere. And he said, "God bless, Bliss. Goodbye, Ty. We'll talk." He kissed his best friend's cheek, then walked away.

Later in the day, Browny appeared at the grave site to share one last sip with the dead. Considering *everything*, he *still* felt cheated. All he said was, "Peace out, ya miserable bastard."

Everyone wondered what happened to Chaz. Was he too distraught to deal? Some would say yes. Five hours after hearing the inevitable news, Chaz Williams suffered a seizure. It was later diagnosed as a brain aneurysm.

Later still, Angel appeared. A thin bruise of a man, he had no words. He poured a shot of *bourbon* over the grave.

LABOR DAY, 1994

Ty sat at his writing desk, talking to Trick. "Obviously, I've got nothing going on, or I wouldn't be stuck here talking to your ghostly ass. It's Labor Day. Jerry *still* ain't found a damn cure for those kids. Muscular dystrophy has gotta be one behemoth-sized bitch! Over 30 years of telethons and still no cure. So what are our chances for a panacea?

"Nothing and no one is so young or pretty anymore. Face is dead, the rest of our goatees are graying. This disease is a teen. For my last birthday, Davy bought me a speed-bag. When I punch it, it becomes anyone or *anything* I want it to be. Can you guess what I want it to be?

"Well, Browny's finally landed a singing gig. He shifted his repertoire from pop to jazz and blues. He knows a little something about the latter. Just loves to flex those falsetto flourishes. The kid's not half bad, though. But didn't we all know that? And the Duch is now officially a *High Priestess of Fashion*. Maybe that's what he was meant to be second. He tested positive, you know. He wanted to get drunk one night, so we did, and he told me. We cried for days. Sometimes I still do.

"But David is a firebird, for real. Today at Wigstock, he decided it was time Davina retired. It was her last public appearance.

Nothing quite as sad as an old queen. Well, maybe there are a few sadder things. It was a damn good performance though. Every year someone steals the show and manages to out-do the most outrageous. This year, in my unbiased opinion, that thief was David. In that three-foot-high Afro wig and six-inch spiked heels, the dancer was stepping lively."

Twenty-Three

And Then There Were Two

"The last time I saw him he was outside The Blue Note in a heavy rain. He stood in the middle of this mean steel-shouldered city, with no fuckin' umbrella. Had on his good overcoat. His "jazz coat," he called it. It was black wool, long and flowing, and it hung along his wet shoulders in a way that made him *elegant*. When he saw me, he smiled a little. But his eyes, they seemed so weary and bankrupt of joy. Maybe it was his time. It seemed like life here had finally just wore him the fuck out."

Once *in another time and place*, David wondered why there was no music written especially for the dejected, lugubrious dancer. Where were the Blue Boy Waltzes, and those Bruised Bangee Boy Ballets? He would've, and most certainly could've, danced the rhythmic bluesy shit out of them. He was in constant search of the right music, and the right singer or dancer who understood and had an answer for his Blues Condition.

Suddenly Victor arrived, and all music was beautiful, *lovely*, vital, alive!

Look at him…my man. My dark, dominant, delish, thick-donged Daddy!

268

To the strains of a sultry samba, Victor asked David to dance. David took his hand, and comically took the floor, walking the *Enchanted Walk*—his head haughty, his limbs mimicking a stiff Bea Arthur meets Bela's Count Dracula glide.

They were alone at last, inside the moody dive they co-owned called Cool Relax.

The old cat with the crying guitar, Browny and the singers backing him, all the players and martini slingers had gone on to tear down and kick around what was left of the night. Outside on a small moonlit street, seedy elegance walked side by side with the hip sneers of leather boys. Ferocious pairings and terminal wet dreamers converged with the lies and cheats and the fictions of an empire. But inside, the cavernous room was brought alive by the soft Latin jazz of Ray Barretto, a favorite of Victor's.

Something in Victor's fragrance had always intoxicated David. Even after a night of entertaining, he smelled as if he'd just stepped out of the warm Caribbean Sea. He smelled and tasted like a new piece of humankind. Now, David's eyes were glued to that protrusion in his pants. Victor's gaze asked, *Are you ready to be seduced, puppy?*

Though 6 foot 3 and at 49 composed of more bulk than muscle, Victor seemed to bulge and muscle all over when they slow danced.

"Music OK, puppy?"

"On nights like this one right here, right now, no other music exists."

"So… Joo in a good mood?"

"The best," David replied, beginning to spritz down his lover's thigh. He wanted to rip those trousers off Señor Love Daddy, expose that proud *papi*'s *pinga* to the atmosphere.

"Good. I have something to say to joo, and it's harder than I thought."

"Oh, yes. It certainly is, Papi!" David chuckled slyly.

Victor sighed a warm trail down David's neck.

Anticipation raced through David. "What is it?" he asked. Then, not used to things going *so right* for him, unfamiliar with things *staying* right, David suddenly panicked, immediately thinking the worst. "What? Please. Please tell me, you're not sick."

"No. I'm fine. Pressure's down." Victor smiled as David silently breathed a sigh of relief. "Wait here. Papi's gonna show joo a night joo'll never forget!"

He vanished, and David lay inside some speechless dream, mad with love, happy in his skin. *Whee-e-e!* Suddenly the jukebox ignited—"In Your Eyes"—and the blue lights dimmed to the softest indigo. David heard breathing, ragged breathing, and realized those breaths came from the amplified speakers surrounding the room. *Ooh!* Victor was the Real Deal Master of slow seduction.

"I'm coming...closer. Can joo feel me? No. Don't joo turn around. Eyes closed! Breathe... Breathe with me..."

David obeyed, inhaled, exhaled slowly, feeling Victor's naked presence behind him. Buttons flew. Music played. Pants cascaded to the floor in a heap. Bodies were bathed in electric blue. And their breaths were not breaths, but small puffs of wind, the kind that make a candle flicker and a flame grow tall. A large, brown, benevolent husk was rubbered.

Atop the bar, David's legs became like straws, thrown over Victor's beefy shoulders. With a smile of seasoned recklessness, Victor aimed through that beckoning brown starfish. "Aw-w-w!" David groaned, washed in those wet eyes, his limbs vining, entwining his lover. Victor pulsed within him, methodical and slow, and David fastened on as that nimble, hollowed place in him conformed with a "Whoa!" to love's profuse width.

"Aw! Aw-w-w! Yes! Do me! Bust that piñata, Papi!"

He gripped the bar's rails, wincing, smiling, meeting, kneading Victor's thrusts.

Victor grunted, catching David's frantic limb and whipping it, inciting sensuous riots in him. "Joo feel me, puppy? Shit, jess, joo do!" His gruff beard raked David's neck, and he planted his kiss there.

David trembled, dripping, wet with sweat. "Yes! Don't stop!" he roared, as Victor bore down. *Tu mesientes*, puppy. *A la chingada—claro que si!*

David danced beneath him, a quaking, shaking body of *joy incarnate!* "Oh, yes, I'm…I'm gonna come for you, Papi. Only you, Papi!" he cried as he erupted.

Victor too vibrated at his deepest depths. And the gush was so strong, both lost gravity and fell to the floor. They laughed hysterically. Victor cradled Davy in a coat of fur, heartbeats, and laughter, their bodies full of jazz and sweat, their chests filled with rapid thunder.

David sighed a short breathless song, and, for once, it didn't sound anything like the blues.

"Joo all right, Puppy?"

"I'm all out of words for 'all right'," he panted.

"Joo happy?" Victor asked.

"More. More than happy. I could lie here ass-naked with you all night. Hey! Let's do it and not give a damn when the cleaning men come tomorrow. I'll just wave a foot over your back, 'Good mornin'!'"

Victor laughed. David often made him chuckle. Then he suddenly rose and walked across the floor.

Oh, Papi! Look at him, damn it! I gots me a man!

Victor returned, grinning, holding something behind his back.

"What you got there, Papi?"

"A little something for joo, of course."

"But you don't have to, baby. You've given me… Look, be careful! You don't want a spoiled little *maricón* on your hands," David giggled.

"Well, this should spoil us both," Victor said, whipping out a little velvet box.

How do you tell someone what you've only begun to realize yourself? That with him, you are the most complete man, person, human you will ever be. Your journey has left you bruised, battered, and bewildered. But not bitter, because you've learned and you've survived. And now, in that most excellent hour of your journey, you're ready—ready to release that Long Blue Moan.

"Oh my goodness, Papi! It's a ring! You're giving me a ring? What does this mean?"

"Everything," Victor said. "Everything."

The two made love again before falling naked, engaged, and fast asleep on top of the bar.

Dave had a dream.

* * *

It started out magnificently in that special violent arena where machismo clashes and sensitivity bleeds crippled red rivers. They called it "The Sweet Sport," and The Champ and The Contender were going at it, dancing, shuffling, mixing it up. Jab for jab, the sting and stun of fists flying, tagging, cutting, jabbing, and soon the river began to flow. With a flurry of uppercuts and a frenzied exchange of blows, each fighter scored points with the judges. But that vile virulent virus of a Champ remained unaffected. Still, even money was on David Donatello Richmond.

Initially, both boxers gave as good and hard as they got, and the hyped crowd settled in for a masterful night of pugilism. But by round 4, The Contender's arms grew heavy, his dancing legs weary. He looked a little wobbly, a bit dazed. He was fading, his will oozing away like the blood trickling down his forehead. Worst of all, he was dropping his fists, not guarding his grill. The crowd began to boo him, hiss him, thinking he would throw in the towel.

Wearily, he gazed back to his corner. No support there. He lumbered forth, resting his head in the hills of his opponent's chest. A few harmless body blows to the opponent's impenetrable torso. The Contender backed away and saw The Champ grinning behind his mouthpiece. Then it happened. The coup de grâce, the death blow. A hellish right cross to the nose that hammered out a spectacular sanguine mist, which drifted slowly to the canvas like a fizz of shattered rubies.

The Contender fell hard.

The hushed crowd watched, shocked, silent.

The referee shouted the count: "1, 2, 3, 4, 5, 6, 7, 8, 9, 10! He's out!"

In the corner of the defeated Contender, Daddy Richmond and Rico Rivera chastised mercilessly: "You let your fuckin' hands down! Why?

You forgot everything I taught you, damn it!" And, "You useless, *boy. Always was! Thought I could make a man out of you. But you ain't no man. You ain't nothing! Wipe that blood from yourself and put on a fuckin' sundress, bitch!"*

Why wouldn't they disappear, just leave him alone? David shouted, "I ain't gotta listen to you bastards anymore. Hell! Be gone! Vanish!" And so they did.

In their place stood Tyrone. A young Tyrone. Smiling and holding something in his hand.

* * *

"I had *that dream* again, Papi."

"Relax, Puppy. It's just a dream. It doesn't mean anything."

"No, I think it does. Madam Zoreena's foreseen hurtful things. I was afraid she was talking about you, Papi. Your heart. Your blood pressure. But now I'm not so sure."

"This dream any different?" Victor asked.

"Well, it starts out like before, where I'm pummeled to a bloody pulp. My father and Rico are tellin' me how worthless I am. But finally I'm strong enough to make them go away. Then Ty appears. But it's Ty from high school, with that long skinny horse face and the Sal Mineo hair. And he's holding this big-ass trophy, smiling his biggest, most goofy smile, and he's telling me, 'Screw the judges, Duchess! Screw the oppressors. Screw 'em all! You're the bravest champion of all the queens and all the queen's men!' I'm so happy to see him there. And when he says it, I *believe* him. I think, yes, damn it, I *am* a champion! But just as I'm about to hug him and bleed all over my goofy horse-faced bastard, he disappears. I wake up, and then I'm scared. What does it mean?"

A kiss exchanged energies. Between David and Victor Medina, there was only silence.

Face Depina was dead.

Bliss was living with HIV in Philadelphia with Face's daughter.

Faison Brown, who was quickly becoming a draw at Cool Relax

and other cabarets in the city, had just purchased Juanita a fully out big-ass mink coat.

And Ty…

After two successful plays and a marginally well-received novel, a sense of *fulfillment* had eluded Tyrone, and that lustrous light at the end of a long tunnel seemed at best anticlimactic.

"It's funny, David," he'd said weeks before. "I worked so hard because I thought the end result would be some money shot into happiness and self-contentment. But you know what? It never happens that way. The money shot is a pitiful little dribble, and the moan of contentment is so low you can barely hear the shit. I've wasted so much time waiting for that money shot. Maybe there's *more to contentment* than a long blue moan."

"Speak for yourself, baby. I'm perfectly happy just to moan with Victor. Well, *happy* is a concept. But I am content."

"Are you really, Duchess?"

"Yes, I am. And yes, I *mean* it. Even at this advanced age, even living with a muscular virus—with the right partner, contentment is a doable dance."

"Well, I'm so glad for you," Ty confessed, his eyes blurring with tears. "I'm glad because *you deserve it.*"

"And you? You still dancin' around 'happy' instead of grabbing it by the dick?"

"I'm not grabbing much of anything. Maybe *happy* is something outside of me, outside of this world I've been inhabiting. But I know there's some meaning out there somewhere. And I'm going to find it."

In the midst of losing friends in the life, losing lovers, losing his bearings, Ty had become haunted by his inability to find a lasting spiritual center. It had worn him down. He'd spent his life attempting to create *better* in himself, in others, and to write or sing, photograph, or carve something beautiful out of the pain of existence. But he grew tired of trying to show the world his scars, and its scars. It was time to concentrate on the business of healing them.

It had been building, erecting, becoming taller in his mind, this higher calling, this *second level to being* a human being.

The metamorphosis began in November of '91, with his first trip to Africa.

Something in Africa, in that time he'd spent wiping the sweltering foreheads of dying children, had resonated in him. Maybe, if he ever found someone *real*, he could adopt a child to love. Maybe he could impregnate a willing lesbian friend. Maybe he could father a child of his own. *Maybe, maybe,* life was full of fucking *maybe's.*

But children were alone and dying on a dying continent. Disease and famine were ravaging both coasts and rocking the interior.

Imani's letters from Liberia were troubling.

Dear Ty,

I write you tonight with a heavy heart. Inside the capital of Monrovia, this conflict has already claimed over 150,000 lives. I believe there are even more. Today a baby was born in my hands. Tonight a child died in my arms. So many others are losing their way. Mothers, fathers lie dying beside their children. But Ty, though people are barely holding on, some are holding on to survival, even in the hot and dry faces of death. I see them, and I am humbled. Even through famine and disease and the guns of rebel factions, these people, my people of the sun are striving to survive!

It was the dawning of an epiphany. In the final analysis, even staring into the eyes of death, the best of us strive for some kind of *existence with dignity.*

There *had* to be something *Tyrone* could do.

* * *

He decided to once again trek to Africa, this time to escape the lies and liars and riots and fires of his life. He approached several editors about embarking on a photojournalistic project on Africa's children. He was promptly rejected. Ty didn't care. *Fuck them!* He was strong-willed and independent. He went on his own.

Tyrone left for the Motherland with the intent to do better by the world.

En route, he wanted to see Paris, just once.

The night turned suddenly golden in the City of Lights. He could appreciate Notre Dame de Champs, The Arc de Triomphe, and still dream of that New York moan of jazz and speeding yellow taxis that ignored Black men. He could still dream of lovers, homeboys, church ladies, and bars and nights when an audience rose and screamed, "Author! Author!"

He was walking down the Champs Elysées, snapping photos, when he thought he saw a face—a vaguely familiar, if slightly older face. *Nah. It couldn't be him*, he told himself.

It was Paris on the cheap, complete with a $70-a-night dive on a winding Parisian street. Inside the lobby, he saw that face again, and that face *recognized him*. "Ty?" a voice asked.

It was a mug Ty hadn't looked into for nearly 20 years.

"Omar? Omar Peterson? What the hell are you doing here?" an astonished Ty asked.

"Starving," he said. "I've been living here for two years. I'm an artist now."

"Really? An artist. Who knew?"

"I did. Sometimes, I feel like I'm the *only* one who knows. So you're a writer now, huh? I read the reviews of one of your plays. Shit, Omar, keep it real. I went to see it, twice, Ty."

"Oh. So *you* were the one."

"So, Ty's in Paris," Omar said in disbelief. "Damn. Is life strange or what? So, how long you here for?"

"Until tomorrow."

"Oh," Omar said disappointedly. "Well, then you have to come with me. I wanna show you something."

What Omar showed him was *his* Paris. The one sprinkled with jazz clubs, out-of-print bookstores, and porn shops. Then he insisted they venture into a little art market, where several of his paintings were for sale. One of them was titled "Sad-face Lust." An oil of a young naked Black man alone on a bed, a single tear drifting down his cheek. That young long-faced man bore a remarkable likeness to a young long-faced Tyrone. "I must've done about 20 sketches of you, man."

Ty stared at the portrait for a long time, silently, then asked, "Why?"

"I was a little obsessed, I guess. I knew I'd hurt you. See, there's a look you used to get when you were hurt and tried like hell not to show it. But I could see it. It was all in those damn *Ty eyes*—so intelligent and sad. Like you *understand* everything—and *everything* just makes you sad. Sometimes, I close my eyes and I still see that look. It wrecks me, because *I* put it there. I'm sorry, Ty," he said. The colors in his voice wore all the hues of sincerity.

The two left the market as it began to pour. Instead of taking the Metro, they ran through the raindrops, laughing like fools. By the time they reached the hotel lobby, they were drenched.

"I've got a bottle of wine in my room. It was a gift. A Château something and it's like over a hundred years old. You wanna…?"

Tyrone's first instinct was to say no. Hell, no! He was on his way to do *noble work*, and he hadn't come to Paris for some bang-bang, peace-out thang.

"Well, just walk me to my room, so I can get out of these wet clothes," Omar suggested.

Tyrone accompanied him, and as they stood outside the door, Omar said. "You look good." He soothed away a bead of rain from Ty's ear.

Then Ty saw in Omar's eyes a hunger as deep and wide as Somalia, and then traces of Kenya in his kiss. After all those years, the taste of betrayal was in no way evident. That one lunging kiss said a million wasted things, spoke a thousand formerly hard homeboy utterances.

Omar opened the door, and nudged Ty inside. Right away, he ripped Ty's leather from his wide shoulders.

"Where's the wine?" Ty asked.

"Fuck the wine! For the longest, I've waited to make things right with you. I'm a man, now. Before, I was just a confused, scared *punk-ass* kid." His hands pulled and tugged at Ty's rain-soaked shirt.

Africa waited. Yet Africa was in Omar's face when he turned to plant a kiss on Tyrone's lips.

Omar moved along Ty's neck, licking downward, suckling earth-brown tits with a hunger that seemed brand-new. He ran his lips against the slopes of Ty's chest and shoulders. With hands tracing, racing the contours of each other's flesh, they fell to the bed, gripping, groping, zippers unzipping.

Yes! Omar thought.

Ty's dark engorged member was looped in a leather-braided ring (a gift from his first *real* lover, Trick Brown). Omar took him in hand, and he slowly swallowed him. And the noise of his slurping drowned out the sound of the rain. His tongue warmed and colored Ty like a beautiful sepia dream.

Omar rose. "Let's do this, Tyrone. I can take it like a man. Wherever it leads."

Ty eased Omar's legs apart and he slowly entered him. Omar watched, as if his eyes were taking photographs of Ty's near-handsome face, remembering that devilish grimace each time Tyrone lit into him. Together, they moved with the flow of water, in a buoyant, warm, and fluid rhythm.

There was only the sound of the rain, the clapping of their flesh, the noise of a gasping rubber and their heated breath. It seemed to last forever, until finally a feeling of consummation grew so intense that Ty had to retreat.

"Oh! Yes, yes, shit! Omar-r-r! It's my baby!" he cried, ripping off the rubber within an inch of its life.

Tyrone arrived in a white torrent on Omar's furry chest.

Omar also pitched and whirled inside that bed in Paris. His charge leapt high to the fuzzy rocks of his belly as Tyrone's essence slowly rolled down his torso.

Yet, even in that eerie afterglow, Ty wondered what had changed?

Even if he *cared* for the man lying in his arms, thoughts of *caring too much* distressed him a little. Where would all that caring lead?

Sensing Ty's uneasiness, Omar cradled him tightly, ran a hand through tousled copper dreads, and whispered, "I'm home. I'm here, Ty. This time, I swear, man, I ain't going anywhere."

"Well, I am. Remember? Tomorrow, I leave for Africa."

Omar lifted his head, and he kissed Tyrone, and it was returned, slowly. And slowly their tongues spun toward the open dark continent of each other's mouths. It was an exchange of spit, a duel of lust and ache and need. And goodbye.

* * *

Sometimes we find ourselves staring into the wilderness of another spirit's eyes, and all that is left between us is a sigh, or a moan. But it's OK. A moan is also a survivor's sound.

Strange, the things the universe hands us…

Tyrone Hunter made his way to Africa, and he was killed in a plane heading home. With Imani by its side, his body was flown back to New York.

"Damn, 'rone? Yo! Always thought out of *all* of us, you was the lucky motherfucka," Browny elegized in his own special way.

David could not talk. All words, all sentiments fell through the trap door of his broken heart.

The services brought out a who's who, and a who's *that?* from Ty's years of do-gooding. There sat a speechless David with Victor, Faison with Juanita, sharing a pew with an inconsolable Bliss and her daughter, Tyra.

Seeing Blur made David want to rise up out of his silence, kick that bastard dead in the throat, and whale all over his politically ambitious ass. But in good Christian etiquette, he chilled. He was surprised by the presence of Omar, and stunned by the gathering of family and homeless friends who attended Tyrone's homecoming.

Loyal to the end, Ty willed his savings, a part of his royalties, even his ghostly apartment to David.

So it became *his* chore to go through Tyrone's things. And in that painful undertaking, he discovered some of Tyrone's most recent journals. *What were you so damn busy trying to tell the world, ya dead half-beautiful bastard?* And then he came across the last passage Ty had written about him: "Today, I am no longer David's mother. I've given up the gig. Besides, he never put in an application for another Moms. I'm sorry I've wasted so many fucking years misusing our friendship. He might've stopped boxing long ago, but David remains my champion. I think I realized that again today. Today, I saw him at Wigstock, rocking the crowd in his big hyper-blond atomic Afro wig, dancing to "I Will Survive." It was like he didn't have one sad bone in his entire body. Later, as I watched him, falling safe and contented inside Victor's arms, I wondered, *Why am I worrying?* David's fine. All HIV-positive queens should be so fine. He's got a good man who's big in the pants and a thriving fashion career. And every now and then when his eyes get weird and teary, I'll ask him if he's OK, and he tells me those tears are because he's *happy!* I have to believe he is, because he looks so much like that queer copper kid I used to know at 15, when all the world's stages were just ahead of him. So I'm not gonna worry about his mercurial ass anymore. The Duchess is happy. Bravo! You go, Baby Boy! Snatch respect!"

And David, who had been raving about unfairness, who'd cried the wild muted tears of a grief-stricken fool for three weeks straight, closed his eyes. He mused about that kid, that long-horse-face almost handsome boy called Tyrone. When he opened his eyes, he thought for an instant that he perceived a flash, a quick piece of light zipping past the corner of his eye. And for some queer reason, that light made him smile.

3469

Acknowledgments

To my peeps and friends on shore: As I've embarked on this journey, you steadied my turbulent course. Thanks for the love and patience.

Cynthia, your voice of experience is a God-Cyn. Terri Fabris—hey, Lady T., maybe you really do be my "Alyson Angel." Scott, the co-rhythm-conspirator and verbal-conductor on this train o' my drama—I send much props and peace to you.

'Renzo, thanks for bein' who you be. Jett, James, Cliff, and Cunning, I do this in memory of y'all.

Shout-out to every believer and nonbeliever in this finite talent o' mine. To the mental-feeders, soul-breeders, and longtime Spirit-teachers, I thank you. To the players, the haters, singers and martini-slingers, Saturday-night-heartbreakers, and you sweet-bitter-long-blue-moan-makers, I'll holla.